TILL MY LAST BREATH

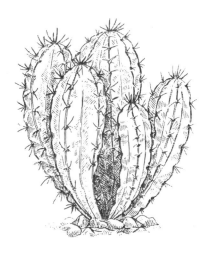

TILL MY LAST BREATH

Book One
Desert Hills Trilogy

Deborah Swenson

Published in partnership with BookBaby,
7905 N. Crescent Blvd., Pennsauken, NJ 08110

Designed by The Story Laboratory
Cover design: Tabitha Lahr; © Shutterstock.com
Cactus vector: Designed by pikisuperstar, courtesy Freepik
www.WriteEditDesignLab.com

Disclaimer
The mention of medicinal plants in this book in no way provides medical or naturopathic advice from the author. Its mention is used for the express purpose of this work of fiction only.

ISBN: 978-1-09833-571-7
EISBN: 978-1-09833-572-4

This book is dedicated to Jean Pennington
For her love, friendship, and encouragement.
Who told me to 'Cowgirl-Up' and finish the book.

Acknowledgments

I WOULD LIKE to thank the following people for their support in making this, my debut novel, a reality.

Jean Pennington, Pam Kieffer Nelson, and DiAnne Rolfzen for their valuable input as readers.

The following award winning authors for taking the time to review my manuscript and provide grateful insight: Jane Little Botkin, Julia Bricklin, and Kathleen Morris. Members of Western Writers of America and Women Writing the West.

Michael Zimmer, award winning author and member of Western Writers of America, for his assistance with period firearms.

Alexander D. Mitchell IV, Vice President of the Grand Canyon Chapter, National Railroad Historical Society. For his assistance with rail routes and local Arizona history in the 1880s.

Krista Rolfzen Soukup of Blue Cottage Agency and Kelly Lydick, M.A. of The Story Laboratory.

Editors: Denise McAllister and Anne Victory with Victory Editing.

And, to all the members of Women Writing the West who put their heart and soul into researching, writing, and sharing stories of the West. Thank you for taking me into your fold.

Thank you for reading *Till My Last Breath*. Visit my website https://deborahswenson.com and subscribe to learn about upcoming events and read recent Blog postings. It is a great place to watch for the release of Book Two in the Desert Hills Trilogy, *Till My Last Day*.

The woods are lovely, dark and deep,
but I have promises to keep,
and miles to go before I sleep.

—ROBERT FROST

TILL MY LAST BREATH

DECEMBER 1880 ARIZONA TERRITORY

Caleb Young

I KILLED A man four days ago.

Today, I find myself sitting precariously on a three-legged chair in a dilapidated cabin in the desert hills. With much to consider, all I have is a cold dinner of mushy pinto beans and dried smoked bacon. Surely not the high-class caliber of Boston restaurants I used to frequent.

Scratching four days' growth of beard, I can't remember when my last home-cooked meal was. Closing my eyes and sniffing, I can almost smell a strong pot of black coffee brewing. I dared not light a fire in that ancient black stove, fearing it might explode. Plus, the smoke would lead them right to me.

I had a bad feeling about the days ahead. Someone was out there looking for me. There always was, after you killed someone. The sun, my only source of light, would soon set as I watched the fading rays of the hot desert orb paint the dirty cabin walls a dingy yellow. That man I shot surely had friends, maybe even family. No matter who they are, they'll come seeking revenge. It's just a stark reality in the West. Dwelling on it only makes it all the more real.

In the fading light, I fingered the worn carvings of unfamiliar names etched into the top of the table, made smooth over the years from greasy hands. A rock-like sensation in the pit of my stomach prevailed, as I dropped my dirty plate into the empty metal bucket that wouldn't hold water if I tried. Staring into its bottom, I laughed thinking I resembled it; empty, dirty around the edges, and without hope of ever being whole again.

I was tired of wandering from one town to another, making money playing poker in cheap saloons where trouble always seemed to find me. Like it had that day. Wandering again, it felt different this time. It held a sense of unease that was boring itself deep into my very soul like a snake slithering into a cold pit, away from the desert sun. I wondered if my luck was about to run out.

Crossing my arms over my chest, I leaned back against the edge of the sink, thinking about what brought me to this place. Dredging up my past was painful, and remembering what I'd done to my father, or more importantly, what he had done to me, would only open crusted wounds. I had to push them aside if I wanted to survive.

I needed to calculate my next move carefully. Looking around, I saw the dry and weathered walls that with one flick of a match, would light up the desert sky. If I remained in the cabin, I was a sitting duck in a tinder box. On the other hand, going outside made me an even easier target. I can't take that chance right now. The hairs on the back of my neck stood up, as that heightened sense of awareness took over. Pushed to make a choice. I had to do it soon.

My Winchester lay loaded and ready on the far edge of the table. Snorting, I realized that one Colt 45, and a rifle, did not an army make, but they were all I had. If there was more than one man out there gunning for me, I'd have a slim chance if any of surviving. The odds were definitely not in my favor.

Popping open the lid of my pocket watch, I stared at its delicate gold hands, not knowing if I wanted time to stand still or rush forward. It was late afternoon, and the sun was losing its height in the winter sky. My time to make a decision was fast approaching.

"Is that River?" Thinking I heard River's whinnying, I moved to the back window. Peering out, I saw him standing calmly at the corral's rail. *"I must be hearing things."* Darting my eyes from side to side, my nerves on edge, I stood at the window several minutes more. Listening, I gazed into the fading light and waited. For what, I didn't know.

Vermin

Sitting astride my horse in the hills above the cabin, I stared down where the man I'd been hunting had taken shelter. Spitting a line of tobacco juice into the dry earth, I patted my horse's neck. *"Patience, Lucifer."* I couldn't give myself away. Not now when I was so close.

Caleb

Moving away from the window, I needed the cover of darkness to make my move when a sense of overwhelming exhaustion caught me off guard. I knew I wouldn't be able to stay upright in the saddle without getting some sleep. The rapidly cooling air at this elevation and thick gray clouds forming to the north meant the weather was about to change. Go, or stay? Either way, I would be caught in a tumultuous storm.

Gritting my teeth together, the muscles in my jaw painfully tightened. I was frustrated at not being able to move out sooner. Taking River's blanket, I placed it over the crossed ropes of the makeshift bed. Intending to use my saddle as a pillow, I set it at the far end so I could safely face the door. My Colt already in its holster, I grabbed the rifle off the table and laid down covering myself with my sheepskin coat, waiting for sleep to come.

Unmoving, I gazed up at the holes in the ceiling listening for any hint of movement. The eerie silence broken only by the rapid beating of my heart, I finally fell into a restless sleep where my demons dwelled.

2

Caleb

A WAKENING WITH A start, I sat bolt upright. Heart painfully thudding in my chest, I aimed at the darkened door as
if waiting for the devil himself to appear. It was River's whinnying
again that woke me. Cautiously, I walked toward the back window,
knowing I couldn't afford to lose my horse. He was my ticket out
of this death trap. Rubbing sweaty palms down my pants, I peered
out between the threadbare curtains towards the corral. In the darkness before dawn, I watched the shadow of River trot anxiously
around. Typically an easygoing horse, something or someone had
him spooked.

I wished whoever was out there would make their move and get
it over with. Waiting to die was not a pleasant experience. Turning
away from the window, I quickly gazed around the cabin. My legs
weak as a newborn foal, I slowly moved towards the door. Without

hesitating, I had to take the risk of checking on River. Drawing my gun, the weight familiar in my hand, I spun the chamber, making sure it was fully loaded.

Placing a moist hand on the bar that did little to secure the door, I thought better of it, pulling my tingling fingers back. Anyone who wanted to get in could just give the door a good kick, and the whole side of the cabin would cave in. I questioned, *why didn't they attack while I was sleeping?* A deep chill passed through my body. Something didn't feel right. Rubbing the standing hairs on the back of my neck, I shook it off as nerves. *"Damn. Someone just walked on my grave."*

My heart hammered against my ribcage while a trickle of sweat ran down my spine, while the bitter taste of greasy bacon threatened to rise. Common sense told me not to open the door. But common sense had not been one of my better traits lately.

Colt ready, I took in a ragged breath, slowly exhaling while lifting the bar. Quickly stepping back, I paused before pulling up on the leather handle. Hearing the rusty hinges creak, I continued to pull. Once open, a stream of golden light from the rising sun flooded the cabin door, framing me in its entrance and blinding me to what lay beyond. Instinctively raising my hand to block the glare, I realized I might as well have drawn a target on my chest.

What in the name of heaven are you thinking son, placing yourself in danger like this? Came a familiar voice from my past.

That's when all hell broke loose, and I lost control of my destiny.

"Arghhhhh!" I screamed, just as searing pain ripped through my left shoulder and the sound of a single gunshot ricocheted through the hills. Its brutal force throwing me back against the door. I didn't know in what direction the shot had come from; it had happened so fast.

Holding out my bloodied arm, I stared at it as if it was no longer attached. An anguished moan escaped my throat as liquid crimson dripped from my fingertips to the dirt floor below. Painfully sucking in air, I realized I couldn't shoot back if I tried. My only chance of surviving was the hope that my assailant would think he had completed his deadly mission and leave.

My next movements were surreal. In slow motion, I grabbed my left shoulder and leaned forward while desperately trying to hold onto my gun. Twisting to my right, I stumbled back inside the cabin, glimpsing the grisly mark my blood had left on the door. Opening my mouth, I took in several ragged breaths like a flopping fish out of water. It was all I could do to make it back inside before being shot again. My strength was leaving me all too quickly.

"God, it hurts to breathe." My labored breaths alternated with shallow surges as I tried taking in precious air. I was in the fight of my life.

Think fast, son. You can't die on me. Again, that voice.

Lifting my eyes heavenward, I searched for the angelic face I had not seen in years. My mother had been a gentle soul, and my lifeline in dealing with my father. I missed her still. Maybe, I would be seeing her soon.

With a raspy voice, I answered her, "I'm trying Ma. But I sure could use a little help here."

Mesmerized by the warm sticky blood oozing between my fingers, I winced as I applied firm pressure to the hole with my right hand. "Damn!" I stumbled to the table as the cabin door behind me closed of its own volition. Angry for being so stupid and caught off guard by a ray of sunlight, I realized I should have expected it to take away my vision the minute I cracked the door open.

How stupid can you be, Caleb Alexander Young? Yelled the vengeful voice of my father. Placing my revolver on the table, I slammed my fist down with what little strength I had left. Answering my father's ghostly presence, I yelled, "Obviously, stupid enough to wind up here getting shot, old man."

"Great, I'm going to die out here in the middle of nowhere, and I'm already talking with dead people." All was not lost on my misplaced humor as I spoke to the empty cabin. Shaking my head, I tried

to clear the encroaching fuzziness. *"Maybe this was just preparing me for my impending descent into hell."* Looking up, I yelled, *"Be ready for me, Father."*

I already am, came his sinister reply.

Leaning harder on the splintered boards of the table, silence fell over the room. Grabbing a dirty tattered towel, I stuffed it into the left side of my shirt in an attempt to control the bleeding. That familiar coppery scent assuaged my nostrils. Unable to control it, my stomach flipped, giving up the contents of my last meager meal.

Swirling acid had me gagging again. Ignoring the nausea, I picked up my Winchester, thankful I'd loaded it before sitting down to eat. Chuckling in a macabre sort of way, "At least I did something right." On that same table lay a small cardboard box of ammunition. Opening it, I cursed, "Damn it!" I had too few left, another act of my carelessness.

Leaving Yuma so fast, I hadn't taken the time to stock up on supplies, including the most important, ammunition. It seemed as though I was willing the forthcoming events to go wrong, causing my life to end on this desert hillside? Scrubbing my right hand over my face, my morbid thoughts drifted to the things people remembered when facing death. *"Dear God, what a place to die."* Staring down at the tabletop, I suddenly realized there would be no one to mourn my passing, no one to place my sun-bleached bones into the barren landscape, and no one to remember I even existed.

Mere minutes had passed when I realized I was sitting at the table in a daze, and the towel I'd stuffed into my shirt was now sticky and cold. Changing it out for another, albeit a dirty one, I tried standing. My Colt in its holster and rifle under my right arm, I unsteadily walked to the back of the cabin. I had only one chance of escape, and that was getting to River. Why I thought the only way to get to River was through the cabin's single window, I'll never understand. Maybe it's because I'd already been shot trying to exit through the door.

Approaching the window from the side, I flinched at hearing more gunshots and a single high-pitched male voice whooping and hollering from the direction of the corral.

"Aahhh, no!" Hearing River's loud whinnying, followed by pounding hooves on gravel, my heart sank as I caught a glimpse of my chance for survival running off towards the hills.

I was trapped.

Whoever shot me was still out there with no intention of letting me escape alive. I wouldn't put it past them to use the volatile timber of the cabin as my crematorium. I could almost feel the heat of the all-consuming flames sucking the life right out of me. Silently I prayed, *"I hope it will be quick because this is not how I pictured myself dying."* Clenching my right fist tightly and raising it heavenward, I yelled, not caring if the devil himself heard me, *"If it's going to happen, I'm going to choose how!"*

Raising my colt, I focused down the length of the barrel, mentally warring with a decision I hoped I'd never had to make. *Can I use the last bullet on myself?*

Leaning against the windowsill, I had my suspicions that the man waiting outside was kin to the man I killed four days ago, and now came seeking revenge. Was he waiting for me to make my next stupid move?

For the right price, any one of the men who had witnessed the shooting that day in the saloon could call it murder and hunt me down for the bounty. Knowing beyond a shadow of a doubt, I'd shot the man in self-defense, it meant nothing in these turbulent times.

Emotionally and physically spent from five years of running, just trying to survive, tumultuous thoughts churned within me. I couldn't come to grips with the fact that my long-unspoken death wish was finally coming true.

As the sun crept higher in the desert sky, I began to devise an escape plan. The bleeding had slowed, but my left arm throbbed to a rhythm all its own and remained too painful to be of use.

Clutching the rifle to the right side of my chest, I began my final move. Still hoping the shooter believed he'd killed me with his first shot, I looked down at my shaking hands, praying I had a chance of surviving this hell.

Nerves hanging by a slender thread, I slowly leaned my head out the window. Feeling a light breeze ripple the threadbare curtain, I shuddered as a cold chill ran down my spine. A rustling noise below the window caught my attention. It was just a tumbleweed rolling by on its journey to the hills. Raising my left leg over the windowsill, I hesitated mid-escape, waiting for gunshots. Hearing none, I slowly lowered my foot, the gravel crunching under my boot. Taking in a deep breath, I remained silent, leaning back on the window casing to catch my breath and the burning sensation in my shoulder to subside. When it did, I leaned forward, maneuvering my right leg over the sill. With both legs out, I waited for gunshots, relieved that nothing cut through the silence. Maybe, I did have a chance.

Taking one cautious step, it happened. A lone gunshot ripped through the right side of my abdomen. Its impact so violent it threw me savagely back against the cabin wall. Shocked? No. But, I didn't know where to grab, the pain was so unbearable. Breathing became near impossible. Clutching the fiery hot pain in my side, I stumbled forward, falling first to my knees as if in prayer, then to my left side, landing on sharp jagged rocks.

My luck had just run out.

Lying with my legs twisted beneath me, I heard sinister laughter coming from the hills above the cabin as a faceless voice yelled, "That's for my brother, Young. You're a dead man."

Coughing raggedly, I tried yelling back as I pushed my fist deep into my abdomen. "I'll see you in hell."

Laughter and the thunder of hooves pounding on dry earth sliced through the silence. Gripping my side, I slowly rolled over onto my back and stared up at the cloudless blue sky, asking, "God, have I finally made it to hell?" In a moment of sheer panic, my body shook uncontrollably as I pleaded, "Please, God forgive me for all I've done."

With each painful shallow breath I took, I drifted towards unconsciousness, knowing it wouldn't be much longer. I only prayed that my physical and mental suffering would soon be over as my chance of surviving alone in the desert was rapidly slipping away.

Thinking I was ready to die, overwhelming fear gripped me. My legs moved without thought. *I don't want to die. Not here. Not alone.* I was scared. With all my regrets, I quickly tried to make peace with my past. I hadn't much time left. Giving in to the fear, I closed my eyes and let myself float away, hoping death would come quickly.

I couldn't understand where my unconscious mind was taking me. In a misty dream, I found myself dancing in the arms of an auburn-haired beauty, whose crystalline blue eyes contrasted with her emerald green gown. I must have been under her spell because I couldn't turn away as I watched the tops of her creamy breasts rise and fall effortlessly with each breath she took. I was grateful for this blessed moment helping me forget my pain.

Embracing her delicate body, her smile lit up the heavens as we twirled effortlessly around a magical ballroom. Pulling her close, the heady scent of her lilac perfume consumed me. Leaning my lips close to her ear, I whispered, "You take my breath away."

This coquettish vision placed one delicate hand over my heart. Her searing touch ignited a flame deep within my soul. I couldn't turn away if I wanted to. Staring down into the endless pools of blue, she whispered, "You're too kind, sir." Demurely, she lowered her eyes, revealing thick black lashes evocatively resting across her pale cheeks. My breath caught, not from pain, but with yearning.

"We've met before, have we not?" I threw my head back and laughed at her answer. It wasn't the response I expected. I didn't care, she felt so right in my arms. Our bodies fit perfectly together in all the right places, and I couldn't help but think this enticing woman was the link to my survival.

The room in which we danced was opulent. Crystal chandeliers hung above the dance floor, casting a golden glow over the ballroom and its occupants. Candlelight gleamed in the mirrors lining the walls and heavy red velvet curtains, tied back with golden cords, embraced the sparkling windows. Off to one side of the room were long tables adorned with fine Irish linen. Four-foot tall silver candelabras dressed with cream-colored candles sparkled as they dripped wax onto the tables below.

More tempting food than any ravenous person could hope for lined the tabletops. Maids dressed in starched crisp black and white uniforms scurried about the room like mice keeping the platters piled high with food. White gloved waiters in long-tail black coats walked through the crowds, carrying silver trays laden with crystal flutes of expensive French champagne.

Women in silks and satins, coiffures piled high, bedazzled with gleaming diamonds and emeralds twirled gracefully with their tuxedoed partners beside us. It was a scene I remembered, yet had once turned away from. I became confused as the music began to fade, and the laughter and spirited conversations diminished. All I heard now was my ragged gasping breaths.

Holding on tightly to this mystical woman, I couldn't let go fearing she would disappear, and I would undoubtedly die. Swiftly, my thoughts turned cloudy, and I panicked. My vision lost focus on her beautiful face. I know I'd seen her somewhere before. Frustrated, *why can't I remember?*

All too soon, my hold around my companion's waist slipped free, and this vision of splendor disappeared, fading into a silvery mist. Reaching out, I yelled into the darkness, *No! Anna, don't leave me.*

The Anna I knew had betrayed me. She was the reason I left Boston five years ago. My pain intensified, and I didn't understand where my thoughts were heading next. Was Anna betraying me again?

Frantically, my eyes roamed over the ballroom, searching for the woman I'd just held in my arms. Gritty and burning, I blinked several times. Gone was the opulence, replaced by a garishly decorated hall with tattered rose wallpaper. The handsome men who had worn elegant black tuxedos were now dressed in threadbare clothing and sneering through tobacco-stained teeth while drinking rotgut whiskey. At each end of the bar, men spit black liquid into brass spittoons from between greasy mustache-covered lips. Women now dressed in flimsy gaudy saloon attire wandered the room flirting with drunken patrons.

Caleb, run you fool, came that little voice in the back of my mind. *Get out of this place. Now!* Each breath I took was more painful than the last. I had to think fast. *Don't you remember? It was Anna who sent you to hell?*

My motionless body betrayed the compulsion to flee. My limbs leaden, I couldn't make my feet do what my mind demanded. This dream scene had become a nightmare throwing me back into the saloon that had led to my imminent demise.

Jerking fully awake, the excruciating pain was taking its toll. *"Damn!"* My head spun as nausea hovered. Opening my eyes, I couldn't focus as the light faded around me, and my rapid breathing had me coughing painfully. I hated that I was losing control. I couldn't stand much more. Giving in, I did what my subconscious told me to do by letting the black void of unconsciousness take me away from this self-imposed purgatory.

$\backsim\!\!\circ$ 3 $\circ\!\!\sim$

FOUR DAYS AGO, YUMA ARIZONA

Caleb

THE STENCH OF sweat, smoke, and cheap perfume permeated the air around me as coins, and small bags of gold dust
filled my pockets. *Just one more game, then I'll head out.* Truth be
told, I'm a greedy gambler. Gold fever, no matter how it was earned,
drove many a man to sacrifice their better judgment, and I was no
different.

After leaving the saloon in the wee hours before dawn, I awoke
in my second-floor hotel room to the sounds of dogs barking and
creaking wagons passing on the street below. Covering my bloodshot
eyes to the bright sunlight streaming in through the open window,
I wished for a breeze. Looking up at the ceiling, I focused on one
corner where the sepia-colored wallpaper was peeling away. There
above me hanging by a strand of spun silk, was a chubby brown
spider, its tummy fat with eggs and its long delicate legs working

furiously on weaving its sheltering den. Fascinated, I couldn't turn away as the spider spun its deadly web. Unexpectedly, shouting on the street below brought me back to reality.

Rubbing my blurry eyes, I opened my pocket watch, attempting to focus on the numbers. It was only one o'clock in the afternoon, still early by a gambler's standard. I'd stayed too long at the saloon last night, playing one game after another. Finally, too many whiskeys made me fold, and head back to the hotel where I fell exhausted into bed.

Moaning, *"I don't want to get up,"* I tried forcing myself back to sleep, but it would be elusive this bright sunny morning. Giving up and tossing back the lye-scented sheets, I sat on the edge of the bed to gauge my balance, when I realized I'd never taken my clothes off. *"Damn! I really must have drunk too much last night."*

When I was sure that I wouldn't fall flat on my face, I raised myself up, extending my arms over my head, stretching to work out the kinks in my back. Removing my shirt, I stood in front of the window, leaning against the sill. I had ordered a bath and hot water to be brought up precisely at one-thirty every day. Anxiously waiting, I looked towards the door and wondered, *"What's keeping that boy?"*

Having no desire to use the local bathhouse, I paid dearly to have a tub and hot water carried up the two flights of stairs to my room. It was well worth the extra two bits to ease the pain and aching muscles from long hours sitting at a poker table. I couldn't say much about the mattress. It felt like someone had stuffed it with pigeon feathers and forgot to remove the birds.

Moving in slow motion around the room, I gathered clean clothes from my grandfather's old carpetbag. Reaching in deep, I located my razor, shaving brush, and soap, when a loud knock came at the door. Pulling my revolver out of its holster, I kept my hand down at my side, when I asked, "Who is it?"

"It's Joey, sir," came a child-like shaky voice. "I have your tub here, Sir. Can I bring it in?"

"Just a moment." While I pointed my gun towards the door, I grabbed the brass knob. *Click*, the rusty device interrupted the silence. Opening the door slowly, I peered at a dirty-faced waif barely big enough to haul the tub up the two flights by himself. "Here, let me help you with that." Carefully placing my gun into the back of my belt for quick access, I stepped out into the hall. Reaching out, I was greeted with a frown and shake of his head as the boy firmly clutched the tubs handle.

"No, sir." Looking down, I saw fear in the small boy's green eyes. His gaze darted behind him as if looking for someone, before adding, "Sorry, sir. I need to do this by myself, or Mr. Adams will give me a whooping."

Muttering a curse, I asked, "Has he beat you before?" My question was met with silence as the boy dropped his head. Reaching out, I placed my hand on his shoulder, lightly squeezing only to have him flinching. "Son, do you want me to speak with Mr. Adams?"

"Oh, no, sir. Please don't go doin' that."

I could see the fear in Joey's eyes increase as he shook his head from side to side. "O.K. Son. I won't say anything to Mr. Adams." *Not yet, anyway.* Placing my finger under his chin, I eased his head up only to see tears threatening to fall over his pale freckled cheeks.

Wiping his eyes with the sleeve of his threadbare shirt, Joey made to move the tub into the room, just as I lifted the back handles to help. Placing the container on the thinning carpet, I faced the boy. "Joey." His head popped up with a trembling smile across his face. "Son, why don't you go down and get me that hot water." Placing two bits into the boy's hand caused his smile to widen. I know I'd just given him more money than he probably made in a month.

Stepping back to the open window, I waited for Joey's return as I surveyed the town below. It was an unusually warm December day, four weeks before Christmas, and the off-key carols playing on the rickety saloon piano across the street didn't do justice to the upcoming holiday.

Staring down the town's main street, I followed it north to the outskirts having plans to head out of this desert mining town, riding towards the Washington Territory. It was the farthest I could get from Yuma before I came to the Northern reaches of the Pacific Ocean. Further yet from my home-town of Boston, where I left shattered memories behind. So far, I'd been able to keep the nightmares tucked away. Occasionally, they snuck in when I least expected it.

Stepping away from the window, another knock came from the door. Placing my hand on my gun, I asked, "Joey. Is that you?" I recognized the boy's voice this time.

"Yes, sir. I have your hot water."

Relaxing the hand at my back, I opened the door to two large steaming pails of water sitting on the floor in front of the boy. The motion of Joey rubbing his hands together and his furrowed brow did not go unnoticed. "Did you burn your hands, son?"

"No, sir," Joey answered, hiding his palms and pointing to the pails, "They're just heavy, sir."

I beat him to the buckets as he bent down to pick them up. "I'll just take those for you." Emptying their contents into the small elongated hip bath, I handed the empty pails back to the boy. Ruffling his red curly hair, I gave him another two-bits. "Thanks, Joey. You head downstairs now and stay out of trouble.

"Yes, sir. I will, sir," he said, smiling. "Thank you, sir." The boy ran from the room just as I began unbuttoning my denim fly.

Misty steam rose up around me as I stepped naked into the steaming bath. Feeling my aching muscles loosen up, I closed my eyes, leaning back against the tub's edge while formulating a plan on leaving Yuma. Usually, I made it a habit never to stay in a town long enough for people to become too familiar with me. I was always passing through on my way to the next town and the next poker game. For some unforeseen reason, my good fortune in this town's only saloon had me returning three nights in a row.

Grumbling, the once steaming water had cooled. Leaning over the tub, I grabbed the towel off the floor. Standing naked, the water sluiced down my body, partially into the tub, partially onto the faded carpet. Stepping into clean denim's, I moved barefoot across the room towards the basin and mirror to shave. The image staring back at me made me wince, as I looked at day-old stubble. *"What a sorry sight you are, Young. You look like something the devil threw back."* Laughing at myself, I asked, *"When are you going to learn that cards and whiskey are going to be your ruination one of these days? Not to mention the pounding headache you have the next morning."*

Completing my morning ablutions, I took special care in shaving since my hands were a bit shaky. *"Nothing like slitting my own throat while shaving,"* I chuckled. Looking down at my trembling hands, I decided I needed lots of coffee.

Buttoning up the starched white shirt I'd picked up from the Chinese laundry the previous day, I noticed my tanned face stood out as a stark contrast to the white of the shirt. Slipping into my well-worn leather vest, that I would never have been caught dead wearing in Boston, I ran my hands down its smooth texture. It fit me like a woman's tender embrace, something I almost forgot how it felt. Picking up the twenty-four karat gold watch piece my father had given me when I joined his law practice, I turned it carefully over in my hands. Despite the memories it elicited, I couldn't part with it.

Moving back to the mirror, I tied a black string tie around my open collar. Last but most importantly, I strapped on my gun belt, letting it hang comfortably low on my right hip. Taking out my Colt, I checked the chambers, before dropping it back into the holster and adjusting its position.

I was ready for whatever the day would bring.

Grabbing my black Stetson off the bedpost where I left it the night before, I placed it snuggly on my head. Taking in a deep breath and grasping the brass handle, I opened the door slowly, keeping my hand over the butt of my gun, not wanting any surprises.

Leaning against a post in front of the hotel, I surveyed the streets of Yuma. Scanning the cactus-rimmed hills and beyond, I peered out from the shadow cast by the brim of my Stetson. Needing to be ever vigilant, I slowly scanned to the right, then left, silently watching.

Gazing across the street, I caught the movement of a familiar child. "Joey." Smiling, I raised my hand and waved, being greeted with his tiny hand waving back. *He's a good kid. Someone's lucky to have him as a son.*

Looking across the road, I read a sign painted in bright red lettering, the *Pick and Shovel Saloon*, my evening's destination. I would be there soon enough. Little did I know that today in this desert town, I would catch a glimpse of what my future held, and it didn't include any of the holiday spirit.

4

Caleb

T AKING MY SEAT in the hotel dining room, I placed my back to the wall as a safety measure I learned a long time ago and had the scar to prove it. Coming towards me with a steaming pot of coffee was the café's plump rosy-cheeked waitress. "Good morning, Miss," I said as she poured me a cup. Turning away, I couldn't help watch her ample hips sway from side to side. Grinning, it had been a long time since I'd held a woman in my arms. I made sure to say it under my breath so she wouldn't hear me. There was a heaviness in my heart at the thought of not having someone to love. Taking a sip of coffee, I knew I needed to remedy that, and soon."

Inhaling the steam circuitously rising from the cup, I allowed myself to relax. Yet, with each chime of the bell hanging over the door, I watched patrons come and go from the café.

"Sir, would you like to order lunch now?"

I must have been miles away since I didn't notice her come back to my table. That lapse in attention could get me killed. Holding my cup up, I smiled, "No, thank you. Just keep my cup full."

"Will do, Sir. If you should need anything from the kitchen, please let me know."

In Boston, I would have been served breakfast on shining silver trays formed by old-world craftsmen, not the chipped mismatched Blue Willow plates in front of me. Once again, lost in my thoughts, the coffee began to work its wonders as my mind wandered back to a time outside my family's stately Boston home in Suffolk County. Well-appointed carriages carrying ladies dressed in the latest fashions, and men in expensive suits would walk peacefully along avenues carrying on the day's business, oblivious to the happenings thousands of miles away. Here in Yuma, everyone that traversed the dusty streets looked at you with suspicion. I deplored this existence. It wasn't the life I intended.

Returning my mind to the present, I picked up a copy of the local newspaper, reading the obituaries first, a habit I acquired while practicing law. This morning's headlines read, "Thomas Edison of Milan, Ohio established the Edison Illumination Company based in New York City." Fascinated, I continued reading. "The system is based on creating a central power plant equipped with electrical generators where copper wires would connect the station with other buildings allowing distribution of electricity." *What will they think of next? Soon gaslighting will be obsolete.* I realized time was moving on in the East, while here in the desert, it seemed to be standing still.

Losing track of how many coffees I'd drank, I checked my watch for the time. It was already three o'clock. I needed to make my way to the saloon. Placing two-bits on the table along with a generous tip for the buxom waitress, I walked out into the glaring sunshine.

Pausing on the boardwalk, I slowly scanned the dusty street. Catching a glimpse of the mercantile, I remembered I needed to purchase supplies before heading out of town tomorrow. Setting off in its direction, I ignored the voice calling from behind me.

"Hey, mishter," an old miner yelled, slurring his words.

I paid him no mind and kept walking.

"Hey, mishter," the old miner called louder.

The tug on my shirt had me drawing my gun and spinning around with lightning speed.

"Don't you know better than to come up on a man that way? You want to get yourself killed, old man?" Seeing the raw fear etched in his weathered face, I looked down at the greasy handprint the miner had left.

"Damn it man!" I swore, attempting to brush off the dirt.

"Sorry, mishter." Pointing in the direction of the saloon. "Just thought you'd want to know about the game in there."

I couldn't be angry with him. Shrugging off my well-intended mission to the mercantile, I resolved that I would have plenty of time in the morning to make my purchases before heading out of town.

With my unlikely companion at my side, I entered the saloon, as the bat-winged doors creaked rhythmically back and forth behind us. Finally, coming to a halt, we made our way to the bar. I needed a whiskey to settle my stomach. My sidekick required it to stop his shaking.

Behind the bar, stood one mean-looking man with a deep jagged scar running from his left eye down to below his stubble jaw, making him look incredibly intimidating. It appeared as if his only mission in the saloon that day was to rub every glass with a worn-out dirty towel. Even though I had seen him daily since arriving in town five days ago, we still eyed each other with wariness.

Leaning his fat hands on the bar, he asked, "What'll it be?"

I knew it was best to keep out of his way since I didn't want any trouble. Holding up three fingers sideways, I asked. "Your best whiskey."

With one foot comfortably on the brass rail running parallel to the floor, I leaned forward, placing down four-bits. Only then did the bartender release his hold of the two shot glasses. Peering into the depths of liquid redemption, I threw it back in one fell swig. It tasted awful. What could I expect? Certainly not the fine smooth bourbon I'd spent good money on in Boston. By the time whiskey made its final destination to the West, distributors and saloons alike, had mixed the spirits with either molasses, burnt sugar, prune juice, or sulfuric acid to increase their profits. In the end, it tasted more like turpentine than a fine smooth whiskey.

Behind the bar, hung an ornately gilded mirror, the same one I'd seen in other bars during my travels. Above that hung a larger than life painting of a voluptuous naked redheaded woman lounging on a velvet chaise. Holding up my glass, I saluted her.

I ordered a full bottle to take with me to a table. Turning away from the bar, I shifted my eyes from one end of the saloon to the other, realizing there were no empty seats in ongoing games. Finding an empty table, I settled in for a long evening. Picking up a deck of cards, I counted out fifty-two laying them neatly down to play solitaire. Before I finished, five of the saloon regulars I recognized from the past few nights was joining me.

Barely sitting upright in the chair across from me, I could see that the devil whiskey had taken its toll on one of the miner's rail-thin body. "Hey Young, ya tink I can win bach the pot I losht to ya lasht night?" he asked, slurring his words through a toothless grin.

"You can give it your best shot, old man." *Maybe, just maybe I'd let the old miner win a game tonight.*

"Gentleman, what will it be, Twenty-one, or Five-Card-Stud?" The miners just shrugged. Not meaning to boast, I dealt the cards with the finesse of a Mississippi paddle-wheel dealer. Satisfied that all men present were ready to begin, I looked each one in the eye and said, "Place your bets."

Time crept by when I noticed the bottle sitting next to me was almost empty, yet it was still early in the evening. Holding it up to the dim light, I didn't remember drinking that much. Catching a sheepish grin on the miner, I'd met on the street. "Why you old devil. You've been nipping at my bottle, haven't you?"

A wary look creased his face. Probably thinking I'd throw him out of the game, he answered, "Sorry, mishter, I was thirsty."

"It's OK, old-timer." I patted him on the back. Holding up the near-empty bottle, I caught the eye of the bartender to order another. That created slaps on backs and toothless smiles all around the table. By doing such, I had another motive. Loose men would only increase my winning pot.

A young saloon girl I'd never seen before, dressed in a short flimsy lace dress, walked towards us, bringing the full bottle. Setting it in front of me, she deliberately leaned over to catch my attention. I was human after all, so I obliged by examining her ample breasts that were barely contained in her low-cut attire. Leaning back, I caught a whiff of stale perfume that caused me to hold my breath. I wasn't interested but definitely amused at the sets of eyes from around the table, staring at the young girl's cleavage.

She was visibly disappointed when I placed a tip in her hand, instead of between her breasts. Standing straight, her bright red lips pouting, she continued to ply her wares, by running her fingers along the back of my collar. Proceeding to tease me with her syrupy Southern drawl, she begged, "Honey, for a few dollars more, I could make your night worth your while."

Not bothering to look up, I answered, "Not tonight, Miss. Thanks."

"Are you sure, Honey? It could be a nice . . . long . . . night."

Looking directly at her, I couldn't make my answer more understandable. "Like I said, Miss. No, thank you."

Hands on her hips, she raged, "Well, Mr. High and Mighty, you don't have to be so nasty about it! A girl needs to make a living around here." I watched as she abruptly turned and stomped back to the bar, her hips swaying and skirts flouncing from side to side. Tempting as the thought was, I still wasn't interested. She wasn't my type.

Coins neatly stacked to my left, gleamed in the light of the oil lamp hanging above the table. As hours passed, smoke from cigars and cheroots, hung over the room like a ghostly fog bank in the Boston Harbor.

Picking up my cards, I arranged them in my hand as an eerie silence fell over the room. All heads turned towards the entrance as the bat-wing doors flung open with a resounding thud. Framed by the yellow glow of the waning sun, there stood a tall man catching the doors as they swung back his way. Dressed all in black from the top of his Champie to his silver-tipped boots, he stood silent, blocking out what little light had been streaming in. He surveyed the dimly lit room before his eye came to rest on me. Looking at the imposing figure, I met his one-eyed icy glare, as a chill ran down my spine. *Damn. I don't need this tonight.*

Before I looked at the black patch covering his right eye, I noted the skin below it puckered, as if having been disfigured from a branding iron. His long shiny black hair was tied back in a queue and held in place with ample amounts of pomade. I would have most definitely remembered this man.

Drawing a commanding presence, evil oozed out of his every pore. The laughter and off-key twang of the piano abruptly stopped as he stepped further into the room. I had to remain calm, knowing nothing good would come of his presence. With each step he took, none of the regulars dared make a move to leave. But his entrance hadn't been lost on the burly bartender as he followed his every move.

Feigning disinterest, I looked down at my cards. At the same time, out of the corner of my eye, I saw the bartender pull up a rifle, placing it in front of him on the bar within easy reach. There would be no serving drinks for a while.

"Girls!" It was all the bartender needed to say. *He's no fool. He's been through this before.* With the back tilt of the bartender's head, the girls left their customers and came to stand next to him.

With calculated moves, I watched the stranger step farther into the saloon, as his silver spurs played their own tune on the sawdust-covered floor. *Clang, spin, buzz. Clang, spin, buzz.* Every nerve in my body went on high alert, knowing this man was going to be trouble of the worse kind.

"Whata yer gonna do, Young?" asked one of the miners. "I don't want ta be caught in no gunfight."

"It's up to you," I replied. I couldn't guarantee that this evening would end well.

5

Caleb

STANDING BEFORE MY table, the stranger chewed slowly on the end of his cheroot, methodically puffing out streams of gray smoke while clenching and unclenching his right fist. I watched a vein near the side of his left eye pulse like a metronome. It was as if the devil himself had come to play poker.

Lowering my head just enough to break eye contact, I remained cognizant of where the stranger's hands were at all times. Keeping my hands in view, I waited for the outsider's next move. Coughing, I let out a strangled breath after catching the foul odor of lard in the stranger's pomade. Pointing to the cards, in a raspy voice, the stranger nodded his head, "This game open, Mister?"

"Your money," I answered, shrugging while pointing to the one vacant chair. My skin crawled, and my heart pounded like a blacksmith's hammer, reminding me to remain calm.

The stranger pulled out the chair causing its legs to grate across the pitted wood floor. Adjusting his gun belt to make a point, he sat down, never taking his eyes off me as one of the old miners sitting next to him stood. "Where you going, Digger?" I asked. "Don't you want to win back some of the gold you lost last night?"

"Nah. Not tonight. I think I'm heading upstairs with Miss Lily. She needs me to keep her warm."

I watched as Digger couldn't leave the table fast enough. If I didn't know better, the brown on the back of his pants wasn't from sitting in mud while sluicing for gold.

Looking around the table, I asked, "Anyone else change their mind about playing?" I was trying to give them all the opportunity to remain alive. No one made a move.

Breaking the silence, I looked at the regulars, "Gentleman, ante-up, and we'll start a new game." Nodding their silent response, I shuffled. "We're playing Five-Card Stud."

The tension in the room relaxed some, and much to my chagrin, the piano music started back up. The saloon girls went back to pouring whiskey and plying their charms as I made a mental note that the bartender had kept his rifle in plain view on the counter.

As he dealt the cards, I wracked my brain, trying to place the stranger. *Did we meet in another town, another game? Certainly not in Boston.* I had come across a lot of evil people in my life, especially in the past five years. Eventually, they all seemed to look alike. But there was something different about this man. I couldn't quite put my finger on it.

An hour passed, and the game had been a quiet one so far. The only words muttered were those of players making bets or folding their hands. With a slow hand, I tilted my hat back to get a better view of the cards. Just as I did, the stranger coughed on his cheroot. I watched him place his right hand over his vest pocket, pulling out a lone card hidden behind his tobacco pouch.

Damn! I muttered silently. *Now, why did he have to go and do something as stupid as that?* I hoped I had been the only one at the table to notice. I certainly didn't want one of the old miners to get himself killed. I continued to look at my own cards, knowing I had a difficult decision to make. I could remain silent or call the stranger out for cheating. I just needed to wait for the right moment.

The stakes were too high, as I watched the regulars fold and slap their cards on the table. All but one remained seated, either out of fear or curiosity. Now, it was just me, and the stranger left playing. The ending would be up to him.

I noticed beads of sweat under his sinister eyes glisten in the gaslight. Appearing anxious to have the game over with, he nervously shuffled the five cards left in his hands. Did he think he could take back what he'd just done?

Funny, but I was drawn to watching the veins in his neck bulge and pulse to an erratic tempo. Sneering, his attempt to intimidate me failed. Was I stupid in thinking this would end well? No, I was scared I'd be on the losing end. Gripping his cards firmly, he placed his final bet in the middle of the table and called the game.

In front of him were four aces and two Queens. One the Queen of hearts. Looking directly at me through bloodshot eyes, he smirked, "I got you beat, Mister."

Before I could lay down my own cards, he began sweeping his hands across the table, pulling bills and coins towards himself.

It was time.

"Now hold on, mister, aren't you the least bit curious to see the hand I'm holding?" Not showing him my cards just yet, I motioned to the rest of the deck. "I say we turn over the remaining cards."

"You calling me a cheat?"

Gripping my cards firmly and taking in a deep breath, I answered, "No, sir, I just like to see the remaining cards when a game with high stakes is over. It keeps us all honest. Don't you think?"

Staring the man down, I felt an emptiness burning in the pit of my stomach. Definitely not a good feeling. It was something I always felt when trouble was about to erupt. Like now.

"That's bull," bellowed the stranger. His left eyebrow twitched madly, and his posture went rigid. "I've never played poker where the dealer asks to turn over the remaining cards."

"Maybe you should. Like I said, it keeps us all honest."

Out of the corner of my eye, I watched the old miner next to me clasp his shaking hands together as the others at the table fidgeted in their seats, obviously anxious to leave before trouble started. Quickly scanning the room, I noticed the tables closest to the door had already cleared of its patrons.

With nostrils flaring, the stranger inhaled sharply. I could almost read his thoughts. His next decision would be critical. Did he know that he could die tonight? I knew I could! I tried shaking off the specter of death that hovered too close.

A mantel of silence fell over the room. I could tell the stranger didn't like being called out. Reluctantly, he unhurriedly began turning over every last remaining card in the deck. There were just a few left when up popped the deck's one and only Queen of Hearts. What he did next was anyone's guess.

My throat was as parched as the desert landscape surrounding the town, but I had the proof I'd been waiting for, and it was in front of a table full of witnesses. Play this cool Young, and no one has to get hurt.

The tone at the table quickly changed, as the stranger began shouting profanities. "You Sonofa . . . you accusing me of cheating?" His face inflamed with fury, "I'll kill you for this, and all your friends here." Pointing to the men around the table, he added, "How do you know it wasn't one of these spineless drunks who cheated?"

"Because, sir," trying to remain calm. "It's simple. The real Queen of Hearts was still in the deck, and never dealt." Moving my outstretched hand around the table, "Why would I, or any of these men randomly slip in an extra card? Besides, I've been playing cards with these same gentlemen the past few days, and at no time did any of them take the opportunity to cheat." I tried placing the ownership on him, knowing he couldn't explain his way out of this one. To avoid bloodshed, I was willing to talk it over.

Leaning forward, my hands visible on the table, I watched the stranger's features tighten. Time slowly ticked by when I finally said, "Gentlemen." All heads turned in my direction. "I believe there is a problem with the cards at this table this evening." With their furrowed brows and confused looks on their faces, I knew my speech was above their local vernacular. It gave a hint to my past that no one in this town would recognize.

One of the regulars at the table looked at me through bloodshot eyes. With liquored speech, he asked, "Whaja say?"

Not taking my eyes off the stranger, I answered, placing a hand on his shoulder, "It means, my dear poker friend that someone at this table has cheated. And you will be getting your money back."

"Well, I'll be damned. That's the bechst news I've heard all night," yelled the miner.

"And, I believe we know who it is," I replied, deploying a bit of sarcasm.

"Shut up, old man," the stranger yelled, spittle spewing across the table.

Scanning the room, I noticed the purveyor of the saloon had a firm grip on the bar, intently watching what was transpiring between us. She had to know the stranger was not going to take my accusation sitting down.

Slowly rising, the stranger pushed the right side of his coat back, revealing his revolver. Exuding evil, fingers twitching, his hand hovered over his holstered gun as we continued our staring match. I was beyond nervous. No pun intended I was scared to death.

"You loaded the deck!" He sneered, slowly dropping his hands to within easy reach of his gun, he paused.

"That's unlikely, sir since you are the one that dealt the cards."
I had him there!

A rustling sound from the bar had all men turning in its direction, except for the stranger and myself.

Abigail

In my years running the Pick and Shovel Saloon, I'd seen too much bloodshed, and I'd had enough of these two men's posturing. I wasn't going to stand for it, not today, not ever again if I had anything to say about it. Slamming an empty glass on the bar, I attempted to break the rising hostility and garner everyone's attention

"Gentlemen, I don't take kindly to bloodshed in my saloon." Moving from behind the bar, much to the chagrin of Henry, my bartender, and dear friend, the only sound heard was the satin of my gown rustling on the floorboards. I knew how this scene could play out, and I had more than one reason to stay out of firing range. But as the owner of the saloon, I needed to try and prevent the inevitable from happening.

My eyes roamed around the table after placing my hands on the back of two chairs. All eyes except the gambler and the stranger's turned to face me as I spoke in a firm voice. "Please, gentlemen. I don't allow cheating at cards, or killing in my saloon. It's bad for business." Standing up straight, intending to command the two men's attention, I crossed my arms tightly over my chest and added, "Besides, it's messy and scares my girls."

Without receiving a response from either man, I asked a bit more firmly. "Gentlemen, do you understand what I'm saying?" Again, no response. My insides began to quiver, and my legs felt like they were going to give out. I wouldn't give up. I was beyond frustrated. I was mad! *Just because I'm a woman doesn't mean these two gun-happy idiots can ignore me!*

I could see Henry was about to come around the bar, holding him back by raising my hand. He knew better than to interfere when I was mad.

Hands on my hips, I tried again. "OK, gentlemen. This game is over. If you must shoot each other, take it out into the street . . . now!"

Caleb

"Ma'am, I'm fine with your suggestion if this gentleman would care to oblige by stepping outside with me." Motioning with my head in the direction of the swinging doors, I was ready to leave the confines of the smoky saloon and face this vile demon in the street. Ready or not, I may be the one to die here today, but for some reason, it didn't matter.

"Damn you to hell, Young, for calling me a cheat." In one fluid motion, I watched the stranger make his next stupid move by reaching toward his vest pocket. I'd been deceived before, and had the bullet hole to prove it. My body wound tighter than a tick. I was ready.

Everything around me moved in slow motion as I watched the stranger pull out a Derringer pocket pistol, encased within a white handkerchief. Small, but effective at close range, he quickly aimed for my heart and fired.

For the past five years, my life had depended on my reflexes. Within a fleeting second of seeing the gas light glint on the stranger's pistol, I drew from my hip and fired. Lucky for me, the stranger's shot went wide, landing in the back wall.

I didn't hear the shrilled screams echo around the room since I had been concentrating on the man across the table from me. The spent gunfire cast a smoky white haze over the table, blurring our vision. We both remained standing, staring at each other as the smoke began to fade. I felt no pain as I mentally assessed myself for wounds. The stranger, on the other hand, had a fist clenched to his chest. Visible to all, was a circle of crimson spreading around a hole in his brocade vest. Luckily, I was still alive, for now.

Letting out a ragged breath I didn't know I'd been holding, I glanced down at the stranger's cards when a drop of his blood fell across the fateful face of the Queen of Hearts. How ironic, the stranger's cheating card had played her final game. At the sound of air being rapidly sucked in, I watched the stranger take a few staggering steps backward. Then came the deep liquid gurgling of impending death.

"I'll see you in hell, Young," Forcing his last words through yellow gritted teeth, he dropped hard into his chair. His effort to grab the edge of the table failed tipping it over as his body hit the floor with a resounding thud. Whiskey bottles and glasses flew through the air, and coins rolled mindlessly in the sawdust with no destination in mind.

"Probably," I replied, watching the light go out in my adversary's eye.

It was over.

The saloon remained hauntingly silent as all heads turned to see the blank stare of death framed on the stranger's face. I stood frozen, looking down at the man I'd just killed. I had no regrets for what I'd done. Unlike previous threatening encounters, I had indeed been afraid of dying this day. I knew the minute that man walked through the saloon door, the poker game would come to a bad ending. It could very easily have been me lying there on the floor, with a hole in my chest, staring up into nothingness. My luck had held out once again, but this life I led, would soon have me six feet under.

6

Sheriff Anders Johansson

"VAT IN DA name of heavens vas tat?" Hearing gunshots break the afternoon silence, I propelled myself out of my chair, sending it crashing into the wall behind me. Grabbing my coat, hat, and rifle, I headed out the door towards the saloon.

At forty, I still had some fast moves left in me despite my old hip injury from the War Between the States. Adrenaline kicked in, and my senses went on high alert at hearing women's screams coming from within the saloon. Cocking my rifle, I stepped up on the boardwalk, staying safely to the side of the entrance. Several men stumbled out tripping over each other in an effort to reach the safety of the street.

My heart pounding like a steam engine, I had good reason to be concerned, knowing the woman I loved was just beyond the doors. Yelling, I pushed past the men flying out. "Get outta my way, you bunch of no goot idiots."

Peering over the doors, I surveyed the room, glimpsing at a man holding a forty-five and standing over a lifeless body. Eyes frantically searching, I cautiously pushed through the doors letting out an uneven breath as my eyes came to rest on Abigail. Pale, and unmoving, she stood like a stone statue.

A tide of relief washed over me, and my heart returned to its normal rhythm. Even though he was dead, the love of my life was mere inches from the dead man.

Making my way through the doors, I slowly moved towards the back of the saloon, never taking my eyes off the gunman. I was expecting to see a cocky young cowhand, not the clean-shaven, well-dressed gambler facing me. My assumptions quickly changed. Motioning towards the gunman with my rifle, "Mister, slowly put tat gun on de floor, and kick it over towards me." Obliging, he kept his left hand in the air as he placed his gun on the floor, giving it a kick.

"Now, step away from the body with your hands up."

I glanced at Abigail, seeing her tremble. "Miss Abigail. Please move away from that man," I indicated with a nod towards the gunman. I could see her hesitate. I needed to keep her calm and focused. "It's OK. I won't let him hurt you."

It near broke me, seeing the raw fear in Abigail's stoic green eyes. Every time she was near me, I wanted to take her in my arms and kiss some sense into her beautiful, stubborn head. My one desire was to carry her away from this filthy place and build a life together. Despite my being head-over-heels in love with Abigail, I had no right to tell her such. It would only complicate both of our lives, more than they already were. I hated it, but it was better to keep my feelings close to my heart, where they'd be safe. As sheriff, I had a job to do, and I couldn't guarantee I'd always come back to her. Alive.

Standing over the body, whose vacant one-eyed stare was unnerving even to the most seasoned lawman like myself, I leaned down, closing the open eye, blocking out the eerie sign of death. There was no need to call for Doc Sweeney. The shot had been a clean one to the heart—a heart whose very existence was emptying itself onto the floor in a pool of scarlet.

Searching through the dead man's pockets for any hint of who he was, I came up empty except for a wallet that held several hundred dollars, a photo of an older woman, a bag of loose tobacco, rolling papers, and lucifers. An unfired forty-five was still in his holster, and a double-shot derringer was clenched tightly in his right hand.

Taking a good look, I didn't recognize the dead man's face from any wanted posters hanging on my jail wall. If there was a bounty out on him, I'd find out soon enough by wiring the county seat. Prying the dead man's bloody stiff fingers from around the derringer, I checked to see if the chambers were empty. They weren't. Only one shot had been fired. Unloading the remaining shell, I handed the pistol, casing, and remaining bullet to Henry, who by this time had come to stand next to me.

Hearing the swinging doors fly open, I watched all eyes turn to the non-opposing figure of the undertaker, Mr. Cribb. Motioning his assistants forward, he stood over the body, waiting for me to give the order to take it away.

"Well, sheriff, this town sure is keeping me busy lately." Raising both hands, "Not that I'm complainin' mind ya, but it seems as though the bodies are mounting up as fast as I can make coffins."

Giving Mr. Cribb a displeased look, I motioned for the man who reminded me of a weasel, to take the body away.

"Well, sheriff, I don't think you're here to welcome me to your lovely town," the gunman said.

I replied in my broken Swedish accent, "Ya, ye be right, mister." I watched the gunman's eyes follow the retreating body. Feeling a bit more secure, I cradled my rifle over my left arm. At the same time, we both turned our attention to the saloon boy, whose only job until now had been to clean spittoons. Hands fiery red from the lye soap and a bloody rag, he cleaned up the stained floor like it was just another day in Yuma.

Caleb

My nostrils burned from the stench of the caustic soap mixed with blood. For the first time since witnessing death, my stomach roiled. It was probably the combination of an empty gut, too much whiskey, and that adrenalin rush, which caused the bile to rise in the back of my throat. Across the room, I watched the saloon matron gag, then quickly run towards the back door with a hand over her mouth.

Turning back to the sheriff, I didn't flinch as he pushed back the right side of his jacket, revealing a forty-five. I knew it would be there. No lawman in his right mind would only carry a rifle. I could see the wary look on his face as he cleared his throat.

"Since ya ver de one standing over te body holding da gun ven I came in, tell me vat you know about de man you yust kilt."

Shrugging, "Other than he was cheating at cards, and drew first, I know nothing about him." Kicking at a hard cake of mud on the floor, I continued. "Until tonight, I've never seen the man before in my life." Shaking my head, confused, I added, "Funny thing, though."

"Vhats funny?"

Brows furrowed, I answered, "He called me by my last name."

"How do ja figure tat?" Pulling a rolled cheroot from his vest pocket, I watched him successfully scratch a lucifer on his rough denim until a yellow flame grew from the end.

"Um," I hesitated. "Don't know. He could be from any of the towns I've been through in the past five years. I've moved around a lot, and one card player starts to look like any other."

The sheriff took a slight step forward before asking, "Any particular reason for tat?"

"Reason for what?" Toeing a roach crossing by the tip of my boot, the lawyer in me told me not to answer any question that wasn't necessary or potentially incriminating.

"Do many people have reason ta come looking for ja?" Tilting his hat back, revealing a tan line and graying hairs, he waited for my reply.

"Look, sheriff, I know what you're getting at, but I didn't come to this town looking for trouble." *It just seems to find me.* "I came here to play cards. That man walked in here tonight knowing he was going to cheat and try to get away with it." Motioning around the room with my hands, "Anyone in this saloon can corroborate what I'm saying." Inhaling a shaky breath, I continued, "He cheated, plain and simple, and I wasn't going to stand for it." Difficult as it was, I tried to remain calm while pointing to the cards strewn about the floor.

"So, ya decided to kilt him," the sheriff asked bluntly.

Pointing to the empty spot where the body had lain, I answered, "No! He and I could have settled this quietly. But, he chose another way." I was nervous. Who wouldn't be? I'd just killed a man and could shortly find myself hanging from the end of a noose, or worse in the territorial prison. Shifting my weight from one foot to the other, I desperately needed to let those in the saloon know. "No matter what you or anybody in here thinks," pointing a finger to my chest, "I'm not a hired gun."

"I never said ya ver." blowing perfectly formed smoke rings into the stale air. "By the vay, vhat's yer name?"

"Caleb. Caleb Young."

Sheriff

The gambler sent me an icy glare. Was he trying to pierce my resolve? If so, I was having none of it. Taking off my hat, I slapped it on my leg to not only clear the dust but break the tension. "Mister, it's my job to ask da questions. A man vas yust murdered here, and ja vere de only one holding a gun ven I came in." Crushing my cheroot with the toes of my boot, I continued to ask. "Now, vether it vas done in self-defense or not, I need to find out da details. So, don't go getting riled up." I took another step closer. "I can yust as easily ask dese questions sitting comfortably in my office vile jar behind bars. So, are ja villing to talk?"

The gambler crossed his arms over his blood-spattered chest. "Look, sheriff, I'm not proud of what I did. But it was either him or me that would be lying dead on that floor. I preferred it to be me left upright and breathing. Besides, that man, made a grave mistake tonight by pulling that hidden pistol. He should have known better."

By this time, the silence in the saloon was unnerving. All the patrons had stopped to listen to my questions and the gambler's responses. What I would do next was anyone's guess.

Caleb

Feeling powerless, my gaze wandered over the room. I'd heard the town hadn't had a lynching in a long time. Maybe, after today's shooting, some might think it was long overdue. *Well, I wasn't going to be this town's entertainment any time soon.*

I watched the sheriff pull out another cheroot, lighting it as he asked, "I know tis may seem like a stupid question, but I need a straight answer."

"Who drew first?" I'd beat him to the one question he'd failed to ask earlier. Staring into the sheriff's steel-gray eyes, I answered with certainty, "He did. But you know as much as I do, it's my word against a dead man's." Motioning to those around me, I added, "You can ask any of the men in the game with us tonight." Turning towards the saloon Madam, I addressed her proper, not wanting to sound too familiar. "Including Miss James, who was standing by the table at the time that man drew his gun. She'll tell you who drew first." *I hoped no one would lie just to have a lynching.*

Nervously, I watched as the sheriff faced the men still standing near the table. Letting the right side of his coat fall over his holstered gun eased the tension some. He looked at Miss James, who now stood behind the bar nodding her agreement to my story.

The sheriff nodded back, then turned to me. "Mister, I vant ja out of my town by sun-up. It's either tat or ja spend time in my jail and get to meet de Territorial Marshall next veek and stand trial for murder vith a stint in prison."

I knew full well the sheriff should arrest me. But I wasn't stupid enough to stand here arguing with him why he didn't. It was my turn to look at Miss James. Her blank expression told me I'd worn out my welcome sooner than I'd planned.

It was time to leave.

I couldn't go on like this. I was about to leave yet another town, luckily, as a free man. Touching the brim of my hat, I nodded politely to Miss James. Shoulders straight, I held my head high and walked towards the swinging doors, pausing at the bar to say my thanks for her agreeing with my innocence.

Standing a moment at the double doors, holding on tightly, I inhaled the profound scent of freedom and life. Without looking back, I pushed through walking out into the dry desert air, realizing for the first time in five long years, I was weary.

Leaving the saloon, I felt the eyes of the town boring into my back as I walked down the dusty street towards the stables. As always, River was waiting patiently. He was the one constant in my life, and we made a good team. I talked, he listened. Silently, of course.

Dusk was falling when I walked into the livery where River was munching on oats. The crunching sounds of his teeth grinding together, and the mewing of a calico cat, broke the silence. "Hey boy," I said stroking River's neck. "Enjoy it now because you won't be having this kind of meal for a long while."

Pulling the saddle blanket from the stall's wall, I laid it over River's back, then my saddle and bridle I'd won in a poker game. Once cinched in place, I led River out the livery's door into the waning light. We walked the short distance to the hotel to pick up my gear. Wrapping his reins over the hitching post, I patted his neck, telling him, "I won't be long boy. I just have a few things to get, then we'll be out of this town for good." River whinnied his reply.

I had an uneasy feeling about remaining in Yuma one more night. So, I made the risky decision to head out in the growing darkness. Looking around the room I'd called home for the past few days, I couldn't help but sigh, thinking this was all I had to show for my life the past five years; dusty trails, hotel rooms, whiskey and poker games.

I exited the hotel and stood on the boardwalk, noticing the sheriff had taken up the position of leaning against a post directly outside of his jail. Watching, he waited for me to leave his town. Without making eye contact, I untied River's rains from the hitching post and leaned in towards River's ear, "Boy, this town wants us gone in a big hurry."

Sitting high in my saddle, back straight, I rode past the sheriff. This time he tipped his hat to me. I nodded my head and whispered to River, "Better not completely burn our bridges boy." The thought of riding into another town made me uneasy because the news of today's events would travel fast. There would be men out there looking for a challenge, but what I needed now was solitude and time to think.

7

DECEMBER 2019, SEATTLE, WASHINGTON

Emily Sweeney, MD

I RUBBED MY FACE as I stared in the tarnished mirror hanging on the inside of my locker door, surveying the tiny spots that danced across my cheeks and nose, *"Dang! I hate these freckles."*

At five foot six, I looked like a teenager barely out of high school. Though my looks were deceiving, I was a woman who loved life fast-paced, making no excuses for it. It defined me personally and professionally. It had driven my parents crazy with my *devil-may-care, face life head-on attitude.*

I'd made it through medical school in record time when forced out into the dog-eat-dog competitive medical world at an early age. Out of my fellowship for five years, I was still trying to maintain that fast pace by working long hours in one of the busiest trauma centers in the Northwest. I was a survivor, having made a respected name for myself in the local medical community in such a short time.

Sitting on a hard wooden bench, I examined the rows of dull green lockers that were reminiscent of my high school's gym. The surrounding gray walls reminded me of the battleships my father used to take me to see when the Navy's fleet came in during Seattle's Sea Fair Festival. Gray was such an appropriate color for this room. It's where my peers and I waged wars within ourselves before entering the ER battle zone.

I had wanted to spend today alone, not here at work. Try as I might, I couldn't bring myself to use my emotional pain as an excuse to call in sick. Unzipping my expensive Italian knee-high leather boots, the ones with the four-inch stiletto heels, I methodically removed one, then the other, when I noticed a hole in the toe of my left sock. My inner child took over as I stuck a finger through the gap, laughing at what an atypical picture I presented: five hundred dollar boots and Dollar Store socks. Hey, I needed to save money somewhere. It's not like anyone else, but I would see them.

Slowly easing down the zipper, I wiggled out of my butt-hugging jeans. Once off, I could finally take in a full deep breath for the first time in hours. Neatly folding them, I placed them on the top shelf of my locker. Lifting the oversized cashmere sweater over my head, a chill ran down my spine. *"Dang, don't they ever pay the heating bill in this place?"* Pulling the clip from my hair, I finger combed the tangled strands, plaiting it into a braid that would keep it out of my face for my oncoming sixteen-hour shift.

It was two o'clock in the afternoon as the rare December sun shone brightly against the adjacent building windows, casting a golden glow into the dressing room. Even though it was still early afternoon, the sun would soon set as the winter equinox approached.

Holding crisp blue scrubs to my chest, I found myself walking in my stocking feet to the only window in the room. Leaning close, my warm breath fogged the wire-embedded glass as I gazed out at my favorite waterfront city. Soon the twinkling lights on the trees along Fifth Avenue would sparkle like a thousand Swarovski crystals, and the Macy's Christmas star would shine radiantly above Westlake Center. Sun dipping behind the snow-capped Olympic Mountains told me that once the city was plunged into darkness, the night air would drop to freezing.

It was on a cold night like tonight, four years ago today, during the Christmas holiday, that my life had taken a dramatic turn. My parents had been leaving a downtown theater when they became innocent victims caught in the crossfire of a drive-by shooting and were killed. The shooters were never found, and the pain of that night still haunts me.

Coming out of my daze, I realized it was still light enough for someone in the adjacent buildings to see me in my underwear. Sucking in a quick breath, I rapidly moved back to the well-worn bench and finished dressing. Donning my white coat, I ran my fingers over my name embroidered in red. Emily Sweeney, MD. If only this simple lettering could tell the world what I went through to earn this coat. Would it matter to my peers and patients? Probably not. Securing my locker, I headed out into the night's unknown.

Sound View Trauma sat on what Seattle locals called "Pill Hill," which overlooked the crystalline blue-green waters of Puget Sound. The Hill was home to three major medical facilities. Still, Sound View was the best in the Northwest for victims of traumatic injuries.

I groaned, staring at the patient census board in the staff control center, noting it was already full. The droning of the medic scanner hummed in the background as I rubbed my cold hands together, saying quietly to no one in particular, *"Let the games begin."*

"Hey, Emily, ready to rock and roll?" My friend Max, and fellow physician across the room called to me. We'd gone out a few times, but it was nothing serious as far as I was concerned. I always felt we were both too busy for a permanent relationship.

"You bet," I answered. I gave him one of my killer smiles to get the energy with the staff pumped up. "I've got my armor on as usual. You know I'm up for anything the night throws at us."

"That's good because I have a feeling it's going to be the typical Saturday night of the crazies coming in."

Walking further into the room, I called out, "Good evening all." Smiling and raising a hand in greeting, I came to stand behind the unit secretary, placing a box of favorite local chocolates on the table that a patient had given me. "What's the score this evening, Sarah?"

Sarah Anderson looked up and smiled. "Dr. Emily, are you trying to ply my good nature with chocolates?"

"But of course," I said.

Picking out the most tempting piece, and taking a bite, I watched her facial expression change as she sighed with pure bliss. I loved it when Sarah was on. She always came to work with an upbeat attitude, very much welcomed in a place that could be solemn and tragic. She had been the swing-shift ward clerk in the ER for the past five years and brought a bit of eclectic style to the group. With her flaming red hair, not the natural kind, piled high on her head, she held it in place with chopsticks. She wore 1950 style eyeglasses, the type with pointed wings, and faux diamonds. Often raving about her clothing finds from the local thrift stores, they were a bit garish. Still, definitely colorful that fit her perfectly.

"Let's see, which do you want first, Doc? The good news or the not-so-good news?"

"I don't care. Just hit me with what we've got," nudging Sarah's shoulder.

"O.K. Well, room one is the only empty one at this time. Then, we have Mrs. Peterson in room two. She's back in with recurrent chest pain. You know, the poor dear, doesn't have any family that we know of, and she hates that nursing home. I think she comes in just because she's lonely and likes all the attention we give her." Brows' deeply furrowed, Sarah sighed heavily. "I just hate to see lonely old people, don't you?" she asked, looking up at me. "This dang healthcare system is getting worse, not better if you ask my opinion." Raising her hand to stop my response, "I know. I know.

But don't get me going on that subject. Sandy's in with her now hooking her up to the monitor and giving her some TLC. Dr. Max said he would take that room for now."

Scrolling down the computer screen, she located the next patient. "Room two is a ten-year-old burn victim." Sarah handed the Medic report to me and continued. "His family didn't have any heat in the house. So, he thought he would help by trying to start a fire in the fireplace using lighter fluid. Poor boy, it blew up in his face." Throwing her hands up. "That's just so sad. Arms and face are severely burned. Dr. Nick is in with him and his parents.

"Then, there's room three, an eighteen-year-old MVA. Head-on crash on Highway 167 that came in via Airflight Northwest. What I hear is they found her cell phone with a message timed just moments before the crash. It looks like she might have been texting while driving. It doesn't sound promising from what I've been hearing. Dr. Drew is in there now talking with the family about the CT results." Coming up for air, Sarah continued to give me a quick rundown of patients.

"So, what's security like this evening?" I asked.

"Three that I'm aware of, but I've only seen the one at the front entrance when I came in."

"OK, I'm sure the others are close by. Wouldn't want the crazies to get out of hand, now would we?" I said, meaning no disrespect to our patients. They all deserved the utmost respect, no matter their plight.

"Please, no. I remember a few months ago when we had those two 'working girls' screaming and going at each other in the waiting room like vipers. It was like watching a Saturday night wrestling match." Chuckling, "In a sick sort of way, it was fun to watch."

"You, Sarah Anderson," I said, pointing my index finger at her, "Are one crazy woman. But I love you anyway."

"Thanks, Doc. Love you, too," she replied, batting her fake eyelashes.

Rolling my eyes upward, I laughed while giving Sarah a nudge.

Pop! Pop! Terrifying gunshots rang out as blood-curdling screams emanated from the waiting room. Within seconds, the overhead paging system announced, "Code Gray in the ER waiting room." Repeating. "Code Gray in the ER waiting room."

Hearing the announcement indicating an Active Shooter, I immediately turned to leave the glass-enclosed area as Sarah yelled out for me to stop.

"Emily, don't go out there. Let the police handle it. It's too dangerous."

Ignoring her request, I pointed my finger at her, "Make sure that SPD has been notified." Stopping short of the exit door, I looked in both directions before entering the hallway.

"Dang, that woman," I heard Sarah yell as the clicking of her heels, and the rickety wheels of the crash cart trundled over the tiled floor. "Get Dr. Max and call 911," Sarah yelled to whoever could hear her.

Having heard screams, and with little thought for my own welfare, I raced forward into the foray. My heart nearly exploded out of my chest as I clutched the doorjamb with clammy fingers. I could feel warm sweat run down my temples along with a slow trickle between my breasts. All I could think of was *it's my job to make sure that the patients are safe.* With only a thin wall between me and the yelling, I smelled the acrid scent of spent gunpowder. Momentarily stopping to formulate a plan, I felt someone grab my shoulders firmly from behind. Not turning around, I knew it was Sarah as she whispered in my ear. "Dr. Sweeney, what in heaven's name are you doing? Are you trying to get yourself killed?" Voice escalating with fear, Sarah took a firmer grip on my shoulders, "You can't go out there! Let the police handle this. Please."

Not turning around. "There may be staff and patients hurt in the waiting room. I need to find out."

"Well, you can't help them if you're dead." Tightening the hold on my arm as if she could stop me. "Please, wait, and think a minute. Don't do anything stupid."

I reached behind and patted Sarah's hand in thanks for her concern. "I'll be OK. Don't worry." But, as usual, I didn't listen to Sarah or the voice in my head that said, *don't do it.*

8

Emily

P EERING INTO THE waiting room, all I saw was the shocked looks on patients sitting frozen in place. Some had been able to crawl under chairs, while others sat silent, tightly holding babies, companions, and total strangers. A petite Asian woman sitting rigid in a black plastic chair clutched a small child to her chest, rocking back and forth while trying to quiet the weeping child. Next to her, another patient spoke rapidly in Spanish while pointing to the man leaning against the wall.

I hadn't seen him yet, but a man yelled angrily at the Asian woman, "Shut up! Just shut him the hell up!" I caught a glimpse of the gun barrel as he motioned with it toward the crying child. As the woman attempted to rise from her chair, the gunman motioned more firmly with his weapon and yelled, "Sit down. Just sit the hell down and don't move." I could see the woman's pallid expression, as she did as he instructed. The child continued crying.

Peering around the corner to the waiting room, I found myself staring at a scene out of a bloody western, but no Sam Elliot was coming to save the day. I sure hoped Sarah or someone had already called 911 because this was more than what a hospital security guard could handle.

Looking up, to send a prayer heavenward, I saw two bullet holes in the ceiling, hoping no one above had been hurt. Slowly, I eased myself around the barrier of the wall. Before me stood a man wielding a large handgun in a standoff with a young security officer whose face was ashen. Knuckles of his gun hand white, he looked barely old enough to be out of high school.

Standing just inside the automatic doors to the emergency room, I didn't understand why the officer hadn't fired. Wasn't that what he was trained to do, protect patients and staff? The thought of killing someone probably never entered his mind when he took this job. I could only sympathize with him.

Annoyingly, the entrance doors kept opening and closing as the cold night air swirled around the waiting room, sending chills through all who witnessed the scene. Both the shooter and security officer were too young, making my heart ache. If only for a moment.

Beyond my reach, the shooter, dressed all in black, leaned against the wall holding a gun in a blood-soaked hand. He hadn't seen me yet. Looking him up and down, I noted a pool of blood forming on the floor near his right foot. *That's too much blood for him to be still standing.*

I wouldn't let panic set-in as my mind raced through years of training. Nothing in medical school could have prepared me for this.

Gulping down saliva and feeling that familiar adrenaline surge, my heart continued thudding in my chest. A few of the waiting patients caught sight of me. Raising my fingers to my lips in a motion to keep them quiet, I'd hoped they understood. Unfortunately, the gunman followed the direction they were looking. His terrified coal-black eyes pierced my resolve. He was too young to die. And, so was I.

I made the foolish move to come from behind the protection of the wall. All I could think about were the panicked pleading looks in the patient's eyes. They needed my help. Isn't this what I'm trained to do?

"Nooooo! Emily!" I heard Sarah scream as I slipped free from her grasp.

The officer caught sight of me as I rounded the corner. Putting his hands up, I knew he'd wanted me to stay back, but it was too late as I found myself standing face to face with the gunman who, in a moment of panic, fired.

"No! God. No!" I heard Sarah scream behind me.

Shouldn't I be feeling pain? Maybe, he'd missed.

Suddenly, my pain receptors soared to life, and a searing sensation tore through my chest. Stunned, I stumbled backward, clutching a hand to my chest. Rapidly blinking, I struggled to take in air. Was that regret I saw the gunman's eyes? For some reason, I reached out to him as another resounding shot pierced the air. The gunman's eyes widened in horror as he was slammed back against the wall. Staring at me, a trickle of blood slowly oozed out of the side of his mouth. His legs gave out, and he slid lethargically down the dirty gray wall, painting a trail with his blood.

The security officer had finally fired. But it was too late for me. My fate was sealed.

I dropped to my knees next to the shooter. Intense pain shot up my thighs. *Come on, Emily. Don't give up.* I heard people screaming all around me, as with each painful breath I took my pulse pounded in my ears. Clutching my chest tighter, I tried to will the pain away, until I felt the viscous warmth of blood flow freely through my fingers. I couldn't get the words past my lips as I silently screamed, *No, God no. Please, don't let me die.*

Lying on the cold tile floor, I turned my head to the side, staring into the look of death in my assailant's eyes. Unmoving beside me, his gun still clenched tightly in his fist, I thought, *how strange it is to view death from this angle.*

"Hang in there, Emily!" a male voice yelled as strong arms came around me, lifting me off the floor and laying me on a stretcher. *Now I know why patients complain about lying on these things. They're just as hard as the floor.*

Looking up through fog-clouded eyes, I moaned. "My knees hurt, Max." Panic set in. My chest held no feeling, yet coughing sent razor-sharp pains through to my back. It didn't make any sense.

I was jostled from side to side, being pushed rapidly down a short corridor, and then entered what I knew to be exam room one. Glaring lights from above pierced through my closed eyelids. More pain. *White lights. Why are there so many white lights? I want to be left alone. Please, just leave me alone.* I couldn't even tell if I screamed the words. I'd wanted to. *Let me sleep for a while; then, I'll be alright.*

If I didn't move, it wasn't painful. I tried yelling again, *Leave me alone*, but the words never materialized. Finally, I gave in. I had no control over what was happening to me. Here I lay at the mercy of others, it wasn't an easy thing for me to do. People were bombarding my body, as I heard a familiar voice call out orders. At the same time, there were sticks to my arms and pricks to my neck where antecubital and carotid intravenous lines were being placed. Everyone had a specific job to do, like a well-orchestrated symphony.

Hearing the clang of metal and the buzzing of monitors, I drifted in and out of consciousness. "Come on, Emily. Don't leave me now." I recognized that voice. *Max, where am I going?* Feeling weightlessness take over my body, the once-familiar sounds faded away as I tried to tell my friends to *wait for me.*

I couldn't feel my arms. They'd gone numb! Silently screaming, *God. Help me!* Opening my eyes, I found myself staring down at an all too familiar scene. What was I doing looking down? People were working feverishly over my body, my face obscured by their hovering heads. Good Heavens! My chest was naked, covered in blood.

Lots of blood! My exposed breasts were no longer visible with all the monitor leads, drapes, chest tubes, and instruments.

Turning towards the beep of the cardiac monitor, I was acutely aware of my heart's precariously slowing rhythm. *Beep, beep...* [Pause]. *Beep, beep...* [Pause]. *Beep, beep . . . beep.* Another long pause. Then, the beeping stopped, and the monitor's low droning silenced the room.

"We're losing her," someone yelled out.

"Get me the epinephrine." It was Max again. I watched him push one of the critical medications into an intravenous line as he simultaneously called for chest compressions. With each compression, I felt intense chest pain and blood surge to my head.

"Nothing," called an unfamiliar voice.

"Get the paddles," Max yelled. "Come on, don't leave us, Emily."

Max held the paddles, one in each hand, as a nurse squeezed on the conductive gel.

Placing the cold paddles on my chest, he yelled, "Clear!" Hands went up, everyone but Max stepped away from the stretcher.

Leaning his body away from the metal rail, he pressed the buttons sending shockwaves to my heart. I lurched upwards, head back, then fell limp onto the stretcher. The monitor remained flat, and someone restarted the chest compressions as critical seconds ticked slowly by. The room fell silent. At the same time, everyone was staring at the cardiac monitor, waiting for what seemed an eternity for a beep to resume.

"Come on, girl, show us what you've got," Max yelled. With no response, he once again applied the paddles and yelled, "Clear!" Again, my body lurched. Silently, I prayed as orders for more medications were methodically called out and given.

I hadn't seen it coming when a long sharp needle stabbed my chest. *Max that hurts.* Max was trying intra-cardiac epinephrine as a last resort. I knew my chance of survival was slim, but I didn't want to die. I had too much left to do. *I won't give up!*

"We need to open her chest," Max yelled.

Just then, a soft white mist flowed over the stretcher impeding my view. Not able to see what was going on below, I was drawn to the cardiac monitor hanging on the wall. Gasping, I watched my once active heart pump its last pulsing force.

I heard someone in the room call, "Time."

"Wait, Max. Don't give up on me. I'm not ready to go."

Max yelled, "No! Give me more epinephrine and keep up the chest compressions."

"That's it, Max, keep trying." Max wouldn't give up on me. I knew he cared too much to stop. Then, someone, I didn't recognize grabbed him by the shoulders. "It's over Max. You have to stop." He did. All their efforts were to no avail. The bullet must have hit a vital organ, and my fate was sealed before I collapsed to the waiting room floor.

Knowing they couldn't hear me, with my hands over my silent heart, I let my co-workers know that it was alright to let me go. A nurse I had worked with stepped up to the stretcher. Hands shaking, with a warm washcloth and towel, she stoically began washing the blood off my body.

My spirit had already left my earthly form as I watched tears stream down my co-worker's faces. Respectfully, they covered my cooling body with a clean white sheet. I longed to be back at their sides, yet knowing never again would we laugh and work together. Max took that moment to lean over, pulling back the sheet and placing a gentle kiss on my cold lips. "What am I going to do without you, Em?"

"I'm sorry, Max. What I did was foolish." It was then I realized that Max had genuinely cared for me. Possibly, he even loved me. I became angry. *Why hadn't he said anything before? Why hadn't I said anything?* Now, I'd never get the chance.

The exam room looked like a MASH unit from a far off war zone. Looking at the clock, I realized that my friends had been working over two hours trying to save my life.

Sadly, not everyone who came through the emergency room doors lived.

Now what?

Frightened, I felt a feather-like touch on my arm, drawing my attention away from the scene below.

9

YUMA, ARIZONA TERRITORY 1880

Mathew 'Doc' Sweeney, MD

I POSSESSED A GIFT. I preferred to call it a curse. A gift not seen with the naked eye nor felt with trembling hands. A gift passed down through generations of my Celtic ancestors that I'd tried ignoring my whole lifetime. A gift that gave me the ability to change lives. Forever.

Unfortunately, there was a catch.

There always was.

I'd been one of the fortunate Irish immigrants who made well in America. After hard work, sweat, and tears, I attended medical school in the East, married, and became a young widower shortly after the birth of my only child. After raising my daughter, she married and lived with her husband in New York. It was then, I answered an advertisement in a newspaper that a town in the Arizona Territory needed a doctor. Much to the chagrin of my daughter, friends, and patients, I headed west, leaving everything behind.

Now aging and lonely, I felt that my time on earth was coming to an end. Then, one cold winter night as I slept, I was awakened by movement at the end of my bed. With an increased sense of awareness, I rubbed my eyes to clear my vision, only to glimpse at a woman shrouded in a billowing white mist. Her beauty and gentleness, I thought I would never see again.

Floating effortlessly across the room, my mother stood before me. Her once black tresses, now gray, hung loose down her back as she hovered in the faded blue dress I remembered so well. Shuddering, she pulled her wool wrap tightly around her shoulders.

Placing my hands on the mattress behind me, I struggled to sit up as she spoke to me in Gaelic. Her brogue reminding me of what I missed most about my homeland.

Mathew, she called out.

"Mother, is it really you?"

Yes, my son.

Is this really happening? Pressing a hand to my abdomen, I asked in Gaelic, "Are you here to take me home?" Throwing off the stiff white sheets, I dangled my legs over the side of the bed as my eyes searched her face for any clues of why she was here.

No, my son. Remember your gift! With no further words, she faded behind the mist just as quickly as she appeared.

Nervously twisting my thinning wedding band around my arthritic finger, I tried understanding why, after all these years, the gift was needed.

Emily

"Emily, dear." Turning, I faced an older gentleman dressed in a dusty black suit. He seemed out-of-place. Wire rim glasses sat precariously on the bridge of his nose. His tan face, outlined with graying salt and pepper hair, made him look distinguished, yet older than what he probably was. Outside his small vest pocket hung a shiny gold chain, and a black string tie secured snuggly around the neck of his faded white shirt, finished his look.

"Emily, I've come to take you home," the old man said, a tear slowly running down his fading freckles.

"Home, I have a home!" *Where did he come from?* Holding my breath, I thought this was just a bad dream, and I'd soon be back in the ER where I belonged. I'd never seen this man before, yet he looked so familiar. *It was his eyes. Yes, that's it. They're the same color as mine!* With a look of sadness etched across his sun-withered face, he reached out to take my hand.

He seems kind enough. Besides, what choice do I have? Without questioning his motives, I grasped his gnarled fingers. Turning away from the scene below, I was leaving the only life I'd had known. A life that no longer existed. Reality hit, and I anxiously muttered, *"I can't go…"*

Just as quickly as I accepted my mortality, overwhelming fear engulfed me. Thoughts running wild, I couldn't remember how my day had started but turned so deadly. *Why was it so hard to remember something from mere minutes ago?*

Pulling my hand free from the old man's, I yelled, "No, I can't go with you. I'm not supposed to be here." The old man reached out again for my hand. I quickly turned away from the misty veil that now wholly obstructed my view below. I could no longer see my lifeless body lying on the table.

Maybe if I ignored the old man, this would all have been a bad dream, and I would wake up standing next to Sarah listening to her go on and on about the patients I'd yet to see.

This can't be real! Deep breath in, Emily. Deep breath out. I'm not dead. Repeating the mantra, I drew in one last ragged cleansing breath and closed my eyes, trying to relax and ease the tension that

had my whole body in a vice-like grip. Thinking it was safe, I slowly
opened my eyes. It hadn't worked. I still found myself surrounded in
cream-colored light, staring into faded violet eyes.

"Don't panic," I told myself, drawing in yet another deep breath,
then releasing it. If I was dead, why could I see this man so clearly?
My heart was heavy with unspoken emotions. I kept questioning,
who is this man, and why is he here with me?

I was tired and weak. My mind kept playing tricks on me as if I'd
just bungee jumped off the Aurora Bridge. Free-falling into a dark
abyss, touching the murky bottom of the Ship Canal, I was rapidly
being jerked back up into reality.

The reality is, I'm dead.

Shaking my head from side to side, I couldn't get my thoughts
aligned. Becoming more frustrated, I didn't realize that the old man
had grasped hold of my hand again. I tried pulling away without
success. Usually, I was calm and in control. With my control gone, I
found myself rambling on just like dear Sarah.

"Emily, come sit with me," the old man motioned to a bench I
swore wasn't there moments ago. I needed answers, so giving in, I
took a seat at the farthest end and faced him.

"Emily, this is going to be hard for you to understand." He
moved closer and took both of my hands in his. "I need to tell you
who I am, and why you're here."

I told myself to remain calm.

"Emily, I'm your great-great-grandfather. I come from…"

"Whoa!" Abruptly standing, I had managed to pull my hands
free. Not giving the old man the chance to finish, I could feel the
pounding of my carotid pulse in my ears, I wouldn't allow myself to
believe what he was saying. Facing him with both hands on my hips,
I yelled, "You're lying! You're not my great-great whatever!"

Pacing, I whispered to myself, "This can't be happening. This is
just a bad dream, I thought, rubbing my sternum. "It must have been
that sausage I ate for breakfast. That's why I have this epigastric

pain." Raising both hands heavenward in frustration, I yelled out, "God, this is not funny. This can't be happening to me." Regaining my composure, I slowly turned back to the man calling himself my grandfather and asked more calmly, "OK. Now, start over. And, it better be the truth this time."

He remained seated while replying, "I am your grandfather."

Containing another outburst, I watched him struggle to stand when I motioned for him to stay where he was.

Looking up at me, he added, "I mean, I'm your great-great-grandfather. But let's leave it at grandfather."

Out of the corner of my eye, I watched intently at the look of defeat written on his face. Was he trying to understand what I was thinking? Rubbing my temples, I refused to look directly at him. If I did, it would only make his presence that more real. And I didn't want to be here.

Looking up, my eyes pinned him to his seat on the bench, silently conveying, "Don't mess with me, old man." It wasn't my norm to yell, but that's just what I did. Rubbing my hands up and down my arms, I paced. My nerves were getting the best of me. "Oh my God, I'm dead. I'm really dead." Waving my hands madly in a rage unbecoming of a lady, I yelled, "It's true, isn't it?" Tightness in my chest had me whirling back around and dropping down on the bench, only to rise again just as quickly. Speaking more to myself, I continued to rant. "Yes, of course, I'm dead. You don't wind up in a fog talking to a strange man, in odd clothes, with a peculiar accent, who wants to take me home with him. Oh, ewe!"

I could feel the heat emanate from my face and neck, knowing they were probably turning redder by the minute. Finally, beyond exhaustion, I gave in, sinking back down on the bench with a plop, and let the tears flow.

A comforting arm came around my shoulders, as my grandfather whispered in Gaelic to me, *"Tá mé chomh brón orm mo chara."*

"What did you just say?"

"I said, 'I'm so sorry, my dear.'" Pulling a thin handkerchief from his breast pocket with the initial "S" embroidered on it, he handed it to me. Wiping my tears, I waited for further explanation.

"My dear, dear child, you've been through so much, and it's a very long story."

"Try me. It's obvious I now have all the time in the world, thanks to you," I interjected a bit sarcastically.

"Where do I begin?"

"Try starting at the beginning," I firmly insisted.

"Well, as a young lad in Ireland, my dear Ma told me of a gift I possessed. I heard naught of it before this night."

I watched as he paused, probably waiting for me to interrupt him again. I was too tired, so I let him continue.

"It was a gift passed down through generations of our Celtic ancestors. I told my mother that it was just a folk tale, and I wanted no part of it."

Pausing again, he chanced a look my way. I remained silent, sitting still, and listened.

"She told me stories about how the gift had come to be and that I didn't have a choice but to accept it. That it was a part of who I was."

I turned to face him, wringing my hands in my lap, waiting for him to continue.

"So, when I was fifteen, I left Ireland to come to America, hoping to leave the gift behind."

The tone of his voice softened as he went on. "I thought I'd been successful, until a few weeks ago when I had a vision of a future family member's impending death. Thinking it meant that I could choose to intervene before the death occurred, but I was wrong. Then I remembered my Ma saying, the gift must be used only at the exact time of death. Not before. So, you see Emily, I couldn't prevent your death."

He squeezed his hands together so tightly, his knuckles turned white. What was this so-called gift he possessed?

"I never understood why I couldn't prevent a death since I'd never used the powers before. I had never wanted the bloody gift. Until you."

His facial muscles tensed. Was he pleading with me to understand what and why he did what he had?

"Can't you understand? You were about to die at the hands of that vile man, and I couldn't watch that happen when I could give you a second chance at living by using the gift."

Biting his lower lip, he took hold of my hands. "Please, Emily, try to understand I did it for your own good."

Pulling my hands from his grasp, I yelled, "My own good. I don't even know what that is anymore." Facing forward, I asked, terrified of his answer, "Am I really dead? Like, no going back dead?"

"Yes, dear, you are."

"Wait. Why didn't I think of this earlier? If you've never used this so-called gift before, how do you know you can't send me back?"

His brows pulled together while shaking his head. I could see he was struggling with his answer. "I don't."

"You don't?" Standing up, I ran both my hands through my disheveled hair. "What do you mean, you don't? Did you ask your mother? Did you maybe ask your Celtic ancestors how to reverse this so-called gift?" I refused to take his answer as final. "You have to find a way to send me back." Like a spoiled girl, I stomped my foot, "I am not staying here with you!" A long silence ensued, and I was afraid to ask but needed to know. "Where are we?"

"In a town called Yuma, in the Arizona Territory."

"Arizona Territory! Yuma! How can that be?" I was so scared, my hands shook. "What year is it?"

"1880"

Clenching the damp handkerchief in tight fists, I spun around, yelling, "You have got to be kidding me." Pacing, I stopped, turning to look directly into my grandfather's eyes. Asking bluntly, "This is a joke, right?" Not waiting for an answer, I continued, "How in the name of heaven did I get to Arizona when I live in *Seattle?*"

10

Emily

COLD AND DISORIENTED, one minute I had been speaking with
my great-great-grandfather, and the next, poof, he was gone.

"What, in the name of heaven, just happened?" Clutching my chest
with one hand, I rubbed my temple with the other attempting to dis-
pel the throbbing in my head. Slowly opening my eyes, I looked about
the darkness with no clue as to where I was. All I remembered is, I'd
been at work in the emergency room with the familiar sounds of friends,
machines, and bright lights when all of a sudden, my world spun out-of-
control. I had watched myself die. Then, there was this old man grabbing
my hand and telling me he was taking me home with him. *Where was
he now*? Looking out into nothingness, all I felt was unfathomable fear.

Should I scream? Would it do me any good? My faith had been
shaky since my parents were killed, but this was probably as good a
time as ever to start praying. If only He would hear me.

No matter how much I stretched, the pain in the middle of my back wouldn't go away, until I realized I was leaning against something cold and hard. Wincing, I felt a lump the size of a golf ball on the back of my head. Ouch. When did I get that? Bringing my hand away, I was relieved not to see blood. Feebly, I pushed myself forward. My vision was blurry, but I could see that my head had been resting on a huge rock. "What in the name of heaven's?"

Running my hand through my hair, I pulled out small pieces of dirt and bits of twigs. Stopping, I watched as the pink sky before dawn changed colors. It was beautiful, but I couldn't understand why it was so dark when overhead there should be the bright lights of the exam room.

Confusion warred within me while I stared into the fading darkness. "OK, last I remember, the exam room didn't have rocks in it. So, where am I exactly?"

Overwhelming helplessness hit as I yelled between my hands, "Help! Somebody help me!" Looking from side to side, I hoped someone would hear me. Temper rising, I screamed again, this time louder. "Where the hell am I? Somebody, please help me!" Suddenly, I cried out as a sharp stabbing pain zipped through my left temple, followed by flashing lights dancing behind both eyes. Inhaling quickly, I tried to quell diffuse nausea that followed.

Then, I tried standing as the pain eased. Turning around on my knees, I pushed myself up along the edge of the rock. Cautiously peering over it, I knew I was no longer in the emergency room. I felt more like Dorothy in the Wizard of Oz, waiting for the flying monkeys to attack while hoping Toto would come scurrying over to comfort me.

The air surrounding me was eerily still. Without warning, somewhere in the darkness, a single gunshot rang out, jolting me into reality. I dropped to the ground fighting back a primal scream as the memory of my last evening at work came flooding back. Instinctively, I grabbed my chest as the shot ricocheted in the distance. Running both hands over my chest, there was no hole. No blood. No pain.

Gulping down breaths to remain quiet, I leaned forward on the rock with both hands while lowering my head onto its rough surface, and prayed. Flashes of a man dressed in black wielding a gun in my emergency room painfully came into view. With a distorted sense of time, I remembered all too quickly what had happened.

An emergency room's worst fear was never knowing who would walk through its doors. But I remembered vividly watching from above as my friends worked frantically to save my life. There was blood, lots of blood—my blood coating the shiny floor.

Turning around, I sat in the dirt. Hands wrapped around my knees, I let my head fall forward. Unsuccessful at channeling a sense of calm, I finally gave in, allowing the stillness to engulf me until the howl of a lone coyote brought me out of my despair. Licking my dried lips, I wiped away tears. I didn't know how much more I could take. I needed to find my grandfather, and soon.

I was so tired, I must have dozed off, if only for a moment. Awakening with a renewed resolve, I turned around to inch myself back up the rock, hoping to get a better look at my surroundings. Just as I peered over, another gunshot pierced the silence, followed by sickening laughter, a man cursing, and the pounding of horse's hooves over gravel.

This time I didn't drop down behind the rock. Why? I was already dead. Wasn't I? Momentarily frozen in place, I leaned forward, waiting. Finally, standing up straighter, I held my breath while slowly peering over the rock, waiting for more gunshots to ring out. "Oh, for heaven sakes, I haven't got time for this. I need to find my grandfather and get back home."

I stood watching the sun inch closer over the eastern mountain tops, painting the sky shades of purple and orange. It was beautiful. I stepped out into the clearing, standing still, and waited. Again, nothing. All I could see was dirt, dying shrubs, and scorched hills. How can so beautiful a sunrise be in such a desolate place like this? A cold shiver ran up my spine, and I wrapped my arms tightly around my middle for warmth. Shaking my head, I was unable to understand why my grandfather had dropped me into this frightening place.

About two hundred feet away, I could see the outline of a building. No lights shone from inside, no dogs barked, and no cars were parked out front. Unmoving, I couldn't even hear the sound of city traffic, honking horns, or ambulance sirens. I spoke freely since it was obvious no one could hear me. "This is horrible. Don't they have electricity here?" Panic took a firm hold on my senses as that inner desire to flee escalated.

Fatigue crashed into me as I reached out with both hands, hoping to steady myself on the rock. I only wished this was all just a bad dream. Standing still, again, I listened for something, anything. But heard nothing. My instincts led me to believe that I wasn't supposed to be here.

Doc Sweeney

Slowly coming awake, I found myself sitting in my old rocker in a familiar room that was oddly silent. Out of habit, I rubbed the bridge of my nose when I remembered what had transpired the night before. "Oh, God. What have I done?"

Walking to the window, I gazed at the familiar scene below. A lone wagon passed by on the street outside my picket fence in the early light of day. Grabbing my glasses off the end table, I walked down the hall, past the exam rooms, and into the kitchen. "Emily, are you here?" Silence. Turning around, I headed to the bottom of the staircase, where I called out, "Emily, are you up there?" The only response I received was the creaking of the aging boards on the stairs as the house slowly came awake.

Shaking my head in disbelief. I slumped down on the last stair. She's gone. I didn't know how Emily could have gotten away from me.

Reviewing the events of yesterday; I had hold of her hand, and I was telling her where I was from and where we were going . . . then. How could
I have lost her? Scrubbing a hand over my face, I walked back to the
kitchen, making a somewhat rash decision. I needed to look for Emily.
She couldn't have gone far. Checking the time on my pocket watch,
I couldn't have slept that long. Hurrying around the room, I grabbed
what supplies I would need before riding out to look for Emily.

"Good morning, Doc. You're up early," said Jonas, the owner of the
livery. He extended his hand to me, and I shook it. "What can I do
for you this morning?"

"I need ye te saddle up Miss Maddie for me if ye would."

"Sure thing, Doc. Have an emergency, do ya?" he asked, walking
to Miss Maddie's stall. Opening the door, he patted the horse's neck
in greeting, saddled her, and then placed the bridle over her head.

Nervously, I shifted from one foot to the other as Jonas took his
time. My anxiety increasing with each passing minute. Finally, Jonas
handed me her reins. "Here you go, Doc. She's all ready to ride. Do
you need any help?" Pointing his thumb in the direction behind the
livery, "I can get my son to go with you if you'd like."

"No!" I replied a bit too harshly. "Thank ye, Jonas. But that
won't be necessary. I appreciate yer offer, though." Putting my left
foot into the stirrup, I hopped twice, pulling myself up, swinging my
right leg over the saddle. "I don't know how long I'll be gone."

Settling into the saddle, I asked, "Do me a favor, will ye please.
Let Sheriff Johansson know that I've left town."

"Sure thing, Doc. You want me to tell him where yer going?"

Pausing, I thought about what to say. I hated to lie to Jonas. "Tell
him I've gone up in te hills. That I've . . . ah . . . that I've gone looking
fer something I've lost." I couldn't miss the wary look on Jonas' face.

Hesitating, he answered, "OK, Doc, will do. You be careful out there, ya hear? Watch out fer snakes and them gopher holes. Don't need Miss Maddie stepping into one and coming up lame. Or, worse, breaking a leg and having her throw yer off."

"Thanks, Jonas. I'll be careful." Easing the reins forward, I squeezed my heels into Miss Maddie's sides and kissed her ahead. Slowly trotting down the center main street, I decided to head south, if for no particular reason other than I needed to make a start somewhere.

⤳ 11 ⤳

Emily

FINGERING THE FABRIC and tiny pearl buttons down my
front, I was shocked to see myself in a dress. Good grief, what
am I wearing? Disbelieving, I shook my head as I frantically looked
around for anyone, and not just my grandfather. Half expecting a
reasonable answer, from no one, in particular, I turned in a tight
circle holding the skirt out and yelled, "Okay, people! Help me out
here." Through rushed speech, I yelled, "I don't do calico."

I recalled my grandfather appearing the moment I died, telling
me he was taking me home with him. Then something about me
being needed. Is this his home? Yelling into the early morning sky,
"Is anyone at least going to tell me where I am?"

A nervous laugh escaped through my dry cracked lips. "I look
like something out of Little House on the Prairie." Closing my eyes,
I silently sent a prayer heavenward. *Please, God, if you're listening,*

now's the time I could use a little help. I need to find a way to get home. Where ever that may be.

Moving forward, something sharp pinched my toes. Pulling up my dress, and glancing down, gone were my comfortable clogs. In their place was a pair of narrow pointed high top button boots. "Really?" Was all I managed to say before dropping the fabric in frustration.

Cursing, "This isn't funny anymore, old man." Vexed, I turned my body in circles, raising fisted hands heavenward, "I demand to know what's going on. Now!" As if I could will my grandfather to reappear, I continued with my tirade. My parents would not be pleased by my actions. But, I was dead after all.

No one answered. I was alone. Letting out a huff, I walked in the direction of the darkened building, noting a door half off its hinges. The place looked deserted. Beyond my wildest imagination, I knew I was no longer in my beloved Seattle.

Holding onto the door frame with both hands, I dropped my head forward, sighing heavily. Shuffling one foot in front of the other, I stood within the cabin's entrance when the stench of mold and rodent feces made me cough. "Good heavens!" I needed fresh air. Certainly, this can't be what my grandfather meant by home?

"Oh! I need to find that man and give him a piece of my mind. What was he thinking when he dropped me into this place?" Once outside, I was finally able to take in deep cleansing breaths. My main focus now needed to be on survival, and deal with the what and whys later. With new resolve, I straightened my shoulders and stepped back into the darkened building, calling out, "Hello, anybody in here?" My voice echoed through the small room as I caught the lingering scent of bacon and beans. Despite my nausea, my stomach growled. I hadn't eaten since breakfast. Was that yesterday?

Guided only by the light of the rising sun, I moved cautiously forward, taking short steps to my left, bumping into something hard. "Ouch! If I wasn't already dead, this place would kill me."

Rubbing my hip with one hand while reaching out with my other, I came in contact with a table that wobbled under my touch. Ha-Choo! Ha-Choo! Not having a tissue, I picked up a corner of my dress and wiped my nose. Everything I touched sent moldy plumes into the air.

Caught in the light streaming through a gap in the roof, was the corner of a make-shift bed covered with a faded wedding ring quilt. Running my hand over its tattered pieces, the hairs on my arm stood up as feather-like legs crawled up my arm. "Ewe!" Screaming, I recoiled, shaking it off. "I don't even want to know what that was." Sweeping my hands down both sleeves, I yelled out to absent ears, "Can this day get any worse?"

With each step I took crossing to the cabin's only window, my footsteps churned up dust moats, sending them floating through the air. Leaning out the opening, I inhaled the cool breeze. Running a hand down my exposed throat, I enjoyed the moments of fresh air caressing me. Lost in my thoughts, I heard a low moan. Waiting silently, I realized it was my imagination playing tricks on me? Then I heard it again. Leaning farther out, I looked from side to side seeing nothing. Just as I was bringing my head back in, another, yet louder moan pierced the silence. It was coming from beneath the window. Looking down, I recognized the silhouette of a body slumped against the cabin wall.

Screeching, I almost fell through the window. "Oh, dear God." Running back through the darkness towards the door, I tripped on my skirts, falling to my knees, cursing. Catching my breath, I stood up, holding my dress higher and continued running around the outside of the cabin. How I managed to make it without falling again was surely Divine Providence. Sinking next to the body, I ignored the pain of jagged rocks penetrating my already tender knees.

My heart thumped wildly in my chest, making it hard to swallow. Salty beads of sweat burned my eyes, and I wiped them with the back of my hand. "Focus, Emily, you know what to do."

My hands raced over the warm body, searching upwards towards the jugular for the pulsing sign of life. Weak as it was, it was there. "Thank you, God." Awareness dawned, and I knew that before me lay the victim of the gunshots I'd heard earlier.

You've got this girl. I always whispered to myself during an emergency. It helped me remain calm. Unfortunately, I didn't hold out much hope of that now. I began running my hands frantically from head to toe to assess for injuries, not surprised when I came in contact with warm sticky moisture. The darkness from the shade of the building made it difficult for me to see the face of who lay before me. Thankfully, sunlight would soon peek over the hills, offering a better view of how much blood he'd lost.

As the minutes ticked by, his skin became cool and clammy under my touch. Definitely, not a good sign. He was in shock. If I could save him, and that was a big if, it was going to be one tough fight. I focused on his chest and abdomen, where major organs lay encased behind fragile tissue. Without scissors, I ripped the buttons of his vest and shirt free from their bondage, sending them flying through the air. "God, please help me," I was doing a lot of praying lately. Despite the heartaches of my past, I still believed in the power of prayer. What else did I have at this point? Now, I just hoped He heard me loud and clear.

Trying not to panic, a surging power rushed through my veins, urging me on. Used to working with a team at lightning speed, I desperately needed more hands. But, it was just a scared me alone trying to save a man's life. Moving my hands back up to his chest, I pulled out a dirty blood-soaked towel—his desperate attempt at staunching the flow of his own blood.

Feeling along his scapula, I felt a perforating wound. Grateful, I wouldn't have to go probing for that bullet since the shot had been a through and through. His belly wound was a different story. Although far enough to his side that it didn't appear to have hit any major organs, there was no exit wound. The bullet remained inside, and I would have to remove it before sepsis set in. Even so, I still might not be able to save him, given the primitive and unsterile surroundings.

Belly wounds could become deadly depending on the trajectory of the bullet once it entered the body. I wasn't complaining now about the extra fabric as I ripped my petticoats into strips. Folding the cloth into a thick pad, I placed it over his abdomen and firmly applied pressure. Just as I did, he let out a pitiful moan. "Stop . . . leave me alone." His hands moved futilely against mine as he slumped deeper into the gravel.

"I'm so sorry," I said, continuing to apply pressure. "I have to press hard to stop the bleeding."

"No . . . stop," he moaned louder. "Get away from me. Just let me die."

Grasping his hand, I placed it on his chest while holding on. "Please. You have to stop fighting me!" I didn't mean to be harsh, but I had no choice. Looking heavenward again for guidance, I stared at the rising sun. "Lord, I don't know where I am, but I now know why I'm here. I need your help keeping this man alive!" After remaining stoic for far too long, I let my tears run unbidden down my face. "Please, show me how to save this man."

Despite the coolness of the early morning, sweat ran between my breasts and anger coursed through my veins. "I'm a doctor for heaven's sake. I should be able to help this man."

"Am I dead?" came his faint question.

"What?" Suddenly, my world shifted with those three words. I realized then, I needed to do everything within my power to save this man's life, despite my friends not being able to save mine. So, I kept talking while gently running my hand over the side of his face to calm him. "No. No, of course, you're not dead," I answered, brushing back a lock of unruly dark curly hair that covered his right eye. "You're here with me." *Wherever that might be?* Leaning in close to his face, I said, "I'm here to take care of you."

I could have sworn the right side of the man's lips rose up in a feeble attempt to smile. I felt a strange stirring deep within my heart as I gazed down at the life I held in my hands, hoping my twenty-first-century skills could save a man in 1880.

⤜❧ 12 ❧⤛

Emily

I GAUGED THE MAN to be well over six feet tall and muscular with long dark wavy hair, giving him a rugged look. An appearance I could come to like. Maybe, more than like. What was I thinking? Was his hair dark brown or black? I couldn't tell you. Did it really matter? This wasn't the time for a foolish woman's infatuation. I needed to keep him alive.

Releasing his empty gun belt, I pulled it free from the constraints of his body. A ray of sunlight flashed off the weapon lying near his feet, for all the good it had done him. Gingerly, I picked it up between my thumb and forefinger, moving it out of my way. I had no use for guns, being well aware of the grief they caused. Next, I turned my focus to undoing the buttons down his denim fly. "Buttons? Who puts buttons on denim anymore? Where's the dang zipper?" Struggling, I cursed my way down the

76

row to free the metal from the stiff fabric, as I yelled, "Thank you, Mr. Levi!"

I was almost at the last button when the man let out a deep guttural groan and grabbed my wrist. Squealing at his contact, I was shocked at his remaining strength. My breath caught, and my heart skipped a beat as his intense smoky eyes stared up at me.

"Mister, if you think I'm trying to seduce you in your current condition, you're sorely mistaken." Fisting my hand, I tried unsuccessfully to pull it free of his grasp. "Nor, would I even think of doing such a thing if you were upright and not full of gunshot." Again, I tried to pull free, but his grip only tightened. Pleading, "Mister, please let go of me. I'm just trying to keep you alive." With that, his hold eased, but he didn't let go.

Coughing deeply, I could see the pain it caused him. Surprising me, he drew my hand to his chest. "Miss, it's nice to think I still have it, considering I'm a dying man." Brows furrowed, he let out a ragged breath, pushing my hand away. With labored breathing, he ground out, "I appreciate what . . . you're trying . . . to do. But don't bother wasting your efforts on a dead man."

"Stop talking like that. Your shoulder wound went straight through, so I don't have to go digging after that bullet. And I don't believe the bullet in your abdomen hit any internal organs, like your liver, pancreas, or your kidney." He probably didn't understand what I was saying about his anatomy, so I ended with, "Unfortunately, the bullet is still in there, and I need to get it out."

I feared he may be right, and his death was imminent. Laying my hand reassuringly over his heart, I felt its thready beat under my palm. I had to do all in my power not to let the devil of death take him. For some unknown reason, this man intrigued me, and I needed to know more about him.

Maybe, just maybe, he could help me get back home. Meanwhile, in my effort to calm him, I covered his clammy hand with my warm one. "Mister, dead men don't talk. Now, please let me do what I need to. I'm trying to keep you alive." Shaking my head, I added, "I'll try not to cause you too much more pain." I was lying, and wasting my time talking when what I needed to do was find something with which to dig the bullet out. "You've lost a fair amount of blood, and you need to keep still. If you start thrashing around, you'll start bleeding again. Do you understand?" Silence ensued as I waited for him to answer. Then . . .

"At least I won't die alone," he hissed out.

"Don't say that."

Reaching up, he laid his bloody shaky hand along the side of my face. Without opening his eyes, he said, "I'll die in the arms of an angel."

Instinctively, I leaned into his hand, taking hold of his wrist and closed my eyes. Even though he was weak, his calloused palm still held a tenderness I'd never felt before. My heart was aching for this man whom I hadn't known existed until an hour ago. He'd barely finished speaking when his hand slipped slowly from my grasp, and I watched him succumb to the darkness of unconsciousness. Body limp, he lay infinitely still as his spoken words hit home. I knew he didn't hear me when I said, "I'm no angel, mister."

Gripping the edges of his blood-soaked vest, I implored him, "Don't you dare go dying on me. You hear me? I don't want to be left out here alone. I know you have the fight left in you to stay alive." Grabbing the hem of my dress, I wiped my eyes with the dirty fabric. Trying to regain my composure, I stared into the early morning rays. The only sound I heard was that of a bird and the light breeze swirling dried mesquite leaves over the ground.

Doing a mental run of internal anatomy and the bullet's entrance site, I surmised that it must have missed his spine since he could still move his legs. "*It must have missed all the major vessels and arteries, otherwise . . . he'd be dead.*" I ran my hand down his abdomen as if tracing a roadmap and continued with my self-lecture.

My nerves kept me reviewing age-old anatomy books like a video in my mind. "*A bullet hitting either of these major arteries would have him bleeding out before I'd ever found him.*" Still, there was no telling what real damage it had done internally to his gastrointestinal tract and surrounding vessels. "*Dang it! I can't do a thorough examination out here. It will kill him for sure if he doesn't die of sepsis first.*"

Regaining my composure, I tore another long strip of fabric from my petticoats, folding it into squares to make another pressure dressing. The man was dead weight, no pun intended, and I had to struggle to work the long piece of fabric behind his back and around his abdomen. Thankfully, his bleeding had stopped for the time being. Touching his forehead with the back of my hand, I gently pushed back a damp curl of hair that hung over his left eye, my fingers lingering a bit longer than necessary.

Even though the man beside me remained unconscious, his presence brought me some comfort. Glacial fingers crept up my spine. I didn't know where I was or if I was still Emily Sweeney, MD. Time was ticking, and I needed to remove that bullet, but, "I need something long and sharp. Think Emily, where would I hide a knife on my body?"

Then, it dawned on me from watching old Westerns with my father. Unfortunately, like some of my former patients, weapons would be hidden strapped beneath pant legs or tucked into belt backs. Running my hands down his legs, I stopped feeling a bulge at his right ankle. Lifting the fabric, I was relieved at seeing a large knife sheathed within a bead-encrusted leather case. Pulling it out, I realized it might be a bit large for my needs, but I wouldn't argue; it would have to do. A larger incision was better than leaving the bullet in his abdomen. I had nothing to clean it with, no fire to boil water, or alcohol to sterilize the blade. Certainly, using a non-sterile knife would hasten his death from sepsis. Leave it in, or take it out? Either way, he was at high risk for dying. I knew what I had to do.

As the sun crept higher in the sky, and the temperature rose to a comfortable degree, I carefully wiped the blade several times in the cleanest area of my petticoat. Then laid it down within easy reach on another piece of clean fabric. I had arrived in nothing but a worn-out cotton dress that now had more tears in it than a sieve, but I was thankful for all the extra material.

I had to be crazy to think I could do this, without anesthesia, suture to tie off blood vessels, sterile bandages, or pain medication. I could go on and on with a list of things I didn't have, and stalling wasn't going to help him. What I did have was my faith, skills, and sheer determination to remove the bullet.

Thankful he was still unconscious, I hoped it would make my job manageable and less painful for him. "Not bloody likely!" I remembered in fine detail every jab, poke, and stick I'd endured after being shot. It had been pure hell.

Moving him from leaning against the cabin wall to lying flat on the ground, elicited a low groan. I had to be careful not to restart his bleeding while moving aside the abdominal bandage. Peering into his agonized features, I knelt closer to his side, praying that God would guide my hands, and he would survive what I was about to do.

Knife poised above his abdomen, my left hand held the skin around the entrance wound taut between my thumb and middle finger. "Aahhh!" he screamed loudly between clenched teeth at the penetration of the blade. Instinctively, he tried to curl up into a ball.

"Mr., you need to lie still. I'll go as fast as I can." A low guttural sound escaped his lips, and his body stilled. I took this opportunity to enlarge the opening with the blade and probe deeper. His eyes flew open, and he grabbed my hand. Pulling his knees up, he yelled, "Stop!" Choking out ragged breaths, the sound echoed into the hills. "You're killing me."

Pushing his hand away, I calmly answered, "You have to hold still. I need to get this bullet out, or you'll die."

Eyes closed, he nodded his assent. "Do . . . what . . . you . . . have . . . to do." His knees slid down to the ground, jarring his abdomen.

Closing his eyes, I knew he remained conscious. "This is going to hurt like hell, but you can't move."

Probing deeper, he arched his back and screamed loud enough to wake the desert dead. "Aahhh . . . God, help me! Make her stop! Just let me die!"

I tried hard to ignore his desperate pleas. I really felt terrible about the pain I was inflicting. What I wouldn't give for some anesthesia and Kelly forceps. Finally, I hit the top of the bullet. It was deeper than what I'd hoped to go. Blood began a steady ooze from the opening, making visibility difficult despite my attempt at keeping the site dry. Not use to doing this alone while kneeling in dirt, the whole procedure went against all my training in maintaining a sterile field.

My strength was giving out, and my arms and neck ached to the burning point. Edging the end of the blade under the narrow rim of the bullet, the glint of metal shone at the entrance of the wound. Grasping the shell and pieces of germ-laden fabric between two fingers, I pulled up and out.

Thankfully, he'd passed out at some point after his plea for me to let him die. Laying still, his breathing was shallow. I knew the worst was yet to come. Drenched in sweat, I placed a petticoat bandage, sans lace, over his abdomen, his color matching the white of the fabric. I was exhausted. My body ached all over as I sat back in the dirt, sighing heavily, afraid I'd just placed the final nail into his coffin.

Before pulling his bloody shirt over his bare chest, I checked his shoulder wound one more time, satisfied the bleeding had stopped. Stretching my neck and shoulder muscles, I leaned back against the cabin wall, sighing deeply. It was anyone's guess if he would survive.

Emily

A S THE DESERT sun rose higher in the sky, the air around us became warmer. Soon, it would be too hot for either of us to remain outside without cover to ward off its burning rays. Remembering the quilt inside the cabin, dirty as it was, it would still provide some protection. Rising on stiff legs, I brushed off the dirt from my dress, looking down at the body lying at my feet.

This time, I remembered to pick up my skirt before turning. It wouldn't do to have me fall flat on my face over his body and break an arm or leg. Pausing at the entrance long enough to allow my vision to adjust to the dimness within, I cautiously made my way to the bed by sheer memory.

Feeling totally out of my element, I sat on the edge of the bed, hunching my shoulders and cradling the musty quilt to my chest. "It would be so easy just to sit here and wait." Wait for what, I didn't know. Wait for someone to rescue us? Or, wait for death to take us both?

I'd hoped by walking through the cabin door, I would find myself back in the emergency room, and the events of that fateful evening would all have been a bad dream. "Didn't my grandfather say that I had someone to save? Well, I did. Now, it's his turn to take me back home to Seattle. Hopefully, where I could make better choices and not get myself killed."

This is crazy. Despite my efforts, I knew the man's chances of surviving were slim. But, there was something in the way he called me Angel that touched a soft spot in my heart. So, dying was not an option for either of us. I desperately wanted to live—a second time.

Wiping my tears with the back of my hand, I gave myself a good talking to. "Emily Sweeney, you're a competent physician. You can handle this. Now get it together."

Rummaging around the darkened room for anything that would be of use, I located a shearling coat and a half-full canteen hanging from a nail next to a dry sink. On a crooked shelf above the stove, I discovered a tin. Opening the lid, I recognized something similar to extra-large saltines. Shaking it gently, I wanted to reassure myself that weevils hadn't taken up hibernation. Satisfied, I wrapped the tin and other items in the quilt for easy carrying.

As I came around the side of the cabin, I heard the crunch of gravel and a loud pitiful moan. My stubborn patient was trying to push himself up with his right arm and failing miserably. I couldn't believe it. I'd just dug a bullet from his gut, and now he was . . . "Stop," I yelled from between cracked lips. Dropping my armload of supplies, I rushed to his side. "What in the name of heavens do you think you're doing?"

Looking up through wisps of hair covering his eyes, he grunted and continued to shift in the gravel. "Isn't it obvious? I'm trying to get up." He reached out, trying to grab my arm in an apparent attempt to use it for leverage. "I have . . . to find . . . my horse," he said, nodding towards the empty corral.

The raspy noise raking through his chest alarmed me. Was it the dry air irritating his throat like mine, or was fluid accumulating in his lungs? I shook the latter thought off knowing if it was fluid, like blood, he would soon be dead, and there was nothing I could do.

"What you need to do is be still," I implored, easing him back down.

"Why? What good will it do?" Feigning a chuckle, he added, "I thought you finally came to your senses and left me to die."

"Don't talk so foolishly. Besides, you're in no condition to go anywhere." Nervous, I chewed on my lower lip, while gathering the quilt from the dirt beside him. A small sense of false relief washed over me that he was still alive, but barely. Didn't the dying sometimes have one last burst of energy? Had this been his?

Applying gentle pressure to his shoulder, not meaning to sound irritated, I implored him, "Please, you need to lie still. I'm glad you're awake, but you don't want to start bleeding again." As I stared at his ghostly pale face, I didn't want him to notice my shaking hands, while assuming the worst impending scenario. Plying the hem of the quilt nervously through my fingers, I mentally listed off what I needed to do next to keep him alive. First and foremost, I needed to ask him a question. Looking away, I didn't know why I felt so nervous when I asked, "What is your name?"

Stiffening, I could see the turbulence in his eyes. It told me all I needed to know; his pain was unbearable. Cursing, he clutched his side rasping out sarcastically, "Why? You want it for my tombstone?"

"That's not funny." Taking hold of his forearm, I tried distracting him from the pain.

Bowing his head in mock propriety, I felt the muscles in his arm tense under my grasp as he answered, "I'm sorry. I didn't mean to sound, you know, ungrateful. It's Caleb. Caleb Young, at your service miss. Sorry, I can't get up to introduce myself properly to a lady. But, as you can see I'm a bit, how would you say?"

"A bit indisposed," I answered for him, trying not to sound glib.

"Yes. I guess you could say that."

He gazed up at me, and I felt a searing heat that wasn't from the sun, rise along my neck. He had me blushing like a young schoolgirl.

"I'm sorry, I didn't mean to stare, but you have beautiful violet eyes."

Sensing his struggle to hold on to consciousness, he graced me with a heart-stopping smile and asked, "What is your name?"

"Mine?"

"Yes. You're the only one here," he said, placing his hand over mine.

"It's Emily. Emily Sweeney." Purposefully, I'd left out the MD. It was my turn to stare and watch the strained features on his face relax, and his raspy voice turned to a weakened whisper.

"Under different circumstances, it would be a pleasure to meet you, Miss Sweeney." He continued holding my hand. "I'm glad you're here with me."

I could see Mr. Young's strength leaving him. He needed to salvage what little he had left. With great difficulty, he reached up to my face. Too weak to accomplish his task, I grasped his hand in mine. With eyes closed, he whispered, "Tell me where you come from, Miss Emily?" I could tell he was afraid to stop talking and drift back into unconsciousness.

"Not far from here." I'd lied. I hated lying. But, in this case, I wasn't, since all I'd known I'd left behind in a place and time Mr. Young couldn't possibly understand.

Where is that old man?

"How did you wind up here in the middle of nowhere, taking care of a dying man?"

A round of coughing had him grabbing his abdomen tighter and leaning painfully to his side rasping out, "Not that I'm ungrateful . . . mind you."

Laying my hand gently over his, I exerted a light downward pressure, bracing his abdominal muscles from the jarring sensation caused by his coughing. "Please, Mr. Young, you must stop talking and conserve your energy. You're going to need it." I ignored his questions, mostly because I didn't have the answers, and didn't think anyone was about to enlighten me any time soon. Distraught with my negative thoughts, I couldn't help but think, *what difference does it make? If he dies, he'll never need to know who I am and where I came from.* My stomach clenched in knots as I shook my head. Angry with myself, I silently questioned, *when did I become so cold?*

Watching, he took in a quaking breath. Not heeding my request, Caleb continued to ramble, "I didn't think anyone knew I was here."

Frantically turning his head from side to side, beads of sweat covered his brow. I didn't know what he was looking for?

"It's obvious someone did, or I wouldn't be dying on this God-forsaken hillside." Suddenly, eyes wide as saucers, Mr. Young's sudden vacant stare sent my medical instinct on high alert. Clutching the front of my dress, he pulled me forward. Feeling his rapid shallow breaths on my face, he rushed out, "I need to get out of here!" I was scared that his sudden anxiety, increased shortness of breath, and disorientation were indicative of a pulmonary embolus. If so, there was nothing I could do out here. It would mean imminent death for Mr. Young.

"She's coming," he choked out, throwing his right arm in the air. "We've got to get out of here."

"Who's coming?"

Pushing his heels into the dirt, he tried sitting up. "She'll kill me." His dark eyes pulled me deeper into his mounting fear, and icy chills ran down my spine as he added in a whisper, "Watch for her. She'll kill you too."

Confused, I looked around for another woman. Had this woman been the one who shot him? All I could see was an empty corral. Beyond that, dry, desolate earth. Mr. Young's hallucinations compounded my fears as he rattled on about a woman, a man, and his father. None of it makes any sense. Gazing on his pallid face, I placed my hand over his, which still clung to my dress with a death grip. I couldn't pry it free, nor did I want to. It tied him to me. "Shush, Caleb." Gently running my hand over his forehead, I tried encouraging him to rest. "Stop talking. I'll make sure no woman comes near us."

Rushing out, as if they were his last words, "What if all I have is tonight with my angel?"

Angel? "It's Emily. It's Emily who's here with you."

"What? No, you're my Angel."

His eyes had turned to a dusty gray, and his tense muscles began to relax.

"Emily?" he questioned between clenched teeth as if he'd never seen me before. Groaning, his hold tightened on my dress, and I could barely hear him when he said, "I don't want to die. Emily, please, don't let me die. Not here."

Squeezing his eyes tightly shut, a single tear ran down his cheek. With my thumb, I gently wiped it away then tenderly cupped the side of his face, hoping to bring him some peace. My breath caught then hesitated when I sent another silent prayer heavenward. "There will be another tomorrow for the both of us, Caleb. I promise."

He squeezed my hand, "Ah, I hear that quiver of doubt in your voice, Miss Emily. In your heart, you don't believe it any more than I do that tomorrow will come for me. My only regret is that I won't get to know you better."

Bowing my head so our eyes wouldn't meet, I choked out, "Please, don't say that, Mr. Young. You'll live to see tomorrow." *You have to.*

"Hush sweet angel," raising his shaky hand towards my face.

His attempt to comfort me was my undoing. I choked back a pent up breath when he said,

"I hate to see a woman cry."

"I'm not crying!" Wiping my eyes with my dirt-covered dress.

"It's OK. You've done your best." Smiling faintly, "I've lived a life of joy in this short time spent with you by my side."

My heart clamored in my chest. I couldn't figure out what led Mr. Young to say such a thing. Had his past been that traumatic to only have these moments with me mean so much? To take my mind off what he just said, I busied myself and took one last look at his bandages to check for any fresh bleeding. Thankful, they remained dry. Reaching over him to grab the quilt, I inhaled the strong scent of leather, sweat, and blood as his warm breath caressed my cheek.

"Umm, you smell like sweet lilacs," Caleb said.

I thought he was still hallucinating because he surely couldn't be smelling my lilac lotion after all this time. *Wasn't it yesterday I applied it? Before I died.*

With renewed strength and without warning, he reached up, drawing my head down so our lips softly touched. Caught off guard, I quickly pulled back, touching my fingertips to my burning lips. My head spun with crazy thoughts at his unexpected tenderness. How could one kiss be so powerful?

"What are you afraid of, Emily? Won't you grant a dying man his last wish to kiss a beautiful angel?"

He's delirious. With all his blood loss, he must be thinking I'm someone from his past, as I told him, "I'm no angel, Mr. Young. You must be thinking of some other woman." Rolling my eyes heavenward, I couldn't believe what a man in his dire condition had done. I could only explain the kiss to be nothing more than his hallucination—an amazing one at that.

Eyes closed, his breathing slowed as I stared down at his face hearing him say, "I certainly hope there's no one else like me kissing you."

"No!" was all I could say.

There had been no man as bold as him in my life. Caleb, his name smoothly flowed off my lips. How could this stranger stir such feelings inside me? Don't go there, Emily. You're going to leave here as soon as you find that old man. In reality, I seriously wanted to find out more about the man who lay before me. In the meantime, I needed to keep him alive, no matter the cost. He was possibly the key to my returning home.

Trying to be resourceful, I opened the quilt and lay it on the windowsill, securing it in place with large rocks. I then spread it over Caleb just enough to create a tent to ward off the sun's rays, hoping the scorching heat wouldn't penetrate through. Securing the quilt to the ground with more rocks, I climbed underneath, pulling the canteen and meager food supplies with me. Gently patting Caleb's shoulder with my hand, I asked him to raise his head so I could place his folded coat under him for a pillow.

Trapping my hand firmly in his, he spoke in a faint whisper, "*My spirit is too weak, mortality weighs heavily on me like unwilling sleep, and each imagin'd pinnacle and steep of godlike hardship, tells me I must die like a sick Eagle looking at the sky.'* "

Astonished, my head snapped up. "Keats. You know Keats?"

"Yes. John Keats. Do you know him?" he asked breathlessly.

"Yes, I do. Well, not personally of course," I animatedly gestured with my hands. "He died over a hundred . . . I mean some years ago." I smiled wistfully, remembering my undergraduate years and the quiet times I'd spent at the University of Washington's Suzazallo Library reading the classics. "I remember him from my college English Lit . . . English classes. He was a wonderful romantic poet like Byron and Shelley. Unfortunately, he died way too young at the age of twenty-five from tuberculosis." Catching myself, "I mean consumption."

"An appropriate verse for a dying man. Don't you think?"

"Mr. Young, please stop talking of dying." My intrigue for this man only increased with each passing minute. He certainly had more stories to tell, and I desperately wanted to hear them.

"Alright, I won't," he said, exhaling a slow breath. "But only if you'll call me Caleb. Mr. Young was my father, and it doesn't bode well for me to hear his name."

"Of course, Caleb." I knew it. There were more stories for him to tell. I just had to be patient to hear them. Rearranging the rocks, dirt, and bits of twigs underneath my derriere, I tried to get comfortable. Finally, as comfy as I was going to be, with my back to the cabin wall, I uncorked the canteen. Giving Caleb a few sips, I asked him to, "Drink slow. I don't want you getting nauseated." Taking a sip myself, I had to ration what we had. Who knew when I could locate water?

Inhaling deeply, I moved my head from side to side, shoulder to shoulder, hearing the releasing cracking along my spine. From long-held tension, the pain had built up taking its toll on my body. Gradually, I felt my aching muscles relax one small fiber at a time. I had no idea what time it was when I leaned my head back against the wall, ready to get some well-needed sleep.

As the sun rapidly rose in the east, I couldn't slow down my thoughts. It was still early in the day, but we both needed sleep when all I could think of, *What if his hallucinations increase? What if he develops a raging fever? What if he dies?* Too many "what ifs." My imagination was running wild. Despite my fatigue, I knew I wouldn't sleep, as my eyes slowly drifted closed, remembering, *this is just like an internship, pulling all-nighters.*

His scent mingled with the desert breeze, had me sending another silent prayer heavenward that we would both survive the night and see the light of a new day.

My head nodded, and I was unable to keep my eyes open when Caleb's faint whispering caught my attention.

"Emily, don't leave me," he asked, his hand firmly gripping mine.

"I won't leave you, Caleb, I promise." *I didn't think I could survive out here alone without him.*

ᓂ 14 ᕼ

Emily

S LOWLY COMING AWAKE, I found my head resting on
Caleb's uninjured shoulder with my hand over his heart, as
if willing him to live. Feeling its steady beat beneath my palm,
and the slow rise and fall of his chest brought me comfort. Every
muscle in my body ached. Stretching, I pulled back our quilted
shelter, watching the waning sunlight over the mountains bring
closure to another day.

Caleb looked ghostly pale after losing so much blood. His
eyes, framed with thick sable lashes, were sunken and rimmed
with dark circles against his tan cheeks. The skin on his fore-
arms tented, indicating signs of dehydration. It was alarming. If
we'd been in my emergency room, I would have had the means of
treating him with intravenous fluids, plus other life-saving medications. But it wasn't to be.

Unfortunately, it would be almost fifty years before penicillin would be discovered in 1928 by Sir Alexander Fleming. These were medical luxuries I would never again take for granted if given a chance. I could only rely on old school medicine of hands-on examination and observation.

I half-expected Caleb to have a raging fever by this time when I laid the back of my hand on his brow. Surprised, that it was cool and clammy, knowing it would only be a matter of time when a fever would rear its ugly head. Then, all my ingenuity and training would be put to good use.

As I moved, my hand was pulled firmly against Caleb's chest, creating a link between us. Sighing deeply with relief, knowing he was still responsive, I attempted to push myself up, but he wouldn't let go. "Caleb, you need to let go of my hand so I can get up."

Mumbling, he moved his head from side to side. "No, don't leave me, Rebecca. I'm sorry I left you behind."

Half asleep, he pushed his feet into the gravel. I sensed his pain to be the culprit of his delirium as I tried easing him back against the ground. Fearing all this movement would open up his wounds, I gently touched his shoulder, asking him, "Caleb, wake up, you are having a bad dream. It's Emily. I didn't leave you."

In a moment of clarity, he mumbled, "I kept dreaming I was dead and finally made it to hell."

My heart ached to hear the torment in a man fighting for his life. "Hush now," staring into Caleb's contorted features. I needed to reassure him. "You're not in hell." *Although, that was debatable.* "You're here with me."

I dreaded what the days ahead would bring. Would he survive, or would we both die alone here in the desert? I couldn't share my worst fears for our immediate future. What would be the point? But somehow, I thought he already knew. When he finally calmed down, I decided to stay by his side a while longer. Still, I was exhausted and could barely keep my eyes open when I finally allowed the fatigue to take control of my body. *"I'll just close my eyes for just a bit longer. I won't sleep."*

More tired than I realized, I fell into a deep slumber and dreamt of times spent with my parents. I was enjoying the memory when mid dream, Caleb let out an ear-splitting scream. Awakening in a fog, I leaned over, noticing Caleb's damp hair sticking to his brow, and the heat radiating from his face. My worst fear had surfaced sooner than I thought. Apparently, an infection had taken a firm hold on his body. *Oh, please, no.* Looking around, as if someone would come walking out of the desert night to help me, I collapsed back against the side of the building, letting out a breath I didn't know I'd been holding in.

"Think. Emily. You know what you have to do." Oh, how I wished for the advantages and medicines from 2019. Not wanting to waste time, I began mentally formulating a plan. The first thing I needed to do was get Caleb off the cold ground and into the cabin where we both would be more comfortable. There, I would have better access to monitoring his fever and wounds. Leaning closer, I told him, "Caleb, I need to get you into the cabin. Do you hear me?"

He didn't. Instead, he raved on and on about a woman named Anna, and a man named Michael that he was going to kill. In a sinister whisper, he asked, "Is that you, Anna? How did you find me?"

"Caleb, its Emily."

"Where's Michael? I'll kill that Sonofa . . ." His yelling led to a spasm of coughing, which had him rolling to his side.

"Anna? Michael? Rebecca? I couldn't keep the names straight." There were too many players in the story of Caleb's past.

I desperately needed to move him into the cabin. But how? I wasn't sure if he could stand, let alone walk around the building in his state of delirium. Lifting him on my own was out of the question. No pun intended, but he was dead weight. Moving him now would only open his wounds and expend too much energy that he needed for fighting the fever. The rhythm of his breathing increased, and his cough was making a deep rattling sound when I realized I would have to leave him here another night under the tented quilt.

I watched as he struggled to speak. "Anna, its Caleb. Or have you already forgotten me?" Taking in gulps of air, he continued, "Are you and Michael here to finish me off?" His one-sided conversation had me confused. I only wished I had a medication I could give him for his agitation and pain. Moving his legs and free arm in an attempt to flee, he yelled out, "Well, you can't have me. You're too late. I'm already dead."

Gently touching the side of his face trying to reassure him, I murmured what I hoped were words of comfort, letting him know that I was not the Anna of his past. His breathing slowed at my voice, and the muscles in his face relaxed. I wondered if Anna had ever cared this much. From his comments, I didn't think so.

Once he calmed down, I tried getting him to drink what little water was left in the canteen. Raising his head, I placed the metal rim over his lips, asking him to swallow. While much of the liquid dripped out the sides of his mouth, a few precious drops made their way down his throat.

I took one small sip, just enough to wet my lips and tongue that had turned to parchment. Staring down at Caleb, I wondered what would befall us next. Hands formed into a steeple, I tried planning my next move, determined to persevere and overcome any obstacles that God put before us. He may test me, but I knew He wouldn't desert me. I was determined to survive.

Finding water was my top priority. We could live without food for a few days, but not water. Succumbing to dehydration would assuredly lead to a horrible death for the both of us. While the thought of killing an animal for food made me physically ill, I knew I would have to do it. Even though I detested the so-called 'sport' of hunting, I wasn't afraid to handle a shotgun, having gone to the practice range with my father. But there, it was shooting a paper target, not a living creature.

Daylight would soon be gone, and another night on rocky ground was not something I looked forward too. Thinking of my apartment with all of its conveniences, overlooking downtown Seattle and Elliott Bay, I hoped I would see it again someday. Right now, I just wanted two ibuprofen, a glass of Cabernet Franc, and a hot bath.

Awakening before daylight, I was able to move without disturbing Caleb. Lifting the corner of his shearling coat, I could see that his bandages had stuck to his chest from the dried blood and sweat. Placing my open palm on his chest, I felt the raspy rattle beneath my fingers with each breath he took. Worried, his fever continued waging war in his fight to survive.

This morning, my job would be to locate water, clean Caleb's wounds, and attempt to lower his fever. I scooted out from underneath the quilt shelter and stretched to ease the intense aching in my lower back. I hadn't paid much attention to my surroundings the day before, but now I saw just how bleak it was. Beautiful in its own way, the hills were filled with varying shapes and sizes of cacti and scrub brush. It was void of anything green, except for one small area high above the cabin. In hopes of locating water, I would have to head in that direction, approximately one-quarter mile up a steep hill.

Grabbing the canteen, I went inside the cabin to search for anything else that would hold enough water to boil. Finding a bucket that looked debatable, despite some rusting around the outside rim, it would have to do. Heading outside, I shaded my eyes from the rising sun as I looked up into the hills determining how long it would take me to get there and back. I prayed that it would be an easy climb. One because of the uncomfortable shoes I had on, and two, I didn't want to be gone long and have Caleb waking up thinking I'd had left him alone to die.

Following a rocky trail leading west, up and away from the cabin, I hoped to find a water source. These hills were far from my lush Cascade Mountains and icy rivers. Reaching the top of the hill, I heard the welcoming sound of water swiftly flowing over rocks.

Moving through the low dense brush, I scraped my arms and legs
on hidden thorns. Desperate to dip my hands and toes into the chilly
water, I pushed through to the edge of the stream, ignoring the pain.
Almost there, my dress caught on an unyielding branch. Struggling
to free it, the harder I tugged, the more frustrated I became. "Let go
of me. You . . ." I know yelling at the bush didn't help, but it sure
felt good. Giving the fabric a final tug, it broke free with a loud rip-
ping sound. As it did, I stumbled forward, cursing. "Dang it! If only
I had a pair of scissors, I'd cut this thing shorter." Ignoring the tear,
I moved out into a clearing where the water was crystal clear. I could
see the creek bottom as it flowed over rocks and boulders, swirling
into a pool below.

Kneeling on the rocky bank, I viewed my reflection in the water.
Shocked at what I saw, I was tempted to strip down to nothing,
wade into the creek, and rid myself of the caked-on dirt. Instead, I
dipped the canteen into the stream. When I did so, I felt the fabric of
my dress soak up water at my knees. Purring like a satisfied kitten,
I would have jumped in naked if I didn't have to get the precious
liquid back to Caleb. Instead, I swirled my hands in the aqueous gift,
let it run over my face, and scooped up a handful to drink my fill.

Swirling it inside my mouth, I hadn't realized how parched
I was until I welcomed the tasteless life-saving liquid. Lost in my
thoughts, I was quickly brought back to the present by the sound
of a low throaty growl. Looking up, there standing on a rock across
the stream was an imposing Puma keenly watching my every move.
Inhaling sharply, I froze in place, never having seen one this close
before. He was magnificent yet terrifying.

As hard as it was, I was trying not to panic, but the pounding
pulse in my ears said otherwise. "OK, Emily, remain calm, and
maybe he'll go away." A macabre chuckle passed through my lips as
I added, "Not bloody likely." It became a staring game between me
and the animal's sandy-colored eyes. I thought at any minute I would
become his next meal. Shifting into survival mode while trying to

rise, I found myself frozen with fear. *Remember what Da taught you. I can't remember! Oh heavens, am I supposed to stand still, or make a lot of noise?* Questioning myself, I was wasting precious time, and running would only cause the Puma to charge. Squeezing my eyes shut, I flinched at any little sound he made. So, I decided to wait, and not so patiently, I must say.

As time slowly ticked by, I could feel streams of warm sticky sweat run down the sides of my head. I had no idea how long I knelt in the mud while I tried gathering my courage. *How stupid could I be in not bringing Caleb's rifle with me?* I probably wouldn't be a good shot with my nerves so frayed, but at least I could have scared him into believing I meant business. Flinching, the animal emitted another loud growl, readying himself to jump.

"I'm a dead woman."

Doc Sweeney

I hadn't ridden far from town when Sheriff Johansson caught up with me. Rubbing the back of my neck, I doubted him showing up was a coincidence. *Dang it! Jonas must have told him I rode out without telling him where I was going.* Scratching my beard, I thought, *Just because I'm an old man, doesn't mean I need a baby sitter.*

What am I going to tell him? As I watched the sheriff ride closer, I felt like a kid caught with his hand in the cookie jar. *Think, Mathew. What excuse am I going to give him? The truth. That's always the best.* It was so unlike me to just ride off and not tell anyone where I was headed. *If I tell him the truth, I'd be taking a chance at being hauled back to town and declared insane.* The sheriff wasn't stupid. He knew I had no patients that lived this far up in the hills. *I'll tell him the partial truth. I'll just omit one significant fact that my great-great-granddaughter was from another century.* I'd never told anyone before that I had a family, always letting the townspeople assume what they wanted of my past. It was easier that way.

"Hey Doc," Sheriff Johansson called out. "Vat ya doing up here?"

"Don't suppose you'd believe that I just wanted to take an early morning ride."

"No," the sheriff replied bluntly. I watched him shake his head from side to side. "It's not like ya ta just ride off, least of all, not tell Jonas vhere you're going." His Swedish accent grew more difficult to understand every time he had too many questions and not enough answers. Reining his horse around, we faced each other. Rubbing his hand over day-old stubble, he continued to ask me questions I didn't want to answer.

"Vant to tell me vhat's going on? Maybe I can be of some help."

I felt my horse's muscles tense under my knees as he sidestepped away from the sheriff's mount. I don't know who was more nervous, my horse, or me. Reaching down, I patted Miss Maddie's neck to calm her, then focused on the ground. "Sheriff, you wouldn't believe me if I told you."

"Try me."

I must have been too slow to answer when he pushed, "I'm listening, Doc!"

"Ah . . . I'm looking for my granddaughter." Waiting for a surprising response, and receiving none, I continued. "She was supposed to arrive at the clinic three days ago. I fear something has happened to her."

"Vhy didn't you say something sooner? I could have formed a posse to go out and look for her." Leaning forward on his saddle horn, he asked me, "How vaz she coming? On the stage?"

Avoiding his question, I knew it was time to tell the sheriff what was going on. He was too smart to realize I wasn't telling the truth. "Sheriff, we need to talk." Palms sweating, I pointed to a shady area under a mesquite tree. "Why don't we sit a spell over there? I have some things to tell you."

"OK, Doc. My horse could use a break." The sheriff sauntered over to the tree while I dismounted, throwing the reins over a low hanging branch, I waited for the sheriff to do the same.

Before I broached the subject of my granddaughter, the sheriff asked. "Doc, do ya remember te man tat gambler murdered te other day?" While filling his hat with water from his canteen, he held it out to his horse, waiting for my answer.

"Yes, I remember. I only saw te body after Mr. Cribb had me take a look at it. Why?" Taking a long swig from my canteen, I felt it was an odd subject for the sheriff to bring up now.

"Funny ting. Te gambler who murdered him. I had him leave town shortly after te shooting. Guess I should have arrested him."

"Why didn't you?" I asked, sitting down under the shade of overhanging branches. Even though we were at a higher elevation, the sun gave off enough heat to make standing directly in its rays, uncomfortable. "I remember ye telling me that. But why are ye telling me all this now?"

"Don't know," he answered, raising his shoulders. "His horse wandered back into town this morning, minus a rider and looking a little worse for wear. Looked like he'd been wandering up in the hills alone for a few days. Plus, his bridle and saddle were missing."

Glancing sideways at the sheriff, I wondered silently, does *he think my granddaughter has run off with the gambler?* I had to know, so I asked. "Do you think he may have something to do with my granddaughter?" I didn't usually lie, but I couldn't reveal too much, and fabricating a story at this point seemed the best for all involved. Even so, I wondered if the sheriff would tell me the truth.

$$\sim 15 \sim$$

Emily

C LOSING MY EYES, I whispered another prayer heavenward. *"Hi God, it's me again needing your help. I know I've asked this many times in the past forty-eight hours, but . . . "* As I continued to pray, I'd hoped the large Puma would have retreated by the time I opened my eyes. No such luck! *All I have is this stupid broken bucket to defend myself with. Why can't just one thing go as I planned?* All my backcountry trekking experience about what to do when faced with a wild animal flew out the window. I was so angry with myself. If I was going to be his next meal, I just wanted it all over.

Emily, please remain calm, spoke that soft loving voice.

Breaths painfully bursting in and out, I replied, "Not now, Gran. Can't you see I'm a bit busy here?"

Of course I can, dear. What do you think I am, blind?

Clenching my fist tightly around the bucket handle, I continued kneeling at the water's edge, knowing I couldn't play stare down with the wild animal much longer. At least there was a stream between us. One of us had to make a move and, I'd rather it be me. What little comfort it brought me, I remembered just how fast these animals could run.

Slowly rising with a death grip on the canteen and bucket, his gut-wrenching growl had me picking up my skirts and running back through the bushes as fast as my pointy-toed shoes allowed. I knew I couldn't outrun him. It was stupid even to think so. But, that fight or flight instinct kicked in as I fled for my life.

Hearing another growl from farther up the stream, I picked up speed. "Great, he's brought his friends to breakfast. Don't look back, Emily. Just keep running." I had too. Crazy, considering all I'd been through in the past few days. All I could think of was the pain he and his friend would inflict. Halfway back to the cabin, I stopped and turned around to see how far back they were.

I was never so happy to see that dilapidated cabin in front of me. Considering I was already dead, I felt it a miracle I'd survived. *Can I die again?* What a silly question, or was it? *If I ever saw my grandfather again!* I still wanted to give him a piece of my mind.

Racing through the door, I slammed the bar in place. Leaning back, gulping in air, I tried easing the stitch of pain in my side that had taken hold halfway down the hill. It was one thing to take a leisurely jog around Green Lake, but quite another to run for my life down a steep rocky ridge.

After all that, I had no bucket of water to show for my valiant efforts. At least I'd been able to fill the canteen. Little consolation knowing I'd have to go back up the hill, find the bucket, and get back to the cabin without spilling a drop. This time, I'd take Caleb's shotgun.

I'd left Caleb lying outside next to the back wall. Rushing around the cabin with the canteen in my hand, I found he hadn't moved a muscle, and it frightened me. Touching his forehead, I knew why he was in the same position. His temperature had risen to a critical state, and he was semi-conscious. Desperately needing to cool him down, I tore off a damp portion of my dress, wet from the stream, then added more water from the canteen. Placing it on his forehead, he moaned lowly at my touch but didn't attempt to open his eyes.

"Caleb. Caleb, open your mouth. You need to drink some water." Putting my hand behind his head, I eased it forward. His eyes remained closed, but his mouth opened to allow the cooling liquid to trickle in when a jagged cough had him abruptly stopping. "Caleb. I need to go get more water. I'm going to take your rifle and head back to the stream. I won't be gone long. Do you understand me?" Head only nodding, he continued to lay soundlessly still.

My stomach growled loudly. "How many days has it been without food?" I asked myself, rubbing my hand over my midsection. More determined than ever, I grabbed Caleb's rifle and ammunition, then headed back up the hill. Pushed to my limits like now, I wouldn't hesitate to shoot the Puma or any other two or four-legged animal that dared threaten me.

Trudging forward, I soon spotted a lone rabbit peeking out from under a bush. Saying a prayer of forgiveness, I aimed and shot, amazing myself that I hit it with my first try. Luck had been with me. God was answering my prayers one small step at a time. Gingerly, I picked it up, holding it at arm's length and gave thanks for the nourishment it would provide. Using Caleb's knife, I took a deep breath and cleaned it at the stream. Filling the bucket above where I'd cleaned the rabbit, I headed back down the hill, thinking, "How did pioneer women do this day after day?"

Caleb

I grabbed my stomach jumping at the sound of gunfire. On impulse, I reached for my rifle only to find it gone. Frantic, I yelled, "Emily!" Again, louder still with my last ounce of strength, "Emily, where are you?" All I could think of was that whoever shot me had come back and taken Emily. Or worse, killed her. I couldn't live without her. I cried out her name again, "Oh, God, no! Emily."

I was helpless as a newborn babe. Attempting to rise up, waves of nausea crashed over me, drenching me in sweat. Falling back onto the rocky ground, I realized it was no use. Emily was gone. "She finally left me?" I never felt so alone.

Emily

"I hear rabbit stew is good." I was trying to convince myself of it on the way back to the cabin. "Keep talking, Sweeney, and maybe you'll believe it."

Hearing Caleb scream, I set down the bucket, canteen, and rabbit. Cocking the rifle, I cautiously approached the side of the cabin, prepared to find whoever shot Caleb had come back to finish him off. Instead, I found him thrashing around. The quilt no longer making a protective tent over his body. He'd probably thrown the quilt and his coat off in an attempt to cool himself down. I could see from the wet stains on his shirt, that in his turmoil, he'd caused his wounds to bleed.

Reaching his side, I took hold of both arms, talking to him softly. "Caleb, its Emily. You need to calm down and lay back. You're bleeding again." His thrashing slowed down, and he settled at the sound of my voice.

Staring through vacant eyes, he yelled, "Get away from me, you murderer!" Trying to push me back, I let him talk since fighting him would only make his thrashing escalate. "Can't you see, I'm dying? Let me die in peace, Anna." Caleb's speech was almost inaudible as he continued, "Go back to your lover! Oh God, we'll go to hell for what we did." Taking in a shallow breath, he added, "No one will ever know what we did. I'll go to my grave with our secret." His speech weakened, "You once said you loved me."

My heart broke at his barely coherent confession. Placing my arms around his shoulders, I pulled him tight against my chest. With his head resting within the softness of my breasts, I rocked gently back and forth while whispering words of solace. "Hush, Caleb. I'm here. I won't let anyone hurt you."

Stroking his feverish brow, I hoped Caleb would understand I wasn't the woman that had brought so much pain to his past. Finally, exhaustion won out, and his thrashing stopped. But his moaning continued, making me feel so helpless in easing his physical and emotional pain. If only there were an emergency room nearby. But all I had to give him were the comfort of my arms and kind words. I feared they wouldn't be enough.

Drifting back into unconsciousness, Caleb's body went limp. His hair, curly from sweat, glistened in the sun as I swept a rogue lock from his forehead. Laying a hand at the base of my neck, I glanced around, looking for answers to the emotions surging through me. My stomach was in knots, in a way I couldn't explain. All I really wanted was to go back home to Seattle. I didn't belong in this place. "Why isn't my grandfather coming for me?"

"Who are you, Caleb Young?" I asked. Moving the bucket containing the precious liquid close to my side, I tore off more fabric from my inner petticoats. "Mr. Young, if I keep tearing fabric off for your bandages, I'll soon be left with nothing but bloomers and a camisole. And won't that be a sight for your weary eyes?"

Dipping the once white fabric into the now lukewarm water, I placed it on his feverish brow. The second piece I laid on his chest as his firm muscles rippled under my touch. Moving the cloth in circles, I carefully cleaned dried blood from the area around his abdominal and shoulder wounds. The site on his shoulder was pink, containing normal serous drainage. It was his abdominal wound that concerned me the most. In his thrashing, it had begun to bleed, and a foul odor now permeated the bandage. The skin surrounding the entry site was red, warm, indurated, and puffy extending out in a circle about three centimeters. His breathing, now rapid and irregular, scared me. My worst fear was that the infection, now septic, was wildly racing throughout his body. If so, he could die within the next twelve hours. Or, sooner.

Doc Sweeney

"Vell Doc, I didn't know ya had a daughter, let alone a granddaughter."

I could see Sheriff Johansson's wheels churning inside his head as he mentally did the math at how old she would be. I hoped I'd given the sheriff just enough information to be convincing.

Lighting up a cheroot, he suggested, "Listen Doc, why don't we head back to town where I can gather up a search party and go back out looking for your granddaughter?"

"I don't know, sheriff. Ye don't need ta be wandering around out there looking for me family," I said, pointing to the hills. "Besides, I have no idea where te start. She could be anywhere. She could even be . . ." I couldn't finish. I didn't want to think Emily could be lost to me again. This time, forever.

I watched as the sheriff puffed out gray circles of smoke, holding up his hand to interrupt me. "Doc, don't go thinking like tat. Besides, it's vhat I do. You need to stay in town in case you're needed."

I could see he was watching for my reaction, probably hoping I'd provide him more information. "I guess you're right, sheriff. I should be close to te town. Never know what might come walking into the clinic. Besides, Abigail might need me." I couldn't help but notice the sheriff's expression at the mention of Ms. Abigail's name. To his credit, I was pleased he didn't go asking questions about her.

Placing his hat back on his head, he said, "OK, then let's head back te town. Ve still have plenty of daylight left, and the sooner ve get back, the sooner the search party can head out. Not waiting for my reply, he turned his horse around and rode off.

16

Emily

IT WAS DAY three of what I called my desert imprisonment. I desperately wanted to run as far away from this hell my grandfather had thrown me in. Stomping my foot, I cursed. "Where will I go when I don't even know where I am?" Looking down at Caleb's still body, I couldn't leave him alone to die an agonizing death.

Furrowed brows, hinted at his pain, while his thick black lashes lay flush against his cheeks. Gone was the ruggedly handsome stubble, replaced now by a growing beard framing his face. Leaning in close, I again whispered words of comfort and encouragement. I didn't know what else to say. All my endearing words may be for naught, knowing I couldn't change a preordained outcome.

It didn't take long for the cloth on his forehead to dry from his body's heat. Dipping it again into the cool water, I hoped it would bring his fever down, knowing it wouldn't be enough. "There's got to be something else I could be doing." Suddenly, I remembered taking a three-day course on medicinal desert botanicals put on by one of the Arizona arboretums and universities. I didn't need to add to his misery. Still, I desperately tried remembering what plants I could use to treat Caleb's infection and fever.

Hope restored, I mentally ticked through the list of plants from the class that could hopefully be useful. First, I needed to locate a cottonwood tree back along the stream. It's part of the willow family, containing a property called salacin, like aspirin, that I would boil the bark, buds, or leaves. Having him drink the tea should help reduce his fever, inflammation, and ease his pain. Better yet, I remembered seeing two chubby prickly pear cacti in the dry hillside behind the cabin. The buds were edible, sweet, and would provide us both with much-needed vitamin C. Then, I would fillet the large flat pads of the plant and place the raw edges over Caleb's abdominal wound, hoping it would soothe the inflammation and draw out any poisons. This time of year should be right, and the cactus would still have some red fruit buds left.

I also remember seeing several huge saguaro cacti on the trail to the stream. Unfortunately, it was too late in the season for it to bear fruit, which was in June and July. "It being December, I won't have to worry about that prickly task, no pun intended."

Last, I hoped to locate a creosote or chaparral bush. Having been taught that the plant had been a major pharmaceutical player for the early Sonoran Desert dwellers, the leaves when dried, could also be steeped into a tea. I knew today's pharmaceutical regulations warned that it was a dangerous plant. Still, despite its dreadful taste, the leaves contained antibacterial, antifungal, and antioxidant qualities. What else did I have? I had to try, knowing it had been used traditionally for thousands of years. "Well, I'm not in the twenty-first century anymore, and I don't have western antibiotics available. So, I'll use what I can gather from nature."

Feeling a renewed sense of purpose, I only hoped the botanicals I used would potentially keep Caleb alive.

Vermin and Stubb

Sitting at a table inside the Pick and Shovel saloon, I watched my dumb brother, Stubbs walk back to the table with a bottle of whiskey in one hand and two glasses in the other. I cursed my dead mother for leaving me with this half-wit. I had no use for him. He was like a ball and chain around my neck that tightened every day he lived.

It was time to celebrate successfully revenging our brother's murder. Stubbs and I had wandered the hills surrounding Yuma in an effort to find the murderer. After killing the card cheating killer, we kept to the countryside to avoid any questions from the law. Not that it seemed anyone would have cared to find the gambler dead. What really had me fuming was his mount had escaped. I had to resolve myself to the fact that I'd lost good horseflesh to the desert.

Licking my dry lips, I watched a young skimpily clad saloon girl wander over to a table next to mine. Tonight, I didn't plan on sleeping next to my brother in the dirt. "Hey, darlin'," I drawled. "Come on ov'r here and warm these ol' legs?" It wasn't a request. Throwing back a whiskey, I leaned my arms onto the table. She'd ignored me. I wouldn't have it. Yelling louder, I caught the attention of a bunch of drunks. "I said, come over here!"

Throwing my half-empty bottle to get her attention, the girl jumped as it hit the table in front of her and shattered into razor-sharp shards. Turning towards me, I said, "Now, that's better, girlie." Reaching out, I grabbed the hem of her skimpy dress and pulled, hearing fabric rip. Screeching, she landed with a hard thud on my lap. I wiggled in my seat and sneered, hissing like a contented cat into her ear, "Now, that's much better."

She was young and soft in all the right places. Just how I liked them. I trailed my dirty hand down the side of the girl's pale face, then over her silky collar bone, searching lower. Feeling her still at my touch, I cupped my hand around one of her small firm breasts and tightly squeezed. "These could be a might bigger for my tastes, but they'll do for tonight."

Her blood-curdling scream pierced my ears as she tried to thwart off my grip. Laughing, I said, "I like the feisty ones." Without letting go of my prize, I leaned back, rotating my hips up, while bellowing my pleasure so all present could hear.

Out of the corner of my eye, I caught the bartender reach under the bar, pulling up his Winchester. My unwilling companion calmed in my arms as we both watched the bartender take calculated steps to my table, rifle in hand. "Damn it, he's going to ruin all my fun."

The imposing barkeep came to stand over me with his rifle cocked and ready. "Mister, take your hands off, Miss Lettie."

Sneering, I let him know, "She's mine for the night. I paid for her comforts." With a nod up of my head, "Go get your own."

Raising his rifle just enough to get my full attention, he answered me, "Not tonight. Like I said, let her go."

Not budging, the barkeep waited for my next move. I was ready for a fight, but looking at my brother's unease, not that I'd cared about him, I knew tonight wasn't the night to tempt fate. Mentally placing the barkeep in the back of my mind, I'd take care of him another time. My brother exhaled loudly. I relented, pushing the frail saloon girl to the floor. Hitting with a thud, I kicked my boot into her backside as she scrambled to stand. Looking directly into the barkeep's eyes, I told him, "OK, you can keep the whore for yourself." With both hands at my sides, I motioned with my head to Stubbs that we were leaving.

As much as I suspected he wanted to, instead of bullets, I sensed the barkeep shooting fiery holes into my backside. Stubbs and I headed out the saloon doors. Stopping, I turned back and said, "We're not through you and me!" Spitting a line of blackened tobacco juice onto the sawdust-covered floor, we continued out into the streets of Yuma.

Emily

I had to work quickly, having been successful in locating the botanicals, I set to work making poultices and drying leaves in the sun for tea. I was surprised that Caleb was still alive. I made sure we had enough botanic supplies to last for at least the next ten days, never knowing if I would need them for myself. Touching the hash marks on the cabin wall with my broken nails, one day seemed to run into the other. So far, five sunrises had passed, and I could only hope we wouldn't be here much longer.

Standing over him, I noted that Caleb's breathing appeared less arduous and shallow. The rattling was still there, but not as deep, and he was finally responding appropriately to my questions. I thought this was the best time for me to clean the cabin and attempt to make a fire in the old stove. Finding a frayed straw broom, I swept the floor free of what appeared to be some disgusting animal droppings. Gagging at the thought of spending a night in this hovel, I would try hard to make it as livable as possible.

Clumsily, I removed the iron lid of the stove. It was heavier than I realized. Peering in, I decided it was somewhat safe to use. I knew enough to make sure the damper was open. I added small bits of kindling and dried leaves I'd picked up around the cabin. Without matches, I located a piece of flint on the stove's top-shelf. Striking Caleb's knife to the flint. Nothing.

My Girl Scout days were a distant memory. Clenching my teeth, I was determined. "I will get this dang stove going if it's the last thing

I do!" Striking the flint harder, success, a spark, then a thin line of white smoke rose from the center of the leaves. I was excited as a kid on Christmas morning. Blowing gently at the base of the leaves, a small flame emerged, and the kindling took hold. Now, I could boil water to make the herbal tea that Caleb so desperately needed.

Day seven, and so far, Caleb had been able to take in several cups of cottonwood tea, plus other water. To my relief or wishful thinking, he seemed more at ease. His fever was slowly coming down, and his breathing sounded less raspy. The prickly pear poultice was reducing the inflammation around the edges of his abdominal wound. Days ago, I had been able to remove all the larger sharp rocks from under him, but if all went well, today would be the day I could get him off the ground.

"Caleb, I have to get you into the cabin." Kneeling close to his ear, I told him, "You can't spend another night out here." Despite the warmth of the day, I rubbed my arms from an inner chill. "The nights are getting colder." After the grueling week behind us, I prayed he'd have even the slightest amount of strength left in him to make this monumental move. Placing my hand on his right shoulder and speaking louder, "Caleb, you have to wake up and help me. Can you do that for me?"

"Heavens, woman! You don't have to yell. I've been shot; I'm not deaf. I heard you the first time."

"Then why didn't you answer me the first time?" *Men!* Shaking off my frustrations, I apologized. "Sorry I yelled, but I didn't think you were awake enough to hear me." Astonished at what strength he had left, I leaned back on my heels, trying to figure the best way to get him up.

Before I could help, Caleb began the grueling process of pushing himself forward. Wincing, the pain brought him to a halt. Eyes wide open, he reached up and took my hand and whispered my name, "Emily."

"What Caleb?" I asked, gripping his hand firmly.

"Thank you."

"For what?" Seeing the raw pain etched across his face.

"For saving my life. I'll never be able to repay you for what you've done." His energy was fading fast, and he wasn't even standing yet.

"You're welcome. I would do the same for anyone in your position." Motioning with my hands, I added, "Now, don't try and move on your own. First, I'm going to take your coat and this quilt and put them in the cabin. I need to get that so-called rope bed ready for you. And, before you move, I'll take a look at your wounds."

His lips turned up as he rasped out, "Bossy woman! First, you tell me to get up, then you tell me not to move. Which is it?"

Ignoring his attempt at humor, I put on my best doctor's voice and gave him instructions. "Stay put. Don't move. I'll be right back." Clutching the coat and worn quilt to my breasts, I couldn't get inside the cabin fast enough. Once in, I let my head fall back against the wall and cried. Thankful, he was alive.

17

Emily

PUSHING AWAY FROM the wall, I walked over to the rope bed. Folding the quilt in two for thickness, I laid it on top of the crossed ropes. His coat would cover him, and I'd use the saddlebags for a pillow.

Heading back outside, I saw Caleb on his knees, leaning forward on his right hand. "What in heaven's name are you trying to do, Mr. Young? Didn't I tell you not to move?" Placing my arms under his, we groaned in unison, me with the effort of lifting him, Caleb with pain.

"Damn it, woman, you'll be the death of me yet with all your squabbling and tugging."

"Squabbling? You haven't heard anything yet! If you think this is squabbling, just you wait Mister Young!" Nerves frayed, I rambled on. "Can you push up with your knees a bit?"

"Yeah. Just give me a minute. It's hard to breathe."

"Take in some slow deep breaths. As deep and as slow as you can." I demonstrated. "In through your nose, out through your mouth. In through your nose, out through your mouth." I could see him struggling, but wanted to keep encouraging him. "Yes, that's right. Let your body relax."

Who am I fooling? Neither of us could relax. Even so, it was a good distraction.

He pulled in a deep breath and his rigid muscles he'd been holding relaxed. It took several more breaths when he asked, "How long have I been like this? Do you know when I was shot?"

"You've been here for seven days."

"Seven days! How can that be?"

"You've been in and out of consciousness," I said, looking into his eyes.

"Seven days." It wasn't a question. "When I got shot the first time, I thought my lungs had exploded. It hurt so much to breathe. This morning it's not as bad. It's just that it hurts to . . ." He didn't finish when a coughing spasm caught him off guard.

"That's understandable. Your shoulder wound was close to your lung.

Pointing to his shoulder, I added, "The base of your lung is up here near . . ." *Stop it, Emily, he doesn't understand your medical terms.* Changing the direction of the conversation, I took in a shaky breath and told him, "OK, I'm going to count to three, and we'll stand up."

"Ha!" Caleb laughed. "Easy for you to say, lady. You're not the one whose gut shot."

Containing my sympathy, I added, "It doesn't have to be straight up just enough so you can move your feet under you and get around to the cabin door. Do you think you can do that?"

"I'll try my damndest."

Watching him struggle, he slowly brought one foot underneath him. "Don't worry. We'll make it inside." Securing my hold, I started the backward countdown. "OK, here we go, three, two, one." On one, I had Caleb up, despite his groaning. Finally, when his feet were underneath him, he continued to lean forward against my shoulder, guarding his belly.

"You made it, Caleb." I smiled, pleased with our success. Sweat streamed down between my breasts like a river, realizing now came the hard part of getting him to walk around the cabin. It was going to be the longest walk we both would ever make.

"Give me a minute," he asked, blowing out a winded breath.

"Take your time," I reassured him, accepting his full weight against my shoulder with one arm around his waist, the other holding up yards of my skirt and petticoats. I didn't know how long I could hold this position as the muscles in my back screamed with pain. I eased my foot forward. With every two steps I took, Caleb took one. The process was agonizingly slow. What should have taken mere seconds turned into an eternity. But, at least Caleb was upright and moving in the right direction.

Sweat dripped from his forehead as the warming sun rose over the eastern hills. Reaching the cabin door, he grabbed onto the frame with both hands as I supported him from the back. Letting his head drop forward, he stared at the same roaches I watched scatter back and forth on the dirt floor below us.

"I can't . . . catch my . . . breath."

"Hold on." Never letting go, I made my way under his arm, coming to stand in front of him. Placing my hand on his chest, "Caleb, slow your breathing down. You're starting to hyperventilate."

"I'm what?"

"Hyperventilate. It's when you're breathing too fast like you are right now."

"How'd you know all this?"

"I just do. Right now, what's important is for you to slow your breathing down so you can make it over to the bed." With my hand on his chest, he did as I asked. Looking up, our eyes met. I couldn't look away if I wanted too. What this man did to my emotions with just one glance! *Oh Emily, you're in so much trouble.*

All too quickly, a mixture of fear for his survival and the longing I had for him to live, shattered the shield I'd raised to protect my heart. Finally, able to avert his eyes, I shook off his look as nothing more than gratitude. "Are you ready to take your final walk to the bed?" I spoke before realizing what I'd just said. *His final walk? How thoughtless of me.* My words went unnoticed. Praying I was wrong, I looked up, asking, "Do you want to lean on my shoulder, or have me support you from the back?"

"I'd rather lean on you if that's okay." A slight smile appeared despite his rough breathing.

"That's fine. Let's just get you inside and lying down as quickly as possible." My knees began to shake as I edged him forward. *Emily, you can do this girl,* echoed my grandmother's voice.

"Whoa! What's the hurry?" Stopping midway between the door and bed, he turned his head towards me, his voice now ice-cold, he asked, "Are you anxious to be rid of me?"

Feeling as though he'd just slapped me across my face. Two could play this game. "How can you say such a thing after all I've done to save your sorry hide?" Angry, I wanted to let go of him. But, I didn't dare, knowing he'd topple to the floor. "Stop saying those things, or I will drop you on your head. And it won't be because I want to run; it'll be because my arms and legs are ready to give out."

Urging him forward, "Now, let's get moving. I don't know how much longer I can hold you up." Readjusting my grasp around his waist, I propelled him forward. "Just keep putting one foot in front of the other," motioning him forward with a nod of my head. I could feel the muscles in my back seize up with every step I took. "A few more steps and you're there."

Raw pain was written all over his contorted features. "Please. I didn't mean . . ."

"Hush. Just keep moving."

Stopping to catch his breath, he added, "It's just that . . . women usually leave . . ." Trying to continue, he was caught by a deep rattling cough, and the phlegm in his chest rattled in its quest to be free.

Stumbling forward, I was no longer able to hold him upright. Grabbing onto a bedpost, he dropped down hard against the wood frame letting out a forced moan. Swearing, I feared he would fall forward and hit his shoulder, or worse, his abdomen. Instead, I was able to turn him in one fluid motion and drop him down onto the quilt with a plop. Drenched in sweat, I wiped my hand over my brow while declaring, "Mr. Young. You are going to give me heart failure."

Looking at me with concern, he asked, "What's wrong with your heart? Are you in pain?" Grasping my free hand, he pulled me forward.

"Yes. No." Flustered, I pulled back. "My heart's fine. It's just a figure of speech."

Caleb was breathless. Placing my hands on his shoulders, I grinned and leaned down close to his face. "You did it. You made it inside."

Taking in a ragged breath, he replied, "No, we did it."

Innocently, he rested his forehead heavily on my abdomen. I didn't know what to do with my hands. Overwhelmed, I let them fall instinctively to the nape of his neck, entwining his long damp wavy hair between my fingers. Pulling back, I knew I couldn't allow my heart to give in to this vulnerability.

Reaching up, Caleb took my shaking hands in his, "Emily, I'd be dead if it wasn't for you. For that, I'm forever grateful."

Wiping away a rogue tear with the back of my hand, I stood up straighter, sniffling unladylike. "I know you are Caleb." *He can still die.* The thought of losing Caleb now was unimaginable. This man had come crashing into my life and burrowed his way into a corner of my brittle heart. I wouldn't; no, I couldn't allow these feelings to grow. Even so, I didn't know if I could ignore them. This had become more than a doctor-patient relationship.

I was scared. Scared that these emotions would prevent me from returning home. *What am I thinking?* I never made irrational decisions without having all the facts. But, isn't that what I'd done that ill-fated night in the E.R? I had no idea who this man was or where he came from. How could I trust him? Self-doubt was irrationally painful.

Reaching up, Caleb touched my nose and ran his calloused fingers gently across my cheek. "You have freckles."

Despite not liking anyone mentioning my freckles, I didn't jerk my head back. Instead, replacing his hand with my own, I covered up my blemishes, ignoring his comment.

"I need to lie down," he said. "I can't hold myself up any longer."

"Of course, let me help you." Thankfully, that ended my wandering thoughts. "I'm sorry I didn't have more padding to put on the bed to make it more comfortable." Using proper body mechanics, I placed one hand behind his upper back, the other under his legs, lifting and pivoting in one motion.

Caleb's face wrinkled up with pain, but he remained stoically silent. Rolling up his coat as a pillow instead of the saddlebags, I lifted his head and tucked it underneath him. What little color remained in Caleb's face was now replaced with a gray tone. I didn't think he could take much more. Sensing my thoughts, he squeezed my hand, "It's OK, Emily."

18

Emily

FEELING LIKE I'D just finished a sixteen-hour shift, I placed one hand behind my back and stretched, hoping to work out the tightness in my aching muscles. Looking down at Caleb, I had that niggling sense I was failing him somehow, that I should be doing more. The reality was, patients had died under my care. It was an unfortunate fact in medicine that not everyone we saw come through the emergency room doors survived. That sense was becoming all too real now.

Exhausted, I crossed the short distance to the table, collapsing on the only seat available. Looking around, cobwebs hung from every corner and places in between. A tattered red checkered curtain drooped from a nail over the back window. It was a dirty place, but the possibility of the dreaded Hantavirus was the least of my worries.

"Well, this is home sweet home until I find my grandfather or he finds me." Giving way to a pounding headache, I applied deep pressure with my fingertips to my temples in hopes of easing the throbbing. "I'm hungry and thirsty, and that's why I have a headache." I felt so vulnerable. It was a side of me I'd learned long ago to keep hidden from the outside world. But, here it was, in all its glory, and frankly, I didn't care who knew. Yawning, I leaned my head forward over my crossed arms and quickly fell asleep.

I didn't realize how much time had passed when I awoke, but by the waning sun streaming through the gaps in the cabin's ceiling, it must have been several hours. Looking over at the bed, Caleb's eyes remained closed in sleep.

Selfishly, I didn't go to him. Instead, I focused on how I would get us out of here so I could head home. Having no idea of where we were, and with no means of travel, other than walking, it was apparent the man in the bed couldn't be of help. That niggling fear kept creeping in. "When is my grandfather going to show up?"

In search of clues, I went over my daily work routine in the emergency room that fateful night. Nevertheless, none of it made any sense. It had all been surreal. "We both can't be dead. Could we? Ghosts don't bleed!" But, the man on the bed behind me did. He breathed, he suffered, and he showed emotion. He was most definitely alive.

Until now, I hadn't been able to take a good look at Caleb's features. Even though he lay sleeping and virtually helpless, he was a ruggedly handsome man. His facial bone structure was nearly perfect, as if chiseled by Michelangelo. Below high cheekbones, his jaw squared off, now covered in several days' growth of dark beard. Other than the crooked grin I'd witnessed last evening, I could only imagine the smile that would grace his face. Just thinking of it made my insides tremble with a deep-seated longing.

His thick wavy black hair reached his shoulders and curled over a tanned brow. Now quiet, his long legs hung over the end of the bed. Having popped most of his shirt buttons to tend to his wounds, I glimpsed at the dark curly hair covering his mid-chest, ending in a deep V below his waistline. He had a six-pack that would make a twenty-first-century man envious and grown woman weep. I couldn't look away. Watching his chest muscles expand and relax with each breath he took, I wondered what it would be like to lay my head on that chest, with his comforting arms securely around me.

Enough! Good heavens, Emily. What the heck are you thinking? Blushing heatedly, I refocused, fanning myself with my hands. I couldn't ever remember being this flustered over a handsome man. But those men hadn't been Caleb, with a ruggedness that made this girl fall fast and hard. Blushing, I could feel my cheeks heat up at having such sensual thoughts. I was human, after all. "Don't be so stupid. How many naked men have you seen in your career?"

Despite him drinking several cups of cottonwood tea over the past twenty-four hours, he still felt feverish. I was afraid to push much more of the herbal concoction on him with the possibility of eliciting toxic effects, of which I knew nothing about. Instead of more tea, I would remove his damp clothes and lower his temperature with cool compresses.

"I don't know if you can hear me, Caleb, but I need to take your clothes off." I felt moisture pool under my arms. I fanned myself using the hem of my dress. I admit, it was warm out, but there was something very different about undressing Caleb versus one of my male patients. In the emergency room, the undressing was usually done by a registered nurse or a male orderly, but here I was on my own. Caleb was beginning to stir feelings in me that I'd intentionally kept hidden for years.

A welcomed breeze floated in through the back window, surrounding me as I heard a familiar voice I loved, speak to me. *Oh, for heaven's sake, Emily, you're a doctor. The man's unconscious, and it's not likely he can lust over you in his current state.*

Letting out a low groan, I couldn't believe my grandmother was paying me a visit in this very awkward moment. Eyes wide open, I realized it was my Gran. How could that be? "Good heavens, I'm not really talking with my deceased grandmother, am I?" Looking up and pointing one finger heavenward, I replied, "Don't answer that, Gran. You're confusing me, and I'd prefer to handle this one on my own; do you mind?"

Of course, she didn't take my hint seriously.

Dang it Emily, but he is a cutie. I bet he'll even look more handsome with his clothes . . . uh, that beard shaved off. You know, I never did like it when your grandfather grew a beard in the winter. He said it was to keep his face warm. But I think he did it just to irritate me. Huh! No pun intended.

"Gran, please," I groaned out as she continued.

It tickled. Plus, it took away from his good looks. I don't know . . .

"Know what?"

I'd be nervous too if I had to take Caleb's clothes off. Good thing he's unconscious or I'd be . . .

"Whoa! Gran! Enough. Besides, you're rambling, and I got your point some time back." Running my hands through my tangled hair, I added, "It's just a little bit embarrassing to have my grandmother say those things. Right now, it's not a pretty visual I have going through my head imagining you and Grandpa doing . . . well, you know what?"

Oh, for heaven's sake, girl. Listen to me, how do you think your mother got here? And, you, for that matter. You undoubtedly didn't fall off a turnip truck. Nor did it happen by just making eyes at each other. It took . . .

"OK, Gran! Point taken. Please, enough of the visual explanations. Now, can you please leave us alone for a while?" Using a shooing motion with my hands, I hoped my grandmother understood the uneasiness her celestial presence made. "You're dead, Gran. Remember?"

I spoke to the walls as I paced the cabin, "I can't believe I'm having this conversation." Hands waving, I kept prattling on. "I know. I know. It's just that I'm tired and my mind is playing tricks on me. That's all this is."

Then, there she was again. *My dearest Emily, as much as it pains me to tell you this, you too are dead. Albeit, much too soon in your young life. You had such an incredible career as a doctor. Your grandfather and I are so proud of you. And yes, we can have this conversation. That's the gift of us both being dead. But somehow, you're still in the living form. Which, I don't understand how that part works. But I digress. I'll leave you now and wish you well in saving your handsome man. If you need me for anything, don't hesitate to call. I love you, dear.*

Oh! How my grandmother could ramble. Smiling and looking up, I said, "I love you, Gran." Pointing my index finger, "Oh, and just so you know, he's *not* my man."

Whatever you say, dear.

I could have sworn I heard my Grandmother chuckle. Despite it being hard to believe, I knew I was dead. What I also knew was that I was alone in a dirty cabin, in the middle of a desert, trying to save a strange man's life.

Before being interrupted, I had turned my focus to removing Caleb's damp clothes. Touching his arm, "Caleb, I'm going to help you sit up so I can remove your vest and shirt." His only response was a grunt. Proceeding, I leaned him forward and pulled his vest and shirt down off his shoulders. In doing such, he groaned louder, but he didn't try to stop me.

Laying his coat over his bare torso, I replaced his saddlebags for a pillow, then commenced taking off his boots. Turning my backside to the bed, I braced myself legs apart and grabbed hold of one boot between my legs and pulled. The determined motion sent me careening into the back wall, landing with a huff. "What have you gotten yourself into this time, Emily?" Thankfully, the other boot came off much easier. Once the buttons on his pants were taken care of, came the task of pulling them down over his hips. It wasn't going to be easy. He was tall, heavy, and unable to help. Hands shaking like a newlywed, I grasped his waistband coming in contact with dried blood that had soaked through his pants. I realized they would have to come all the way off. Grabbing and tugging at each side of his hips, and rolling him from left to right, brought loud moans, but no attempt from Caleb to stop me. Task completed, I ran a shaky hand through my hair, pushing back dirty strands that had come loose from my braid.

With his outer pants off, I chuckled. All that was left was his racy long underwear. *Men really wear these?* I pulled the top down to his waist, making the decision not to even try tackling the job of removing them completely.

As the sun dipped towards the western hills, the room remained warm. By the time I got through undressing Caleb, replacing his bandages and the prickly pear cactus poultice, I was exhausted again. Even more so, I was relieved that the puffy redness surrounding his abdominal wound had decreased. *Maybe those botanicals really did work!*

The tension in my shoulders had coiled tighter, and my headache had returned. Dull at first, then came the pounding at my temples like a jack-hammer. Sitting on the edge of the bed, I gazed at Caleb's face while sipping a cup of cold cottonwood tea. I hoped it would work on my headache as it had on Caleb's fever. At the end of the day, all I had left to do, was pray. Pray that God would continue giving me strength, and care for us both.

His face pale, dark circles bordered his tortured eyes. Leaning in close with the canteen. "Caleb, you need to drink some more water." Opening his eyes, he firmly grasped my hand, spilling some of the prized liquid. No smile, brows wrinkled, his face held a look of pleading while he spoke through cracked lips.

"Promise me . . . one thing, Emily." His grasp held my hand firmly. "Can you do that?"

Unable to speak, I nodded my reply.

"When I die . . ."

Quickly interrupting him by holding up my hand, "Caleb, you're not going . . ."

He cut off my protest, "Shush! Just listen to what I have to say since I don't have much time left."

Closing my eyes, I acquiesced.

"When I die, you'll leave this place and find yourself help." A coughing spasm caught him off guard before he could continue, and I reached again for the canteen. "Please, will you do that for me?"

"Yes," I replied, feeling tears slip down my cheek. He tightened his hold on my hand, anchoring it over his heart.

"Caleb, you have to know I won't leave you here. I'll come back to you."

"I know," was all he said before closing his eyes again.

Cursing myself, and without thinking, I did what I believed I'd never see myself do; I placed a gentle kiss on Caleb's warm lips. Feeling him tighten his hold on my hand, I vowed I would do all in my power to save this man who'd stolen my heart.

19

Sheriff Johansson

I T WAS A cold December afternoon when I rode back into Yuma, bone-tired and road-weary, my oil duster covered in trail dust. Passing by the saloon, Abigail chose that moment to wander out onto the boardwalk as I rode by. Tipping the edge of my hat with my fingers, I hid a smile below its wide brim. Despite her advanced pregnancy, I still thought she was the most beautiful woman I'd ever laid eyes on.

It was none of my business, but ever since noticing her delicate condition, I desperately tried to work up the courage to ask her who the father was. Believing we'd once shared a secret I held sacred, my heart broke in-two thinking she'd been with another man. Shaking my head, I whispered to myself, "I must have been wrong." Even so, whoever the father was, it wouldn't stop me from loving her. I remember the first time we met. I fell head-over-heels in love. It was a memory I'd carry with me the remainder of my days.

I reigned my horse to a stop in front of Doc's house. Walking up the sagging porch steps, I knocked on the door, hearing Doc's boot heels click on the entry hall's wooden floor.

"Sheriff, you're back." With a hopeful look, he opened the door wider, motioning for me to come in. "Come in, come in. Can I get ye something to drink? Coffee, or, some of my fine Irish whiskey?" he asked, pointing in the direction of the parlor.

"Coffee vould be fine if ya have any," I answered, rubbing my hands up and down my arms to generate some heat. To make it back before dark, I had ridden long and hard through biting cold.

"Yes, of course. Please make yourself comfortable. I'll be right back."

Standing in front of the welcoming warmth of the hearth, I nervously twirled my hat slowly around in my hands while waiting for the Doc's return. Finally, feeling the heat seep in, I turned to take in the room's sparse furnishings. I'd been in this room many times before, but this was the first time I noticed a small picture sitting on the mantel. It was of a beautiful young woman that shared the same features as Doc. I found myself asking, *Is this the granddaughter he's searching for?*

Coming up behind me, Doc brought me out of my wayward thoughts. "Thanks, Doc," taking the offered mug. Steam rising, I inhaled its rich aroma before taking a cautious sip.

"Well," I started before Doc interrupted me.

"Have you . . . I'm sorry. You go first," Doc apologized and motioned for me to have a seat.

"No. Tat's OK. I'd rather stand." Looking down at my dirty boots, I was anxious to tell him. "I'm sorry, Doc, but ve didn't locate ya, granddaughter." Pointing my finger at the picture on the mantel, I asked, "Ist tat her?"

I watched his expression change when he looked at the picture, "No. That's my wife, Maggie. It was taken before we married. But, my granddaughter looks just like her."

I broke the awkward silence that had fallen over the room, while Doc continued to stare at the picture. Placing my empty mug on a side table in my haste to leave, I explained, "Doc, I better take care of my horse." Putting my hat back on, I added, "Te boys and I . . . vell, ve didn't even pick up a hint of a trail. The posse and I will be heading back out in twenty-four hours. This time, we'll head towards the northwest. The disheartened look on Doc's face said it all.

Emily

Staring at yet another charcoal mark on the cabin wall, I remained hopeful that my grandfather was out there looking for me. It had been nine days since arriving in the desert. In reality, my chances of ever being found decreased each time the sun set in the west.

By the grace of God, prayer, and the desert botanicals, Caleb was still alive. He seemed to be improving despite his restless nights. I noticed he was more lucid and able to talk without struggling for each breath. Yet, he still hadn't been able to walk around inside the cabin. His only movement was to sit on the edge of the bed to relieve himself using a rusted can, left by the previous inhabitants.

My stomach growled daily with hunger, and this calico costume now hung off my shrinking form. Though thankful, I was becoming tired of eating rabbit. What I wouldn't give for fresh-off-the-boat alder smoked salmon from Anthony's. Better yet, fresh Dungeness crab. Foraging for food and wood meant lugging around Caleb's heavy rifle while spending my days going ever farther up into the hills. Thankfully, the stream continued to run full, providing us with continual fresh water.

My main concern, besides Caleb's well-being, and our survival, was that we had little ammunition left. What he'd started out with, was now down to less than ten cartridges, and I needed them to shoot meat, not ward off nefarious intruders.

Another evening was drawing to a close. Each day that passed, the night air grew colder. It was December after all. While Caleb slept, I sparingly poured water into a clean tin plate. Dipping in a strip of my dwindling petticoat, I slowly drew it over my face and neck, as visions of soaking in the hilltop stream came to mind.

The howl of a lone coyote broke the silence. Shivering, I'd heard them nightly since arriving, but I didn't know if it was my imagination running wild, or the real thing. Tonight the howling seemed closer, and it definitely was real. Banking the fire in the stove, I ignored the sounds while allowing fatigue to wash over me. Pulling the bench close to Caleb's bed like I'd done every night since being inside the cabin, I lay down on the hard wood. Using my hands as a pillow, I would maintain my nightly vigil.

Awakening sometime in the middle of the night to a rattling noise, I thought someone or something was trying to get inside the cabin. Grabbing the rifle from the floor, I pointed it in the direction of the door while deciding my next move. In my silent thoughts, I realized the sound wasn't coming from outside, it was coming from Caleb. Behind me, he shook uncontrollably, rattling the bedframe against the wall. Touching my hand to his forehead, his once abated fever had returned with a vengeance.

"Cold. I'm so cold," Caleb chattered through clenched teeth as he tried curling up on his side.

"I'll be right back." Turning towards the stove, I only wished I had more to cover him with than his shearling coat.

"No, don't leave me," he said, pulling back on my hand before I was able to move away.

Leaning down, I told him I was going to the stove to heat up some leftover broth for him to drink. With his determined grip, I could tell he was reluctant to let me go. Helping him lift his head high, he drank his fill, despite half the liquid dripping out over his chin. Wiping it off with the hem of my skirt, I gently laid his head back down, placing the cup on the floor.

Next, I took the warm stove plate and covered it in a piece of petticoat, placing it near his feet. It cooled too quickly and wouldn't be sufficient enough to warm him. I knew the only real warmth would be from my radiating body heat.

Even though the cot was narrow, I lie down beside him. Wrapping my arms securely around his waist, I pulled him close, hoping to generate enough heat without falling off.

Intuitively, Caleb placed his arm over my waist, asking me to stay with him through the night. Lying beside him felt natural, but stirred feelings I'd tried so hard to deny. I couldn't allow myself to enjoy his closeness, or let the ember of my emotions flame out of control. He was sick and still could die.

Unsuccessful at sleeping, I firmly held Caleb close to my warm body. Sometime near dawn, his shaking subsided, but he remained restless, frequently talking out loud, rarely coherently. Everything he spoke of was a mystery to me. But, I understood enough to know that Caleb's past haunted him.

In his sleep, he muttered of his mother's loving heart and his father's unending hatred. He spoke of a Rebecca left behind in Boston, of law school, working with his father and the fact that he never could please "the old man" no matter what he did.

Then he mentioned Anna. *Ah, the elusive Anna.* His words of love, intermingled with betrayal, torment, and death, were strung together with "leaving it all behind." None of it made any sense. It was a mystery, one I'd like to solve. But, I had no right to pry into Caleb's past.

∽◦⟋⟋◦∼

Caleb

Warmed by the closeness of my sweet Emily's body, I drifted in and out of a vivid nightmare that had haunted me for the past five years since leaving Boston.

Shortly after my mother's death, and definitely not within society's proper mourning period, my father had taken himself a young bride. Beautiful, she was the daughter of a wealthy Boston banker, and young enough to be his daughter. It had been another agreed-upon societal marriage. Anna Bennett, for the money, my father, for his incessant sexual needs. Love had never figured into the equation. I, like my father, couldn't help myself and was drawn to Anna like a moth to a flame. She had a way about her that made men do things they usually would never dream of doing.

Loving my mother dearly, and knowing what she would think of the whole debacle, I couldn't bring myself to betray my father, no matter how much I despised him. The new Mrs. Young had other plans. She was a well-played vixen who wouldn't leave me alone. Seducing me became her game, one she had no intention of losing.

While firmly holding onto Emily, my anchor in this stormy sea of emotions, I sank deeper and deeper into my nightmare.

At night, Anna's taunting and flirtatious looks across the supper table sent my pulse racing. One night, I watched her lick whipped cream off her slender fingertips, one, slow, finger at a time. I became hyper-aware of what she could do to my body. I didn't know how much more of her seductive overtures I could stand. Her icy allure became harder to resist.

One night during supper, Anna's game went from teasing to pure unadulterated lust. When under the table, she slowly ran her dainty toes up my pant leg, and beyond.

Unaware of what I was doing, I pulled Emily closer, hoping I could satisfy the physical needs Anna created.

That night at dinner, I rapidly lost control, squirming painfully in my chair. Placing both hands, palms flat on the table, I attempted to rise up and adjust my . . . , how should I say, embarrassing discomfiture? All the while, my father sat across the table from us, oblivious to his wife's adulterous actions.

Restless in Emily's arms, I was not to be calmed, remembering my father's stern criticizing manner. "What's the matter with you, son?" he asked disdainfully. You coming down with something? Stop that squirming."

"No sir. I'm fine," I ground out as I glared across the table at Anna, warning her to stop.

After that night, I made excuses to stay away from the evening meal. Soon, even that didn't work. Living under the same roof, albeit a large one, and floors apart, I still couldn't escape my father's wife.

Deciding to take dinner in my room one night, I pulled the cord for a servant to come up. A knock at the door had me answering only to see Anna standing before me. 'What in heaven's name are you doing here?" I asked. Pushing Anna back into the hallway, closing the door behind me. The last thing I needed was for her to enter my room. I'd never get her out. Keeping my voice low, I whispered, 'You shouldn't be here."

As I dreamed of Anna's searing touch on my bare skin, I could feel myself stiffen in Emily's arms. Anna had reached her warm hand through my open shirt, curling her fingers in the hairs on my chest. Just then, one of the maids rounded the corner, stopping short at seeing the lady of the house with her hand on my bare chest.

"Miss Anna, I'm not feeling well this evening." Grabbing her wrist, I pulled her hand away from my burning skin. Driving home my point of frustration, I sternly added, "Please, let my father know that I will be taking dinner in my room this evening. Alone."

Closing my eyes tightly, I let my head fall onto Emily's soft shoulder, remembering Anna's dagger-like glare piercing my heart. I knew she was angry with me, but I didn't care. She would have to eat alone with my father, whom she called her 'insufferable husband.'

Looking back, I recognized Anna to be a selfish spoiled woman who was used to getting her way. "This is not over Caleb," Anna said to me. "I'll have you know. I will win!" Tapping my bare chest with her finger, she added, "I always do."

❧ 20 ❧

Emily

Another night over, I awoke before dawn. I was more tired than I ever thought possible. It had been forty-eight hours since Caleb was feverish. Trying not to disturb him, I pushed myself up off the cot. Gently touching his brow, I sighed with relief that his fever had not returned. Since then, he had been able to eat small amounts of cooked rabbit, which contained more nourishment than the broth alone. His color remained pale, but in sleep his face finally looked peaceful and rested.

As promised, I leaned down and whispered to Caleb that I was going after fresh water. Before walking through the door of the cabin, I picked up the piece of charcoal and made another hash mark indicating it was now day eleven. With sheer grit, determination, and prayer, I had successfully managed to keep us both alive. Despite it being a daunting task, I was grateful for having my medical knowledge and skills. Holding onto the doorframe, I bowed my head and prayed once again that this nightmare would soon end.

The sun was coming over the horizon, casting a glow on the red rocks to the west in shades of pink and purple. Feeling the warmth of the day to come, I headed out with rifle in hand. As hot as yesterday had been, the night had been colder, and I could see a light dusting of snow now covered the higher mountains to the west. As the days grew shorter, the winter solstice edged closer. Chuckling to myself, I remembered a local weatherman in Seattle saying, "The difference between rain and snow is just one degree." As crazy as it seemed in the Northwest, snow at sea level was a rare thing. But when it happened, Seattle commuters went literally into a tailspin. Reminiscing was hard to do. Hoping, like a child for that rare white Christmas, I would sadly miss sharing the upcoming holiday with my friends.

Returning to the cabin, Caleb appeared to be sleeping. I added wood to the stove, then filled a pan with fresh water, placing it to boil. Covered in dust and caked-on dirt, I desperately needed to bathe, not just a once over spit-bath.

Waiting for the water to heat, I stood near the radiating warmth of the stove and stepped out of my tattered dress. Untying the many petticoats that hung like rags around my waist, I chose the middle one as the cleanest to use as bandages when I checked Caleb's wounds later this morning.

Sitting down at the bench near the table, I struggled with the eyelet straps around the tiny buttons on my shoes. Freeing my feet, I sighed, wiggling all ten toes, not caring about my chipped pedicure. Happy to be out of the leather constraints, I stood barefoot near the stove in threadbare pantaloons and a once-white camisole. The gossamer fabric showed the outline of my every curve, leaving nothing to the imagination.

"Beautiful. My angel is so beautiful," Caleb said in a hushed whisper.

Caught by surprise, I quickly covered my breasts with my hands as the straps of the camisole fell well below my shoulders. "How long have you been watching me?" That devilish smile of his had me wishing things I shouldn't.

"Long enough to know that I can't wait until I can get out of this bed."

"Mr. Young, please cover your eyes and provide me a moment of privacy whilst I bathe."

"Oh, so now it's Mr. Young. How proper. Well, Miss Sweeney, I'll have you know that I am a man who respects the boundaries of propriety and a lady's boudoir. Unless . . ."

"Unless what?" I asked, shaking my head. I'd cut off his response, "Really?" Raising one hand in mock protest, while the other held up my camisole, "Never mind. I don't need to know what you're thinking, or how you know about a lady's boudoir."

I was about to turn my back to him but thought better of it. "Well, it's obvious you're feeling better and gaining some strength back, but I think the fever's addled your brain some." With a shooing motion of my hand, I asked, "Now, turn over and close your eyes, tight." Not complying, I repeated, "I said, close your eyes!"

Finally obeying, he said, "Here I am, admiring a beautiful woman, and I can't even move. Let alone do anything about it."

I never took my eyes off Caleb as he turned back to me. I felt him caressing my half-naked body with his eyes as they roamed over my dust-covered form. Dropping one hand, I realized the movement had caused my camisole to slip farther down, exposing a bit more of my skin. Without thinking, I took one slow step forward, watching Caleb inhale sharply. Dead, or not, I still had what it took to tempt a man. Pulling in my bottom lip, a smile of satisfaction crossed my lips. Just then, a cool breeze drifted in from the window, caressing my body and pulling my nipples taut under the gauzy fabric. When did I become such a seductress?

Pleased with the look on Caleb's face, I continued forward without hesitation. "I'm far from an angel Mr. Young. You should know that by now. Now, tell me, just how many boudoirs have you found yourself in?" Considering the beads of sweat on Caleb's brow wasn't fever-induced, I recognized I was becoming a dangerous tease.

Emily Sweeney, you're playing with fire here!

Looking heavenward. "Gran, I know what I'm doing. Trust me." Of all the inconvenient times for her to show up.

Frankly, dear, I don't trust you, and I don't think you know what you're doing. I've never seen that look in your eyes before. It's a look of . . . well . . . why it's the look of . . . love! I remember seeing that look in your mother's eyes when she first met your father. But they'd known each other for quite some time. You, on the other hand, hardly know this man. It's not even been two weeks. You have no idea who he is, where he's from, or what kind of family he has.

Gran once again rambled on. *Well, that man is definitely awake now and can see more of you than he should. Emily Sweeney, you need to turn around and put that dress back on.*

"Oh, good heavens," I stammered, shocked by what my Gran eluded to. What was I thinking? Looking heavenward for that familiar voice of reason, I pulled up the straps of the camisole and turned away from Caleb.

"Wait! Where are you going?" Caleb asked, reaching out for my hand. I quickly retreated back to the stove when he questioned, "Who are you talking to?"

Embarrassed, I couldn't respond, nor did I turn back around to face him. *Whatever possessed me to do such a thing?* Playing with Caleb's emotions wasn't fair to him or me since I planned to get out of this place as soon as I could.

"To tell you the truth, Emily, there's never been another woman like you." Clearing his throat, he continued, "The last woman I loved or thought I loved, got me into this predicament in the first place." I heard his sarcastic chuckle as he added, "It was the stupidest thing I'd ever done."

I found his confessions hard to believe. But who was I to judge? Thinking better of challenging him, I pondered my own romantic life. Or, the lack-there-of. *Questioning his past doesn't make any sense. I won't let myself fall in love. Not here. Not now.* Standing in front of the stove, I ignored Caleb's pleas, forgetting my morning ablutions.

Caleb

Caleb Young, you know better than to lie to this lovely woman. You've had the habit of lusting after every girl you've known since finishing grade school. After all she's done for you. Now isn't the time to think about Emily in that way!

"Mother!" I groaned out in a whisper, so Emily didn't hear. "I can't believe you're here." Covering my eyes with my hands, I thought of all the times for her to show up.

Well, if my son thinks he's dying, the least I can do is make sure he sets his life straight before he meets our Maker.

"Mother," I stammered, "I um . . . I don't know how to tell you this. But I don't think I'm going to make it." Hearing my mother gasp, I pushed on. "What I meant to say is, I don't think I'm going to make it up there with you. I haven't led the most pristine of lives since Boston."

Don't talk nonsense, son. You'll be coming up with me.

"Wait! Do you know something I don't?" I solemnly asked. "Can you tell me if I die here? Now? In this place? Do I leave Emily alone?"

Emily

While Caleb was busy mumbling, I put my dirty dress back on, then waved my hands to catch his attention. "Who are you talking to? What was the stupidest thing you've done?" Hands on my hips, frustrated, I asked, "Well, I'll have you know that I . . . Oh, never mind."

"Wait a minute. One question at a time," Caleb said. I surmised that he needed me to understand. "That is not what I meant." Pleading, he whispered, "You have to know you're different."

I was angry with myself for even starting this complicated conversation. But I couldn't let well enough alone. I needed the facts. "Oh, really! I'm different? How so? Please, do enlighten me." Frustration got the best of me; I asked sarcastically, "And, while you're on the subject of your other women . . ."

"Yes? Other women," he answered. "Wait, what do you mean, other women? There are no other women."

I softened my questioning tone, "Then tell me who this Rebecca is." I wasn't angry. I just needed to know who she was and if he stilled loved her. If he did, I didn't know how I would handle it. I could see in his eyes that my blunt questioning had struck a chord.

"Who said anything about Rebecca?"

"You did when you had a fever and delusional."

Caleb's voice dropped to a bare whisper as he stared at the ceiling, unsure if he was avoiding me. Finally, he blurted out, "Rebecca's my sister. I haven't thought about her in months."

Caleb wasn't telling the truth. Not about Rebecca being his sister, but that he hadn't thought about her in months. He wasn't fooling me, he probably thought about her every day.

With a shaky voice, he added, "She's such a beautiful woman." His trembling lips turned into a thin line as he added, "She lives in Boston with her two amazing sons and her . . . rotten cheating husband."

"I'm sorry, Caleb. I wouldn't have brought up Rebecca if I had known how painful the memories were. Please, forgive me." Walking back to the bed and kneeling, I took hold of his hands. "You'll see her again."

It was time.

Fearful Caleb wouldn't understand what I was about to say, I had to tell him. No matter if he believed me or not, he deserved to know my story. "Caleb," I said, looking into his tormented eyes, "There's so much I need to tell you. Things that even I don't understand." Coming to stand next to him, I took his hand in mine, feeling a strange electricity pass between us. "I don't know where to begin." I searched his face for any sign of understanding. When I didn't see any, I proceeded ahead. Hesitating, Caleb reached up with his right hand, gently brushing at my tears with his thumb. Staring intently into his empathetic eyes, I began to explain how I came to be here. It was a long circuitous story, and the questioning look on Caleb's face gave me the nerve I needed to continue.

Caleb remained silent, holding my hand the entire time. Nerves beyond frazzled, I caught myself holding my breath several times as I waited for him to respond. *He must think I'm crazy. I wouldn't blame him if he did. Even I wouldn't believe my story.* Anxious, I had to break the silence that dragged on between us. Rapidly speaking, I blurted out, "Caleb, I don't blame you if you think I'm crazy, but please stop staring at me like I have two heads." Tugging on his hand, I asked, "Say something! Anything!"

"I'll take care of you," he replied endearingly.

"What? Is that all you have to say?" Had he heard anything I'd said? If so, he was choosing to ignore it all.

Catching me off guard, he reached up behind my head, pulling me down to his warm, inviting lips. I didn't resist. Instead, I felt myself losing control at his searing touch. His slow tender strokes up and down my arms were driving me over the edge, sending a symphony of inner vibrations throughout my body. At that moment,

I felt wanted and loved. What had started with a tender kiss soon deepened into a flash of scorching heat.

Lost in the moment, I wanted more from him than I could give back. Without thinking, I encouraged his passion. Cautious of his left side, I placed both my hands on his chest, feeling his heart's erratic rhythm pound against my palms. Overcome with emotion and fueled by desire, I didn't want him to stop. Was I such a fool for letting this go this far?

Parting his lips, a deep low groan came from a secret place within his chest. Entwining his fingers in my hair, he firmly held my head in place against his lips. The once chaste kiss, turned into a frantic overture I'd never thought possible, as we both took advantage of the moment.

"No!" I cried, realizing what we were doing. Struggling to break free, I touched my fingers to my kiss swollen lips. "You don't understand." Catching my breath became painful as I choked back a torturous sob. The hold he had on my arms tightened as he drew me closer to his powerful chest. Once again, he captured my lips as I tried shaking my head in protest. This time, his kiss was so demanding, I wanted to tell him I'd changed my mind. I wanted to stay with him. Forever.

But I didn't. Instead, I told him, "You don't understand. I'm not staying here. I can't." I wouldn't let our eyes connect. "I have to go home."

Clutching my hands, he made me look at him. "I thought you just said you couldn't go back?"

My heart wounded, I felt it shatter into a million pieces. Wiping at tears, I tried making him understand. "No. What I said was that I didn't know if I could go back. There's a big difference." Holding onto his hands tighter, I forged forward, "If there is any chance I can go back, I'm taking it. You have to understand!"

Releasing my hands, he curtly asked, "So, you want to leave me?"

"Yes. No." Confused, I waved my free hand in front of him. "Oh, you know what I mean. It's all so complicated, and I can't become involved with you." *Any more than I already am.* I was losing control, not only of my mind but my heart. *Stop it right now!* *You can't do this and leave.* As painful as it may be, I had to make a choice. And soon.

"Caleb," I faintly said. "I shouldn't have encouraged this." Staring into his dark and mysterious eyes, I'd come to love, the eyes that seized my tenuous soul every time he looked at me. I asked myself, *how can I ever leave this man?*

"Stay here . . . with me," Caleb asked, taking my hands firmly in his as if he could capture a receding tide. I know you want to." Before I had a chance to interrupt, he pleaded, "We can start a new life together. I'll take you anywhere you want to go. We can even go to the Washington Territory, where you can see what it was like before your time."

I felt myself slipping like sand through his fingers. Relief washing over me like stormy winter rains, his words died out before he could finish. I sat silent, shaking my head. "I can't stay." *There, I've said it.* "Caleb, I understand your idea of chivalry, but women in my time not only take care of themselves but their husbands, children, family, and friends." Pausing, I added, "It's what women have done for centuries. It's just that some men can't comprehend it."

Hearing the pure frustration in his voice, I knew I'd made a big mistake in telling him who I was. I had to stop him from wearing himself out, or he'd pay a price. "Caleb. Look, you have to stop and rest. We can talk more about this later. You haven't been able to talk this much since being shot. It's not good for you."

Drawing in a slow steady breath, his anger only increased. "No! I won't rest. I want to talk about it. Now! Like you said, I may only have today to understand who you are. You can't possibly know how I feel about you. It has nothing to do with gratitude. Besides, if you're going to leave me, I need to understand why."

"I never said you only had today. Please don't think like that. And stop putting words into my mouth. Yes, women like to be taken care of. But, more importantly, it's about being respected and capable of working side by side with the ones we love." *Especially the men who hold our hearts.*

Eyes wide, I watched Caleb study my expression before he spoke. "I'm sorry. I guess I have a hard time understanding why a woman would ever want to do the same jobs as men when they could remain home taking care of their family." Shaking his head, he asked, "What's their reasoning?"

"Some women have no choice. Besides, here in 1880, women already work beside their husbands in the fields all day long then come home to do what you call chores until well after the sun sets. And still, others have to work at less-respectful jobs. They all do it for the same thing, survival. They need to work and keep themselves and their families fed, clothed, and a roof over their heads. Women, in my time, are no different. Some are single mothers or widows and still must fight to have the right to work despite being insulted and looked down upon in the process."

Finally, my nerves getting the best of me, I stood pacing the small room as I continued. "Women in my time are doctors, nurses, lawyers, and yes, sheriffs. They run ranches and large corporations. The list goes on and on." I was on a roll and couldn't stop. "Take your mother for example. It sounds like even though she was married and was afforded many comforts, she raised you and your sister by herself. Granted, she may have had the help of a nanny and house staff, but she was the one who was always there for you, made sure you were fed and clothed. And most importantly, loved." I waited for a response, but none came, so I continued. "This may be even harder for you to believe, but women in my time are in the military and fight battles, all the while still being wives, mothers, and strong women."

I continued to pace, feeling Caleb's eyes watch my every step. "Being an independent woman doesn't take away from the fact that we can be mysterious and sexual, while still wanting to be loved, cared for, and needed. To say we are complicated creatures is an understatement. That will never change. I, will never change." Pausing to catch my breath, I pushed forward. "Caleb, it comes down to a matter of being given a choice. And, the opportunity to be who we want to be while being respected and not looked down on because we are women. Can you understand that?"

Stopping in front of him, I caught a slight grin crease his face. Why was he grinning when I had just 'taken him down a notch' so to speak? I envisioned his mental wheels churning with all the information I'd just provided. Tired, I sat down next to him on the bed, adding, "I pray that someday if I'm graced with the wonder of a daughter, I'll be there to encourage her to be whatever she desires, and provide her with the tools to be a successful woman."

Caleb smiled deviously. Pushing himself up, he caught me off guard, giving me the gentlest of kisses that held more than longing. It held understanding. Behind the kiss, he whispered, "I hope it's a boy."

"What an infuriating man you are, Caleb Young. Didn't you hear a word of what I just said?"

With all the strength he had, Caleb crushed his lips to mine, holding me firmly in place.

After all I'd just confessed, I didn't know what came over me. I gave no resistance to his advances. Accepting his strong arm that tenderly enfolded me in his warmth. *Oh, Emily! You are going to be so sorry for allowing this to happen. But what if he's right and I can't go back? Do I want to miss the love this man has to give me?*

Before I realized what I was doing, a quiet release settled over me as Caleb deepened the kiss. Grasping the sides of his face, I pulled back, glimpsing the fireworks behind his gold-rimmed irises. Slowly running my hands through his unruly hair, I foolishly gave in and welcomed his advances. What harm can kisses be? Caleb's hands drew me closer. Breathless, I sighed, releasing a soft moan of pleasure. Discovering each other like young lovers, our hands roamed freely over each other.

Reality hit when my hand came in contact with the bandage on his shoulder. Trying to push away, Caleb continued to hold me firmly in place. With such gentleness, he traced kisses over my eyelids, the tip of my nose, my cheeks, and back to my lips where he'd started his journey. This time, with determination, I asked, "Caleb, please stop. We can't do this. We have to stop this now." Placing my hand firmly on the cot, I pushed back, successfully breaking our embrace. Confused, both breathing heavily, we stared into each other's eyes, silently questioning what had just happened.

"Did I do something wrong?" Watching his eyes search my face, he would find only sadness. Running his hand from my hair to my cheek, he would also see my vexing emotions.

Was he silently questioning my love for him? Is that what he wanted? My love. It wouldn't do either of us any good if I did love him. We were from two different worlds, two different centuries. One of us was bound to get hurt. Closing my eyes, anger won out, as I screamed internally, *I won't let that happen.*

Standing, I hung my head without answering him. Moving back to the stove, I felt Caleb's hand brush mine. Pulling away, I needed to distance myself and think.

"Emily, I'm sorry if I did something wrong. Please, look at me."

Slowly facing him, I was unable to meet his eyes. Wringing my hands tightly together, I said, "Caleb, I can't. I just can't do this right now." My chin trembled as I took one small step towards him, "Please understand. I care deeply for you." *I love you.* "But it won't work. You have to know that." I was trying to rationalize my feelings when I added, "We've only known each other for less than two weeks."

"What do you mean it won't work?" Letting out a trembling breath, his hands fell over his chest. Had I broken his heart?

"I don't care if it was just one day. It could have been a year. This feels right to me. Besides, friends don't kiss the way we just did." His tone demanding, he added, "I know you feel something. You can't deny it."

No, I couldn't deny my feelings for him. But, neither could I declare them.

Standing silent, I needed to find out what my future held. Was I to remain here in 1880 or return to 2019? Either way, I didn't need the emotions of love to interfere in my search for answers. If I let this relationship go further, and I did return to 2019, I would die all over again—this time, from a broken heart.

Silently screaming for answers, I had to find my grandfather and have him send me back to Seattle before it was too late. I couldn't let these feelings for Caleb go any further. It was horrible to say, but he was a hindrance to my leaving.

Feeling as if my throat was closing up, I struck him hard with a verbal assault. "Caleb, this is just your gratitude speaking for me saving your life. Nothing more!" Steeling myself for a fight, I continued, "I have things I need to deal with, and you're not one of them!" *Maybe, not ever*, I whispered. I'd just committed suicide with my heart.

Watching the pained expression on his face give way to defeat, I realized I'd hurt him beyond all measure. It was worse than if I'd been the one who shot him.

Caleb

Sitting up on the edge of the bed, I was stunned at Emily's cruel blunt confessions. Looking down, I realized that I'd been clutching my coat so tightly that my knuckles had turned painfully white. Her answer wasn't the one I'd hoped for. Slumping my shoulders in defeat, I could honestly say that I had never felt this way for any woman, not even Anna. I've been fooling myself for far too long. Anna had been just a means to get back at my father.

Leaning forward, elbows on my knees, Emily's proclamation left me dead inside. Cursing to myself, I wondered how I would survive without her. Better yet, did I even want to? The wounds she'd inflicted on my heart hurt like the depths of hell, leaving me with a sick longing to die. Emily was like no woman I'd ever met. She was resilient, intelligent, self-reliant, and witty. Self-assured without arrogance, carrying confidence that I couldn't help but admire. She had shown me a compassionate tender side of her that abetted my surviving. When I'd given in to her magical charms, her passion exceeded any woman I'd ever known. One thing I'll never forget was the kiss we'd just shared. If I survived, I would by no means meet another woman like Emily Sweeney again. *I couldn't allow myself to lose her! She would be mine!*

"I need to find out why I'm here, Caleb. And you'll only complicate matters."

Brought out of my numbing thoughts, her words struck dead center like a shot to my heart. Before I could ask, my speech stilted, and I croaked out, "What do you mean, why you're here?" The tightness I now felt in my chest wasn't from my wounds. It was her mortal words that were killing me. "Emily, I don't understand what's going on in your mind right now." Holding out my hand, I struggled to ask, "Can't we talk this through?" Stepping back away from me, I stared into her eyes, gone dim behind a blank expression.

"Caleb, please. I can't. I just can't do this right now. You'll just have to trust me."

Confused and emotionally spent, "OK," was all I managed to hiss out. Laying down, I stared up at the rafters and began counting the knotholes in the decaying boards as fatigue won out. All I wanted to do now was fall into a deep sleep and forget we'd even had this conversation.

⤳ 21 ⤶

Emily

THE TENSION THICK between us extended into the evening, speaking only to each other when the need arose. There was no food left, and I hadn't been out to search. Tonight's evening meal would consist only of leftover broth.

My stomach growled loudly, knowing tomorrow I'd need to find something, anything to keep us from starving. Even though Caleb was still too weak to walk around, I understood his anger with himself for not being able to provide for us. But, he hadn't been that weak to . . . I had to stop thinking of his kisses.

We both slept fitfully—Caleb alone in the bed and me at the table with his rifle by my side. Awaking early the next morning to the sounds of gravel crunching outside the door, I picked up the rifle and checked the chambers. Previously, I'd pledged to protect us both against any intruders. Still, I didn't know if I could actually shoot another human being, knowing firsthand the suffering it caused. But I would do it if need be.

The crunching stopped just outside our useless door. Standing, legs apart, I braced the rifle butt against my right shoulder and leveled it at the door. Taking in a deep breath and holding it, I was ready.

My shoulders were tighter than a coiled rope that I'd almost forgotten to breathe. Hearing a horse whinny, I let out my breath as a loud knock sounded at the door. Frozen in place, I was unable to reply. With another louder knock, I answered, "Who is it?"

"Tis da sheriff, ma'am. Sheriff Johansson" came a gruff reply. I was almost sure he was staring at the dried blood stains on the outside of the door, making him wary of entering. He probably had no idea what he was getting himself into, and I understood if he was hesitant.

Arms aching with false bravado, I asked, "What do you want?"

"I saw da smoke from da chimney as I vas riding by, and thot ja might need help."

"How do I know you're the sheriff?" Momentarily taking my eyes off the door, I looked in the direction of the bed seeing Caleb with a pained expression creasing his face. With his gun in hand, he was in the process of sitting up.

"Ja don't, ma'am. Ja just needs ta trust me."

"Well, sheriff, I'm not a real trusting woman right now," I replied with a ring of sarcasm.

Caleb's huff sounded like an express agreement, and I couldn't help but turn a stern face his direction.

"Ma'am, if ja'd like, I can turn around and ride out of here right now if ja'r sure you're OK."

I waited for Caleb to sit up and take aim at the door before answering the sheriff, "No, please wait a minute." I didn't move but looked to Caleb for advice.

Not speaking, he motioned with his gun for me to slowly open the door. In his condition, I could tell he was just as mistrustful as I was, no matter who was at the door.

We were both ready to shoot if need be. But, what would happen if Caleb or the man on the other side of the door shot first? Would I be caught in the crossfire and die all over again?

"I need to tell you that there's a rifle pointed at the door sheriff. So, if you make any fast moves, you will be shot. Do you understand?" Taking one last glance at Caleb to make sure he was ready, I moved to lift the bar.

"Ya, ma'am. And, I need to tell you that I have a forty-five pointed at the door and will do the same. Do you understand?"

Nodding as if he could see me, I finally answered. "Yes, perfectly." Taking in a deep breath, I raised the bar with sweaty palms while hearing the sheriff mumbling on the other side, "Crazy voman."

The door creaked on rusty hinges, as I feigned bravery, never lowering the shotgun. We now stood face to face. "Show me your badge," I demanded before I let the sheriff take one step over the threshold.

"OK, lady, yust stay calm." Raising his left palm, he added, "I'm going ta reach inta my jacket and pull it back real slow so ja can see my badge." Watching his left hand move in slow motion, the sheriff pulled back the side of his coat, revealing a shiny brass star engraved with 'Sheriff' across its center.

"Yust don't go gettin' trigga happy. I like be'n a live sheriff."

I didn't flinch. I was used to dealing with these types of people in my E.R., who tried to bargain their way around my better judgment. *Just let this one try to put something past me, and I will have no problem shooting him.*

Sighing with relief, I kept the rifle in position when Caleb called out from where he sat on the bed. "Sheriff Johansson. I can't believe I'm saying this, but you're a sight for sore eyes."

The sheriff slowly peeked around the door to see who knew him, mindful that there was still a rifle pointed his way. Once Caleb recognized the sheriff, he lay back on the bed, still clutching his weapon.

Astonished, I asked, "Caleb, you know this man?"

"Yes, we've met. He's the sheriff in Yuma. The town he ran me out of."

"Ran you out of?" Lunging at the sheriff, I screamed, "Why you Sonofa . . ." My words were lost against his chest. I was swearing enough to burn his ears while I beat him with both my fists. "You shot Caleb and left him here to die?" My fiery Irish temper was rearing its ugly head, as my eyes drilled holes straight through his heart. "Why, I ought to shoot you right here and now and leave your sorry carcass for the buzzards."

"Vhoa, little lady." The sheriff got lucky by ducking my final blow by grabbing both my wrists. "Now, yust hold on a minute."

I sent a swift kick to the sheriff's shin and struggled against his grip. "Let go of me, you animal!"

"Ow!" he yelled, sidestepping any further assault. Shaking me a bit forcefully, he said, "Stop it! Listen to vhat your man has to say."

"He's not my man!" I replied. Lifting my chin, I forcefully pulled back against his hold.

"Vell, vatever he is, you may vant to hear him out before ya try beating me to death."

Sherriff Johansson

I remembered banishing Mr. Young from Yuma over two weeks ago. By their disheveled looks, the woman before me, although beautiful underneath all the dirt, had probably been at the cabin the same length of time. I didn't recognize her from any of the wanted posters hanging in my jail. Or, anyone else I'd seen in town. But, there was a familiar resemblance to someone I knew.

Looking her up and down, I could see her visible despair and tired features. Her dress was torn and covered in desert filth. The long braid hanging down her back was tangled with bits of grass and twigs. It looked as though it hadn't seen a comb in weeks. Which it probably hadn't.

The looks Caleb sent my way meant the woman I now held in my arms was off-limits. No matter! I wasn't interested in her that way. I had Abigail. Or, I wanted to believe I did. Whom, by the way, I was anxious to be getting back to town to see. I'd been gone for four days hunting down a gunman who killed a miner outside of Yuma. So far, I hadn't had any luck in finding him or his trail.

Clutching my coat in a firm grip, the woman had finally stopped pummeling me. Spent, she now leaned her forehead against my chest, and I could feel her warm heavy breathing through my wool shirt. Relief washed over me as I effortlessly eased her down onto the nearby bench.

Watching, she stared blankly at the floor as a roach scurried across her bare foot. She didn't move or scream, only appeared emotionless and drained of all physical energy. If I hadn't shown up when I did, they might have had just days before both she and Mr. Young would have succumbed, leaving this earthly plane.

Raising her head, she looked blankly in Caleb's direction, not at me. Lying on his back, I watched Caleb turn his head to face her. A look of raw pain drew his features taught.

What now? I thought.

Sensing her resignation, I cautiously walked over to speak with Caleb. Standing over the bed, I asked, "So, Mr. Young, vat has you out here in the middle of nowhere flat on ja back? And, in ja long johns, no less."

Before Caleb could reply, his woman brought over the bench she'd just been sitting on, indicating for me to sit. I thanked her. Then, both Caleb and I watched her walk out the cabin door, into the bright sunlight, without saying a word or looking back.

At my insistence, Caleb began to relate their story of the past weeks, all-the-while watching the door and waiting impatiently for the woman's return. By the time he was done talking, he was exhausted and covered in a sweaty sheen.

"Where could she have gone?" Caleb asked.

"Don't worry, I'll find her." Placing my hands on my knees, I pushed myself up. You yust lay back and rest."

"That's all I've been doing," Caleb huffed out.

Before I could move away, Caleb grabbed hold of the hem of my jacket. "Sheriff, listen. That woman out there . . . Emily, she saved my life. I owe her everything. Do you understand that?"

"Of course I do," I replied, setting my Stetson back on my head.

"I don't think you do. I don't know what I would have done without her." Coughing, he added, "If she hadn't come along when she did, you'd be digging me a six-foot hole out back right about now. She means more to me than you'll ever know." Gripping my coat tighter, he added, "Please, make sure she stays safe if anything should happen to me."

Placing my hand on Caleb's shoulder and squeezing, "Notting's going to happen to ja now. You have my word. I'll go check on her. You rest now."

I could see that Caleb would give his life to keep that woman safe, so I added, "I promise, ja going to be fine once ve get ja back to town, and the doc takes a look at ja." Pointing to the door, "It looks like that little lady there has done some fine doctor'n herself. Ja're a lucky man."

"You don't have to tell me that. I know. She's my angel sent from heaven," Caleb said with a faint smile.

Leaving Caleb's bedside, I stepped through the door, finding Emily sitting on the ground, her head leaning back against the cabin wall. Knees pulled up to her chest, the morning sun enhanced the dark circles under her eyes. Kneeling beside her, I looked into eyes of compassion that I hadn't recognized during her fit of anger.

"Sheriff, I'm sorry for what I said and did in there. That's not like me."

Her hands moved through the air as she talked. "It's just that I'm so tired of trying to figure out where I was going to find our next meal, let alone how we were going to get out of here. When Caleb's wounds became infected, I was frightened he'd die, and I'd be left out here alone."

Before I could respond, Emily's chin trembled as a single tear fell down her cheek. "Sheriff, I don't want Caleb to die." Gracing me with a beautiful smile, she touched my arm. "Thank you for coming to our rescue. You're my knight in shining armor."

"Jar vhat?" I asked, confused.

"Never mind." Removing her hand. "I'm just so glad you found us. I was running out of options."

"Oh, I doubt tat yung lady. Jar pretty resourceful," nodding my head in the direction of the cabin. "Ja did pretty well in keeping tat young man in ter alive. I know tat he is more tan grateful."

Standing, I extended my hand to help Emily rise. Taking hold, I pulled her up, not letting go, as she searched my eyes, then placed a soft kiss on my cheek. Without saying another word, she turned and walked back through the door.

Stunned, I stood holding my cold fingers over my now warm cheek that Emily had just kissed. The only woman to thank me that way was Abigail. And I rather liked it.

Following the young lady back into the cabin, I wanted them both to know that I wouldn't desert them. Nodding my head in Caleb's direction, I said, "Listen, I only have te one horse, and tis man here ist in no condition to ride. It's a day's ride back te town, and a day te return. I'll leave you some provisions te make it through until I return in about forty-eight to seventy-two hours, maybe sooner wit a vagon and extra men to help. Then I'll get you back to town and have the doc take a look at both of you."

Taking off my heavy coat, I handed it to Emily. "This will help keep you warm at night while I'm gone." Pointing to the table where the rifle lay, "I'll leave some extra ammunition in case you need it." Turning, I went to get the extra supplies from my saddlebags. Placing a sack of biscuits and some beef jerky on the table along with a small bag of coffee and beans, I handed Emily my rolled blanket.

"Sheriff, I..." stopping, she looked in Caleb's direction before continuing, "We can't thank you enough. Please be safe." Whispering so only I could hear her, she said, "I have a suspicious feeling that whoever did this to Caleb may still be out there."

Nodding my understanding, I had to agree with her. Loud enough for Caleb to hear, I proclaimed, "I'll be back."

Emily placed a hand on my arm, giving me the faintest of smiles. "Please do."

"I will Miss, you can count on tat."

Walking over to stand next to Caleb, I let him know I would return with help. "Remember your promise, he uttered."

"Caleb like I said, not'ing is going to happen, ja're in good hands wit tat little lady. She cares a great deal for ja. Jer knows that, don't ja? Besides, I keep my promises. Ja doesn't have to worry about tat."

Caleb

Deep down, I wasn't so sure. Especially after the conversation, or should I say heated discussion, Emily and I had had that morning before the sheriff arrived. I only hoped that we could remain on peaceful terms until the sheriff's return. "Thanks again. And, safe travels, sheriff."

Tipping his fingers to the brim of his hat, he turned and walked out the door, leaving Emily to stare after him, while I stared at her back. What was she thinking? That we'd never see the sheriff again? That he'd left us to our own devices and that of the desert?

Once the sheriff left, I pushed myself up off the quilt, letting out a low moan. I could finally ask her, "Where did you go?"

Emily didn't rush to help me sit up as she usually would. Nor was her answer swift in coming. Instead, she walked to the stove, giving me a short answer, "Not far."

"I was worried about you."

"There was no need."

✒ 22 ✒

Emily

THE DAY AFTER the sheriff left was spent in silence. Neither Caleb nor I asked what was to happen next. In less than twenty-four hours, the sheriff would return, and we would go our separate ways.

It was midafternoon when I turned my attention to the rumbling in my stomach. I was just about to fix us both something to eat just as Caleb called out to me.

"Emily, we need to talk."

"Not now, Caleb," I replied, refusing to face him. "I'm going to make us something to eat first."

Turning my attention to the stove, I placed the pot of water on to boil for coffee. Cutting the biscuits in two, I placed them and a piece of jerky on the one tin plate. I couldn't take a chance to waste food in case the sheriff didn't return like he said he would.

What will I do if he doesn't return? We were both so hungry that the hard biscuits were a treat, and the jerky, to me, tasted like a filet mignon.

Standing back, I watched as Caleb struggled to sit on the edge of the bed. "Caleb, you need to eat," I said curtly, handing him the plate.

"What about you?" he asked, holding the plate between us.

"I'll eat after you. We only have one plate and cup between us." Looking down at the floor, I felt terrible for being so distant towards him. Confusion warred within my heart. Stay or leave, once we reached Yuma. "Caleb, I'm so sorry about the other day." *Here I go again.* Feeling the tears ready to spill. *Dang these waterworks!* Why couldn't I keep them in check?

"I don't know what came over me. You've been nothing but kind to me." I stuttered, "I know we need to talk, but it will have to wait until we get to Yuma, where we both have a chance to relax. And you have a better chance to recover. I promise we'll talk then."

"It's OK. You don't owe me any explanations." Coughing on the dry biscuit, he dropped his head, staring at the floor. "Emily, I've done things I'm not proud of. I've hurt too many people in my past. And, I've given it some thought. You're a genteel lady who deserves a better man than I."

"Caleb, you don't have to tell . . ."

Raising his hand, he interrupted me pushing forward, "Let me finish. Like I said, I don't want you to feel obligated. I can't ask that of you, knowing who I am and what I've done."

"What are you talking about?" I asked, running my hands through the loose ends of my hair. "It doesn't matter Caleb." Pointing a finger to myself, "We've all done things we're not proud of, but we move on hoping to make better choices."

Bluntly, he asked, "Have you killed before?"

Whoa! I didn't see that coming. What I did see was the raw pain of regret and loneliness in his eyes. I wanted to take him in my arms, tell him that his past didn't matter and that I'd come to love him. Surprised, with my confession, I decided to keep it to myself for the time being.

"Don't you understand Emily? I won't pursue our relationship further once we get to town. You'll be free to leave and go home."

The air chilled around me as I raised my quivering chin. "Fine, I understand." Turning as if to leave, I stopped and faced him directly, raising my voice. "Who am I to try and make life more complicated for the two of us? We're from two different worlds. Like you said, it just won't work, and neither of us can ever be together. Not now. Not ever." Taking the plate from his hands, I walked back to the dry sink, dropping it in with a clatter, then walked out the door into the fading light.

I had no idea where I was going. Winding up at the empty corral, the cavernous void within my heart could never be filled. I was out of my element, let alone out of my time, with nowhere to go. My only mission now was to find my grandfather and demand he send me back home.

Holding back tears, I leaned my head on the top rail. It was no use. I couldn't hold them back any longer. Like my grandmother use to say, crying cleanses the soul, and I sure could use a good cleaning right about now. Washing away all the pent-up anger and emotions from the past two weeks, relieved from the weight Caleb and this century had placed on my shoulders.

Pushing away, I dried my face with the sleeve of my dress. Picking up my skirts, I began walking quickly up the rise to where the creek ran down from the hills. I wasn't making any sense as I started talking to myself. "I am not going back to that cabin as long as I have a breath in me."

Breathing labored, I panted as the incline increased. The sheriff would be here tomorrow, and he could take care of getting Caleb back to town and medical help. I was just stubborn enough to fend for myself and find my own way back.

Emily dear, I'm so sorry to interrupt the conversation with yourself but, where do you think you're going at this hour? It's going to be dark soon, and once again, you didn't bring the rifle.

"Gran, is that you?" I asked, looking heavenward. "I thought you'd left?"

Yes, dear, it's me. Listen, that man back there loves you, can't you see that? He's just scared. Everyone he's ever cared about has hurt him. Oh, not in a physical way. It's just that he hasn't had any luck with love. He doesn't want that to happen between the two of you. He's setting you free, Emily. Free from potential emotional pain. Can you understand that?

Sniffling, I answered, "Oh Gran, why does love have to hurt so much? It doesn't make any sense at all. You'd think the love between a man and a woman would be simple. You know I care a great deal for Caleb. Don't you?"

Stopping midstride, I asked, "Gran. How can I be dead and fall in love?" Wiping my nose with the tattered hem of my dress, I knew I wasn't making any sense. "Anyway, it's too late, I'm not going back to the cabin." My stubbornness prevailing, "I'll find my own way to town."

Sweetie, you have a lot to learn about men and love. They are fickle creatures and wouldn't know up from down if it wasn't for women. You both have "issues," as you often say. And, you need to deal with them before your love can take a firm hold.

"But, Gran, love isn't some fancy words on a greeting card. And this certainly isn't a Hallmark movie, as much as I love watching them." Asking grimly, I continued, "What if he really doesn't love me and he's mistaking love for gratitude? It's just like he said, he doesn't think I could deal with him loving me." Turning in circles, on the hillside, arms wide open, I yelled, "I know my feelings for Caleb are real. Why does it have to be so difficult for men to figure out theirs?"

Dear, it's like you females in the medical world like to say, it's the short Y male chromosome that's messing with his heart.

"Gran, I love you and miss you so much. Being able to talk with you like this, it's like having you sit on my bed when I was a young girl, and we talked about all sorts of things. You were right when you use to tell me that life and love were not an easy task, but it was sure worth all the effort we gave it."

I didn't realize how far I'd walked until I noticed the sun drifting behind the Western hills. Soon darkness would surround me. Thunder rolled in over the mountains, and lightning struck a tree below. My thoughts wandered back to Caleb alone in the cabin. "Is he wondering where I've gone? Would he make a foolish attempt to come looking for me?" I hoped not. "Oh, God. Please help me. If you can hear me, I've messed things up and need your help now, more than ever. *I love that man.*"

Despite what I said about not going back to the cabin, even if I'd wanted to, my options were swiftly shrinking as the dark gray clouds rolled in around me. Picking up my skirts, I headed in its direction just as a roll of thunder boomed directly overhead, and lightning struck the ground behind me. Screaming, I ran faster. As I was getting closer to the cabin, the first fat raindrops splattered to the dry earth. Soon, pools of muddy water were surrounding me. Surging down in torrents, I was soaked to the skin. Frightened, the weight of the yards of wet fabric slowed me down. I wasn't used to this downpour. Most of the time, it only drizzled in Seattle. This was so much more. This was a full-body soaking rain that even an umbrella would be of no use.

My braid had come loose and hung in wet, limp ringlets down my back. Each drop of water that dripped from the tips of my hair sent icy chills trailing down my spine. Shivering, cold and soaked to the bone, I slipped in the mud, landing painfully on my backside. Pushing up, I saw the edge of the cabin in the distance. "Not much farther," I said. "Keep going Emily."

Caleb

I awoke disoriented in a cold room that was darker than the depths of hell without fire. Thunder pierced the night air and shook the cabin walls. I was concerned that Emily didn't have a fire going in the stove like she usually did. Suddenly, the room lit up from a bolt of lightning shooting through the sky, causing the hair on my arms to stand straight up.

During that one bright moment, I was unable to make out Emily's form within the cabin. "Where is that woman?" With renewed energy, I pushed up off the bed as rain pummeled the roof like pebbles.

"Emily, where are you?" I yelled over the pounding rain and thunder. Feeling a drop trickle it's way down my nose, I looked up, seeing the roof was no protection. Water maneuvered its way through the gaps, coming to form a puddle at the foot of the bed.

I yelled again for Emily. Still, no response. Steadying myself, I made sure I didn't fall flat on my face as I listened for any sound Emily would make. Before taking one tentative step forward, I reached the table as another raindrop hit me on the back of my neck, sending needle-like chills down my spine. This time, lightning struck even closer, giving concern that a strike to the cabin would turn it into an inferno.

Cringing, I prayed, "God, please don't let her be out in this." Rubbing my hands over my bearded face, I had to assume that Emily knew nothing about desert flooding. Letting out a tightly held breath, I thought, "She'll die out there."

Standing barefoot in my long underwear, I couldn't go out looking for Emily in the muddy mess without first putting on my boots. Chilled, I shook from head to toe. With much effort, I moved back to the bed, groaned, pulled on my boots, and groaned some more.

Grabbing my shearling coat from the bed, I put it on, hugging the front closed. Taking a step forward, then another, I was determined that weakness would not deter me. I would do anything to find Emily.

The pain in my shoulder was bearable. It was my abdomen, which was another story! The motion of standing up, sitting down, pulling on my boots, then walking again, sent tearing sensations from my belly down the front of my right leg. I was terrified my legs would buckle underneath me. Right now, the only thing keeping me upright was the fact that Emily was out there. Somewhere, alone in this horrible storm needing me.

Grabbing my hat off a peg, and my rifle, that Emily had left lying on the table, I slowly made my way to the door. Pulling it open, I was assaulted by fat icy raindrops. Still, I had to find her. Leaning against the doorframe, I yelled her name at the top of my lungs with what little air I could take in, "Emily, where are you? Please. Come back to the cabin. It's not safe out there." I had no idea where she was or how far she'd gone, or if she could even hear my pleas over the thunder and pounding rains.

Caleb

T O PROTECT MY eyes from the blinding rain, I pulled my hat down over my forehead. I didn't see Emily approaching. All I was thinking about was I couldn't live another day if I lost her. Desperate, I needed to tell her again that I loved her and wanted to be with her no matter what life dealt us.

Despite my watch saying it was early afternoon, the storm had turned daylight into darkness in a matter of minutes. The dirt around the cabin was now a pool of thick sloppy mud. Sliding to a stop, Emily nearly ran straight into me. Catching myself, I leaned against the doorframe, desperately trying to stay upright.

As if sent a gift from tempestuous heaven, Emily stood before me. Letting out a jagged breath, I said, "Thank God you're alive." Holding my abdomen, I coughed, and the shooting pains almost brought me to my knees. If it hadn't been for Emily catching me, I would be lying face first in the mud. My energy faltered, and I found myself sagging into her arms. Supported in her embrace, I looked down into her violet eyes, I said, "You didn't leave me." Reaching my hand up to cup the side of her face, I felt sticky dampness on my fingers and saw the red mark I'd left on her cheek. "Damn!" My wound had reopened. Trying to make light of the situation, I showed Emily my hand and said, "I know, you're going to kill me for this if I don't die first."

Staring at my hand, I tried gauging the amount of blood I was once again losing. I didn't care, Emily was back. Pulling her wet body tightly to my chest, I whispered in her ear, "I love you, Emily Sweeney. Don't you ever leave me like that again!"

Emily

My face burned as much from Caleb's declaration, as from my exertion running through the storm. Not letting go, I tried moving past him to help him inside the cabin while taking a good long look at what he was wearing. He had on his Stetson, shearling coat, cowboy boots, and red long johns. It would be funny if the mood weren't so dire.

"Caleb, you're bleeding again," I said, trying to open his coat and examine his abdomen. "You shouldn't have tried looking for me." Walking him back towards the bed, I could feel his body shudder in my arms as I tried moving the wood frame away from the wet wall and puddle. "Let's get this wet coat off, then you need to lie down."

While I tugged at his coat sleeves, my emotions warred within me. *I have to tell him.* Gently running my palm along the side of his bearded face, I leaned forward, placing a kiss on his cold lips. "I love you Caleb." For the first time in my life, I had finally admitted what my heart truly felt.

Pushing back, the doctor in me took over. "Now, let me look at your wounds." There appeared to be less blood than I'd first thought. It was the combination of his red underwear and being wet that had caused the stain to look to be more substantial than it actually was.

"I . . . I need to tell you," Caleb said through chattering teeth.

"Hush," I said, placing my fingers over his lips. "We'll have time enough to talk. Right now, I need to start the fire and get us out of these wet clothes." Shivering, I added, "I'm soaking wet and freezing."

"Um! That sounds nice," Caleb teased.

"What's sounds nice, freezing?" I asked, knowing exactly what he really meant.

"No, I've been trying to figure out a way of getting you out of your clothes for days," he said, trying to be glib. "I mean . . ."

"I know what you mean Cowboy. And it isn't going to happen." *At least not now.* But still, I couldn't help but smile. I had just declared my love for Caleb. It was a commitment I didn't think I would ever make, whether in 2019 or 1880. Now, what do I do?

"I like it when you smile." Caleb let out a deep shaky breath. "I haven't seen you do that, but maybe once before." Changing the subject, he added, "Sheriff Johansson will be here in a few hours."

"I hope he comes back like he said he would."

Firmly squeezing my hands, he pulled my attention back to him. "Why wouldn't he?"

"I don't know. It's just a feeling I have." Retreating to the stove, I added, "It's silly of me. He promised he'd come back. In the meantime, we need to dry off and get warmed up."

I could no longer deny my love for Caleb. It was not just a city girl's infatuation with a cowboy. The fact he'd risked his life, and tried coming after me in torrential rains, wounded, in pain, and wearing nothing but his sexy red underwear, made my heart over-flow with love.

Using one end of the quilt, I tried helping Caleb dry off as the room began to warm up and ease the bone-chilling dampness that had permeated the air. Caleb shivered uncontrollably. Touching my hand to his brow, I once again felt heat radiate from his hot skin. "Dang it Caleb, you have a fever again. I need to get you to a hospital." His spiking fevers were definitely not a good sign, and rapidly decreased his chances of surviving. I helped him drink some leftover willow bark tea, then instructed him to lie down until the sheriff came.

Stripping down to my underclothes, I rubbed my hair and face only to find it futile. The mud wasn't coming off without soap and a hot bath. Hanging my muddy dress over the chair, I moved it in front of the stove to help it dry. Hoping to generate heat, I rapidly rubbed my hands up and down my cold bare arms, while pacing back and forth across the cabin's muddied floor. Waiting for the sheriff was painful in itself. My voice echoed through the cabin, "Why isn't he here?"

"He'll be here," Caleb said through chattering teeth. "He told us he'd return, and I believe him. Besides, with the weather this bad, the horses may be having trouble getting up the muddy hillside."

"Why do you believe him after what he did to you in Yuma?"

"The sheriff did what he thought was best. Besides, it could be worse. I could be sitting in the Territorial Prison right now waiting to hang for murder."

The pattering of rain had stopped when I answered him. "You're right." Sitting still was out of the question. My body ached from head to toe, and I would give anything for two ibuprofen.

Hearing the crunch of wagon wheels on gravel, I was out the door in seconds, in nothing but my underwear. Running down the path, I met the sheriff as he jumped off his horse in one fluid motion. Ignoring my skimpy attire, he grasped my arms before I fell. Short of breath, "Caleb," was all I could get out. "Caleb," I sputtered again.

"Miss Sweeney, vat's wrong?" the sheriff asked, holding me steady while staring in the direction of the cabin.

By then, my damp hair had fallen across my mud-splattered face. Placing my palms on his chest, I inhaled deeply and began telling the sheriff what had happened since he left. Once finished, I noticed four men astride horses next to a wagon, eyes wide open silently watching us.

"Caleb's in the cabin," I pointed towards the door. "He has a fever. We need to get him to the hospital as fast as possible." Easing me away, Sheriff Johansson turned, giving an order for the other men to get Caleb and bring him to the wagon while I ran in to put on my dress. Thank heavens, someone had had the forethought to lay fresh hay and several worn quilts in its bed. I pleaded with the sheriff and his men to be gentle, as I watched them lift Caleb into the wagon bed.

Before realizing it, I too was being raised into the back of the wagon by Sheriff Johansson. Once safely settled, he yelled to his men to move out. Covering Caleb with the quilts, I cradled his head in my lap. He didn't make a sound or open his eyes. At the wagon's first lurch forward, I took hold of his fevered body with one hand while grabbing onto the sideboard with my other. Holding on for dear life, it seemed the ride took forever. I was sure the driver hadn't missed one rocky rut on the way down the hillside. We couldn't get to town fast enough for my liking.

Emily

I T FELT AS though my kidneys were being jostled up into my throat as the wagon descended the hill. *Oh! What I wouldn't give right now for my SUV.* Bouncing from side to side, I could only imagine what Caleb was feeling. Holding firm, I tried to keep his head from rolling back and forth in my lap. His fever raged, and he drifted in and out of consciousness during the tortuous journey.

Approaching the town, my head was on a swivel trying to take in everything around me. Nothing looked familiar. Forgetting my surroundings, I again focused on Caleb. The sooner we got him to the clinic, the sooner I'd be able to search for my grandfather.

After what seemed like hours of grueling travel, the wagon finally made it to the edge of town. I was stunned to see the scene before me. Men on horseback, dressed like Caleb and the sheriff, rode by on their stately mounts. Women strolled along the boardwalks wearing long calico dresses, their hair pulled back in tight buns covered with bonnets. Looking down, I realized I had on the same type of dress, but in much worse condition. And, my hair hung free in a tangled mess.

Unconsciously, I tried pressing the wrinkles out of my dress with the palms of my hands. The women who stared at me, held their hands over their mouths while whispering to each other. I had always been so meticulous with my presentation. Now, for the first time in my life, I felt uncomfortable. Turning my head from their direction to hide my embarrassment, I looked down at the grime that covered my hands and clothing. If they only knew what I'd been through in the past few weeks, their first impression of me might change.

My curiosity won out. Holding my head high, I gazed from one side of the street to the other, taking in everything before me. To heck with their stares. I had a right to be here.

The town looked as if it had been here for more years than I could imagine. Down the street, I noticed the jail, a laundry, the barbershop, stables, saloon, and hotel. *Oh, thank heavens, a hotel. I can finally soak in a hot bath and wash my hair.*

The wagon slowed, and I noticed a stunningly attractive young woman standing in front of the saloon. It was late afternoon, and she was dressed in a form-fitting pale yellow calico, not what I expected of saloon attire. Looking up, she was smiling demurely, but not at me. Following the direction of her gaze, she was looking at the figure of Sheriff Johansson sitting astride his horse. Back straight, with a staid expression on his face, not once did he glance in her direction.

What caught my attention was the way her clothes fit snuggly across her midriff. *Silly man.* I knew that look of longing in her eyes, and my heart ached for her since it was apparent the sheriff paid her no consideration.

The wagon came to an abrupt stop in front of a white two-story building surrounded by a sagging white picket fence. Within the yard, clinging to the slats, were thorn-covered rose bushes that at one time had probably been lovingly cared for. Stunned into silence at what I'd seen in the past few minutes, Sheriff Johansson stood at the back of the wagon, waiting for me to make my move.

"Miss Sweeney," the sheriff said rather loudly, catching me unaware.

"Yes, sheriff." I glanced at his outstretched hands, not taking them. "I thought you were taking us to the clinic?"

"This ist ta clinic, Miss Sweeney."

"It is?" I barely choked out. Staring in disbelief. *He can't be serious? Could he?*

"Yes, ma'am. It tis."

"Good heavens." What was I supposed to do? I couldn't believe this was the clinic I was to surrender Caleb's care too? Resigned, I had no other choice. I nodded and pleaded with the sheriff, "Please be careful with Mr. Young when you carry him inside."

"Yes, ma'am, ve vill," he answered as his men moved forward to assist him. Taking hold of the edges of the dirty quilt, they pulled Caleb ahead until they were able to lift him encased in the fabric's folds.

I slid towards the tail of the wagon bed since one of the men had stayed behind to help me down. Holding out his hand for me to take, I was reassured in his strength, never having experienced such chivalry.

"Ma'am," the young man said, looking up at me. "Let me help you into the clinic."

Slipping my arm through his, I allowed him to escort me up the short walkway. I was glad to be holding his arm when I stopped short at the base of the steps and looked up. I almost tripped on the hem of my dress when he asked, "Is there something wrong, ma'am?"

It wasn't that warm out yet, but rivulets of sweat ran between my breasts and down my back when I read the sign hanging from the intricate gable above the steps. I couldn't believe it. There in bold black letters read, 'Mathew Sweeney, MD.' Re-reading it several times before it sank in, I placed my fingers over my lips, "This isn't possible."

"What isn't possible, ma'am?" Concerned, my escort took hold of my elbow to steady me. "Ma'am, do you need to sit down?"

I ignored him, not to be rude, but because I was in shock at what I had just read. Bringing my hand to my throat, I tried to swallow the words lodged there but found I could only choke back the dry dust that had settled in my mouth over the long journey.

I couldn't tell if my eyes were deceiving me? Shaking my head from side to side, no they weren't. I knew my great-great-grandfather's name was Mathew Sweeney. Indeed, he'd been a physician living and dying somewhere in Arizona.

"Ma'am, Are you sure you're OK? You're lookin' a might peekid." Slowly, he led me to the steps. "Why don't you sit down here, and I'll go fetch you some water?"

"What? I'm sorry. I wasn't paying attention to what you were saying."

"Yes, ma'am. I asked if you needed some water since you're lookin' a bit peekid."

I didn't doubt it. I was staring at him as though he was speaking a foreign language when I realized what he'd asked. Laying a hand on his arm, I replied, "Yes, water would be nice. Thank you." Lifting my head upward, I looked at the sign from a different angle, hoping the wording had changed. It hadn't. I was sitting under my great-great-grandfather's name.

Oblivious to the swirling dust and the town noises, I prayed, *OK, God, I asked you to guide me to my great-great-grandfather so he could take me back home. But I didn't think I would be this lucky and have it happen so soon. Now, what do I do?*

No matter how much I tried to moisten my lips, they remained dry. *Where was that young man? I could really use that water.* Willing myself not to faint, I didn't know if I was able to face my grandfather right now. I wouldn't have much further to go to succumb to the strain of the past two weeks.

Typically, I was a woman on top of my game, knowing what to do and when to do it. Today, however, I was lucky if I could remember how to put one foot in front of the other.

The cowboy returned. Noticing my distress, he was beside me in short order. Cautiously, placing the tin cup of lukewarm water in my hands, he held onto it until he was confident it wouldn't spill.

"Thank you," I said, raising the cup to my lips. Catching movement behind me, I looked up at an aging man with thick silver hair and a tanned wrinkled face watching me. Speechless, I stared back at him as our eyes locked. It was like looking into my father's deep violet eyes, the same color as mine. Though this man was older, he had a handsome face, etched with lines produced by years of hard work.

It was the moment I'd been waiting for. I was peering at my past. Suddenly, my memory was inundated by flashes of bright lights and people yelling for me to *stay with them*. Then this man behind me was taking my hand, telling me he was taking me home. As if on cue, a dog barked, bringing me out of one nightmare into another.

By the looks he was giving me, he knew who I was. Straightening, I glared at the Doc, daring him to say something.

"Well, girly! Are ye coming in, or are ye going te sit there all day?"

"I'm coming in!" I said, stomping up the stairs, walking right past him without a "Hi, how are you, or nice to meet you, grandfather."

Walking down a long hallway in the direction in which the sheriff and his men had carried Caleb, I found that they had placed him on an old table, covered with a brown-tinged sheet. Shuddering, I hoped it was clean, or at least bug-free. Covering their noses, the men quickly turned and left, as the scent of chloroform lent a dizzying redolence to the room.

Caleb moaned and moved restlessly on the table. Reaching his side, I tried calming him by holding his hands and speaking in a soft tone. His frantic movements slowed as Dr. Sweeney came up beside me. Our shoulders touching, he looked down at Caleb.

Without looking at me, he asked, "How long has't he been like tis?" Removing his coat, he hung it on the back of the door then began rolling up his sleeves.

Not taking my eyes off Caleb, I answered while pushing a wayward lock of damp hair from Caleb's brow. "Since early this morning. I was caught in the storm, and I didn't realize he'd come after me until I found him standing outside the cabin, soaked to the skin and shaking violently."

I pulled the doctor's attention to me by touching his arm. "He was shot almost two weeks ago." Dropping my gaze, I hesitated. This was Caleb's life, and the doctor, my grandfather, needed all the details. "He was doing fine until we fought." Stroking the back of Caleb's hand, I added, "I was angry and left him in the cabin while I took a walk to clear my head."

The Doc looked up just as I said, "I know now it was foolish of me. Then the storm hit." Waiting for a response and getting none, I asked, "What do you plan on doing? Can you take care of him here, or should we move him to the hospital?"

"Hospital?" he responded incredulously. "Miss, there are no hospitals around here. Tis isn't New York City. Besides, I wouldn't put one of me patients in those rat-infested hell holes te die."

Stunned at his description of hospitals, I stammered, "I, ah. I just thought he would get better care in a hospital."

"Miss, are ye questioning me ability to take care of yer man?" placing the wire of his glasses over his ears.

Anxiously, I stammered, "No! Yes! No. Not really."

His bushy brows shot up when he asked, "Well, which is it? Yea or nea?"

"Please, I'm sorry. I'm just tired."

Turning my attention back to Caleb, "Let's just take care of him. Without any antibiotics, I was irritated that I couldn't do more for him."

"Those be pretty fancy medical words ye'd be using girlie," he said as he began taking off the bandages.

"Wait!" I yelled, holding up my hands and eliciting a groan from Caleb. "We haven't even washed our hands." Pointing to his dirty fingers, I asked, "Where's the hot water?"

"In te kettle on te stove, where it should be," he answered, pointing in the direction of the kitchen.

"Don't touch him until I come back with hot water and soap." Pointing my finger at the doctor, "Don't even think of touching your instruments with those hands. Matter-of-fact, don't touch any of your patients ever again with dirty hands." Taking hold of my grandfather's hands, I turned them over. "Ugh! And, clean under those nails." Turning to leave, I had to ask, "Haven't you heard of washing with soap and water before and after touching a patient to prevent the spread of microorganisms and diseases like influenza and cholera?"

"Good heavens girlie. Such a lecture you're giving me. That's a lot to take in. Besides, I've just come from tendin' te me horse before ye arrived. I hadn't a chance to wash."

Shaking my head, I didn't know how people survived the eighteen-hundreds. Rushing down the hall, I found the kitchen retrieving what I needed. Simple as the items were, I placed the basin on an empty table and washed my hands with what I believed to be lye soap. My fingers tingled. "At least they'll be clean from all the dirt I've come in contact with recently. Emptying the water out the back door, I refilled the basin with clean water, instructing the doctor to do the same.

He did as I asked while I peered around the room in fascination, wondering what it was like to practice medicine in 1880. To one side stood a large glass front cabinet stocked with brown and clear colored bottles in all shapes and sizes, filled with different solutions. Next to it was a long wooden table covered with a sheet that held his instruments. Some, I recognized as those I still used in 2019, and a few that looked like instruments of torture. I hoped the doctor had no intention of using them on Caleb.

Coming to stand beside me, the Doc showed me his hands. "Do they meet with ye approval, Miss?"

Giving him a tentative smile, I replied, "Yes, doctor. Much better, thank you."

So far, neither of us had mentioned that we knew each other, let alone were related. For now, keeping our relationship professional was what Caleb needed. The timing wasn't right to broach the subject. It was better saved for a later date when I was assured Caleb would survive.

"Well now, let's take a look at yer man." Turning back to Caleb, he removed the old bandages as the stench of necrotic flesh filled the small room. "This man has wound fever. That's why he's been shaking so badly."

"I know. But, I didn't have the instruments or medicines to use."

Examining the wounds closer, he added, "We'll have to clean and debride the dead tissue. When we're done, I'll use bromine." Pausing, he turned to me and asked, "Do ye think ye can help me?"

Looking from Caleb to the doctor with grave concern, I answered, "Yes, I can help, but please don't use the bromine. It will damage what healthy tissue there is surrounding his wounds." Placing my hand gently on the Docs forearm, I added, "We'll find something else just as effective and less harmful."

"You may be right," he said. "I never did care for that stuff. It's painful to use too."

In this instance, I knew I was right. The untoward side effects of using bromide on open wound infections in the 1800s had been well documented.

"Even though we do all that we can, yer man may still die anyway from the fever."

My heart sank at his discouraging words. I was upset at Caleb for getting shot. Not once, but twice. I was angry with him for chasing after me in the storm. And, angry with him for getting wound fever. But, most of all, I was angry I'd allowed my heart to become involved.

Why couldn't he be like any other patient I've cared for with no romantic attachments?

Moving my hands towards Caleb's bandages, "Please, let me do that." I needed something to keep myself busy and my mind off the fact that Caleb may yet die. Leaving his sole care to this country doctor, grandfather or not, was not something I was comfortable with. Doc graciously acquiesced, stepping back and allowing me to proceed. Two weeks of hellish living and not knowing whether either of us would survive had finally caught up with me. Crying right now would do me no good.

"Do you know what yer doing?" Of course, he already knew I did?

Surprised at his question, I answered, "Yes, sir." Caleb lay deathly still as I removed the bandages, and the doctor pulled his table of instruments closer to the bed. Once removed, we both looked down at two wounds, the worst inflamed, red, and oozing blood-tinged thick-yellow fluid. Feeling emotional ties to the man lying before me, I was committed to doing everything in my power to keep him alive. Neither of us said a word as we worked diligently side by side as if we'd done it this way for years.

The elder Doctor Sweeney probed deep into Caleb's abdominal wound, bringing him to a semi-conscious state. Yelling profanities, Caleb tried pushing away our hands when he let out a blood-curdling scream, startling both of us. Doc tried holding Caleb down at his shoulders as he looked at me. "Do ye know how ta use an ether inhaler?"

Shaking my head, "No, but tell me what to do."

"It's the domed shaped mask on te counter over there," pointing to the back table. "See te gauze next to it?"

I nodded, coming to stand close to the table where the mask lay.

"Take te gauze and set it inside te mask, then close te lid. Now, bring it over here wit te brown bottle marked ether."

I obediently did as he asked, careful not to drop the bottle for fear of wasting the precious liquid.

"Set te bottle down on te counter nearest you, but far enough away tat he can't knock it over before we have him asleep. Now, draw up some liquid in the glass dropper." Raising his voice, he added, "Be careful not to inhale any." In all seriousness, he was cautioning me. "Or, I'll let ye lay on the floor until I've finished with te surgery."

Out of good practice, I rotated the bottle and read the label out loud. "250 Grammes, ETHER for Anesthesia, Manufactured by E.R. Squibb & Sons, Brooklyn, NY." *Good heavens.* I would have preferred using chloroform since it was faster acting and non-flammable. But, it too had its risks. Administering too much of either and the patient could die. "Do you have any chloroform?" I asked, "I've seen that used before." Goosebumps formed on my arms when I realized I had taken more than one giant step back in time. Practicing medicine like this seemed barbaric to a doctor trained in the twenty-first century.

"No. Now come on girl. Times a' wastin." Doc Sweeney hurriedly instructed me on how many drops of ether solution to place in the cone. Carefully drawing up the full length of the dropper, I replaced the bottle cap securely.

"Now, place the mask over his nose and mouth, then add several drops onto te cloth. When he inhales, he'll breathe in vaporized ether, and it will put him to sleep."

My hands shook while I slowly counted each drop. Adding them to the mask, "Is it safe to use this in his condition? What if I give him too much? Or, what if he goes into a coma and never wakes up?"

Looking over the rim of his glasses, he replied, "Ye can't have him moving around and in this much pain while we're stabbing his insides wit instruments. I need him te lie still until I'm finished. Besides, I won't let ye give him te much." Looking directly at me, sensing my fears, he reassured me. "I'll talk ye through it."

I administered the ether as instructed, watching as Caleb's taut muscles relaxed under the drug's influence. Thankfully, he lay still until the Doc finished his grisly task. I applied the clean bandages then located a clean sheet and a soft woolen blanket to cover his bare torso.

As Doc washed his hands, I watched the once clear water in the porcelain basin turn crimson from Caleb's blood. In 2019, gloves were within easy reach hanging in boxes on every imaginable hospital and clinic wall. It had been second nature for me to put them on along with masks and protective eyewear before encountering bodily fluids. Here in 1880, it was just a healer's bare hands.

During medical school, I had been fascinated with the history of the development of surgical instruments and supplies. I explored my memory bank for the first recorded use of latex gloves in 1883 by physician John Stewart Halstead at Johns Hopkins Hospital. At the time, he'd had them developed by the Goodyear Tire and Rubber Company. How bulky they must have been. Shuddering, I also remembered that in the late 1700s, surgeons wore gloves made of sheep's intestines. "Ugh!" I unknowingly said out loud.

"Are you alright?" my grandfather asked.

"I'm fine. You should get some rest. I'll stay here with Caleb," I told him.

"Yes, that sounds good." He didn't argue. "Call out if ye need me. I'll be upstairs."

I could see that the combination of blood loss and the ether had taken its toll on Caleb's body. I couldn't help but stare at the contrast between his pale white cheeks and dark beard. His cheeks, now sunken, showed the agony of what he'd endured. By the grace of God, he'd survived thus far. But I knew he couldn't take much more.

Caleb could use a transfusion. But how? I could have my grandfather do a direct exchange transfusion, where whole blood from a donor flows through a tube directly into the recipient. It was a good thought, but problematic since there was the issue of where to get the tubing, let alone the needles, and how to sterilize them. Rarely done, the risk of a reaction could be disastrous if Caleb and my blood types didn't match. I would have to try other measures to build up his red blood cells and iron stores. I did remember reading in a history journal once that people would boil rusty nails and drink the resulting liquid to replace their iron. I shivered at the horrible thought.

Finally, Caleb looked peaceful in his ether-induced sleep. I smiled, knowing I'd lost my heart weeks ago to this man and would have some difficult decisions to make in the coming days.

Placing an innocent kiss on his cheek, I pleaded with him, "You're going to live, Caleb Young." I wiped my misty eyes with the back of my sleeve. "You have to. I have too many things to tell you." Placing my warm palm lightly on his chest, I leaned forward and whispered, "I love you, Caleb. Do you hear me?"

⤳ 25 ⤶

Stubbs and Vermin

M Y BROTHER VERMIN and I sat at a back table in the Pick
& Shovel Saloon. Working on his third whiskey, Vermin's
temper escalated as I sat silently, sipping sarsaparilla. Out-of-the-
blue, Vermin slugged me in the left arm. He never needed a reason
since pure evil ran through his veins.

Being mute myself, I grabbed my left arm where he'd hit me,
and lightly moaned. Most of my life, I'd given in to the abuses my
brother doled out. Fearful, if I retaliated, Vermin would either leave
me behind to die in some out of the way place, or just plain shoot me.
It was that simple for him.

Abruptly standing, Vermin headed to the back door without
looking back. I, on the other hand, remained seated sipping on the
last of my drink. Vermin may think I was stupid, but what I astutely
heard, loud and clear, was the men at the bar tell of a gambler who

was brought in alive the previous day. Their conversation had my eyes widening in astonishment. What I heard would infuriate my brother. That's why when he walked through the back door, wiping his filthy hands on his pants, I remained silent, waiting for the right moment to spring this news on him.

Emily

The same men that had carried Caleb into the clinic were now tasked with moving him to a small room in the back where he could begin his recovery. What Doc called the recovery room held a small metal-framed bed, with at least a better mattress than ropes strung between wooden posts. I looked about the room while the men lay Caleb carefully on the bed. Against one wall was a dresser with a cracked mirror overhead. In one corner was a stand holding a porcelain washbasin and pitcher filled with tepid water.

The only window looked out over the back of the building with a view of the desert hills. The fading winter sun filtered in through faded yellow curtains, casting flickering shadows on the wall. On the floor at the side of the bed was a sizeable hand-woven rag rug that had seen much use. In another corner stood a caned rocker waiting for its next occupant, to sit and rock.

Rocking was a solitary affair, reminding me of a wise old crone. Running my hands over its rim, I wondered how many people it had held over the years while waiting for the healing hand of God, or the devil's clutch of death to take their loved one. Despite my dark thoughts, it was a pleasant room compared to the cabin Caleb and I had shared the last few weeks.

"Ma'am?" the same cowboy who helped me out of the wagon, spoke softly coming to stand in front of me. "Excuse me, ma'am."

I looked at him blankly, "Yes. Did you need something?"

"Yes, ma'am." Turning his hat around and around through calloused fingers, he took in a deep breath. "The boys and I were just wondering if there is anything else we can do for you before we leave."

"No, thank you. You've been very helpful," I answered, moving to the bedside where Caleb lay.

The cowboy left just as Sheriff Johansson moved in to take his place. "Miss Sweeney, will ya be needin' a place ta stay tonight?"

"No. Thank you sheriff. I'll be staying here with Mr. Young. I need to be here when he wakes up." Laying my hand on the bedpost, I added, "Or, if the good doctor is called out during the night, I'll be here to watch over Mr. Young."

Looking over at Caleb's still body, "Tats probably wise. If ya need anything, yust send vord over ta the jail. Myself, or one of ta boys will come right over."

I followed the sheriff's gaze. "Thank you again, sheriff, but I'll be OK."

"I'll ask Doc if he has a cot for ya to sleep on. If not, I'll have one of da boys bring one over from ta jail. They're not fancy, but it beats the floor. I hope ya don't mind."

"That would be nice. Anything is better than sleeping on rocks. At least, Caleb, I mean, Mr. Young should rest more comfortably tonight."

Leaving the room, he returned not ten minutes later with a cot. "Doc said he would bring you some linens.

"Sheriff." Coming to stand next to him, I placed my hand on his forearm and said, "I can't thank you enough for your help. From what I understand, you and Mr. Young got off to a rocky start." Looking down at my dry, cracked hands, I added, "And so did we for that matter. You could have easily left us up in the hills. But I don't think you're that kind of man to do such a thing. I only hope that what happened between the two of you, and between us, you won't hold it against Caleb."

"No, miss, I don't." Placing his hand over mine, "No one deserves vhat he got. I yust hope he pulls through for yar sake."

Not surprised for once, I knew the sheriff's words were sincere. "Sheriff, I do have one question. Running my hand over my threadbare dress, I asked. "Do you know where I can get some clean clothes for myself and Mr. Young?"

"I tink I can handle that, miss. I'll have one of Miss Abigail's girls bring over clothes for ya tis evening. Tomorrow, I'll bring over some for Mr. Young."

"That would be wonderful. Thank you again. If there is ever anything I can do to repay you, please, don't hesitate to let me know." I gave him my best smile, considering how tired I felt.

Sheriff Johansson made it to the door before I thought of one more favor to ask of him. "Oh, sheriff," holding up my hand to stop him. "I'm sorry, but I have one more favor to ask. If I may impose upon you to send a message to Mr. Young's sister. I believe she lives somewhere in Boston. She should be informed that her brother has been gravely injured." Pausing, I added, "Actually, I don't think she even knows he's still alive. From what I gathered, it's been years since they last saw each other." Feeling like I was giving him too much information, I caught myself wringing my hands. "Or maybe you could tell me how to contact her?"

"Yust give me her name, and I'll get a telegram off to the Boston Police Department tomorrow morning."

"Thank you, sheriff. That would be very helpful."

I heard Sheriff Johansson softly talking outside the door with the Doc, letting him know that he was available to help if needed. "I feel partially responsible for vhat happened to Mr. Young since it vas I tat ordered him ta leave town."

"Sheriff, ye had no way of knowing this would happen. You've got to understand, it's not your fault. You were only doing yer job. Now go home son, and get some rest."

Pulling back the cover to check on Caleb's bandages, I was pleased to see they remained dry. His fever still had its frightening grip as I placed my hand against his cheek. Pouring fresh water into the basin, I took the damp cloth and gently wiped it across his flushed face. "If only I had antibiotics."

Frustrated, I felt the overwhelming exhaustion of fighting an uphill battle with none of the tools I usually worked with. I hated feeling so helpless! Sending another prayer heavenward, I moved down the top sheet to Caleb's waist and continued with my cooling ministrations.

"Ahum!" I heard Doc Sweeney clear his throat behind me to get my attention.

Turning towards the door, I saw him leaning against the frame, looking as tired as I felt. So many questions needing answers rattled around in my head, but now wasn't the time to ask. They'd have to wait for another day. Strange, but no words passed between us as he turned away from the door.

Satisfied Caleb would be resting for a while, I followed my grandfather into the kitchen. It reminded me of my grandmother's house, where I'd learned to bake cookies and cinnamon apple pie. Moving into the room, I stood at the end of a long wooden table that had seen years of wear. It felt like home. "I thought you were going upstairs?"

Not bothering to look up from reading a newspaper, he answered, "I was, but I won't sleep. I'm all wound-up."

"May I heat some water?" I asked.

"Of course ye can dear." Laying the paper down, he took his glasses off and squeezed the bridge of his nose. "Do ya need any help?"

"Maybe. It's just that I've never used a pump or a wood cook-stove before."

Doc painfully pushed himself up from his chair, its legs scratching the worn wooden floors beneath. "*Dang rheumatism*," he swore under his breath. Slowly, making his way to the stove, "Here, let me show ye how tis one works."

Grateful, I stepped aside.

"Always make sure that te flue here tis open ta the outside or ye'll have the room filled with smoke."

Lifting the round plate that covered the flames, he further instructed, "Place da kindling in here, making sure it's to the back of the stove, like this. There still are some hot embers in da back tat should take hold in a few minutes. Once they've caught, ye can add a few larger pieces. But, don't put in te many. Ye don't need to burn te house down."

Gracing me with a sincere smile, I placed my hand on his arm, realizing the curmudgeon I'd first met was actually a kind and gentle man. Despite him being the one who brought me here, I kept my anger in check. "I haven't thanked you enough for all you've done. So, thank you, especially for what you've done for Mr. Young. I'm grateful," I added, averting his gaze.

Patting my hand, Doc Sweeney replied, "It's indeed me pleasure, my dear. Ist what I'm here fer. I'm te only doctor tis town has, and probably fer a hundred miles around." Turning away from the stove, he added, "Besides, it's always nice te be in te company of a beautiful young lady like yerself."

Feeling the heat of a blush rise on my cheeks, I said, "Thank you, Doctor Sweeney."

Using a pump looked easy. You just pick up the handle, pull it up and push it down. "This can't be that hard to do." I soon realized it was not as easy as the movies portrayed. "Dang those pioneer women needed muscles to get these things working." After several hard pumps, my biceps started to burn, and the water finally began to flow.

Returning the kettle to the stove, my grandfather asked me to sit with him while I waited for the water to boil. Remembering the old adage, "A watched pot never boils," I was happy to oblige. Taking a seat at the opposite end of the table, I ran my hands slowly over the worn wood, waiting for the doctor to speak. He remained silent.

Caught wool-gathering, the kettle began to whistle. I pushed it to the back of the stove when I noticed a chipped flowered teapot on the counter. Holding it out towards my grandfather, I asked, "Can I make you a pot of tea?"

"Tat would be nice. Thank ye," he replied. "Please, will ye join me for a wee cup?

"Maybe another time, I really would like to clean up. It's been a very long day," I answered. Adding loose tea leaves I'd located in a tin, I poured in hot water, watching it turn a golden brown before replacing the lid.

"Of course, dear. It has been a long day for all of us."

Pouring a cup, I handed it to my grandfather. "Sheriff Johansson said he would have one of the girls bring over some clean clothes for me this evening." Holding the hot cup to his lips, he blew on the steaming liquid. "But right now, I'd like to shower off the dirt, then check on Mr. Young again."

"Shower?" looking over the rim of his cup, he questioned my comment.

"What I mean is bathe." I quickly corrected myself, realizing the Doc was probably not familiar with the concept of showering.

"I understand, dear. Ye go right ahead. I'll have ta clean clothes brought back to ye as soon as they arrive."

Thanking him, I took a towel off the counter and wrapped it around the handle of the kettle. Excusing myself, I carried it down the hall to the room where Caleb slept. Opening the door slowly, so as not to wake him, I walked to the stand and poured the warm water into a flower-rimmed porcelain basin. *Oh, what I wouldn't give to be at the hotel soaking in a tub filled with steaming hot water right now.*

I visualized myself at home in Seattle, leaning back against my soft tub pillow, my favorite lavender soap, and a glass of fine wine in my hand. Every tight muscle fiber in my body would relax to the bubbling massage of the Jacuzzi jets. Instead, I was standing next to a small bowl with its contents rapidly cooling and an empty tea kettle in my hand.

Shaking my head, I stared in the mirror and ran my hands over my dry face, then through a tangled mess of hair. Pulling the chair over, I sat down to take off the boots I'd come to hate. With every inch of their freedom, I couldn't even imagine putting the tortuous devices back on my feet. Rolling down the scratchy black wool stockings, I gratefully placed my bare feet on the cold hardwood floor and sighed.

Standing, I unfastened the tiny buttons down the front of my dress. With several hip wiggles, it dropped to the floor in a pool of tattered calico. Only in my camisole and pantaloons, I stole a look at Caleb before proceeding to further disrobe. Thankfully, he remained asleep, unaware of my state of undress.

26

Stubbs and Vermin

I WATCHED MY BROTHER walk back to the table we shared. Cautiously, I touched his arm to gain his attention. As usual, Vermin shrugged me off like I was an annoying insect. His disdain for me was getting to be more than I cared to endure. Soon, I needed to be free of him.

With my own form of communication, I tried to convey to Vermin what I'd heard the saloon patrons discussing. Vermin watched as my hands moved rapidly about. I knew the moment it suddenly dawned on him what I was telling him about the gambler he thought he'd killed. Leaning in towards me, Vermin whispered so as not to have the whole saloon hear, "You mean to tell me that gambler is still alive?"

I vigorously nodded my head up and down in acknowledgment.

Nostrils flaring like an angry bull, Vermin slammed his fist on the table, sending our glasses crashing to the floor. Grabbing the collar of my shirt, he pulled me towards the swinging doors and out into the street.

Emily

The small room darkened as night approached. I lit the kerosene lamp with one of the matches left in a glass dish on the dresser. Turning down the wick to dim the light, I was confident no one could see me. Considering what I'd been through the past two weeks, I didn't care if they did. Quickly slipping out of my undergarments, a soft knock sounded at the door. "Who is it?" I asked, grabbing a blanket from the rocker.

"It's Samantha, miss. I'm one of Miss Abigail's girls," she whispered.

The voice sounded so young. "Just a moment." Wrapping the blanket firmly around me, I moved to the door.

"I brought you some clean clothes, just like the sheriff asked."

"Thank you, Samantha," Clutching the blanket to my breast, "Please leave them on the floor outside the door, and I'll get them in a minute. And, please, tell Miss Abigail, thank you. And thank you for bringing them over."

"You're welcome, miss," came a soft reply.

Hearing soft footfalls retreating down the hall, I opened the door just a crack, picking up a brown paper package from the floor. Closing the door behind me, I placed the packet on the chair, then proceeded to take off my pantaloons. Naked, I looked into the mirror that hung over the basin, not recognizing myself. Turning from side to side, what I saw scared me. I had lost so much weight. Gone was the luster of my hair and once velvety complexion. Replaced now with a sunburn, dirt, and ghostly circles under my eyes. My once manicured nails, now cracked, looked like I had crawled through the desert.

Turning my focus back on the basin, I took up the bar of lavender-scented soap, inhaling its delicate perfume. "Where did the good doctor get this?" Not caring, I lathered up the washcloth, closed my eyes, and with slow circular movements, began gently washing my face and body.

Despite it being winter, my once alabaster skin had been exposed to the desert elements, turning my freckles a darker brown. "Just look at my face, will you?" Despite my disdain towards those blemishing dots, the warm water and lavender soap felt heavenly against my skin. Lost in the moment, and delighted in the simple act of bathing, I turned out the events of the past two weeks.

Caleb

With an overwhelming sense of drowning, I found myself sinking deeper and deeper into a panic state as my thoughts turned to Emily. *Where was she?* Had something happened to her? *God, please don't let her be dead.* Struggling to surface from the nightmare, I heard a familiar voice humming sweetly. Groaning and feeling drugged, I opened my eyes. I didn't recognize where I was. Nausea threatened, and the incessant beating drum in my head kept up its constant rhythm.

Sucking in air, I tried to sit up, failing miserably. Giving in and collapsing back, my head landed on something soft. With my good arm, I slowly reached above my head, coming in contact with a soft pillow. Sighing heavily, I placed my hand across my chest, feeling the warmth of a smooth blanket over my body.

Despite its warmth, I shook uncontrollably unable to understand why I felt so cold. Touching my face, my hand came away wet with sweat. *I'm dying. That's why I'm hearing angels sing. Mom was right. I did make it to heaven.* Painfully, I turned myself to my uninjured side and looked about the room, when my eyes landed on a vision, standing naked before a mirror. It was Emily. She was alive.

Slowly inhaling, salty tears of relief streamed unbridled down my face. *I'm not dead. Emily's safe. Thank you, God.* If I should die today, all I wanted was to memorize the vision before me and carry it with me to my grave.

She was so beautiful. Hoping she wouldn't disappear, I smiled, quietly giving thanks that we were together. All I had the strength to do, at this moment, was to watch her every move. If I looked away, I was afraid she would disappear. Still, unable to control the last vestiges of ether, I fell back into a deep drug-induced sleep.

Emily

I was surprised at how well the borrowed clothes fit regardless of being faded from several washings. I didn't care, I was clean, my dress was clean, and I could burn the calico I'd worn for two weeks.

Looking around the room for a place to dump the water, there was no sink to pour it down. Opening the window, I looked out, spotting a rose bush that obviously could use a drink. Without a second thought, I emptied the basin's contents on the bush.

Moving to the side of the bed, I looked down at the peaceful expression on Caleb's face. His brow was still warm, and I knew the fever still lingered. When done here, I would go down to the kitchen and boil the remaining cottonwood bark I'd brought from the cabin. Making a mental note to locate more for future use.

Pulling back the blanket to check his dressings, Caleb moaned something unintelligible at my touch. Relieved that both bandages were dry and the foul odor had dissipated, I began the task of washing him. Only to find he was completely naked under the covers. Somehow, the men who'd carried him into the clinic were able to relieve him of his blood-soaked long-johns.

Blushing, heat crept up my neck at the thought of what lay beneath the blanket. The good doctor, or one of the sheriff's men, would have to bathe Caleb any further. "I am not going there," I snickered. Looking at Caleb's face, beneath that beard lay high cheekbones and a square jawline, I already knew what his tantalizing lips held.

A soft knock sounded at the door. "Miss Sweeney, may I come in?"

"Yes, of course," I replied. "I just want te check on me patient," Doc said, holding onto the edge of the door frame.

"I just finished bathing him as much as I could. Looking down at Caleb, "I'm worried." Brushing a wayward lock of his hair back into place. "He still has a fever." Looking directly into Doc's eyes, "Do you think he'll die?" I asked, already knowing the answer.

I watched the warring emotions play out on his face before coming to stand next to me. Placing a hand on my forearm, "I will be honest with ye. You know as well as I do, it will be touch and go te next few days. Let's just hope he has enough fight left in him."

Laying my hand over his, "I'm praying he does." Holding back tears, "Do you know where I can locate a cottonwood tree?"

"Yes, there are several trees just outside of town along the river as you head towards the hills. I can send one of the boys to fetch some."

"If you think they know what to look for, that would be helpful. I don't feel like wandering around in those hills again." *At least not for a very long time. Hopefully, never, if I had anything to say about it!*

Washing his hands in freshwater, my grandfather checked Caleb's bandages, then asked, "Are ye hungry? You haven't eatin' since ye got here."

I'd almost forgot how hungry I'd been upon arriving in Yuma. Due to rationing out our food, I'd eaten little in the past few days. "To answer your question, yes, I'm famished. But I don't think I could eat much. "Something light like bread and jam?"

"Ist that all ye be eating now?" he asked with concern.

Patting my abdomen. "Even though I'm hungry, I'm afraid I wouldn't be able to keep down a large meal right now."

"Ah!" my grandfather paused, smiling, and nodding, his question drifting past his lips. "Ifin' ye don't mind me asking," he said, staring at my stomach, "Are ye in the family way?"

"What!" Following the direction of his eyes, I repeated his question to make sure I understood, "Family way?" After a minute of stunned silence, I looked down at my abdomen, then back up to my grandfather. Emphatically, I answered, "Good heavens. No! I most certainly am not in the family way."

Pointing towards Caleb, I sputtered, trying to sort out my words, "I. He. We didn't. We haven't been together in the way you're thinking. I hardly know the man." I needed to make sure he knew I spoke the truth.

"Beggin' your pardon, I misspoke. I didn't mean any offense. It's alright, girl. You owe me no explanation. I just want to make sure that yer well. That's all." With that, he turned for the door, stopped, and looked back, seeing only kindness and concern in his eyes. "I'll bring you some tea, bread with butter, and a wee bit of jam."

Flustered, I was too embarrassed to look at the doctor for fear he would guess just how much I really cared for Caleb. "That would be nice. Thank you."

After eating, I pulled the chair up close to the bed. I was afraid if I left Caleb's side, he would die alone, and then what would I do? No, I was staying right here as long as I could.

The day had been uneventful with Caleb sleeping through it. The only time I left the room was to use the privy. Doc checked on him one last time before letting me know he was turning in for the night.

Settling back in the chair, I looked out at the beautiful star-studded sky. Bone tired, my aching muscles gave way, and the tension released its rigid grip. Closing my eyes, I wondered what I would be doing now if I was still back in Seattle. *There would be work, the staff Christmas party, shopping, more work, more shopping, and yes, fighting that I-5 crazy-person-making-traffic.* Even though I longed to be alive once again in 2019 with its modern comforts and medicine, I would not have this adventurous life I was now experiencing. Most importantly, I wouldn't have Caleb.

27

Emily

I WAS THANKFUL TO be clean, warm, and safe as I held onto Caleb's hand. I'd just drifted into a restless sleep when Caleb's blood-curdling screams wrenched me awake.

"God, help me. I've been shot," he yelled, gasping for air and throwing the blanket off his chest. "Don't take her. Please, don't take her from me", he sobbed. "I need her." Eyes wide open but unseeing, his muscles rigid for a fight, he tossed his pillow at me. Still drowsy, my reflexes weren't quick enough to duck as the pillow hit me directly in the face. No harm done, I placed my hands on his shoulders, trying to keep him from falling out of bed. "Caleb, its Emily. I'm here. You're safe." I feared that the fever was taking its final hold, draining what little strength he had left to fight off the infection.

Continuing to struggle against my restraint, Caleb yelled even louder. "No! You can't take her." His arms flailed out to protect himself against an unknown foe. "Leave her alone."

Sweating, I held on, struggling against Caleb's naked body while it moved as if demon-possessed. Breathing heavily, I heard Caleb whisper in a choking voice, "Take me instead. It's me you want. Not Emily. She's done nothing wrong."

The door flew open, crashing against the wall as Doc rushed into the room. *What a picture this must make? Caleb, thrashing about naked, and me practically lying on top of him.*

Rushing to my side, Doc took over and held Caleb down, while commanding me to "Go get the laudanum. It's in te glass cabinet in te surgery."

I stared at him like he had two heads. I'd read the horror stories of people using this addictive medicine. But this wasn't the time to voice my concerns. Caleb needed it now.

"What's wrong with ye girl? Do as I say. Now!"

Running down the hall to the surgery, I located the cabinet and grabbed the brown bottle. Clutching it to my chest, I ran back to Caleb's room.

Holding it out to my grandfather, he grumbled. "Can't ye see I'm a wee bit busy here lass? You'll need te open it." Struggling against Caleb's movement, he said, "I'll tell ye how much to give him."

I did as he ordered, placing the dropper of laudanum into Caleb's mouth and squeezing. With my fingers under his chin, holding his mouth firmly shut, he shook his head fiercely from side to side. Trying to spit out the bitter liquid, I was committed to keeping his mouth closed while counting, "One . . . two . . . three . . . four." Seeing his Adam's apple slide up, then down, I was convinced he'd swallowed before I released his chin. Gasping for air, Caleb spewed forth the foulest of obscenities.

"You Sonofa . . ." was only part of his expletives. It took several minutes before the laudanum began to take effect. His strength fueled by anger, he continued fighting us both. Reaching out into thin air with trembling hands, he said, "I'll kill you before I let you take her." Pushing against me and my grandfather's hold, he yelled out through slurring words, "Emily, where are you? I'm so sorry. I tried to save you."

"Caleb, I'm right here." Placing my hands on both sides of his face, speaking softly into his ear, "It's OK. Calm down. I'm here. I won't leave you. I promise."

Caleb's glazed eyes opened, staring blankly at me. "No," he slurred. "He'll come for you." Gripping my hands, "You have to get away."

Confused, I asked, "Caleb, who will come for me?"

Caleb's breathing slowed as I watched his hands fall to the mattress as he descended into a drug-induced sleep. Looking at the Doc, I declared, "I gave him too much laudanum. I know I did." I panicked. Searching his eyes for answers, I shouted at him, "Do something. Don't you have any Narcan to reverse the drug's effect?"

He must have seen the panic in my eyes. Letting go of Caleb's arms, he took hold of my hands, shaking them to get my full attention. "No lass, ye didn't give him too much. Now calm down." Patting the side of my face, he explained, "The laudanum is doing what it should. He should sleep the rest of te night. Now, why don't ye go down the hall te sleep, and I'll stay here with ye man."

"No!" I pulled away. "I'm staying right here in case he calls out for me again."

"Ye be doin' yerself and him no good if ye don't get ye rest."

"I don't care. I'm staying here."

Out of the blue, he asked me, "Emily, do ye love this man?" motioning to Caleb with a nod of his head.

Stunned, I replied with my own question. "Why do you ask? We've only known each other for a few weeks. I can hardly say that I love a man after that short of a time."

"I knew your grand . . ." Catching what he was about to say, he amended, "my wife, less than that. Ye could say it was love at first sight for her and me."

I was lying to my grandfather. I couldn't let him know my true feelings, or he wouldn't help me get home.

In the last few weeks, my world had been turned upside down, where chaos and confusion reigned. Even though I had declared to myself my love for Caleb, it had been in a moment of . . . Oh, who knew what? Too hard to comprehend, I wasn't ready to give in to the possibility of never seeing my home again. Committing to loving one person in this time and place could only mean one thing, I would never go home. And I couldn't allow that. I was being pulled between two centuries.

"It was just a question," my grandfather said. "Ye do as ye wish girlie," walking towards the door. "Why don't ye try sleeping on te cot. It's probably more comfortable than tat there chair." Reaching the door, he asked, "By ta way, what is tis Narcan you spoke of?"

"It's a drug I've seen used," I replied cautiously.

Ignoring my response, he left the room.

Exhausted, I wanted nothing better than to lay my head down. I didn't care if it was on a pillow or a rock. Preferring the pillow, I sat on the edge of the bed, clothed in borrowed calico. Leaning to my side, I rested my head on the corner of Caleb's pillow and fell fast asleep, with my arm across his chest.

Caleb

Sometime during the night, I awoke with blurred vision and another splitting headache. Touching my forehead, it was cold and damp. Running my tongue along my blistered lips, the bitter aftertaste of laudanum made me pucker.

That feeling of being trapped brought back a familiar sense of angst I remembered all too well. Pulling on the sheet that restrained and tangled beneath me, I came in contact with something warm and soft. Turning my head to the side, I sighed with relief, seeing Emily lying beside me, with her arm draped across my chest. Taking in a slow deep breath, I treasured the moment, inhaling her fragrant scent of lavender. "You smell so good," I whispered. Thankful for her presence, I softly kissed the top of her head and ran my hand slowly up and down her arm, finally feeling at peace.

Whimpering softly, Emily stretched her back but didn't wake. Each time she breathed in, then out, I felt feather-like caresses flow across my bare chest. Taking pleasure in such a sensual moment, I anchored her hand over my trembling heart. I was thankful to have her close, knowing she hadn't been hurt, or worse, left me. Looking down at her freckled face, a smile curled at the corner of my lips. I didn't know how I'd come to deserve this beautiful woman. She was the reason I was still alive.

Fully clothed, the softness of Emily's breasts through the thin calico pressed closer with each rise and fall of my chest. I could hardly keep my mind off the reaction she caused, both physically and emotionally. Whispering to myself before I fell back asleep, "Loving this woman is the best thing I've ever done."

Emily remained beside me as I awoke several hours later to bright sunlight filtering in through the window. Aching all over, I groaned while attempting to stretch the kinks out of my neck and back. Placing a gentle kiss on the crown of her head brought her fully awake. Smiling, I looked into her sleepy violet eyes, thankful I wasn't standing on weak legs.

"Has anyone ever told you, you're the most beautiful woman in the world?"

"Caleb, you're awake." Running her fingertips over my brow, she said, "Your fever broke. How are you feeling?"

"Better, having you here with me." Pausing, he added, "Truthfully, I feel like a herd of stampeding bulls ran over me several times."

"I'm so sorry," Emily said. Easing up on one elbow, she placed a chaste kiss on my cheek. Her smoldering eyes had me shivering, and not from a fever. Streaming kisses along my bearded jaw, I welcomed her advances. Needing no encouragement, I followed her with a tempered sense of passion. Emitting a low growl from deep within my chest, I clasped her head in both my hands and deepened the kiss. Urging her on, I was ever so thankful to be alive and feeling. Surprised with Emily's eagerness, I responded intently to the woman who'd saved my life, not caring if I'd survive her ardent attentions this beautiful morning.

Breaths labored, I tried pulling Emily closer. "You're going to kill me girl," I rasped out, letting my arms fall limp to my sides. "But, oh, what a way to die."

Pushing herself up and away from my side. She babbled, "I don't know what I was thinking. It's just that . . . It was so unprofessional of me. I didn't mean to kiss you. I was just happy to see you awake." I watched as she pushed back loose strands of hair behind her ears. I'd noticed her doing the same thing when she was flustered. She then asked, "Would you like some broth and a cup of tea?"

"What? Wait! What did you mean when you said you didn't want to kiss me?"

Turning her head away, Emily answered, "I said, it was unprofessional of me. Not that I didn't want to kiss you."

Reaching up with one hand behind her neck, I drew Emily's head towards my face, and said, "Unprofessional? That's not what I felt. And, you know it."

Ignoring me, she repeated, "Broth and tea?"

"Fine! Starve me in more ways than one." Catching her eyes with my angry glare, I added, "And, you know what I mean by that!"

Making light of an awkward situation, Emily said, "No steak dinner for you mister. You need to take it slow with your first few meals post-surgery. It's just . . . you need to make sure your insides are working OK."

Patting the side of the bed, it was my turn to try and lighten the mood. "Come back here," I motioned with my hand. "I'll show you just how slow I need to take it."

Hands up, Emily answered, "Oh no, you don't. You need to rest. And, so do I."

"Emily," I called out, raising my hand towards her. "I don't know how many times I've said this. But, thank you again for all you've done."

I could see Emily's eyes glistening in the early morning light, with threatening tears. Nodding, she walked out the door, leaving me alone.

Emily

Closing the door behind me, I leaned back against the wall and let the tears flow. That's where the Doc found me.

"Oh, my dear," he said, rushing down the hall and taking my hands in his. "I'm so sorry. I'm sure he was a good man. Why didn't ye call me when it happened?"

I stared at him, confused. "When what happened?" I replied, suddenly realizing what he meant. "Oh! Good heavens, no. Mr. Young didn't die. If that's what you're thinking." Pulling my hands free, not able to face him directly, "Matter of fact, he's very much alive." *A bit too alive.* Pointing down the hallway, I pushed myself away from the door and added, "I was just going to the kitchen to get him some tea and broth."

"Oh dear, what a mistake I've made. I thought when I saw ye leaning against the door crying . . . Tea and broth? What that man needs is a good stiff shot of Irish whiskey."

"Ah . . . I don't think that would be a good idea for his first meal," I said before catching his teasing. "Maybe you can save it for another day, and we'll all imbibe." *After all this, I could use a good stiff drink*

"Top o' the mornin' to ye, son," I heard Doc say as he walked into Caleb's room.

Caleb hadn't seen me standing behind him when he answered, "If you say so."

Moving to Caleb's bedside, Doc asked, "How are ye feelin'?"

"Fine."

Pausing, I saw Caleb turn his attention to the door where I stood. Fists tightly clasping the quilt, I knew he was lying, he was in more pain than he let on.

"I'm sorry, Doc. Better, thanks to you. I appreciate all you've done for me."

As I re-entered the room carrying a tray with tea, broth, slices of bread, and jam, Caleb looked directly at me. Not knowing what was going on in his complicated mind, I placed the tray on the dresser next to the window. I looked out over the dry earth and struggling rose bushes below, wondering what they would look like if I took care of them. *Thoughts like that, Emily Sweeney, will get you into a heap of trouble. You are not sticking around long enough to worry about some drooping rose bushes.*

~ 28 ~

Emily

ROCKING SLOWLY BACK and forth in the chair to the cadence of the lighthearted banter between Caleb and the doctor, I placed the warm cup to my lips. Smiling behind its rim, I relaxed for the first time in weeks at hearing Caleb's laughter, and the lilting brogue of my grandfather. Both voices were a balm to my wounded soul. Closing my eyes and leaning back, I sent up a silent prayer of thanks that we were safe, and Caleb was going to live.

Pressing a palm to my heart, I tuned out the men's conversation, hearing only the sound of the rocker's clicking on the hardwood floor. Outside the window, doves were cooing in the trees, and the sun shone brightly through the glass, casting a golden halo around Caleb's head. My heart, now entangled with Caleb's, went out to this man and what he'd endured the past several weeks. It amazed me that in this primitive time, he'd survived. Even in 2019, with all the medical advances, he still could have perished. But here he was alive, making me smile, and my heart beat a bit faster every time he looked my way.

"Well, son, it's almost six-thirty, and time I started my rounds," my grandfather said bringing me out of my deep thoughts.

"Yes. Is there anything I can do while you're gone?"

"No, thank ye dear." Taking the empty cup from Caleb, he added, "Ye need to get ye rest today. I'm sure that once ye man here is better, he'll be anxious to be movin' on."

Move on! I couldn't begin to think of Caleb leaving. What would I do?

Following my grandfather out into the hall, I motioned him towards the kitchen. With my hands gripping the back of a chair, more for courage than support, I cleared my throat and proceeded, "Doctor. I believe there are some things that we need to discuss. Am I correct in surmising so?"

Walking towards the back door with his bag in hand, he turned to face me. "Yes dear. We do. When I get back this evening, we'll talk. Just the two of us."

Nodding, I was almost relieved by the delay. It would give me more time to formulate my questions. I was anxious to hear his answers but feared they might not be the ones I sought. It wasn't going to be an easy conversation for either of us: questions needed to be asked and honest answers given. My future depended on it.

The day was uneventful for Caleb and me. We both avoided each other unless necessary. Towards the end of the day, our moods turned tense. I had spent all of my time in the kitchen preparing meals, while Caleb remained sequestered in his room. I gave him his liquid lunch while he sat up in the rocker for the first time. Fatigued after sitting up and drinking the weak tea and beef broth, I left him to his own devices to get himself back into bed. If he was going to leave, he should start doing things for himself.

I'd left Doc's dinner in the warming oven since both Caleb and I had already eaten by the time he arrived home sometime after dark.

"That was a fine dinner ye made. I don't remember when I had a home-cooked meal that tasted so good." Patting his stomach, he added, "I thank ye."

"You're welcome." My response short, I continued to wash Caleb's and my dishes.

"Shall we go into the parlor to talk?" he asked from across the room.

Not answering, my hands shook as I nervously went to pick up his dirty dishes off the table.

"Those can wait," he said, placing his hand over mine. Straightening, I felt his hand behind my back. My muscles tensed under his touch as he led me towards the parlor.

Afraid I was going to lose my dinner, I stopped mid-hallway, bringing my grandfather up short as anxious nausea threatened. Taking in several long deep cleansing breaths, I willed the sensation to subside.

In an effort to remain calm, I sat down on the horsehair-covered chair opposite the Doc. Back straight, legs together, and hands clasped in my lap like a proper lady of the time, I waited for the inquisition to begin. *I'm not going to cry. I won't cry, and I won't yell.* I repeated the mantra under my breath several times.

"Emily."

Jumping at the sound of my name, I looked up into his eyes.

"Ye look as if I'm about to give ye bad news girl."

"Well, aren't you?" I answered. "I mean, give me bad news." Wringing my hands within the fabric of my dress, I had so many questions. But, could I handle the answers?

Sitting forward in his chair, he added, "Please understand. I mean ye no harm. Ye have to know that."

"Why am I here, Doctor?" I asked politely. "It's not a coincidence that we share the same name. Is it?" Staring into a face from my past, I waited for a response from the man who held my very future in his hands.

Clasping his hands together, the Doc answered, "Emily, it pains me to tell ye that I brought ye here for yer own good."

With my arms around my stomach, I squeezed my eyes shut. Leaning slightly forward, I asked, "You're sure it wasn't for your own good doctor? I was doing just fine where I was. You had no right to bring me here."

Voice calm, he replied, "My dear, you weren't doing fine. You'd just been murdered. And, if I hadn't brought ye here, you would have been lost forever."

"No!" I screamed at hearing his words. The vein on the side of my head began to throb. I hadn't meant to yell.

"I had to make a choice to use the *gift*." Taking off his wire-rim glasses, I watched as he squeezed the bridge of his nose, something I'd see him repeatedly do during our conversations. I tried to feel bad for him, but right now, all I wanted was to be angry and run from the room.

"Me dear," he said, holding out his hands towards me.

"Stop calling me that. I'm not your dear!"

"Alright. Emily. Let me try ta explain meself better. First, I need ta tell ye that I'm your great-great-grandfather."

Abruptly standing, I began pacing the expanse of the small room. "I already figured that out since we share the same last name. I remember Da telling me that one of his grandfathers had been a doctor. When I saw your name on the sign over the steps, I surmised it was you." Stopping in front of him, I asked, "How can I be standing here talking to someone dead for close to one hundred years?" Raising my voice, I didn't give him a chance to answer. "Don't you understand? I don't belong here!" Dropping down onto the divan, I felt like I was about to explode.

"This can't be happening to me." Thinking, it hit me, "Gift. What gift?" I blurted out, imagining a box wrapped in bright colored paper and tied with a shiny satin bow. "Why should I care about a gift?" Nervously, I ran my hands through my hair and continued.

"Please, I just want my life back!" Clutching my hands to my chest, I pleaded, "Can't you understand that?" Standing again, directly in front of him, I asked, "What are you going to do to make it right?"

This wasn't going as I'd hoped. I had no preconceived ideas it was going to be easy. Still, I'd expected my grandfather to have better answers.

"Now dear," he jumped in to speak, reaching out to take my hands, "Please calm yeself and be rational about this. I can explain everything."

"There you go again with the 'dear.'" Pulling my hands back. "Rational. You want me to be rational. What are you thinking?" Angered by his suggestion, I countered, "Oh, dear grandfather, I'm just getting started." I sat. I paced. And in one breath, I spewed forth a diatribe of pent-up anger.

Counting off on my fingers, "First, you rip me from my previous life. Two, you dump me in the middle of a heaven-knows-where desert, have me sleep on rocks of all things, then in a filthy bug-infested cabin. Three, you have me trying to save a shot-up gambler I've never met before, without any of my medical supplies. And, alone, no less!"

Inhaling, I continued, not letting him get a word in edgewise even if he begged. "And, four, as if being dehydrated, hungry, chased by a cougar, surviving torrential rains, having to shoot poor innocent animals, skin them, and eat them wasn't enough. Now, I'm in 1880 in a desolate desert town, and you expect me to remain calm and stay here with you, in this filthy place without a hospital. You have your nerve!"

I wasn't done yet. Proceeding before letting my grandfather speak. "I don't think so!" I stood directly in front of him and leaned over towards his face, "Are you out of your ever-lovin' Irish mind, Grandpa?" Why I didn't stomp out of the house right then and there, I would never know. Maybe it was because this was all too hard to believe, and I wanted more answers. Or, I was just too frightened and didn't know where to go. I was a stranger in a strange town. Rubbing my temples, another blinding headache emerged with flashing lights and throbbing pain.

"Are ye done with yer fit of rage girl?" my grandfather asked curtly.

Snapping my head up, I glared. "Done! A lot you know. This is nothing compared to what I can do when I really get mad." Sucking in air, I couldn't believe I was speaking to my elder this way, let alone my grandfather. It wasn't like me. Of course, I'd never been murdered before and ripped away from everything I knew and loved.

"Well then, I surin' don't want to be around ye when that happens," he said, injecting with sarcasm.

"No, ye don't!" Realizing how I sounded, I tried to curtail my attitude. "OK. I'll sit down and listen calmly to what you have to say. But it doesn't mean I'll understand or agree with you."

"Of course, dear," he replied, rubbing his graying beard. "When I'm done explainin', ye will understand why I did what I did." He came back with a temper resembling mine and added, "Ye may not be likin' it, but it can't be undone."

Sitting as patiently as I could, I listened as he proceeded to explain how I had come to be with him and why. "Born in Ireland, I knew as a young lad that I possessed a gift. One I tried to ignore over my lifetime. The gift was rare, consisting of time travel that gave me the ability to save only a blood relative of the Sweeney clan, whether they be young or old, at the time of their death." Pausing for my reaction and receiving none, he continued.

"Before ye died, my dearly departed mother came to me one night through a mist, speaking in Gaelic and reminding me of the gift. She told me that it would soon be needed to save a family member. What she didn't tell me was who I'd be saving. She quickly vanished before I could ask her more. I already knew the only catch to the gift was, that whoever I saved and gave new life to, I wouldn't know where they would come to be the minute I took hold of their hands. You could have gone anywhere in the world, at any time, just not back to your former life. But you would be alive."

I sat silently listening, taking in everything he said while staring at the pained expression on his face.

"You were lucky enough to come to be here with me."

Pausing and looking into my eyes, he waited for me to speak. When I didn't, he continued. "Ye were at work and been fatally shot. Yer friends tried to save ye." Bowing his head and pausing, "I watched it all unfold. I came to ye prayin' that ye'd live, and I could go back to my life here, satisfied to live out my remaining years, alone. You know they tried, Emily. You watched them. But, in te end, they couldn't save you. It broke me heart when I was standin' beside ye as they declared ye dead. So, I did the only thing I knew I had to do. I made the quick decision te take ye hand, bringing ye with me or let them put ye in the cold ground next to yer Ma and Da. I couldn't let that happen; I wanted you here with me. But . . . something went wrong. I lost you in your crossover. That's why you landed in the hills and not here with me."

Finally, I answered him, "I remember you standing beside me. And Max . . . Max didn't want to stop." My grandfather now sat with his head in his hands.

"I made a selfish decision to take ye hand the minute your friend declared ye dead. If I hadn't, ye wouldn't be here now. I'm so sorry. I should have cursed that gift and let it rot with me in hell."

Coming to kneel before my grandfather, I pulled his hands from his face. "Grandfather," I pleaded. "I don't know why you made the choice you did, because I would have been satisfied to lie with Da and Ma eternally." Taking a deep breath, I wiped at the tears flowing down my face. "But you did what you thought was right at the time. Now, you need to help me find out how to get back."

Feeling the roughness of his hands on the sides of my face, he placed a gentle kiss on my brow. Looking longingly into my eyes, "I'll do anything in me power te make it up to ye, lass. Please believe me."

"I believe you will. But tell me one thing grandfather."

"Surely, ifin' I can."

"Are you positive I can't go back?"

29

Emily

THE LOOK ON my grandfather's face had me worried. "My dear child, I just told you, you can't go back. It's impossible. You can't escape yer fate. Listen to me. You're an amazing young woman with Celtic blood running deep through yer veins. You remind me of Meadhbh, the Celtic warrior goddess. She was strong-willed, ambitious, determined in her ways, and with unwavering strength. You'll survive here."

He was avoiding my question. Instead, he asked, "What about yer man? Do ye want ta leave him?"

I lost all composure. I couldn't reveal my love for Caleb. Instead, I yelled loud enough for the whole town to hear. "How many times do I have to tell you? He's *not* my man. He was a man who needed my help. And, I just happened to drop out of who knows where to care for him." Facing my grandfather head-on, I blurted out, "You know who I am and where I come from? You know my knowledge of medicine?"

"Yes. Of course I do," he managed to say.

Closing my eyes, I took a calming breath. "Look, Caleb and I are from two different worlds. As a matter of fact, two different centuries, for heaven's sake! You know as well as I do, I can't stay here, with you or with him. I need to go home." Insistent, I pushed on, "Certainly, you can understand that. I only did what I was trained to do by helping him." Pointing a finger between us, "We, you and I, took the Hippocratic Oath to help those in need." Motioning down the hall, I added, "That man would have died out there without my help." At that moment, I didn't know who I was trying to convince my grandfather or me.

Caleb

I'd been lying awake, staring at the ceiling and listening to Emily and her grandfather argue. She had made it very clear that I had no place in her life, and she was only here because of some gift. As soon as she could, she would be leaving. "Damn it, then why did she say she loved me?"

Emily

"Emily, dear, listen to me. This gift is complicated. Ye died in 2019. When ye took me hand, yer fate was sealed from ever going back to living in that time. By bringing ye here, I gave ye a second chance at life. I know, it's not the one ye want, but it's one ye can't walk away from."

Raising my hand, I cut my grandfather off, "That's what you say. But have you ever known anyone who's tried to go back?"

"No. But, I know what te gift entails, and tat means not being able te return te one's time and risk final death without another chance at living. Are ye willing to take that risk?"

Without hesitation, I replied, "Yes, I am." What was I thinking? I needed to know if there was even the slightest chance I could go back. Kneeling down before him, I placed my hands on his knees and looked up into his fading violet eyes. "Please, Grandfather, you must understand how I feel. I need to find a way back." Squeezing my fingers into his thighs, I pleaded, "Whatever you do, don't say a word to Caleb about our conversation. I'll tell him when I'm ready."

My grandfather nodded his agreement to my request. I could see the emotional pain written all over his face. He'd just found me, and now I was asking him to let me go. Part of me was angry, while the other part felt sorry for him. But, he was paying the price for putting me in this awful position. Without further conversation, he got up and walked from the room, leaving me to stare after him.

Slipping quietly into Caleb's room around ten that evening, I found him asleep. Changing into the borrowed nightshift, I took a blanket and pillow from the armoire, and walked down the hall to the spare bedroom. The sooner I distanced myself from Caleb, the easier it would be for me to leave. So I thought.

Sitting silently in the dark, I leaned my head back against the headboard, needing to be alone with my scattered thoughts while trying to put the pieces of my life back together. "Why did I have to die? It's not fair." I knew why my grandfather had done what he had by bringing me here. He wanted me to live. He wanted my help. "But does Caleb, and he love me enough to let me go?" It was all too confusing. Sleep would not come easy this night.

After tossing and turning, I gave up on the idea of sleeping. Sitting on the edge of the bed, staring into the darkness, my mind raced through different scenarios of what-ifs. Thinking. Hoping.

Praying. What had I left behind in Seattle that was so important? Was it a life I truly longed to have back? "Oh God, how can I even think of staying here? This town has nothing for me." *This will never feel like home.* Raising a glance towards the ceiling, I asked, "Why did you let this happen to me? I want to go home!"

That familiar comforting voice entered my thoughts. *My dear Emily, you know that God did not let this happen to you. God answers our prayers in His own time and in His own way. You should remember this from after your parents died. As time passes here, you will come to know the answers. It may not be in the spoken word, but in the form of a comforting hand, the look in a certain someone's eyes, or the security of loving arms around you. I don't mean to diminish how you're feeling right now, but did you ever stop to think that this might be where you were meant to be all along, using your talents to help these people? To find love?* Pausing, with no response from me, my grandmother continued. *You have a gift, Emily, one that these people need. Besides, you will come to love your grandfather and that young man down the hall.*

"Oh, Gran, I wish I could believe you. I know God didn't do this to me. It's just . . . I'm terrified that I will be stuck here for the rest of my life." Shaking my head, "I can't do it." Brushing tears from my eyes, "Can't you see that?"

Would that be so bad dear child? Your grandfather has given you a second chance. Don't wish that away by trying to go back. Have you thought of what could happen if you fail?

Sitting up straighter, I had a thought. "Gran, do you know anything about this gift?" Not letting my grandmother respond, I rushed out another question. "You need to find out more. You must speak with grandfather and find out why I can't go back. I need to know. Please, will you do that?"

So many questions. Dear, you heard what your grandfather said. I know nothing about this gift. I've never even heard of it. It's from your father's side of the family. I'm sorry, but I can't communicate with your grandfather like I can with you. And I can't see what your future holds.

Frustrated, I persevered. "But what if I wasn't really dead and grandfather reacted too quickly in bringing me here? Can you answer that? Besides, how would I ever know if I don't try and go back?"

Emily, think back to what happened that day. You watched your friends try so hard to save you. Do you really think they could have succeeded considering the injury you sustained? If they'd put you on life support, don't you think it would only have delayed the inevitable? You would never have been able to lead the life you once knew. Besides, if your grandfather hadn't acted when he did, you would have been lost to a cold grave, or worse, on endless life support. At least here and now, you are alive, feeling, and doing what you love, practicing medicine.

Rising, I sat in the rocker next to the room's only window, and stared up at the stars, waiting for the night to be over, knowing my grandmother was right. It was still a bitter pill to swallow as I continued to overanalyze my situation.

All I ask, Emily, is that you give it some time and thought before you rush into trying to go back.

"I don't know if I can do that, Gran. You know I'm not of this time. How does Grandfather expect me to fit in as if I've always been here?"

You're a strong lass, as your Da always said. You'll find a way to fit in. These people need you. Your grandfather needs you. And, most definitely, Mr. Young needs you. Silence ensued before my grandmother added. *Just think about what I've said, Emily, and remember I love you.*

In a hushed whisper, I responded, "I love you too Gran." My Gran was right, I had come to care deeply for Caleb with all my heart, but was it enough to jeopardize trying to return to 2019? Feeling weighed down by despair, one thing I knew, even if I could find a way to return, Caleb couldn't come with me.

30

Caleb

SOMETIME AROUND MIDNIGHT, I reached for Emily's hand. But she wasn't there. I couldn't imagine where she might be. Turning my head from side to side, I couldn't locate her form in the darkened room. Calmly, I called her name. With no answer, I painfully struggled to get myself up and out of bed. Thankfully, my strength was improving. It had been almost three weeks since being shot. Now was as good a time as any to start moving on my own. Taking in slow deep breaths, I cautiously walked towards the door by gripping onto the tops of furniture with one hand while grasping my abdomen with the other. "You can do this, Young."

By the time I reached the door, my legs were shaking. Opening it, I painfully walked down the narrow hallway by leaning my weight against the walls for support. It might have been only ten feet in distance, but it felt like ten miles. Taking one unsteady step at a time, I became weaker the farther I went, when I finally found myself standing at the closed door to the spare room. I knocked.

"Come in."

With no moonlight to guide me, my vision adjusted to the darkness, and I located Emily's form sitting in a rocker. I could barely see her hugging a quilt to her chest while staring out the window.

"Caleb?"

"Yes. I woke up, and you weren't there. I was wondering where you were. Are you alright?" She didn't respond.

With a gripping ache in my chest that wasn't from my wound, I added, "I didn't mean to disturb you. I'll just go back to bed and see you in the morning."

"Fine." Emily didn't engage me in further conversation, and I was at a loss for words.

Surprised she hadn't offered to help me, I braced myself firmly, knowing the rolling spasms of pain would come as I maneuvered back to my room. Wincing, I dropped down on the edge of the bed, drenched in sweat. My heart was breaking as I thought, "She's going to leave me over some damn gift."

Emily

It had been a fitful night. I hadn't slept a wink after last night's encounter with my grandfather. Then Caleb's showing up at my room. Right now, I couldn't bring myself to go down the hall to check on him. Instead, I went directly to the kitchen, bypassing his closed door. Busying myself with filling the tea kettle, I turned to find a note left on the table from my grandfather saying, '*Gone to the saloon to see a patient.*' "Now, who could that be?"

Finding the ingredients in the cold storage cellar underneath the pantry floor, I proceeded to make breakfast consisting of bacon, fried potatoes, and scrambled eggs. Chuckling to myself, "Well, if this won't clog up the ole' arteries, nothing will." I hadn't figured out how to make toast on the woodstove yet, so I spread thick slices of bread with fresh butter and berry jam. All the while, I was thinking of ways to tell Caleb I was leaving.

Turning from the counter with the tray I planned on taking to his room, Caleb suddenly appeared at the entrance to the kitchen. He'd shaven, making him look even paler with the contrast between his tanned forehead and cheeks. How long he'd been standing there, I didn't' know. Speechless for the first time since arriving in town, I couldn't help but stand there unmoving. Looking at Caleb's finely sculpted features, I thought, *oh, girl. You are in such deep trouble.*

Afraid I'd drop the tray, my hands tightened on the handles, at the sight of him. His shirt hung open except at a single white button. My eyes wandered up, then down, coming to a stop at the fine dusting of dark hair trailing all the way down to . . . Well, to below where I shouldn't be looking at this moment. Heat rose up my neck as I continued to gape. His left arm crossed protectively over his chest, while the other splinted his abdomen. Inhaling slowly, I realized that if the wall hadn't been there in his fragile state, he would be lying flat on the floor.

With a trace of bitterness, as if I meant nothing to him, he bluntly said, "Good Morning, Miss Emily."

Placing the heavy tray on the table, I ignored his sarcastic inflection. All I wanted to do was put my arms around him and tell him I loved him. Restraining myself, I couldn't do it. He was taller than I expected, and if he didn't look so sickly thin, I could only imagine the way his bleached white shirt and faded denims would hug his once muscular frame.

"Why are you barefoot?" I asked, pointing towards the floor. "Where are your boots?"

He followed my gaze downward and answered, "I couldn't bend over to pull them on."

"Oh." I averted his eyes as I wiped my sweat-dampened hands on the apron. "I'll help you put them on after you eat." Motioning to the chair, "I don't want your food to get cold. So, please sit down."

As he moved to the table, I thought, *something's missing*. His face was a blank slate. Gone was that rakish grin I'd fallen for. Something was definitely wrong. *Was it because I didn't speak with him last night when he came into my room?* I was afraid to ask, so putting the tray of food on the table, I went to help him into a chair.

Holding up his hands, "No. I'm fine. I can do it myself."

His words stung, so I stepped back.

"If I don't start moving around, I won't be able to ride. And I need to be ready to move on before the New Year."

So, he's going to leave too? Where's he going? Wait! He can't leave. Not yet. It's too soon. He needs more time to heal. As I watched him sit down, so many questions scrambled around in my head. I couldn't get them past my lips. How do I tell him? *I don't want you to leave.* Moving to the stove, I retrieved the pot of coffee. *Here I am making plans to leave myself. I haven't the right to tell him what to do or when to go.*

Looking at Caleb, but not really seeing him, I stumbled over my words, "You can't leave yet. I . . . ah. What I mean is, you can't leave until your wounds are healed. I'm sure that the Doctor will let you know when it's safe for you to travel." I found myself shifting my weight nervously from one foot to the other. Setting the coffee pot down next to the tray, I took the plate of food, placing it before him.

"Would you like some coffee?" Standing close enough to touch him, I stopped myself just before I was going to put my hand on his shoulder. That tender touch wouldn't do. And making eye contact would only have me fall apart—something I definitely couldn't handle right now.

"Yes, please." Not looking up, he pushed his food around his plate. He hadn't even taken a bite when I asked, "Do you take anything in it, cream, sugar, or both?"

Cursing, "Damn it woman! What is with all this wife-like small talk?" Slapping his napkin on the table, he looked up at me. "Any other time you'd be talking non-stop and driving me crazy."

In obvious pain, I watched as he inhaled sharply. *Wife-like small talk! What did he mean?* "We have nothing more to talk about," I said calmly. "We're each going our separate ways. Let's just leave it at that."

"Just black then," he ground out. "Thanks!"

Screaming inside, I had enough of his short caustic answers. "Caleb, what is going on with you?" I asked curtly. His bold dark eyes had me taking a step back. *I will not let him see how much he affects me.* Hands on my hips, I stood my ground on the opposite side of the table and asked, "Have I done something to make you mad?"

"I don't know, have you?"

The anger inside me hit the boiling point. I couldn't stand it when someone answered a question with a question. "Oh, for heaven's sake Caleb. Are we going to play this game all day long?"

"You tell me, Miss Sweeney."

The tone of his voice hurt. Turning his face away, he took a sip of the hot coffee. He wouldn't admit it, but he'd just scalded his tongue. *Serves him right.* "Miss Sweeney, is it?" Nostrils flaring in indignation, I could feel my face was flaming red as I continued my discourse. "Why you sanctimonious back end of a mule," I cursed. Not prone to violence, but if he wasn't already in pain, I'd smack him one good. Leaning both hands on the table, I leaned forward, facing him head-on. "Mister, you better tell me what's going on right now!"

Taking in a deep breath, I was resigned to the fact that Caleb must have overheard last night's conversation between my grandfather and me. *How stupid can I be? Of course he heard. I was yelling loud enough the whole dang town could hear me. He found out that Doc Sweeney is my grandfather. I'd told him that Caleb isn't my man, and I was leaving. That I only cared for his physical wounds because I'd taken an oath. That it had nothing to do with love.*

Turning away, I faced the window and asked myself, *who was I kidding?* Crossing my arms over my chest, I fumed. *Now what?* Muttering an oath, I realized I had been such a fool for so many things the past few days, most of all, how I'd come to love Caleb. *Dear God, I'd fallen in love! I tried not to. Really I did.*

Turning back to the table, I noticed Caleb hadn't touched his food. My breath hitched as our eyes met, and I waited for Caleb's response. None imminent, I decided to tell him the truth. I was going back to the life I'd left. *I'd have to lie to him and tell him I didn't have feelings for him. Oh! What a mess I've created.*

Caleb

I sat silently watching Emily move about the kitchen, dying inch by inch as the seconds slowly ticked by. If I could, I'd walk out the front door, head to the stables, and ride River as far as humanly possible out of Yuma. I never wanted to see this dried-up gulch of a town again. My only problem, I couldn't stand to leave the woman I loved. I just couldn't do it.

Despite the short time we'd known each other, I had to make her see that we were meant to be together. We needed more than chaste kisses. I needed to feel the fire and passion I knew was hidden in her heart. *She can lie to me all she wants, but I know she loves me.* Time dragged into eternity, waiting for Emily to speak was like having the local barber agonizingly extract a painful tooth.

The longer I sat up, the weaker I became. I could feel beads of sweat forming on my brow and upper lip. Like an unmoored ship floundering in the Boston Harbor while it searched for an exit to the sea, my mind drifted to what life with Emily would be like. There were no words to describe what it could have been like. Damn it! Why couldn't I have just died up in the hills? It would certainly have made things easier, at least for me. *I'm really in love. Shouldn't I be happy?* Shaking my head, I thought, *what a mess I've created.* Leaning on the table, I asked myself, now *what?*

Emily

"Obviously, this conversation is going nowhere, Mister Young." Taking off the apron, I threw it on the back of an empty chair. "I'm going out." Walking past Caleb, he didn't try to stop me.

"Fine! I don't care!" he replied.

Grabbing a shawl from a hook near the front door, I wrapped it around my shoulders. With a firm pull, the door slipped out of my hand, banging against the parlor wall. At the same time, I turned my head towards the kitchen and saw Caleb flinch. Grabbing the handle again, I pulled harder. Stepping through, I let it slam closed behind me, hearing the rattling of the glass panes.

My eyes squinted at the sun bearing down from a cloudless sky as I stomped down the porch steps. Pulling the shawl tight across my chest, I could feel my blood pressure rise. My frustrations playing out, I tried taking deep breaths to relieve the pent-up tension, when I caught the fragrance of long-ago faded roses. *"How can that be?"* I searched the yard for a live bush, but there was none, so I continued on my way.

I couldn't remember when I'd been this upset with a man. Right now, I was mad enough that if anyone crossed my path, I'd spit nails at them. With no destination in mind, I veered across the street and down the boardwalk. Hands clenched, I was having one heck of a conversation with myself, and not watching where I was going when I ran straight into a brick wall.

31

Emily

"I AM SO SORRY," I said. Reaching up with both hands, they rested against a firm muscular chest, just as two strong arms came around me, keeping me from falling backward.

"Miss Sweeney. Ver are ya going in such an all fire hurry?" asked Sheriff Johansson, securing his hold.

On impact, my breath rushed out, leaving me unable to answer him right away. Willing oxygen into my lungs, I looked up. I had to be a foot shorter than the sheriff, making him look down at my flustered face.

"Not having a gut morning, Miss Sweeney?"

I answered breathlessly, "I'm so sorry, sheriff. I wasn't watching where I was going." Removing my arms from his chest, I looked down at my shoes.

"Vell, tat's obvious miss, since ya yust about bowled me ov'r," he added teasingly, then graced me with a wink.

Not in the mood for the sheriff's humor, I attempted to move past him. My mind had been elsewhere trying to get a certain Mr. Young out of my head. But, most importantly, out of my heart. It was proving to be more difficult than I could ever imagine.

"If you'll excuse me, sheriff," I said, grasping the ends of my shawl to move pass the formidable man. "I'm just going to continue my walk." Pointing forward, I didn't want the sheriff to read any of the emotions swimming behind my eyes. That would only lead to questions and answers I wasn't willing to admit. "I'll just be on my way."

I couldn't help but notice that Miss Abigail James had chosen that moment to come out of the saloon and see my hands on the sheriff's chest. *Dang. This doesn't look good from where she's standing.* Swiftly turning around, Miss James marched right back into the saloon, leaving the batwing doors fiercely swinging behind her.

Thankfully, Sheriff Johansson had missed her display of over-analyzing the scene she'd just witnessed. Tipping his hat, the sheriff allowed me to pass by.

Unable to calm my anger, I walked past the saloon, when I decided I needed a beer. Shaking the few coins in my pocket that my grandfather had left me that morning, I figured that beer in 1880 wouldn't cost as dearly as it did in 2019. "Why not? There's no one here to stop me!" I said defiantly. Setting my plan in motion, I turned around and slipped through the swinging doors, walking straight up to the bar.

Vermin

"Stubbs. Stubbs!" I yelled, slapping my brother on the shoulder. He stopped rolling his quirley and followed the direction my finger pointed. There, across the street, we watched the most beautiful woman I'd ever laid eyes on entering the saloon.

Pulling my brother by the collar into the alley, I pushed him against the outside wall of the jail, where I had Stubb's undivided attention. "That's sure some fine-looking whore orer' there. I'm goin' ta have some fun with that one," I said, spitting a line of tobacco juice on the toe of Stubb's boot.

My brother rapidly shook his head from side to side, obviously disagreeing with me.

Emily

Walking through the saloon doors, I headed straight to the bar finding myself standing in front of the burliest bartender I'd ever seen. He was a bit intimidating, but that wasn't going to stop me from drinking this early in the day. I had no idea what I was doing when I watched his eyes pop wide open at my approach. With three feet of chipped wood separating us, I stood my ground. I didn't care what he thought of me being in his saloon. In a subdued voice, he asked, "Can I help you, miss?"

Tersely I replied, "I'd like a beer please. And make it ice cold." It was unlike me to be impolite, but right now, I didn't feel like being cordial. To anyone! I just wanted a cold beer. *Is that too much to ask?* My taste buds were becoming impatient. It had been too long since I'd enjoyed the flavor of a Washington craft beer. Today though, I wouldn't be so lucky.

"OK, lady! But we don't have ice. Wouldn't hold up in the heat."

"Oh, I hadn't thought of that," I said, disappointed.

"You still want the beer?" he asked while wiping some invisible stain on the bar.

"Yes!" I answered, bolstered by the thought of having alcohol dull my senses from being in this retched place against my will.

"You want a whiskey chaser with that lady?"

"Oh, why not? That sounds even better." Slapping my hand lightly on the bar's damp wood.

"That'll be two-bits," he said, nodding his chin up.

"OK." Reaching into my pocket, I pulled out a silver quarter and placed it on the bar in front of me. "What's your name?" I asked.

"Henry" was his one-word answer. I didn't chance to push further.

The saloon was quiet as a church on Sunday morning. All the patrons had stopped to stare at me, the woman who'd just sauntered in off the street asking for a beer with a whiskey chaser.

Behind Henry's bemused look, I watched his eyes roam up, then down my form. What was he thinking? *Can she hold her liquor?* Henry slid the mug of beer down the bar top. Surprisingly, I deftly caught it in my right hand as if I'd done it a hundred times before.

Dear, do you think you should be drinking this early in the day?

"Not now Gran!" I answered forcefully. "If you say one word about my drinking, I swear I'll walk out that door until I find the ends of the earth. Or another bar." Silence ensued, "I don't need your help right now, so please, just leave me alone."

Well! If you put it that way, I will leave you alone. But remember, Emily, you will regret your actions come morning. You wait and see!

"Gran, regrets are all I seem to have right now. So, don't worry. One more is not going to hurt."

"Who are you talking to, miss?" Henry whispered, leaning over the bar to direct his question for my ears only.

"My dearly departed grandmother, who at this moment is trying to convince me that drinking comes with consequences and regrets." Taking a swig of the warm, bitter liquor, I choked, almost spewing the foul-tasting liquid across the bar. *Oh! This isn't going as planned. Just keep drinking Emily, and you'll soon feel the numbness.*

Snorting, "Your dead grandmother you say?" Henry leaned back, attempting to distance himself from me.

Waving my hands at him, "Long story," I said. "You wouldn't understand." Taking another swig, but smaller this time, I pointed a finger to my chest, "Even I don't understand it."

He did what most bartenders do, he listened intently as I prattled on about a town named Seattle, things called cell phones and computers, and of all things, the year 2019. Henry stared at me as if I was speaking a foreign language.

I didn't much feel like a lady right now, more like a confused woman who was slowly losing her mind. Having conversations with my dead grandmother added more fuel to my craziness. Today was the best day to drink away my troubles, hoping it would make me forget what I'd been through the past several weeks and the unknown future that lay before me. Better yet, I hoped when I awoke from this self-induced stupor, I would find myself as far away from Yuma as possible and back in Seattle.

In my short stay, I had had enough of this town, 1880, and definitely enough of Caleb Young. Downing my second beer in less than five minutes, the warm liquid quickly made its way to the bottom of my stomach. Unsettling, a very un-ladylike burp slipped up and out.

Picking up the whiskey glass, I threw the liquid fire back in one swallow. None of this sipping like I would have done in a cocktail bar. Choking, the liquid slid down, burning the back of my throat as it flowed south. "A few more of these and I should be golden." Looking Henry squarely in the eyes, I put the glass firmly down on the bar and ordered my third round.

Grinning, I felt a buzz while a fuzzy blanket of warmth enfold me. I was loosening up to a point where I actually began enjoying myself for the first time in weeks. Unaware I'd drawn a crowd, I leaned on the bar, chatting loudly with Henry and the saloon patrons. Snickering, I guessed none of them had seen a citified woman drink beer before.

Several miners tried unsuccessfully to vie for my individual attention. To their dismay, I ignored their offers until the sorrowful piano music drew my interest, and one of the toothless miners asked me to dance. I couldn't resist. By this time, I was feeling no pain, and definitely no shame at who noticed my lack of sobriety.

Being twirled around and around the dance floor in a dizzying pattern, the liquor took a firm grip on all my senses. My insides felt like an old-time washing machine, churning its contents up and over.

"Oh, my aching head," I whimpered, trying to forget what was going on inside my cranium. Leaving the dance floor, I grasped the sides of my head between both hands, pressing inward, hoping the counter-pressure would relieve the pain. It felt like a jackhammer was trying to pound some sense into me. Unsuccessfully. "Another shot will take care of it," I said, fooling myself.

By the time I finished my fourth round, I was having difficulty focusing and keeping my thoughts in order. The origin of my mission accomplished, I gripped the bar top, the only thing between me and the floor. If you'd asked me, I couldn't have told anyone my name, let alone remember who Doc Sweeney or Caleb Young was.

"Little lady," Henry tapped on the bar in front of me to get my attention. "I think you've had enough to drink for one day." Coming around, I let him put one arm around my waist and guide me to the chair in the far corner of the saloon.

When I looked up and smiled, Miss Abigail was standing next to Henry, staring at me. What was she thinking of me now? First, she sees me come riding into town in the back of a wagon the sheriff was leading, then she finds me with my hands splayed across his chest. I sure could get myself into some crazy situations.

"I know where that lady belongs," Miss Abigail said. Motioning with her head, "She came out of Doc Sweeney's clinic earlier this morning. She didn't look none too happy when she reached this side of the street." Turning her back away from me, she continued to address Henry in what she thought was a whisper. I could still hear her as she spoke. "I think she's staying there. I'm positive she's the same one who came into town riding in the back of the wagon with that gambler who'd been shot. Remember him? He's the one who killed the stranger in here last month. The same one the sheriff sent packing."

I heard the whoosh of satin as she walked away from the table, stopped, then instructed Henry, "Henry, make sure you sober her up with some coffee. While you're doing that, have one of the boys get Doc Sweeney to come retrieve her. She's going to need a lot of help getting back across the street."

Vermin

I'd been sitting in the corner of the saloon waiting. As luck would have it, that woman was just drunk enough for me to make my move. Then, I overheard the saloon madam and her bartender talking about a killing that had taken place in this very bar over two weeks ago. It was my brother they were talking about.

Furious, I cursed slamming my fist on the table. *Damn it! It can't be. I thought I'd killed him. Can't believe that murdering gambler 'ist still alive! I had unfinished business to take care of.* Pulling my brother by his collar, I headed out the saloon doors. I needed a plan to end this once and for all.

Emily

I jumped in my seat, hearing a fist slam on a table nearby. Looking through blurry eyes, I watched a filthy man stand abruptly and scratch himself in places I didn't need to see before he headed out the saloon doors.

"Little Miss, let's get you sobered up some before sending you home," Henry said, setting a steaming cup of coffee in front of me.

"Home?" I muttered, "I don't have a home!" With tears in my eyes, I repeated over my uncooperative tongue, "I don't have a home." Blinking several times, I added, "Wait! I need to pay you for all my drinks. How much do I owe you?" Fumbling to find the pocket hidden deep in my dress, it suddenly dawned on me that all I had left was twenty-five cents in coin. Not enough to cover all I'd drank. Embarrassed, I informed Henry, "I'm sorry. I don't have enough money. I'm sure my grandfather will cover my tab? Or, I can work it off here somehow."

"It's OK Miss. You can pay me whenever you get the money. And no, you won't be working it off." Patting me on the shoulder, Henry walked back to the bar, hopefully, to make more coffee. It was going to be a long afternoon.

Two hours had gone by, and I was still sitting at the table, occasionally groaning into my cup. And no offense to Henry, sipping the worst coffee I'd ever tasted. Hands wrapped around the warm heavy mug, I inhaled the burnt scent of beans, which seemed to be doing their trick. My liquor induced fog was slowly lifting. At this point, I didn't care, all I wanted to do was crawl under the table and die. "Oops!" I snickered. "I'm already dead."

I felt like I was hovering over 'the' porcelain bowl, waiting for someone to flush. "Oh!" I felt horrible. Grabbing my head, I rolled it from side to side, as my vision spun out of control. Groaning, I decided to give up and dropped my forehead onto the cold tabletop.

"Of course you feel horrible," said a snappish voice behind me. Not looking up, I knew that voice as she continued stretching the truth a bit, "You drank half my beer and whiskey supply, and now you tell us you can't pay. I ought to send for the sheriff and have you thrown in jail."

Still not looking up, I replied, "That's OK with me lady, as long as there is a bed I can lay down on."

When I was finally able to look up without my head spinning, I said, "I'm really sorry. I've never been drunk before." Moaning, I laid my head back on the table. "Oh, my splitting head."

"I saw what you and Sheriff Johansson were doing outside on the boardwalk. You should be ashamed of yourself."

Why was this woman still yelling at me? Her voice grated on my brain like fingernails on a chalkboard. I couldn't for the life of me, remember even seeing the sheriff today. "What was it I'd done with your sheriff?" I asked, my mouth feeling like it was full of cotton balls.

I felt her warm breath next to my ear as she hissed out, "You had your hands all over the sheriff's chest! Don't deny it. I saw you."

"Oh, that. That's nothing," I answered, swinging my hands in the air and coming close to falling off my chair.

Quick to the rescue, Miss Abigail caught me before I tumbled to the floor. "What do you mean, nothing?"

Indignant, my head popped up, coming face to face with Miss Abigail's protruding belly. "Lady, don't be so uptight." Rubbing my blurry eyes, I continued, "Pregnant women shouldn't stress out like this. Besides, it was nothing. I wasn't looking where I was going, and I bumped into your precious sheriff. He grabbed my arms to keep me from falling flat on my azz... fanny. So, there!" Rapidly running out of steam, I could no longer hold my head up or continue the conversation. But, I had to ask, mumbling into the tabletop, "Do you have any ibuprofen I could take?"

"Ibu ... what?" Miss Abigail asked.

"Never mind," I said, palming the air, "I'll ask Doc Sweeney when I get back."

Vertigo made my eyes twitch rapidly back and forth, adding to my nausea. After several minutes, I cautiously stood with awkward grace. Unfortunately, my off-kilter equilibrium had me plopping right back down into the chair, sending it tipping backward with me in it. If it wasn't for a miner sitting behind me catching the chair, I would have landed with my head in a spittoon.

In my not-so-graceful moment, my grandfather and Caleb just happened to walk through the saloon doors. Neither of them looked too pleased with what they saw. I watched as Caleb ran his hands through his hair, something he did when he was angry. His look of annoyance told me all I needed to know. He was not happy with me. But I didn't care. I don't know how he'd made it across the street in his weakened state. But, here he was standing before me.

Slapping the top of each man's shoulders, Henry said, "Gentlemen, this fetching little lady here, has had quite the appetite for beer and whiskey chasers."

"She what?" Caleb asked in a high pitched voice that made me flinch.

"I'm going to be sick," I yelled. Gagging, I covered my mouth, not knowing which way to turn my head.

I heard Miss Abigail yell, "Henry, hurry, get a spittoon." He was too late. Caleb had been standing too close, his shiny black boots paying the price. When I was able to raise my head, Caleb was looking down at the foul mess. Others smart enough took several quick steps back, just in case I missed again.

"Feeling better, are we dear?" Miss Abigail asked sarcastically, patting me on the back.

Looking up at her with my best evil eye, I answered, "Just dandy lady!"

I heard my grandfather chuckling. My vision was clear enough to see him looking between me, his intoxicated granddaughter, and Caleb. "Gentlemen, I do believe tat our der' sweet Miss Sweeney here is't half-in-te-bag."

From what I could see, Caleb wasn't amused. His legs planted apart, not to make a statement, but more than likely to keep himself upright. I watched as his eyes narrowed and glared at me. It was enough to make me want to crawl under the table and slither like a rattler out the back door.

Caleb

Sweat ran down my back in rivulets. The longer I stood over Emily, the weaker I became. A chill raced through my body when I recognized this as the exact spot where I'd killed the cheating gambler. The very place my life began its downward spiral. I was only standing here now because I thought something had happened to the woman I loved. But no, here she sat inebriated, hanging over a spittoon. *What was she thinking? Better yet, what the hell am I thinking? This woman is intoxicating in her own right, with trouble written all over her!* Chuckling to myself, *maybe that's what I like most about her.* Watching Doc Sweeney lean down to face his granddaughter, I wondered if anyone knew what Emily meant to the both of us.

"Emily dear. Tis' time for ye te get back te the clinic and rest. We'll help ye."

"I don't want any help from him," she said, pointing to me. "Get away from me. You . . . you! Don't you touch me," she screeched, trying to push my hand away.

"Fine! Sit here and drink yourself into oblivion!"

Before I had the chance to turn around, with a quick jerk of her right leg, Emily struck home. "Argh!" I yelled. "What the hell did you do that for?" I hissed out before bending down to rub my shin.

"Cause I wanted to, and you deserved it."

"Deserved it? Why you little . . .!" I said, moving towards her. I wanted to shake some sense into Emily. What was she thinking of getting drunk, and now attacking me?

"Now children," Doc Sweeney said, smiling while urging me away from the table. "Enough of this fighting." Reaching out to Emily, he said, "I think we need to get Miss Sweeney back to the clinic, so she can sleep today's bit of fun off."

"You're right Doc," I replied, turning to some of the patrons I trusted to handle Emily with care. I asked them to escort her to the clinic. If I physically could, I would do it myself. But I was afraid we'd both find ourselves brawling in the middle of the street.

～ 32 ～

Emily

I SLOWLY AWOKE, THINKING I must have had one atrocious night in the emergency room to feel this dreadful. Gradually opening one eye and gazing into the sunlight pouring through the window, daggers of pain shot through my head. Quickly, I covered my eyes with my forearm and skimmed my tongue over my dry, cracked lips. My mouth tasted like the bottom of a litter box, and my breath held the lasting evidence of alcohol.

Groaning, I concluded that I wasn't in my Seattle apartment, and I hadn't been at work last night. Woefully, I pulled the pillow over my head to shut out the glaring light and the sound of an obnoxious dog barking below my window. It was the sound of a sweet little bird's repetitive chirping that was about to do me in. Grabbing my head with both hands, I willed the pain to cease and the bird to go away. *How can a dead person feel this miserable?*

Just then, that familiar voice chimed in with a touch of sarcasm, *Well, dear, but I must say you indeed tied one on yesterday. I did try to warn you. But no, you wouldn't listen to me. It's that Irish stubbornness you possess.*

She was right. I'd been so foolish. Never had I done something like this before. "Gran, please don't talk so loud," I pleaded, placing my hands over my ears. Her voice this morning, which only I could hear, sounded like screeching train wheels on warped tracks.

Whining, I added, "My head really hurts, Gran. Can't you show me some sympathy?

My Gran added with a wee bit of smugness, *Oh! Not feeling so well, are you dear?*

Through gritted teeth, I answered her, "Nooooo, I'm not! Now, please help me get rid of this hangover, or leave me alone to die in peace."

Alright, dear. As they say, whoever they may be, 'Fools suffer alone,' or something like that.

"I get your point, gran. Now, please go."

Why, of course, dear. Just let me know when I can be of help.

My stomach suddenly lurched and rolled like a ship fighting rough seas. Leaning over the side of the bed just in time, I heaved into a nearby basket, hoping it wasn't one of my grandfather's treasures. I couldn't remember in all my college years of having drunk this much. With studying to get into medical school, my intern years, and fellowship, I hadn't the time to waste on partying.

Yesterday was a blur. I didn't know what this town made their whiskey out of, but it was correct when they called it *rotgut.* All I wanted was to moan, sleep, and moan some more when I was startled out of my self-pity by pounding on my door.

"Go away. Let me die in peace," I ground out.

"Oh, if it isn't Little Miss Sunshine," Caleb replied, having let himself in.

"Stop mocking me and go away," I grumbled, pulling the pillow over my head.

"I remember those exact words from a dying gentleman you saved not too long ago," Caleb added.

Peeking out from under the pillow, I saw him leaning on the doorframe, his crisp white shirt hanging open, revealing his healing wounds and firm tanned muscles.

"Go ahead and laugh Mr. Young, but I'm in real pain here. And, for heaven's sake, button up that shirt and show some mercy." Waving a hand towards him, my eyes fixed on his chest. *Good heavens but he's . . . gorgeous.* Rolling my eyes, I asked, "Please, just leave me alone. I'm not getting out of this bed for the rest of the day. Do you understand?"

"Suit yourself," was Caleb's only retort as he pushed away from the door, leaving me to suffer alone.

True to my word, I slept the day and night away without eating a thing. Neither Caleb nor my grandfather made any attempts to get me up. For that, I was thankful. Drinking was one thing, but getting drunk had definitely not been my smartest move since landing in 1880. At this point, I never wanted to see another glass of liquor for the rest of my life, even if it was for medicinal purposes.

The next morning, I didn't feel the warmth of the sun that had streamed in through my window the previous day, only the lasting chill that had crept into my room overnight. Keeping my face covered by the sheet, I wondered what day it was. If I calculated right, it was just two days before Christmas. Yet, neither my grandfather nor Caleb had mentioned the holiday. It would be just another day on the calendar. Rolling over, I felt a deep stabbing ache of missing family and friends.

Sometime later that morning, the sun finally broke through the gray dawn as Caleb touched my shoulder and whispered, "Good morning Angel."

I jumped at his touch. Throwing back the covers, I came up swinging. "What are you doing here?" I asked, trying to clear the wooziness from sitting up too fast.

"Well, isn't it obvious? I'm looking at the most stunningly beautiful sleepy-eyed woman I've ever had the pleasure of greeting the morning with."

Reaching out, he tenderly took a wayward lock of my hair, tucking it behind my ear. Stroking my shoulder, his tender touch sent hot shivers down my spine. "Stop that," I said, slapping his hand away and jerking back my shoulder. "Have you been here all night?"

"Yes," he answered, placing a hand over his heart. "Why! You don't remember last night?"

I couldn't tell if he was serious or teasing until I saw the shocked expression on his face.

"Miss Sweeney, I'm truly offended. I thought I left you with earthshattering memories of our night together."

"No!" I groaned loudly. "Please tell me we didn't. Ah . . . you didn't." Making circles with my hands, I fell back onto the mattress and covered my head with the sheet, "You know what I mean." Peeking out, I caught the sly grin on Caleb's face. "Why you wretched man . . ." I yelled, taking aim and hitting him with the pillow.

Catching the pillow midair, Caleb stood over me, running his free hand up and down my arm. I felt both strength and gentleness in his calloused hands, leaving me to wonder. *Wonder what? Stop it Emily! You're asking for trouble.*

I watched him raise his eyebrows mischievously, then sincerely pointed out, "Oh sweetheart, I would never take advantage of you. Last night you were in no condition to think straight, let alone be intimate."

Taking my hands in his, he pulled me up. "Emily, you have to know how I feel about you." Squeezing my hands tighter, he bowed his head, "Of course, I'll always be grateful to you for saving my life." Raising his head, Caleb confessed, "But somehow, somewhere, in this crazy journey of ours, I fell in love with you."

Stop! Don't say anymore. I swallowed the lump lodged in my throat as Caleb's eyes pierced my wavering resolve.

"Emily, did you hear me? I've fallen in love with you!"

Looking down at my hands in his, the words *I love you too* wouldn't come. *It would make it all the more painful when I leave.*

He continued to stare at me. "Besides, when we make love, I want you to know that it's me," pointing to his chest, "Loving you."

At his bold confession, my heart shattered into a million pieces. *When we make love? Oh, no, no, no. That is not going to happen.* Unexpectedly, that little voice in the back of my head wasn't my gran yelling. It was me. *Tell him. Tell him you love him.* All I could say was, "Caleb, yes, I have feelings for you."

I watched Caleb's endearing expression falter, knowing he'd hope I'd confess my love for him. Rubbing my temples, I groaned. Confused, I watched his eyes drift to my lips as I moistened them with my tongue. My breath hitched. *Please, kiss me Caleb. Make me change my mind.*

The mattress dipped as Caleb sat down beside me. Clearing his throat, he brought my attention back to him. His voice had gone husky. "More importantly, Emily, when we're intimate, it needs to be what you want."

What I want? Oh . . . what do I want? Stay? Go? Caleb was now part of my heart. It would shatter if I left him. Cursing silently, I stoically sat still. If I'd been standing, I'd be stomping my feet like a child having a temper tantrum. Every time I glanced at him, that devilish grin of his was my undoing.

Leaning forward, Caleb made sure I understood his intentions. "First, and foremost Emily, you need to know that at some point, we will make love. There's no doubt about it!"

Fully awake now, I slapped his arm and pulled the sheet up higher to cover my nightdress that had fallen off one shoulder. Looking down, I wondered how I'd come to be undressed. I didn't remember taking off my clothes last night. Was it last night? As a matter of fact, I don't remember much. *That means only one thing! Oh, good heavens.* My lips thinned into a fine line as I boldly conveyed to Caleb,

"We will not be making love Mr. Young. I can tell you that right now." Pausing, I asked, "Did you really sleep in here all night?"

"I did," he replied honestly. "Does that bother you?"

"Ah, no. It's just that. Why would it?" Surprising myself, I placed my hand on his forearm, "It's nice to know that you slept with me." Catching my meaning, I pointed a finger across the small room. "In the chair over there, I mean."

As Caleb snickered, I fell back onto the mattress, holding firmly onto the sheet while rolling to the opposite side of the bed. Covering my eyes with my hands, I mumbled, "I was so stupid drinking all that liquor yesterday. I should have known better, but I wasn't thinking straight. I was angry."

"Angry at who?"

"You!"

"Me? Why me? What have I done?" Caleb repositioned himself on the side of the bed, leaning forward. "Emily, I care about you. You should know that by now, with all we've been through."

Rolling back over to face him, I could see the hurt in his eyes. "Caleb, don't turn gratitude into love. It's entirely two different things, and I know how some people can mistake one for the other."

Caleb squeezed my hands firmly. Was he afraid if he let go, I'd disappear in a misty cloud? "Listen," I said. "I have some things I need to deal with. And drinking yesterday seemed like a good option at the time." I read the confusion and pain in his eyes, knowing I needed to be completely honest with him. Pulling his hands closer, "I know you appreciate what I've done for you, but it's what I would have done for anyone in the same circumstances. It's my job."

Caleb flinched at my declaration as if he'd been gut shot all over again. Abruptly letting go of my hands, he stood. "That's great. Now you're making me out to be a charity case." Turning towards the window, his voice escalating, he began to scold me like a child. "I don't need your damn pity lady." Pointing out the window, he added, "I could have gotten along just fine out there on my own."

Propping myself up on one elbow, I responded snidely, "Of course you could have. The only problem being is that you would have been dead by morning." Reaching out to turn Caleb towards me, it was my turn to raise my voice, "Is that what you wanted Caleb? To die out there alone."

"Dead!" he chuckled, running a hand through his unruly hair. Turning back towards the dirty window, he added, "Right now, that would be better than what I'm going through with you."

It was my turn to flinch. I'd hurt Caleb badly. His increasing anger would be detrimental to his healing. Watching his face become redder by the minute, the muscles in his neck stretched like tight coils ready to spring. I pleaded with him, "Please listen to me and try to understand. I don't want to argue with you."

Moving farther away, Caleb stopped at the door. Turning, in a calm voice he replied, "You think you're the only one in pain?" Waiting for me to respond, he jabbed his index finger towards his chest, frustration evident. "I'm the one being tortured here." Inhaling sharply, his hands moving as he spoke, "Lady, ever since I met you, there's been nothing but trouble between us." Moving back into the room, I watched as he paced the floor, his arms moving up and down as far as his wounds allowed. "I can't think of anyone else but you. You're in my thoughts during the day and my dreams at night. I haven't had a good night's sleep in days." Walking to the window, he looked up at the sky as if seeking divine guidance. "There isn't enough laudanum in this damn town to make this kind of pain go away."

Stopping in front of my bed, towering over me, Caleb placed his open palm on his chest. With a half-hearted shrug, he continued his declaration. "I know it's wrong, but all I can think about is holding you against me, loving you, and feeling our hearts beat as one. I never, ever want to let you go. But it's obvious now that I can't make you stay. You'll do anything to leave." Sighing disconsolately, he couldn't stop. "Stupid me, I was willing to fight anyone or anything to keep you in my life, even that damn gift."

I knew it. Caleb had heard the conversation between my grandfather and me.

Raising his voice, I could see in his eyes that he wasn't giving up. His determined stubbornness persevered. "How many times do I have to tell you Emily that I'm in love with you? I can't even breathe without you near me." Leaning down, Caleb grabbed hold of my hand, placing it over his heart. "Feel it? This heart beats only for you." Tears, I'd never seen him shed, glistened in his eyes. "Emily, you deny my love, and it stops beating." Hands shaking, he asked, "Can you live with that?"

I was stunned into silence. *What was I going to do?* I couldn't pull my hand away, not that Caleb would let go, but because I didn't want to. Feeling the steadying rhythm of his heartbeat beneath my palms broke my resolve. *Damn it. I loved this man. Didn't Da always say, 'Grab hold of love when you can because it may not come your way again?' He was right.*

Taking in a deep steadying breath, I cursed silently. Damn it. He'd done it. He'd torn down my barriers. But, that one chance of returning to Seattle kept niggling in the back of my mind. "Caleb, it appears you overheard my conversation with my grandfather. But you must know it won't work between us." Shaking my head, "I can't let this happen." Pulling my hands free, tears escaped, rolling down my flushed cheeks.

Caleb gently brushed them away. Taking my face in his hands, he searched my eyes. "It doesn't matter. We can work things out. We have all the time in the world."

"No! We don't!" pulling my face away.

"I know there's been a wedge between us since we arrived in town," Caleb said, looming over me. "Something has happened to you since coming here. I want to know what it is. Let me help you, Emily." Placing a finger under my chin and raising my face up to him, "Emily, don't shut me out now. I can't bear it, and I don't think you can either."

"Caleb, you . . ."

Raising his hands to halt me, he added, "Please. Just hear me out. Heaven knows I'm no saint. I've done things that I deeply regret, and will have to live with for the rest of my life."

He was tiring. Crossing his arms over his chest, his breath caught. "After I was shot, I was resigned to the fact that I was going to die on that hill, with no one beside me who cared." With a half-hearted shrug, he continued. "With all the explaining I'd have to do when it came time to meet my Maker, surprisingly, I was OK with it." Looking away, he added, "I had made such a mess of my life up until then, it no longer mattered." His voice broke, and his chin trembled, "To be honest, I didn't want to die alone where no one would know who I was when they found my body." His struggle shown in his eyes. "Then, there you were—my Angel. I wasn't alone anymore. And I could die knowing you would hold me as I took my last breath."

Trembling, my heart was breaking as I listened to his story. I wanted him to hold me and tell me everything was going to be O.K. But he didn't. Instead, he sat in the rocker before his legs gave out. This conversation was taking its toll on his waning strength. So, I waited for him to finish.

"Emily, you became my link to life. You kept me alive when I was moments away from death." Leaning forward, he placed his arms on his knees as he whispered the last.

"I remember you telling me then that you'd never leave me. But how can you say you will now?" Sitting up, he stared at me. His eyes searching for answers. "It's not gratitude I'm feeling, Emily, its love." Letting out a breath, he pleaded, "Death would be easier than losing you. Please, don't leave me now."

Shocked and scared beyond all comprehension, I'd already bared my soul to Caleb in the hills. Of course, he'd had a fever at the time and probably didn't remember all the details. I didn't want to have to go through it all again, but I would if it helped him understand my reasoning. Maybe my grandfather was right, and I could never go back to Seattle.

"Caleb, don't you remember me telling you my story when we were in the cabin?"

"Vaguely. I was in so much pain, and with the fever, I don't remember a lot of things."

Hesitantly, I answered, "All right. I'll tell you again. But, remember, this isn't easy for me." I doubted he would be as understanding when I got through. Sitting up straight, I clutched the coverlet to my chest. Chin up, I asked Caleb not to interrupt me until I'd finished. I didn't leave out one detail. Realizing I'd gone too far to stop now, as I proceeded on my no-going-back-confessional path.

Caleb sat stone silent. Waiting, he stared out the window. I grew concerned when he didn't face me. He must be trying to put the pieces of my puzzling life together. I'd asked him not to speak until I was done, but his silence now was killing me. *Why is he not saying something? He always interrupts me.* As the silence drew on, so did my trepidation. Wanting Caleb to say anything, even yell at me, telling me I was crazy, would be better than this.

Finished, out of fear of what Caleb would say, I, too, remained silent. Maybe it was the part of telling him that Doc Sweeney was my great-great-grandfather, and was the one who had brought me here. Or, perhaps it was that I thought I still had a life in 2019. My head was spinning with possibilities explaining his silence. I didn't know what to think. As the minutes ticked away, still Caleb said nothing. I couldn't wait any longer for him to speak. "So, you see Caleb, we're from two different centuries and worlds apart.

Quickly standing, Caleb plunged his hands deep into his front pockets. As if presenting his side of a legal case, he said, "I don't care where you came from or who you were before. All I know is that I can't lose you. Not now! Not ever!" Turning to face me, his face paled. "If you're planning on leaving, I'm going with you." Holding up his hands to stop me from speaking, he said, "I've made up my mind. You can't stop me."

Moving off the bed, I walked to Caleb's side. Taking his hands in mine, I looked into his pain-filled eyes and said, "There is nothing more I want right now than to have you by my side. But, Caleb, you have to understand what I left behind. If given the opportunity to go back, I need to try. Inhaling, I added painfully, "If you love me, you'll let me go."

"No! He said, pointing his finger at the floor. "This is where you belong. Here with me." Holding my shoulders tightly, as if anchoring him to me, he added, "I need to be with you Emily, forever. We'll find a way to make this work."

Could he see the love and pain warring behind my eyes? Pulling out of his grasp, I turned away. I was confused and couldn't continue arguing with him, so I gave him a vague answer. "O.K. Caleb. We'll discuss this later with clearer minds."

Standing, he took hold of my arms, determinedly pulling me against his chest. Staring into my eyes, he said, "Understand this, Emily Sweeney, with every breath I take, you're mine, and will be until I take my last."

Sighing, I closed my eyes, leaning into Caleb's loving embrace. Framing my face with his strong hands, Caleb's lips urgently crushed against mine, hungry and demanding. My mind reeled by the power he held over me. Deepening the kiss, I desperately needed to be loved by this man, as all arguments about returning to Seattle vanished.

Leaning my head back, he trailed tender kisses from my temple to the base of my neck, sending shivers deep to my inner core. Lacing my hands around his neck, I pulled him closer. Moving downward, his kisses gentled until he came to the tops of my breasts, stopping abruptly as warm air escaped his lips. For the life of me, I couldn't control my rapid breathing.

"Tell me to stop, and I will," he whispered in my ear. Staring into his dark smoky eyes, I trembled and shook my head no. "No, don't stop!" Was I doing the right thing? *Yes!* I wanted to shout at the top of my lungs. I wasn't thinking, I was feeling; safe for the first time in my new life. Clutching the front of Caleb's shirt, his quaking kiss was my undoing. Holding onto passion beyond my wildest dreams, I wouldn't let go. Feeling the rapid beat of his heart under my palms, I was consumed with overwhelming joy as we took possession of each other's bodies, hearts, and souls.

As the winter sun shone through the gossamer curtains, I stretched my arms over my head, remembering last evening. Smiling, I reached over to find Caleb's side of the bed empty. I was upset to find him gone. I should have said no to Caleb's advances. But I hadn't. I'd wanted last night as much as he did.

Quickly donning my dressing gown, I mumbled what I was going to say to Caleb as I descended the back stairs to the kitchen. He wasn't going to get away professing his love just to get into my bed, then leave me in the early hours of the morning.

Stopping mid-flight, the realization hit. *Wasn't that what I was going to do? Leave him without any explanations?* Continuing slowly down the back stairs, gave me time to formulate what I would say. Reaching the bottom tread, I heard male voices in the kitchen. Not like me to eavesdrop, I couldn't help it. Caleb and my grandfather were speaking in hushed tones. Straining, I heard my name mentioned. My grandfather was saying to Caleb that he didn't want me to go. He wanted, no, he needed me to stay in Yuma with him.

"Son," I heard him say to Caleb, "I was probably wrong in bringing her here, but she's the only link to a family I have." Sensing my grandfather's wavering voice, I held my breath as he continued, "I'm an old man. I won't be around much longer."

Perching myself on the stairs, I leaned against the wall listening more intently to my grandfather's distressed voice. "I know it was selfish of me. But I want her here. Can you understand that I truly believe I did the right thing in bringing her here?"

I could only see Caleb's shadow reflected on the kitchen wall as he spoke, taking note of what he said. "Doc, I love your grand-daughter more than life itself. I'm not letting her go anywhere! She's staying right here with me. With us."

Caleb must have moved because I heard a chair scrape across the wood floor, and his shadow disappeared from the wall. Watching a shorter shadow traverse the room, I heard my grandfather say, "I believe she loves ye just as much."

"Great," I thought. "Just great." My opportunity to return to Seattle just flew out the window. My grandfather had no intention of letting me go. The real question I should be asking myself was, could I really leave the two men I'd come to love?

33

Caleb

I FELT A SENSE of relief after having declared my love for Emily to her grandfather. Now, all I needed to do was go back upstairs and tell Emily the truth about my past. This could be the breaking point in our already tentative relationship, and I could lose her forever.

With a heavy heart, I stood outside the closed door to the room we shared the night before. Palms sweating, a feeling of dread stole into my heart as I tapped on the door.

"Come in." Sitting in front of the mirror plaiting her thick silky hair, Emily was resplendent in a bright yellow calico with pink rosebuds blooming over the bodice. She took my breath away, and all my restraint to remain standing at the entrance.

Looking into the mirror, she could see that I hadn't moved past the entry. "You can come in, you know. I won't bite."

Rubbing the back of my neck, I moved across the room with heavy footsteps to stand directly behind her. Seeing her ethereal reflection in the mirror, there was no easy way to begin this conversation.

"Emily, we . . . I mean, I need to speak with you." Motioning to the chair next to her, I watched as she nodded her consent.

"What is it, Caleb? Are you not feeling well? Did last evening . . ." She didn't finish. Instead, a pink blush bloomed across her cheeks. Did she have regrets about last night?

"No. There's nothing wrong, physically." Clearing my throat, "It's time I told you about who I really am. I owe you that much." Holding my breath, I added, "Especially after last night."

"Caleb, you don't owe me any explanations. We're both adults. We knew what we were doing. It won't happen again."

There it was—the twisting of the knife. Wounded from Emily's stabbing comment, I couldn't give in to the emotional pain. I would continue on with what I needed to say. Moving about the room, I stopped, turning to face her. She had been watching me in the mirror walk back and forth, deepening the line in the already worn carpet. I began the best way I knew how, from the beginning.

I didn't recognize the hiccupping pitch of my voice. "Emily, there was another woman in my life. I . . . ah, thought I loved her." Thinking this conversation was over before it even started, I looked directly at her, wanting her to stop me. When she didn't, I struggled to continue.

"The life I knew since childhood ended five years ago when I made what some would call a disgraceful and scandalous choice involving a woman." I watched as Emily raised her eyebrows. "My father was the late Mr. Westerly Young, a Harvard Law School graduate, and well-respected Boston attorney. I was born into wealth with the proverbial silver spoon in my mouth. I'll admit, at one time, I enjoyed that life of affluence. But my father was a hard-driven man with little time for his family."

I'd started a story that demanded a finish despite my fatigue. So, I sat in the rocker. Leaning forward, elbows on my knees, I surged on. "My father and mother had an arranged societal marriage merging two prominent Boston families. It was strictly a business deal. Unfortunately, despite my father's cold nature, my mother's only real fault was that she actually loved her husband, and it killed her."

Emily sent me a questioning look. "Well, not in the literal sense. But I believe my father's disrespect and overwhelming lack of attention, not to mention his ostentatious flaunting of his many mistresses, sent her to an early grave. The only love shared in our family was between my mother, my sister, and myself. She lived as long as she did because she wanted to keep us safe from our father's volatile temper." Holding back years of pent-up anger, I remained calm. "To my father, my mother was there only to make his life comfortable socially and share his bed when he wasn't satisfied with his mistresses. He wasn't capable of loving anyone but himself and his money."

I watched as Emily sat stone-cold-still, her vacuous gaze unreadable from where I stood. *Why doesn't she say something? No, I don't want her to interrupt me.*

The pain was still fresh as I inhaled deeply. "Shortly after our mother died. And definitely not within society's 'proper mourning period,' my father took himself a young bride named Anna Bennett, the daughter of a wealthy Boston banker, and a woman half his age. Of course, it was another arranged societal marriage. Miss Bennett was looking to live a comfortable and prosperous life, and my father, well, let's just say it was for his unquenchable physical needs. Again, love never figured into the arrangement."

"Foolishly, like my father, I couldn't help myself. I was drawn to Anna like a moth to a flame. Still, I couldn't betray my father as much as I despised him. But the new Mrs. Young had other plans. She was a well-played vixen who wouldn't leave me alone. Trying to seduce me became a game for her, one she had no intention of losing."

"She spent nights taunting me across the dinner table as my father sat by oblivious. Soon her game turned to lust, and I inanely became her pawn. I started making excuses to stay away from the dinner table. Even that didn't work. Living under the same roof, albeit a large one, and floors apart, I still couldn't escape her temptations."

Finally, Emily asked, "Why didn't you leave?"

"Looking back, I should have. But, I was young, reckless, and becoming just like my father. If he found out, he would have disinherited both my sister and me and destroyed my career. Unknowingly, my sister was his bargaining chip, and I couldn't let that happen."

Emily only nodded. I hoped she understood.

"One night, Anna came to my room. Thankfully, one of the maids came down the hall at the same time and saw her standing at my door. After a brief conversation, Anna left, but not before telling me that it wasn't over between us. She said something to the effect of, 'I always win.'"

"So, I'm supposed to feel sorry for you up to this point? Because, if I am, I'm not. You should have shown better judgment." Turning back to the mirror, Emily picked up her brush, running it through the hair I remembered holding last night with its scent of fresh lilacs. Raising her index finger at me, she added, "Not that you're any different from any other man in the same situation."

Well, I'd been put in my place! Starting to rise, I gave her a quick answer, "Fine. I won't bore you with any more details."

"Wait," Emily said, looking up at my reflection in the mirror. "Please continue."

Swallowing a lump in my throat, "Alright. If you're sure? Anna's taunting continued, until finally, one rainy night, she found me in a darkened hallway leading to the basement. She was a mystical woman, and I could no longer resist her advances and hypnotic charms."

That certainly got Emily's attention. Her lips forming a thin line, she glared up at me.

Catching the hint, I instantly regretted calling Anna 'mystical' and 'hypnotic' in front of the *only* woman I loved. "I won't go into details, other than to say that I made one of the biggest mistakes of my life that summer night, while my father slept in his bed, alone, one floor below."

Emily, came that familiar voice. *Are you going to let what Caleb's telling you get in the way of loving him?*

"Hush. Not now!" Emily replied.

"Did you say something?"

"No. No. Continue," Emily said with a shooing motion. "Wait. You said it was 'one' of your biggest mistakes. What were the others?"

"I'm getting to them." Bowing my head, I shuffled my feet then stared into her violet eyes. I wanted so badly to pull Emily into my arms and ask her forgiveness. But, now wasn't the time if I was going to finish.

"At the time, I was willing to sacrifice anything to be with Anna. Including my father's revenge. I knew what I was doing was a sin, but I hated my father so much from his years of emotional abuse, it didn't matter. Then, one evening, when I was in my study alone, my father came to speak with me, telling me he didn't like the way I was treating his wife. I almost spilled the glass of bourbon I was holding across my desk."

It felt good to be free of all this baggage. I believed my painful confession to Emily was the catharsis I needed to move forward with my life. I found myself standing in front of the only window in Emily's room. Looking out, I continued. "My father always dressed impeccably, despite being a rotund man. When he entered my office that night, he didn't look well. His face was red and puffy, and he was having difficulty breathing." Turning to Emily, I posed, "You want to know what I hated most about our conversation that night?" Emily only shook her head from side to side. "My father dared to tell me that Anna was my stepmother, and I should show her some respect. I was thirty-six years old for heaven's sake! What was he thinking? I was so furious over his disrespect for my mother, I almost choked him to death right there and then. Little did he know, his young wife was most certainly not my stepmother.

Calming, my father and I talked more until Anna flowed into the room in all her billowing glory, unaware her husband was standing behind her at the bar. Walking to my desk, she proceeded to, shall I say, ply her skills at trying to get me up to her room."

Hesitating, I searched Emily's eyes for what, I didn't know. Forgiveness? Acceptance? I couldn't tell if she was coming to hate me with every word I spoke, or if she was hiding her sympathy for a man who'd made some irresponsible choices in his past.

"My father heard every word Anna said. He became a raging mad man, someone I'd never seen before. I knew he could be cruel, but this was different. After throwing his drink in Anna's face, he backhanded her, causing her to fall to the floor. Before I could get around my desk to intervene, Anna's face was bloody and red."

Emily sat quietly on the edge of her seat, where I watched her hand tremble and twist in her lap. Again, I wanted to take her in my arms, but if I did, I wouldn't be able to finish. She deserved to hear it all.

"I was able to pull my father off Anna when he started beating on me. Arms flailing, I allowed the punches to hit home, thinking this was my retribution for betraying him. Before I knew it, he'd picked up a crystal pitcher from the bar and held it over Anna's head. I knew what he was about to do and couldn't allow it. So, I shoved him back. Realizing too late what I'd done, I reached out, trying to halt his fall. But, he hit the back of his head on the edge of the bar with a resounding thud that will haunt me till my dying day."

Standing before Emily penitent, I added, "As much as I wanted to kill him that night, I didn't. It was an accident. You have to believe me, Emily."

Placing her palm on my forearm, "I'm so sorry, Caleb. I do believe you."

"My only saving grace was that Mrs. Haggerty, our housekeeper, heard the yelling and had come to investigate. She entered the room just as my father was raising the pitcher, and I intervened." Catching my breath, "An inquest followed that declared my father's death an accident."

Emily now stood next to me and said, "You couldn't have known your father was going to die."

"No, you're right, I couldn't. But what Anna and I did after that is the most disgusting thing of all. Now a young widow, I immediately asked her to marry me." Shaking my head, "Just like my father, I didn't wait the appropriate time for mourning." Shrugging, "Not that I would have mourned."

"Did you get married?" Emily asked.

I laughed, "No. You could say that I was saved once again."

"What do you mean?"

"Well, I came to find out from my household staff, that Anna had been having an affair and cheating on both my father and myself, with of all people, our law partner." Opening my arms wide, "How ironic. What is it they say, what goes around, comes around? I'd become my father, and Anna had played me like the fool I was."

I had more to tell. But, I wondered if Emily could ever forgive me?

"Having been blinded by lust, I told myself then that I would never again let myself succumb to another woman's charms. So, I started drinking to numb the memories." I was in pain from all the pacing, so I sat on the edge of the bed, and continued, "I no longer had the patience to deal with my law practice and life around me. Gone was my love for the law. In the process, I'd lost the respect of my peers, my clients, and my friends. Life as I knew it was over. The only one who still loved me and became the one constant in my life was my sister Rebecca."

Hanging my head, "I was humiliated and angry at the world. So, I walked away from it all. No more life as a well-respected Boston attorney. No more of the physical, emotional, and social comforts that money could buy. No more taking chances with love. I had to get as far away as possible.

"So, you see Emily, I took what little dignity I had left. I packed whatever I could fit into my grandfather's old carpetbag, and left Boston and the whisperers behind. My only regret was not telling my sister where I was going. I bought a one-way train ticket west and never looked back." Laughing, I added, "I'd never been on a horse or shot a gun before in my life, until heading out west. Hating who I was, I became a gambler, not only with cards but with my life as well."

Emily stood in front of me, gazing into my eyes. If she was angry, she wouldn't be this close. Would she? Could she understand all I'd said and still forgive me? Please, God, don't let her leave me now.

"Caleb, we all have pasts that we're not proud of. I don't think there is anyone that can say they don't have some regrets they wish they could change." Clearing her throat, Emily proceeded, "I have a strong faith that our life is a gift from God; what we do with that life is our gift to Him. He doesn't care for us any less because of our misguided decisions." Patting her palm gently on my chest, she added, "It's what's in your heart that counts. And, it's up to us, standing here in this room, to make the best choices we can for the future. Our future, together."

Pulling Emily tightly against my chest, I needed to feel the heart I loved beat close to mine. Telling her my story had finally freed the demons from my past, clearing the way for our future together.

34

Abigail

I T WAS CHRISTMAS EVE, and I was preparing for one of the busiest days in the saloon. Without the usual atmosphere of loud music, card playing, and drinking, I planned on a quiet day celebrating the sacred holiday. The miners without families depended on the saloon's annual festivities and the meals we served.

This year, in particular, I didn't want any drunken behavior, so liquor was banned for twenty-four hours. Henry, my bartender, and my dearest friend was in full agreement. He, too, was in no mood to break up brawls. My girls were thrilled to be dressed like the other townswomen in pretty floral calicos with lace trim and higher than usual necklines. Most of them had no family, or at least family that would admit to what their daughters or sisters did for a living. So, they were happy to stay, serve the meals, and provide congenial companionship.

The girls had spent their free time during the year knitting. Yes, I said, knitting! Socks of all colors were decked on the saloon's scraggly Christmas tree. All to be given to the miners at the end of the meal. They looked forward to the holiday event, feeling it was the least they could do to bring some joy into their patrons' lives.

The day before, I had felt uneasy spending most of the day in my room. Awakening early, I lay abed, staring up as the sun cast dust fairies on the ceiling. Stretching, I was greeted with a thump, roll, and another thump from my baby. Rising, I leaned back, trying to stretch my waist and relieve the discomfort in my lower back that seemed a bit more intense this morning. Slipping out of my nightdress, I stood naked in front of the full-length mirror, placing my hands over my abdomen. The womb within me protected and nurtured the life Anders and I had created. I couldn't help but be amazed at the precious gift I carried when I was rewarded with a stronger kick. Speaking softly to my cherished babe, "Once you arrive my sweet, we'll leave this town and start a new life together. Just you and me."

Looking back into the mirror, sadness filled my heart at the thought of leaving Anders. But, if he didn't love me, I couldn't place upon him the burden of caring for an unwed mother and child, he may not believe to be his. He'd made it clear that he just wanted to be friends and nothing more. According to Anders, the one night we'd spent together had been a mistake.

I had put a great deal of thought into how my baby and I would survive. I had some money saved up, plus the sale of the saloon would get us to California on the train, where I hoped to purchase a small home on the coast. I'd always wanted to see the Pacific Ocean. Posing as a young widow, no one would ever need to know of my past. Thinking of a future without Anders was painful. But, I would always love the stubborn Swede.

Donning layers of petticoats made of the softest balbriggan and a French lace-trimmed camisole, I sat down at my dressing table to apply a just hint of rouge and plait my hair. Wiping my damp eyes, I looked at the corset lying on a chair next to the armoire. I was so grateful for having relieved myself of it months ago after no longer being able to cinch the stays. Hang propriety, I thought, chuckling to myself, "I may never put it on again."

Rounding my four-poster bed, I was suddenly gripped with intense pain in my lower abdomen. Grabbing hold of the intricately carved bedpost with one hand and clutching my rotund belly with the other, I leaned forward, struggling to catch my breath. It was no use as the pain intensified. "God, no," I cried, looking heavenward. "This can't be happening. It's too soon. I'm supposed to have three more weeks to go. Its Christmas tomorrow, and I have too much to do."

As soon as I was able to stand upright, my breathing eased, allowing me to move to the other side of the bed where I had laid out my best holiday gown. It was red satin with ecru-trimmed lace, the same one I'd worn the first time I'd met Anders. Recently, one of my girls with seamstress talents had taken out the seams and added extra fabric, redesigning it into an empire waist to accommodate my expanding waistline. Smiling, I remembered how Anders had looked at me that day, commenting on how the dress paled in comparison to my beauty. I'd fallen in love with the handsome man, right there and then.

Holding up the camisole, ready to slip it over my head, another wave of pain struck—this one a bit stronger than the last. Attempting to slow my breathing down, I tried concentrating on something other than the pain. Giving up being stoic, I gripped the bedpost with both hands until my knuckles turned white. "Whew, that definitely was a stronger one." Wiping the dampness from under my eyes, I told myself, "I'm sure they'll go away."

Feeling huge, I was tired of being pregnant. Sleep was elusive. Cranky and feeling alone, with swollen feet no longer visible past my protruding abdomen, was getting to be too much. Thoughts that this baby would never come had been haunting my nightly dreams.

I was up, what seemed like every hour to use the chamber pot, and worst of all, the man I loved was as distant as ever. "Dang that clueless Swede!"

My knowledge of birth came from caring for my girls. I never called them 'soiled doves' or 'prostitutes.' I loathed such defiling terms. Despite having been dealt a cruel hand in life, I adored them all. Now, they were fussing over and taking care of me like mother hens.

Truth be told, I was terrified. I never knew my mother. My father told me she had died shortly after giving birth to me. If this was labor, I feared I was destined to the same fate. I couldn't imagine leaving my child motherless.

Dressed, I descended into the smoke-filled room. Head held high, one hand beneath my abdomen, the other on the smooth wooden rail. Waiting for me at the bottom was my dear sweet Henry. He had been my one true constant since I'd acquired the saloon. More like a father than a friend, I walked towards him, seeing the worried look on his face. *Remain calm Abigail, then reassure Henry that I'm fine, and we can enjoy the day.*

"Good morning Miss Abigail," one of my girls called out.

"Good morning Cynthia. How are you this morning?" Usually, not one for small talk, I felt it necessary to keep my mind off the contractions. Moving behind the bar, I spoke with Henry to finalize plans for Christmas dinner. Leaning back against the unforgiving wood for support, another contraction crested. Trying to control my breathing, I placed both hands behind my back, taking one slow breath in, letting one slow breath out. Sighing with relief when the contraction was over. *This day is not starting out as I planned.*

Henry wasn't fooled. "Another contraction?" he asked, touching my arm.

"What?" I replied. *How does he know?*

Coming to stand in front of me, "Listen, missy, you can't fool this ole' mule. When the contractions start coming closer, we need to let Doc Sweeney know. Just give me a holler. Understand?" he added, eyebrows raised.

"Yes, Henry," I replied, dropping my eyes as if I was adequately scolded. "You're too good to me," I said, squeezing his hand. "What would I ever do without you?" Leaning up on tiptoes, I placed a quick kiss on his cheek.

Henry smiled. Since no one was watching us, he placed a fatherly kiss on my brow, then turned away. Oh, how I was going to miss that man when I left. It made my heart ache just thinking about it. During the next hour, I had several more contractions that were milder. Still, I was able to keep the saloon patrons from knowing how I felt—all except for Henry, who watched me intently.

Around one o'clock in the afternoon, I came to a standstill while wiping off a table at the back of the room. Lightheaded, a warm flush cloaked me from head to toe. My legs weakened, and I had a sudden need to sit down. Before I did, I turned towards Henry, mouthing his name. The glass he was drying crashed to the floor. Stepping over the broken pieces, he rushed to my side, grabbing my arms, "Abbie, what's wrong?"

I was thankful he was holding me, or I would have slumped to the floor. My gaze drifted downward. Henry's followed. At my feet was a puddle of water. My shoes and stockings were soaking wet, along with the front of my beautiful dress. Looking back up, I was unable to get any words past my lips. Finally, I managed to say, "I think my water just broke."

"It's OK honey. It just means that you're going to be a mother soon." As he pulled me into an embrace, I tried to look pleased, but he was scaring me, as he held me tighter.

Staring at Henry's ashen face, I knew past memories of his wife and daughter dying shortly after giving birth were crashing into him like a raging bull. The fear of my impending delivery was probably more than he could handle at the moment. Still, I knew he would remain calm for me, doing whatever necessary to keep my baby and me alive.

"Henry, no. It's too soon. Doc Sweeney says I'm not due for another three weeks. I'm terrified," I pleaded, clutching the front of his shirt. "What if something happens to the baby or me?"

Enfolding me in his arms, "Now girl, don't go asking for trouble." His head was on top of mine as he added, "You and the baby are going to be just fine. Trust me." Henry yelled across the room, "Cynthia!"

The young girl came running, eager to please as always. "Yes, Mr. Calhoun."

"Go tell the girls to get Abbie's room ready for her. They'll know what to do. Then run over to the clinic and bring back Doc Sweeney. Tell him Miss Abigail's water broke."

Cynthia stood staring at me with her doe-like brown eyes, then down at the pool of liquid surrounding my feet. Asking no questions, she turned to do Henry's bidding.

Shaking uncontrollably in his arms, I clung to Henry as another contraction crested, more intense now that the cushion of water was gone. Another gush hit the floor between us as I saw my reflection of fear in Henry's eyes.

Shaking my head from side to side, I pleaded with him, "Henry. I can't do this."

Exuding calm, he whispered, "Honey, you have no choice."

"What am I going to tell Anders?" I asked through muffled sobs.

Pushing me back, Henry asked, "You mean to tell me you never let Anders know he was going to be a father?"

"No. I was too scared," I answered, laying my head on Henry's chest.

"Oh good heavens," he responded, shaking his head. "Well, I'll take care of it." Lifting me in one fluid motion, he carried me up the stairs. Inside, my girls were waiting. Leaving me in their care, he kissed my brow and left the room, cursing under his breath. I knew he was just as afraid as I was.

Henry

Downstairs, I washed and re-washed the same glass several times, when finally Cynthia came walking through the swinging doors with Caleb in tow. Staring past them, I looked for Doc Sweeney. Not seeing him, panic set in. "Where's the Doc?"

"He'll be right over as soon as he gets together everything he needs. He shouldn't be but a few more minutes."

Sighing with relief, I determinedly rubbed the bar top over and over.

The room was relatively quiet as I watched Caleb look around. There were still men playing cards in the corner. The piano sat silent, and not a drop of whiskey or beer was being served. Caleb asked, "What's going on? Why don't you just shut the place up?"

"I would have, but none of them want to leave." I shrugged, pointing to the miners, "As long as they behave, they can wait with the rest of us for the baby. Surprisingly, they don't even mind that I've banned liquor until afterward."

I stopped rubbing the bar top when I had an idea. "Caleb, would you do me a favor and go over to the jail and have the sheriff come right over?"

"Sure. What should I tell him?"

Crossing my arms over my chest, I hesitated. Do I tell Caleb the truth? I hated to put him in an uncomfortable situation, but I wasn't going to leave the bar right now. "Tell him he's about to become a father." *Serves him right to find out this way.*

"A father!" Caleb yelled. "Henry, I'm not so sure I . . ."

Before he could finish, I issued an order. "You heard me right. Now get a move on, and get that sheriff over here. Now!"

Caleb

"Yes sir," I whistled sharply. "But, I'm still not so sure I should be the one telling him." Henry gave me that look that told me not to ask any more questions. Smiling like a Cheshire cat, I crossed the street, thinking this may be my payback for having the sheriff chase me out of town. Talking to myself, I tried formulating the best way to broach this delicate subject. "How can the sheriff not know? I'd want to know if Emily was pregnant with our child. Of course, there would be no way of me not knowing since I would have been . . . wait! Could there ever be a question?" Stopping midstride, my heart skipped a beat as I thought, "A baby with Emily would be wonderful."

Never having been at a loss for words in the courtroom, for the life of me, I couldn't think of a way to start the conversation with the sheriff. Continuing across the street, I practiced what I was going to say. "Sheriff, Miss Abigail is in labor." No. No, that wouldn't do. The sheriff would be wondering who the father is. I continued to play out my options. I could just say, "Henry and Miss Abigail need you in the saloon." But then the sheriff would just tell me he was busy and would be over when he had the time. No matter how I put this, it wasn't going to be pretty. Standing at the jail's closed door, I took a deep breath to calm my nerves, then knocked.

"Come in," came a resounding voice behind the door. Letting myself in, Sheriff Johansson came around his desk to stand before me. Something I hadn't noticed that fateful day in the saloon was now that we stood toe to toe, eye to eye, the sheriff was an imposing man.

Reaching out his hand, I clasped it with my sweaty palm, as he said, "Mr. Young, tis gudt ta see jar up and around. Must be feeling better?"

"Yes, sir I'm feeling much better." Hat in hand, I shuffled my feet in one place. As a lawyer, I had faced dozens of defendants, plaintiffs, and jurors in court. Yet, I couldn't remember ever being this nervous. "Sir, we need to talk," motioning to a chair. I desperately needed to sit down before I hastily retreated.

Sitting back at his desk, he motioned for me to take a seat. "I vas yust getting ready to leave. Vhat's so important tat ve can't talk outside while ve valk?"

Despite the temperature outside, having dropped about ten degrees, my face heated. "Ah, sir, I think it's better if we stay in your office for now. It's of a personal matter."

"No vone's been hurt, have tey? I haven't hert any gunshots. No mine explosion?"

I remained standing, seeing the concern written all over the sheriff's face. Rocking back on my heels, I answered him, "No, sir, they haven't." I felt my stomach flip. *Not yet, anyway.*

"Vell, vhat ist it, man? Vhat's so secretive tat ve havt ta talk in my office? I vas yust going to ride over to te Meeker ranch. It seems they're having trouble with a few miss'g cattle.

Rustlers, or someting." Leaning forward in his chair, he waited for me to speak.

"Henry sent me over."

At the mention of Henry's name, the sheriff's clenched his fists on the top of his desk. I deduced that mentioning Henry's name was the same as saying Abigail's. I could see that he was doing his best to remain calm when he asked, "Henry? Vhat's tat ol' coot vant?"

"Henry wants you to come to the saloon right away." Dropping my voice to a muffled tone, I rushed out without taking a breath. "Miss Abigail's in labor, and you're going to be a father." That certainly got the sheriff's attention. Maybe, more than I wanted.

"I'm vhat?" Standing up, papers flew across the floor. "Did you yust say Abbie's in labor? How can that be?"

"Ah," I stuttered, "Sheriff, I hope I don't need to explain how that works."

"Did you yust say I'm going to be a vatter?" The sheriff's color went from bright red to white in mere seconds as he repeated, "I'm going to be a vatter," dropping back into his chair.

"Yes, sir. That about sums it up," I smiled.

Before I could say anything more, Sheriff Johansson was up and at the jail's door, grabbing his hat, coat, and guns. Turning, he yelled at me, "Vell, are ya coming or not?"

Following close on the sheriff's heels, we moved through the batwing doors, causing them to slam loudly against the wall, garnering everyone's attention.

Stomping his way to the bar, the sheriff looked directly into Henry's eyes, and asked,

"Vhat in tarnation man do ya mean I'm going to be a vatter?" Slamming his fist on the bar, he continued, "Abbie never tolt me it was my baby. I should have known by now."

Henry looked at the sheriff's perplexed expression and said, "Well, I can't help it if you're too dim-witted and blind to see how much she loves you." Henry's eyes smoldered with anger, and I could see he wanted to throttle the sheriff.

35

Caleb

I WATCHED DOC SWEENEY walk into the saloon, finding Henry and Anders staring intensely at each other. Thankfully, the bar was between them. Walking over to me, Doc asked, "I take it the sheriff just found out he's going to be a father?"

Leaning in close, so only he could hear, "You'd be right on that, Doc." Rubbing a dull pain in my side, I placed my hat back on my head, before taking a sidelong glance. "What I don't understand is how that man could not have known he was going to be a father. Anyone with eyes in their head can see how he looks at Miss Abigail. What kind of relationship does he have with her?"

"I can't say. But, it seems te be a bit complicated." Making a move to head upstairs, the doc turned back to me and added, "Like they say, love is't blind."

With his last remark, was he hinting at Emily and me? "Well, I wish him luck finding his way, since it looks like Henry is ready to peel the hide right off him." Chuckling, I let Doc know I was heading back to the clinic. "I'll leave you to do whatever it is you do with pregnant women."

Doc grinned, moving past Anders and Henry's stare down, making his way up the stairs.

Emily

A loud knock, then the front door of the clinic flew open before I had a chance to answer it. Quickly stepping back, before me stood a sizable woman dressed in a faded feed sack dress covered with a dirty apron. Clinging to her leg was a towheaded boy, tears streaming down his dirty pudgy cheeks. I couldn't help but smile at the sprite of a boy. I turned my attention to the woman whose pale complexion indicated she was ready to faint. Extending her left arm, crudely wrapped in a bloody towel, she muttered something in a thick German accent. Both Caleb and I rushed to her side, guiding her into Doc's surgical suite as her small boy held firmly to the hem of her threadbare dress, trying to keep up.

I didn't know the woman's name, but with some coaxing, we heard her say, "Mueller." It was good enough since I didn't have the luxury of an interpreter like I used in Seattle.

Removing the bloody towel and dropping it in a basin, I replaced it with a clean compress, instructing Caleb to keep steady pressure on it. "It looks like a nasty laceration. She'll need stitches. But first, I'll need to flush out the wound with some clean, warm water." Looking at Caleb, I said, "I'll hold the compress if you would get me the kettle of water off the stove and a bottle of whiskey. The water should have cooled down enough since breakfast."

Raising an eyebrow, Caleb asked, "Is the whiskey for you or me, Doc?"

I gave him that 'Really?' look and turned my attention back to my patient.

"Sorry," he answered, looking contrite. "If it's not cool, do you want me to add some cold water from the pump?"

"No. Adding water directly from the pump without boiling it would only introduce bacteria." Finally, in my element, I was feeling needed, even if it was in a small way.

Caleb returned with the kettle when I asked him to apply pressure on Mrs. Mueller's wound. At the same time, I prepared the suture and sterilized the instruments in the alcohol. Noticing his pallid complexion, I asked, "Mr. Young, are you all right, or do you need to sit down and have a sip of that whiskey?"

A grin creased the sides of his face, as he answered, "As nice as that sounds, I should be fine. Just give me a second, then tell me what to do."

"Take some slow deep breaths, Mr. Young, and hold Mrs. Mueller's arm still while I finish cleaning the wound." The suture in hand, I nodded my head to Mrs. Mueller then inserted the sharp, curved needle under the stoic lady's tender flesh. Just as I did, the bell over the clinic door rang for the second time that morning.

"Caleb, would you mind seeing who that is? I'm fine here." I couldn't help but notice the look of relief on his face knowing I'd given him a reprieve from his messy task.

I was left smiling at Mrs. Mueller, who remained quiet and looked somewhat unsure about having a woman doctor attend to her injury. Wasting no time, I deftly worked on the wound, having it cleaned, sutured, and bandaged in less than fifteen minutes. I did my best at instructing Mrs. Mueller on the care of her injury, and to return to the clinic in two weeks to have the sutures removed. Or sooner if she had any questions. I just hope she understood.

Smiling and nodding her head several times, Mrs. Mueller and her son walked out the back door of the clinic. Grinning, I realized I had just treated my first patient in 1880 without twenty-first-century accoutrements.

I hurried through cleaning up the instruments in case I needed them before my grandfather returned. Finished, I went into the parlor to see what the earlier commotion was about. Caleb was standing in the doorway with his arms around an elegantly dressed woman who happened to be clinging to him for dear life, sobbing. On the couch sitting quietly were two handsome young boys. Was this the infamous Anna that Caleb had talked about? He hadn't mentioned having sons. But there was some resemblance.

Gray clouds cast an opaque haze through the open front door, and my heart seized with a pang of jealousy at seeing another woman in Caleb's arms. Gracefully, I made my way into the room, coming to stand next to the settee. Crossing my arms in front of my chest, I waited for Caleb to notice me. When he did, he kept his arm around the raven-haired beauty causing me to clench my teeth. I tried not to say anything that would embarrass myself.

Taking his eyes off the woman he held, Caleb said to me, "I almost forgot to tell you. Doc said you're in charge while he's gone."

Heart pounding, I didn't hear a word Caleb said, my concentration was focused on the woman he held entirely too close. Posture stiff, I cleared my throat and asked politely, "Mr. Young, aren't you going to introduce me to your guest?"

"Oh. Of course. I'm sorry," he said, reaching for the woman's hand. "Emily, may I introduce Mrs. Rebecca Ackerman."

I extended my right hand just as I recognized the name. "Why, you're Caleb's . . ."

"Rebecca's my sister," Caleb interjected, squeezing her shoulder. "Rebecca, this is Doctor Emily Sweeney." Rebecca extended her delicate pearlized hand, waiting for me to grasp it. Instead, I held out my arms, pulling her up and into my embrace. "Caleb, that's wonderful." Releasing Rebecca, I turned my attention to the couch. "And these two handsome young gentlemen are?"

"They're my nephews," Caleb answered smiling, pointing to each boy. "Porter and Daniel."

"It's nice to meet you both," I replied.

Rebecca whispered in my ear, "Thank you, Doctor Sweeney, for sending me the telegram and letting me know that Caleb was alive and recovering here in Yuma." Pulling back, she added, "It meant the world to me to get that telegram. I thought I would never see him again." Smiling up at Caleb, Rebecca entwined her arm through his, pulling him close to her side. Caleb beamed. It was apparent to me that brother and sister had been very close at one time, and still were.

Rebecca searched her brother's face, dabbing at her tear-filled eyes with a rose-embroidered handkerchief. "I can't even think of what my brother endured, let alone the possibility of him dying."

"Please, call me Emily. I asked Sheriff Johansson to send the telegram to Boston looking for you. But I never heard back. So, I didn't think you would come all this way from Boston, alone.

"It was quite the journey. But that's a story for another time. I had to come," Rebecca said, looking between Caleb and me. "Pearl came with me. I was so grateful to have her accompany us. She wouldn't let me travel alone with the boys. You remember Pearl, don't you, Caleb?"

"Yes, of course, I do. She is such a dear woman. Where is Pearl now?" he asked, looking towards the door.

"She took a room at the hotel. She wanted some time to freshen up, rest, and let us visit alone. Oh, Caleb, I missed you so much." Running her palm down the side of her brother's face, she continued, "Before I heard from Emily, I thought you were dead." Tears flowed down her cheeks. Caleb tenderly brushed them away. "You never wrote. Why?"

Caleb took hold of his sister's hands, leading her back to the couch. As she sat, he stood over her, "I didn't think you wanted anything to do with me after what happened. But that doesn't matter now. All I care about is that you and the boys are here and safe."

"Oh, Caleb, how can you think that? I'm your sister. I love you." Searching in her reticule for a dry handkerchief, coming up empty, tears continued to run unchecked down her cheeks. Caleb handed her his. "That woman you were going to marry was pure evil," Rebecca said with distaste. "God, forgive me, but she got what she deserved."

Eyebrows furrowed, Caleb asked, "What do you mean?"

"Of course. You wouldn't have any way of knowing," Rebecca answered, patting Caleb's hands. "Your former partner, who Anna had an affair with when she was . . . engaged to you." Looking at me for my reaction, Rebecca's voice caught. "It's a rather horrible story. But you need to know." Twisting the handkerchief repeatedly in her hands, she proceeded, "Your partner murdered her. Then killed himself. The police found them lying next to each other in his bedroom. They said he was still holding the gun."

I watched Caleb's face for his reaction wondering if he had regrets. Motionless, he didn't say a word.

Rebecca continued on with the sordid details of the affair and supposed murder-suicide. "It was horrible. It was in all the newspapers for weeks. Thank heavens, your name was never mentioned. What I heard was that he'd come home early from work one night and found her in bed, their bed, with another man."

Caleb just shook his head.

"That woman was never satisfied, even when she was with you. People talked that she had been seeing more than one man before being murdered. But it seems she was able to keep it secret from him until that horrible night. It must have been too much for your partner to endure, and he snapped." Pausing, "Gossipers said he was justified in killing Anna and saving another man from her infidelities. I guess he saw taking his own life better than spending the rest of it in prison."

Squeezing his eyes shut, "I'm sorry to hear that. I would have never wished her such a violent ending. How did her family take it?"

Head bent Rebecca answered, "Not well, of course. Both her father and mother died shortly after their daughter's death." Taking his hands in hers, "But, dear brother, I don't want to talk about her. I want to talk about you and how you're doing."

Tapping the seat next to her, she urged Caleb to sit. With a familiar show of endearment, Rebecca pushed a wayward lock of dark hair from his face. "Caleb, you must know, now that we've found each other again, I will never let you go. Ever. We're all the family we have left."

Caleb gave his sister a weak smile, then looked up at me as if trying to read my thoughts.

⤚§ 36 §⤙

Emily

I EXCUSED MYSELF FROM the parlor to fix the late breakfast I
was never able to make earlier when chaos struck. Calling from
the kitchen, "Rebecca, can I fix you some tea? And, would the boys
like a glass of milk?"

"That would be lovely," Rebecca answered. "Can I be of
help?"

"No, thank you. Caleb, I'll bring you some coffee." Smiling,
I thought how nice it would be to start every day bringing Caleb
his coffee. "Boys, why don't you join me in the kitchen so you're
Momma and Uncle Caleb can talk?"

Remembering what Caleb said about me being in charge, I
returned to the parlor and asked, "Did you say my Grand . . . I mean,
Doctor Sweeney left me in charge?"

"Yes, he did," Caleb answered, grinning.

Leaving the parlor again, I began talking to myself. "I need to speak with my grandfather about his clinic routines. What medicines he uses? Where does he get his supplies? What type of surgery he does? Suddenly, I realized my thoughts were those of a woman planning on staying in Yuma. For the first time, it felt right.

Caleb had left his sister in the parlor to follow the boys towards the kitchen. All three stood within the doorframe, watching me talk feverishly to myself. Pushing off, he moved into the kitchen. At his movement, I turned to face him. Placing his hands on my shoulders, he said, "Your grandfather left you in charge because he trusts you and knows you are an excellent physician."

I was afraid to respond. Fortunately, I wasn't given the opportunity when yet another knock came from the front door. "Now what?" I asked, raising my hands in frustration.

"Obviously, Doc, the town needs your services," Caleb answered. "You finish up here, and I'll see who it is."

He turned to leave when I stopped him. "Caleb. Thank you for your help earlier today with Mrs. Mueller. I really did appreciate it." Chuckling, I added, "Even though you can't stand the sight of blood."

"You'd be right about that, Doc," he patted my hand. Pointing towards the parlor, "I'd better go see who's at the door."

"Wait," I said, firming my hold on his arm. "I'm so glad that your sister is here. Now, you both can catch up." My hand moved up his sleeve as I added, "Don't let her out of your life again, Caleb. You need each other."

Caleb didn't answer but placed a gentle kiss on my brow. Turning, he left me staring after him.

"Oh, how I love that man."

Turning my attention to the boys, they gazed up at me with questioning looks. I wasn't about to explain what their Uncle meant to me. "I guess if there is any breakfast or lunch to be made, your momma is going to have to make it." Going back into the parlor, I found Caleb speaking with a pretty young girl, who obviously was from the saloon by the way she was dressed. "Is there something I can help you with?" I asked, standing next to Caleb, placing a declaring hand on his arm.

The look on her face confirmed she was frightened. Looking at me, she blurted out, "It's Miss Abigail." Pointing across the street to the saloon, "Doc Sweeney sent me to fetch yer over. He says there's something wrong with the baby."

Placing a sheltering arm around her shoulders, I brought her inside. "It's OK, you can relax. We'll help Miss Abigail." Not wanting to scare the girl further, I asked, "Has the baby been born yet?"

"No miss," the girl answered, standing on one foot then the other. "Poor Miss Abigail, she's doing a lot of screaming o'er there."

"OK. I just need to gather a few things before heading over." Facing Rebecca, I asked, "Would you mind taking care of this young lady while I'm gone?" *She is so young*

"I'd be delighted to," Rebecca replied, holding out her arms to the girl who rushed into her welcoming embrace, crying.

Caleb followed me into the surgical suite. "Doc, what can I help you with?"

"Nothing, thank you. I'm just going to retrieve some supplies since I don't know what difficulties my grandfather is having." That familiar adrenaline kicked in as I silently went through the motions I did every night before heading into the ER. Excited, I hadn't delivered a baby in quite some time.

"Caleb, there is something you could do. Would you please go to the saloon and let them know I'll be there shortly. And, can you tell whoever is there to have clean towels, clean basins, and clean sheets ready for me? Turning to gather the supplies, I added, "Oh, and please have someone boil a large pot of water. Better yet, two."

I would use one pot to sterilize instruments and the other to scrub my hands. I was excited to think, "What a perfect Christmas gift bringing a new life into the world."

Rebecca followed me into the surgery suite. "Is there anything I can do to help? Having delivered the boys, I could possibly be of assistance."

Placing my hand on Rebecca's arm, "No, I think we'll be fine. You stay here with your boys. Send the young girl back when she's ready. If I need anything, I'll send Caleb back."

Using one of my grandfather's leather medical bags, I placed everything I thought I would need into it as I continued to speak with Rebecca. "Please, make yourself comfortable. I started a late meal, but you'll have to finish it for yourself and the boys. I'm sure you're tired and would like to rest. The extra bedrooms are upstairs, and there's clean linen in the hall closet."

"Don't worry about us. We made it across the country by ourselves. We'll be fine here alone."

Smiling, "Since I'll probably be there several hours, I'll send Caleb back as soon as I can so you two can catch up. I don't want to keep him away from you too long."

Stopping at the door, I turned and gave Rebecca a hug. "I'm just so glad that you and the boys are here." Grabbing the heavy wool shawl from the hook near the front door, I headed out into the cold night air. Looking heavenward, I listened to the silence. Were my eyes playing tricks on me? Tiny snowflakes gently drifted down from the dark night sky. Holding my hand out, palm up, tiny cold flakes caressed my warm skin. Snow was unheard of here in Yuma. It certainly was turning out to be an unusual Christmas Eve.

It seemed like the saloon was miles away from the clinic when in actuality, it was just a short walk across the street. Smiling, I crossed the lightly snow-dusted road, wondering what type of father Caleb would make.

All too familiar with its interior, I walked through the saloon doors towards the stairs leading up to Miss Abigail's room. Caleb immediately came to my side, taking the heavy bag from my hands. "Everything is ready for you upstairs." Taking hold of my arm before I took the steps, Caleb placed a soft kiss on my lips, "You can do this, Doc."

Wanting more, I pulled away before I was lost in his embrace. Smiling, I noticed Henry restlessly pacing, a look of concern creasing his brow. Beside him stood Sheriff Johansson, pale as his sheepskin coat, staring blankly into the mirror behind the bar. If I didn't need to be professionally serious, I might have burst out laughing. Instead, I thought, *this was undoubtedly the strangest cast of characters for a Christmas Eve pageant.*

Caleb leaned in to whisper in my ear, "The sheriff just found out that he's the father."

"What!" I said, a bit too loudly, causing everyone in the room, including the sheriff, to look my way.

"Shush," Caleb said, taking my elbow. "I'll tell you more about it when we're alone."

I leaned in close and asked, "But how could he not have known?"

Shrugging, Caleb said, "Like your Granddad told me earlier, love is blind?"

Walking up the stairs, I knocked on the door, answered with a brusque, "Come in!" from my grandfather. Slowly pushing open the door, I was surprised at how elegantly appointed the room was. Rose wallpaper and lace curtains draped the windows from ceiling to floor. In the center of the room was a large four-poster bed where Abigail lay in the throes of labor.

I was pleased to see that in the far corner stood a small wood stove whose glowing embers filled the room with warmth. This was where I would keep a kettle boiling, and the baby blankets warmed. Abigail was surrounded by her girls. Her pale yellow hair with a hint of ginger, lay damp with sweat about her face. Her flushed cheeks paled in comparison to the rouge-painted faces of her girls. If I didn't know this was a saloon, this boudoir could be in any elegant Victorian home.

Abigail screamed as a contraction took hold of her delicate body. "I can't do this," she yelled.

"It's about time ye got here," my grandfather said harshly, trying to remain calm for Abigail's sake. Taking my arm, he moved us both to the farthest corner of the room and away from inquiring ears.

Reading the fear written all over his face, I asked in all seriousness, "What's happening?" Looking back at the bed, I felt for the woman who writhed in laboring pain. It was *the* most strenuous physical undertaking a woman would ever do.

"Te baby . . . ist too big. Tis not coming down like it should. I'm afraid it won't make it through te birth canal." Turning to look at Abigail, he squeezed my hands.

Reading his unspoken words, I said with self-assurance, "We're not going to lose them. Not if I can help it." Tugging on my grandfather's hands, bringing his attention back to me, "Do you trust me?"

"Ye know, I do."

"Then I'd like to examine Abigail. But you need to tell her I'm a doctor. I'm afraid she wouldn't take it well coming directly from me since the last time she saw me I was a bit out of sorts."

I saw Abigail look warily beyond my grandfather to me, then back at him, nodding her consent. Moving to the bedside, I explained to Abigail what I was about to do, receiving a short one-word response. It was all the consent I needed before proceeding with my exam. When complete, I took my grandfather back to the corner of the room to discuss my findings.

"I located the baby's heartbeat to the left, and above Abigail's umbilicus using your monaural stethoscope. The Leopold maneuver shows the baby is luckily vertex, but well above the outlet. You're right, it's not engaged. It's riding too high in Abigail's pelvis at this point in her labor. The baby's head seems much larger than the diameter of her pelvic outlet. It's most likely she won't be able to deliver vaginally. And with her water already broken . . ."

"That's what I thought," he said, pulling off his wire-rimmed glasses and pinching the bridge of his nose. "Have you performed a cesarean before?" he asked me, looking hopeful. "I've done a few in ta field, but not nearly enough were successful. I'm sorry to say that I've lost too many mothers and babes."

"I pray that won't happen here tonight," I said, patting the top of his hands. "I've assisted on a few cesareans during my obstetrical rotation, but it was always with the attending physician. That's why you'll be with me every step of the way." As if trying to escape the swiftly fluttering butterflies in my stomach, I turned my thoughts to what I had to do.

Squeezing his hands, "I believe we can do this. Together." Suddenly, I went from an observer to what I was trained to do, instructing my grandfather and the girls. Leaning over Abigail, I informed her of my exam findings and the need to do a cesarean. My heart ached at the look of terror in her widening eyes. I tried reassuring her as best I could. But, I understood her fear.

"Do what you must." Grabbing my hands, Abigail added, "Just save my baby."

I sent one of the girls downstairs to retrieve the sheriff. He needed to be here. While waiting, my grandfather and I stood over the metal basin, scrubbing our hands. The girls prepared Abigail by washing her abdomen with unscented soap, then covered her upper and lower body with clean sheets.

I'd chosen the most mature of the girls to administer the ether, with my grandfather instructing her. Of course, the ether would have to be light until after the baby was delivered. Neither of us wanted to risk depressed respirations in a baby that may be premature. The initial incision, the pulling and tugging to remove the baby, would more than likely cause Abigail unbearable discomfort. But once the baby was delivered, the amount of ether could be increased to complete the suturing.

A pale and terrified sheriff was escorted into the room when his gaze landed on a basket in the corner containing blood-tinged sheets.

I saw the panic and dread in his eyes as he dropped to his knees. "Oh, God. No, don't take her from me," he sobbed into his hands.

"Sheriff," I called loudly across the room, "What's wrong?"

"Why didn't ya tell me my Abbie died?"

"Sheriff, Abigail is not dead. Now, come over here and sit in the chair next to her head. Doc Sweeney and I are about to perform a cesarean delivery, and we haven't got time to explain." When I saw the sheriff's uncontrollable trembling, I added in a softer tone, "Anders, please take some slow deep breaths and hold Abigail's hands. You're going to do fine."

The sheriff sniffed back tears and nodded as he looked at the draped sheets covering Abigail's perfectly rounded belly enfolding the life the two had made.

Vermin and Stubbs

Stubbs and I stood in the dark shadows of the alley across from the saloon, watching and waiting in the cold stillness of Christmas Eve. Tonight would be the night we'd make our move.

$$\text{\textit{37}}$$

Emily

CHRISTMAS MORNING AND the clock standing in the corner of Abigail's room chimed three. Still the middle of the night as far as I was concerned. The successful surgery and delivery produced a beautiful baby girl whom the parents named Holly Christine in honor of the holiday. After cleaning up, I hugged my grandfather and whispered in his ear that our prayers had been answered. He informed me he was going to stay with Abigail and the baby for a few hours to make sure they were doing well. Recovery was going to be slow, albeit painful for Abigail. Barring any postpartum complications, she should do well with help from Anders and her girls.

Exhausted, I thanked my grandfather then headed downstairs, finding Caleb sound asleep at one of the tables with his head resting on his arms. I was touched that he'd stayed and waited for me this long night, knowing he should have been back at the clinic visiting with his sister or sleeping. Placing my hand on his shoulder, he startled out of deep sleep.

Reaching for his gun, which never left his side, I jumped back as he awakened, realizing it was me that had touched him. Stretching, he graced me with a warm smile. Reaching out, he pulled me into the safety of his embrace. Just having him hold me at that moment made everything right in my world.

I looked over his shoulder to see every remaining person in the bar standing around us waiting anxiously for news of the birth. Finally, I announced, "Merry Christmas. It's a girl!"

Whoops, and hollers went up around the room as Henry rushed towards me, taking me out of Caleb's arms. Planting a kiss on my cheek, he swung me around, the motion lifting my skirts high off the floor. I threw my head back and laughed, seeing the relief and pure joy in Henry's eyes.

"I don't know how to thank you, Miss Emily. I mean, Doctor Sweeney." Setting me back down, I saw the unshed tears pooling in Henry's eyes. His gaze dropped as he toed the loose sawdust covering the floor. Looking back up, he said, "Abbie means the world to me."

"I know. She loves you very much, Henry." I was touched that this giant of a man was actually crying.

Taking my hands in his, he said, "You've given all of us here a wonderful Christmas gift to cherish for a lifetime. This town needed a new life." Henry's expression turned sad as he added, "Miss Abbie is like the daughter I lost years ago. And, losing Abbie would have surely killed me."

"I'm so sorry about your daughter, Henry. Abbie is fine and has given you a beautiful baby girl to spoil." Squeezing his hands, "I'm sure Holly will be happy to call you Grandpa."

Smiling, I indicated the stairs with a nod, "Why don't you go on up. Just know that Abbie might be a bit groggy from the medication we gave her for the surgery. And, please go easy on Anders. He's not going to leave Abbie and the baby." Henry nodded his understanding, then took to the stairs.

"Emily," Caleb said, coming to stand behind me. Encircling me in his arms and placing a kiss on the top of my head. "Why don't you go on back to the clinic and get some sleep? I'll see if Doc needs anything, then I'll meet you there."

Turning, I looked into his eyes, rimmed with dark circles of exhaustion. "I probably won't sleep after all the excitement. No, you go ahead home to your sister. She'll be worried and anxious to hear news of the baby." Patting his arm, "I have to go back up and get my supplies and check on Abbie and the baby one more time."

"Can't your grandfather do that?"

"Yes, he can. But I'd feel better knowing everyone is OK, including my grandfather. Then I'll be right over. It shouldn't take long." Caleb smiled, turning to leave when I added, "Please, have some coffee ready for me. I might as well start the day early. Besides, it's Christmas morning."

"O.K., I will," he assured me with his dazzling smile. My eyes followed him as he slowly walked towards the saloon doors. Finally, healing, he'd gained strength and weight. I couldn't be happier. No man had ever loved me like Caleb. Rushing to stop him before he disappeared, I grabbed his arm, turning him around. Placing my arms around his neck, I drew him down to my lips, kissing him with more desire than I thought possible. Breathless, I broke the kiss, holding his face in my hands and whispered, "Merry Christmas, Caleb."

"Merry Christmas, my love."

Emily, my dear, you and your grandfather did an excellent job tonight with Holly's birth. What an angelic little baby. And that Anders, well, he's smitten. It's about time that man came to his senses. I can't wait for their wedding.

As I listened to my gran, I watched Caleb walk through the swinging doors, as a sense of contentment settled over me. This single moment in 1880 gave me the clarity I needed to know I was in the right place—the place I was meant to be for the remainder of my new life. Standing alone in the empty saloon, I took a deep breath. Looking heavenward, I asked, *Gran, can you tell me something?*

Of course dear. You know you can ask me anything. It's what I'm here for.

Smiling, I remembered the unconditional love we'd shared while my gran was alive. Now, with so many years gone by, she was still here guiding me. How lucky could I be? Exhaling, I rushed my confession out. "Gran, I don't want to go back." Waiting for a response, none was forthcoming. "Did you hear me, Gran? I don't want to go back. I can't leave Caleb and Grandfather. I realize what an amazing, kind, generous, loving man Grandfather is. Then there's Caleb. My Caleb. I don't think I could love another man as much as I've come to love him." I knew I was rambling, but I couldn't stop. "Like you said, Gran, I know I have a lot to give to this town and its people." Looking around the saloon before continuing. "I've come to love it here, even if it isn't Seattle. I realize that I can make anywhere my home as long as I'm with the ones I love. Does that make sense?"

Of course, it does, dear.

I rushed on, afraid my Gran would leave before hearing me out. "But what if I'm wrong. What if I can really go back and restart my life over on that day? Can I go back to that evening in the emergency room and make a safer choice by not putting myself at risk of being shot? Or, if staying here, will I live forever, eventually losing Caleb when he grows old?

In my haste to get my questions out, I dropped my satchel on the floor. "Gran, I don't want to live forever. I just want to live a life with Caleb. I'm so confused right now. What do I do?"

Oh, my dear Emily. If I could just hold you in my arms like I did when you were a little girl and make everything alright, I would. But I can't. Life can be so confusing for both young and old alike. Don't you know it's about taking chances every single day? Not all of them are going to have the outcomes we want. As I always say, it's better to have tried than to go through life with regrets and what-ifs. What I can tell you is, that if you choose to stay here, your life will go on as if you were born into this time. You will live, and die, hopefully at an old age, knowing you've been loved beyond measure.

Sighing heavily, I was too drained to think about our conversation. Sitting down, I leaned back in the chair, my eyes heavy with fatigue. Fixed on the saloon doors slow swing from Caleb's exit, I was hit by the urge to run after him and tell him I could never leave him. Instead, I remained seated, thinking about how loving one man had changed my life. I had to stop second-guessing my decisions. Leaving Caleb was the last thing on my mind.

I was staying in 1880.

Heading back upstairs, I gathered my supplies and checked on Abbie, Anders, and the baby one last time. My grandfather was fast asleep in a rocking chair near the stove. The dark circles under his eyes from the strain of the long night were highlighted by the fires glowing embers. I didn't want to wake him, he needed his rest. Asleep, I saw close-up the creases at the side of his eyes, and the worry lines furrowing his brow, realizing how hard he worked as the town's only physician. It was just another reason I needed to stay.

Before leaving the room, I glanced back at the sheriff, who finally looked content lying on the bed with the baby tucked in one arm and Abigail in the other. It was a scene I longed for with Caleb someday.

Heading back downstairs, Henry was sitting in a chair relaxing, with a cup of coffee in his hand. "Miss Emily, I'll walk you back to the clinic."

"Oh no, Henry. That's nice of you to offer, but I'll be fine. I only have to go across the street. You get some rest because that little girl up there is going to keep you busy when she wraps herself around your heart."

Henry laughed. "She already has. And I'll love every minute." I could see a change in this crusty ol' man who'd put on a good front.

His eyes were brighter now that he had new meaning to his life, and a new life to care for.

Taking the shawl from me, Henry placed it over my shoulders and gave me a fond kiss on my cheek. Pausing, I looked across the street before pushing open the double doors. It was still dark out, but the stars were fading as new dawn approached. When I stepped onto the boardwalk, I could see that the snow had stopped falling, leaving a light dusting on the street. A wintry chill crossed my back, and I pulled the shawl tighter around my shoulders. Inhaling the fresh air of this glorious Christmas Day, I glimpsed a light shining in the parlor window where Caleb waited. Soon, I would be in the arms of the man I loved.

⌒ 38 ⌒

Emily

Poised to step off the curb, a large fleshy hand came from behind covering my mouth. Cutting off a primal scream, my heart pounded in my chest. Dropping my satchel in the remnants of dirty snow, terror coursed through my veins. As that fight or flight instinct kicked in, roaring blood surged in my ears. Drawing on all my strength, I pulled my right leg up, then forcefully kicked back against my attacker's shin. Unfortunately, it was me that yelped in pain when I was fiercely jerked to one side.

Despite the chilled night air, I was sweating profusely. As my abductor's hold over my mouth tightened, my breathing demanded the vital oxygen he was cutting off. Black spots clouded my vision, yet I continued to fight, fearing hyperventilation would soon render me helpless. The light at the surface of my consciousness dimmed, and a sense of drowning cloaked me in darkness.

Unexpectedly, the hand released my mouth, and I quickly surfaced, gasping for air as he lifted me up off my feet. I continued twisting, kicking, and punching with all I had left in me. Exhausted from being up all night, my strength was rapidly fading. But I wasn't ready to give up.

My blows hadn't slowed my attacker as he dragged me back into the alley. I'd never felt so vulnerable knowing a woman's worst fear; he was going to rape me. With clarity, I could only imagine the horror the rape victims in my E.R. had experienced.

With a new surge of energy, I managed to turn myself around, and in one swift move, upped my knee hard into his groin. Letting out a huff, he dropped like a sack of grain in the dirty snow. I turned to run, yelling, "Help! Somebody, help me!"

My screams echoed between the two buildings. *Why wasn't anyone coming to help me? I didn't understand.* Before making it ten feet down the alley, a hand grabbed my lose hair. Pulling me around, he slapped me across the face, sending my head snapping back, hitting the saloon wall so hard that flashes of light blazed before my eyes. Feeling the burn across my cheek, I desperately tried to remain alert and fight. Instead, I crumpled to the ground, drifting into unconsciousness.

Upon awakening, I found myself gagged, blindfolded, and with hands tied firmly to a saddle horn with a hulking body behind me. I had no idea how long I'd been unconscious. *Think Emily. You've got to get out of this mess.* My head throbbed with every jarring step the horse took. Any hope of knowing where I was being taken was out of the question. Whoever my kidnappers were, they were going to make darn sure I didn't get away.

Caleb, where are you?

Thinking hard, I couldn't figure out why I had been the one they kidnapped—me of all people. I had no ties to anyone in town, other than my grandfather, and, for sure, no money. There were plenty of prominent people that would be likelier candidates. Why not the banker or the mine owner? The only possibility I could think of was they know I'm a doctor and need my help? If so, why all the secrecy? They could have just asked for my help.

Tired beyond belief, my body ached all over from fighting, and what seemed like hours of riding. If not for the man behind me, I would have fallen off the horse. With each touch he made to secure me to his body, my skin crawled. His wafting stench, a cross between stale whiskey, wet horse, and foul body odor, had me gagging. I could only imagine what he looked like.

Hearing the crunch of rocks under the horse's hooves, I sensed the animals growing fatigue, from carrying two riders. As it lurched forward, moving up a steep incline, I could feel the air around us grow colder, and I longed for the shawl I'd lost back in the alley. The only good thing about my abductor was the body heat he radiated, keeping me warm.

Heaving and snorting, the horse finally stopped. Suddenly, I was being pushed forward over the saddle horn as my co-rider dismounted. Once down, he grabbed me around the waist, hauling me not-so-gently to the ground. Pulling the gag out of my mouth, I inhaled deeply, glad to breathe freely again. The smell of damp earth and rotting wood reminded me of the musty smell from the cabin. *Are we back at the cabin?*

My sense of hearing went on high alert, knowing my constant vigilance was the only thing keeping me alive. Unexpectedly, a hand grabbed my arm. Flinching, I let out a muffled yelp as I was jerked to one side. Then two giant hands were pushing me firmly down. I landed on something hard. A tree stump or log, perhaps? I was still blindfolded and couldn't tell for sure.

I had no idea where we were or how far we'd traveled. Fear was scrambling my thought process, and I had to force myself to concentrate. Surely whoever they were wouldn't keep me tied up and blindfolded forever. I couldn't devise an escape plan if I couldn't see my surroundings. I prayed that someone, maybe Henry or the sheriff, had found my shawl and satchel by now, and was out looking for me. Silently though, I hoped Caleb wouldn't try to ride in his condition. He wasn't completely healed, and his wounds couldn't take the pounding of riding a horse.

The air in front of me moved. I stilled. Gulping down raging fear, a repulsive stench of warm sour breath filled my nostrils. Someone was kneeling in front of me. Terrified for what was about to happen, I pulled my head back only to feel the touch of rough hands across my face. Thankfully, those hands were only there to remove my blindfold. Squinting to adjust to the fading light, the man before me grinned through broken tobacco-stained teeth but didn't speak.

"Please, untie my hands," I pleaded holding them out.

"Oh no, little lady," the man standing next to his horse said while rubbing his thumb and forefinger over his greasy beard. His cold black eyes made him look like the devil incarnate. *God, help me.* "Can't have yer getting away now, can we?" Turning his head, he spit a line of black tobacco juice into the dirt. Cringing, I had no idea where I was. At least now, I could see my captors and surroundings.

Both men wore holsters slung low on their left hips, their clothes filthy and tattered, and their boots caked with crusty mud. It was easy to imagine they hadn't seen soap and water in months. I could only imagine when their last bath had been. Oddly, the boots on the man who spoke bore expensive silver tips with matching spurs.

Appealing to the speaking man, I looked up with all the confidence I could muster, asking for a drink. I was thirsty from all the dust and grime I'd inhaled during our long ride. The smaller of the two men, the one that never spoke, handed me his canteen filled with tepid water, then nodded. At this point, I didn't care where the liquid came from, as long as it was wet. Placing the opening to my lips, I drank my fill.

Soundlessly sitting, I watched my kidnapper's erratic movements. One would pace, while the other sat, then they changed places. It seemed they were exceedingly nervous. But why? My thoughts scrambled as I tried to understand why they had chosen me. Was there more to this kidnapping than I could figure out?

It had been hours since we stopped, and an empty churning filled my stomach. Finally, the silent man handed me a piece of dried beef jerky. I was so ravenous I didn't care what it tasted like. At the moment, I imagined it a piece of juicy prime rib.

As the evening wore on, the air became colder. I was sure their reasoning behind not starting a fire was to avoid giving away our location. I could only hope the night wouldn't get much colder than it already had, since there would be no coffee to warm me, no matter how bad it tasted.

The speaking man threw me a blanket that had been tied to the back of his horse. You can only imagine how it smelled, but I wasn't about to complain. It was better to be warm than freeze to death on some desert hillside. Instead of lying on the ground, I decided to wrap myself in the itchy wool while leaning back against a log.

Pretending to sleep, I listened to the two men on the opposite side of the fire arguing. The speaking man mentioned a ransom. Now, who in Yuma would have enough ransom money to pay for my release? Biting the inside of my mouth, I didn't think my grandfather did, and certainly not Caleb. *They must have another motive.* My heart ached as I held back tears, longingly thinking of Caleb.

Caleb probably thinks I left him to find my way back home. Well, I had no plans to return to Seattle. If I got out of this mess alive, I was staying in Yuma for good. I missed him so much. To keep me sane, I closed my eyes and imagined his strong arms surrounding me while he told me everything would be alright. But would it?

Somehow, I must have miraculously dozed. Upon awakening, I found myself lying on the cold ground, aching all over, reminiscent of weeks past. Every fiber in my body was screaming with pain.

Emily

I DESPERATELY NEEDED TO make a trip into the bushes. While they slept, I tried wrestling my tied hands under my buttocks. It was no use. The silent-man had secured my hands together so tight he didn't leave room enough to budge. Finally, rocking back and forth several times, I managed to stand. Thankfully, they hadn't considered I would try to escape by not having my legs tied up. It definitely showed their lack of intelligence. Well, I wasn't about to enlighten them anytime soon! As they slept soundly, I was able to step over the log I had been sitting against. Placing one foot on the other side, a branch snapped. Holding my breath, I repeated, *Please don't wake up. Please don't wake up.* Thankfully, neither man moved.

Emily. Are you all right?

"Oh! Just fine, Gran," I whispered sarcastically.

I've been so worried about you. Those vile men deserve to be hung for what they've done to you. If only I had a rope.

"Gran. Where the heck have you been?" If she couldn't help, at least we could talk.

I've been right here, dear, but I couldn't do anything physical to help out. Or, you wouldn't have been taken by those beastly animals.

"Do you have any idea how I can get out of here?" Finding the perfect spot, I struggled with my dress. What a time to be talking. "Gran. Where's Caleb?"

He's coming. And, he has lots of men with him, including that charming Sheriff Johansson.

"Gran, no. You can't let Caleb come. He's not well enough."

Now, dear. Don't you worry about Caleb? You know I don't have any control over what he does.

"No! Gran, you have to stop him. Make him go back. If he opens those wounds, I won't be able to help him."

My dear, that man wouldn't be stopped even if I could.

I didn't know whether to be angry at Caleb or scared for him. "Gran, Caleb probably thinks I've left him to go back home." Pleading, "Please, you need to make him stay away. I can't have him killed." With no response from my Gran, I raised my voice, not caring if my abductors heard. "Gran, did you hear me?" Silence. "Dang it!" Frantic, I didn't know what to think.

I made it back to the fire, looking at the reclining figures when I caught Stubbs beginning to stir. Holding my breath, my gaze darted from man to man, then the tree line beyond. Could I make it to the edge of the trees and start running with all I had in me? If so, I just might have a chance—a slim one, but still a chance. I had to try. Running was better than remaining captive with these two cretins.

Tiptoeing my way around the campfire, I stepped around Vermin's body only to lose my balance. Free-falling, I landed hard on my left shoulder, then rolled next to the foul-smelling body of

Stubbs. In pain, I moaned. Slowly opening my eyes, I found myself staring at a mouth full of rotting teeth.

Vermin came awake at the sound of my hitting the ground. Kicking his brother in the side, he yelled, "You're supposed to be watchin' her. You good-for-nothin' scum."

Standing over me, Vermin grabbed my arm, jerking me to my feet. "I told ya, yer wouldn't get away from me." Vermin's tobacco-stained teeth shone in the firelight as he pulled me hard against his chest. "You, missy, is the bait I've been waitin' fer. I have what Mr. Young wants." Within inches of my face, he sneered. I held firm in my stance. "Next time, I won't miss! He killed our brother in cold blood. Now, he's going to pay for it." I tried pulling away as his grip on my arm tightened. Stricken, I knew this was the man who had shot Caleb and left him to die in the hills. I understood their plan now—as another sickening stream of tobacco juice landed at my feet. I was numb to his scare tactics, finding the less I reacted, the better chance I'd have of surviving. Jerking on my arm, he hissed out, "He should have died in that ole' cabin. But then you came along and ruined everything."

In his grip, my left arm went numb, causing me to lose my ability to focus. I knew I would pay dearly for what I was about to do. I spit in his face.

"Why you whore," he yelled. Raising his hand, I couldn't move fast enough as the slap struck my face with such force, it caused me to plummet to the ground, feeling intense burning the side of my face.

Vermin stood over me with a sick sinister grin. "Maybe, just for fun, I'll let yer man watch you die first. Then I'll finish what I started with him." Pulling me up, he shoved me towards his brother. Yelling through tobacco-stained lips, "Watch her. Don't let her out of your sight, or I'll kill ya both."

I didn't know how much more I could take before giving up. It wasn't like me to do so, but I'd never endured this kind of hell before. At least when I'd been shot, death came quick. This time, the end felt like it was taking an eternity. Centuries apart, the evil made no difference as a sense of detachment encompassed my body.

Stubbs untied my hands from behind my back, only to retie them in front. Before turning away, I thought I glimpsed sadness in his eyes. Picking up the coffee pot, he dumped its remaining contents onto the fire sending a plume of swirling steam into the cold morning air. I could feel my left eye swelling and my vision blur. Reaching up, a sticky warmth oozed from a small laceration on my cheek. Wiping it with my dirty sleeve, I closed both eyes and shuddered.

Opening them, Vermin was standing on the far side of the hissing fire, picking his teeth with the point of a large Bowie knife. He was doing it to scare me. And it was working.

My stomach felt like a desert rattler was bouncing between my ribs and backbone when his disgusting hand raised up. Remaining firm in my stance, knowing there was no place to run, and screaming would only make him angrier. I flinched, waiting for the strike. Instead, Vermin ran his dirty calloused fingers down the side of my left cheek, and over the tender handprint he'd left earlier. His touch, harsh like sandpaper, scraped along my raw skin. Refusing to look at him, I tried to maintain my calm by focusing on surviving.

I couldn't stand it. Jerking my head to the side to avoid Vermin's assault, he took a firm painful hold of my chin, turning my face back. Leaning in, he placed his filthy wet mouth on my bruised lips, as his overgrown beard painfully scratched my skin.

Bitter bile burned in the back of my throat and edged its way up. Vermin's tongue continued to assault the inside of my mouth as I pushed against his chest. It was no use. He held my arms so tight. Choking, I bit down hard, while at the same time, I came up with my right knee hard into his groin. Vermin sent ear-splitting profanities into the air, immediately letting go of my face. Leaning forward in obvious pain, his head slowly came back up. It was then, I found myself staring into the soulless eyes of a sinister killer.

Seething with anger, Vermin placed his hands around my throat so quickly I didn't see it coming. Laughing, like the crazy man he was, his squeeze tightened as I gasped for air. Pushing my tied hands against his chest, I attempted to disengage his hold. Unsuccessful, his fierce grip only tightened around my neck. *I'm going to die. God, please help me.* I saw the first rays of dawn rapidly turn to darkness as I slowly drifted towards the edge of oblivion. With one hand, Vermin swiftly tore the bodice of my dress, exposing the tops of my breasts. Letting go of my throat, he pushed me back against a tree.

Gulping in oxygen, I slowly edged my way back from the darkness. If I survived Vermin's assault, I wanted him to pay dearly for what he was about to do. If not, I hoped Caleb would hunt him down to the ends of the earth and seek revenge. *If only I could grab his gun or the Bowie from his back belt, he'd learn just how much of a fighter I was.*

Pulling me roughly to his body, I felt his hardness. Eye to eye, we stared at each other. One corner of his lip lifted in a sickening smirk. "It's time you satisfied me, little lady."

"Please," I choked out. "You don't want to do this."

Laughing, Vermin replied, "What makes ya think I don't? I haven't had me a woman in a long, long time." Adjusting his gun belt, "You just happen to be the lucky one." Stepping closer, he took out his Bowie and traced the remaining neckline of my bodice, while licking his filthy lips inches from my face. "It's time I showed yer what real lovin' is." Not taking his eyes off me, he began unbuttoning his trousers. Leaning in close to my face, he said, "Your man ain't goin' to like no damaged goods, now is he?"

I would show no fear. But I would fight, even if it meant he killed me in the end. Gulping in deep, ragged breaths and screaming a war cry as loud as I could, I came up under his chin with my fisted hands. Vermin's head lurched back, splitting his lower lip between his teeth. Wiping blood with his arm, he came at me with open fingers. Though my hands remained tied, I moved fast, coming down with closed fists to the side of his head, sending him stumbling back to the ground. I screamed, "I'll show you, you animal!"

Rising up, Vermin swore, "You whore!" As he came at me again, his rage was cut short by a single gunshot. Stubbs stood to the side, holding his gun high above his head as smoke streamed from the barrel. I'd been saved, for the moment.

Pulling his gun, Vermin pointed it directly at his brother. I couldn't have him killing Stubbs. He may be the help I so desperately needed. Without thinking of the possible consequences, I quickly kicked out my right leg, taking Vermin to the ground. His gun fired, then flew out of his hand. While Vermin was down, Stubbs made his way to my side.

Vermin watched his brother, Stubbs make his way towards me. Shoving me aside, Vermin lunged for his brother. They fought until both were bloody, winded, and lying on the ground. I made my move towards Vermin. Stilling, he must have sensed what I was about when I reached behind him for his Bowie. Twisting, he pinned my arms to my side, causing me to drop the knife. "I like a little fight in my women," Vermin whispered in my ear. His overweight body squeezed the breath out of me, and his spittle covered my exposed skin. Screaming, I panicked as he positioned himself above me, pulling up my skirts.

Only dazed, Stubbs must have understood his brother's intent, as he tried to stop him the best he knew how. A gunshot shattered the air, halting Vermin's attack on me. "Damn it! This isn't over little lady," he yelled as he raced towards his brother. "It's time I killed you." His strikes were swift. I didn't understand why Stubbs hadn't shot his brother. So, all I could do was pray that he survived the beating.

An hour later, Stubbs lay on the ground next to me while Vermin ate. His attempts to rape me forgotten, for the moment. Not bothering to offer me any food, I couldn't choke it down if he did. While sitting, I'd been able to take a portion of my tattered skirts, tie it together, and clumsily pull it over my neck. At least I would no longer be so exposed to the elements.

Stubbs finally regained consciousness, looking at me with piteous eyes. I'd seen that same look on my patients before that suffered traumatic physical abuse, and my heart ached for him.

40

Emily

AFTER VERMIN FINISHED eating, we were back on the horses riding farther up into the hills. Rocking back and forth with the cadence of its steps, I tried in vain to relax. Watching my mount heave frosty streams, I shivered in the wintry air despite Stubbs's warm body behind me.

Without a sound, Vermin raised his hand, and Stubbs stopped at his command. I caught a whiff of musty rotting wood. My eyes searched the hillside while the horse shifted his stance from one leg to the other, eager to be free of his burden. It was daylight, but the sun offered little warmth. Turning in the saddle, I caught sight of what appeared to be a dark opening. "Oh, please. Tell me we aren't going in there? That's a death trap," I whispered.

"What did ya say?" Vermin yelled.

"Nothing. I didn't say a thing," I responded, as my eyes continued to roam over the rotted pilings.

Stubbs dismounted, leaving me tied to the saddle horn to watch him hobble the horse.

"Just in case you get any ideas," Vermin grinned sarcastically.

I noticed Vermin appeared to be moving a bit cautiously this morning after our encounter and last night's fight with his brother. Despite my oath, he'd receive no sympathy or medical attention from me. In obvious pain, it served him right.

Neither man wasted any time getting their meager supplies into the mine. Finally, Vermin stood next to my horse. Reaching up, he pulled me out of the saddle, setting me roughly on the ground. Without a word, he took the rope between my hands, pulling me towards the piling entrance, with Stubbs following closely behind. Inhaling deeply, I feared this would be my last breath of fresh air before I died.

Having been out in the bright light of day, it took several minutes for my vision to adjust to the underground darkness. Vermin paused, lighting a lantern hanging on the side of the rock wall. He'd walked directly to it in the dark, making it apparent they'd been here before. As the light broached the darkness, I realized the depth of hell I'd been dragged in too.

Pulled along, I had trouble seeing the ground I walked on. But, what I couldn't see, I heard scurrying along the mine's walls and over my boots. Marching my feet rapidly in place, I tried kicking at what ran below me. "Rats! I hate rats!" Having their domain invaded, they skittered in every direction. *How appropriate. Two human rats amongst the company of their four-legged family.*

Trying to stay upright in the darkness, I became hypersensitive to any touch and sound. Suddenly a thunderous roar passed over our heads, and Vermin was jerking me to the ground. Crouching in the damp earth, a breeze stirred in my hair. High pitched screeching surrounded us, as thousands of bat wings surged overhead. I wanted to run but didn't know in which direction to go, fearing one wrong step, and I would fall endlessly into a bottomless pit.

"Get a move on," Vermin yelled, pulling me forward.

Staring, but not seeing, I stumbled forward, bumping into his backside. He didn't bother to turn around, only picked up his pace, moving deeper into the mine. The lantern he held began to flicker, bringing to mind the sacrifice of the lone canary in a British coal mine. I feared we would go too deep while being overcome with carbon monoxide. Just as that thought ended, Vermin came to an abrupt halt. There in front of us was a wide opening in the path. Holding up the light, I saw boxes stacked high against the walls. Frightened, it looked to be enough supplies to last us several days, if not weeks.

Taking my arms, Vermin stood me in front of several wooden crates, instructing me to, "Sit down, don't move, and keep your mouth shut."

That I can do. Closing my eyes, I forced myself to think of the good times spent with Caleb and my grandfather. What came to mind was how frustrating and argumentative Caleb could be, and yet how gentle and passionate. I longed for his touch and fiery kisses. I was doing everything in my power not to cry. But, to no avail, the tears began to flow down my freckled face, Caleb told me he loved.

In an attempt to generate body heat, I rubbed vigorously at the goosebumps forming on my arms. Stubbs happened to notice and handed me a wool blanket that smelled like a wet horse, among other things. I didn't care; it would provide me with much-needed warmth. All I wanted to do right now was sleep. Laying my head back against the rock wall, I did just that.

I awoke to the sound of Vermin's yelling, while Stubbs was using his hands to crudely communicate with his brother. If only this was 2019, Stubbs could learn to use American Sign Language with confidence. Straining to hear, I couldn't understand what Vermin was saying, but I surmised it wasn't good, as a look of horror framed Stubbs' face.

While the two men fought, hands flying in gestures, I studied the space in the dim lamplight, shocked at what I saw. To one side of the vast area, were boxes stacked one on top of the other with the black lettering D-Y-N-O-M-I-T-E on their side. Wiring exited the boxes, trailing along the walls. "Oh, God, help me." I realized Vermin's plan for Caleb and myself. He had kidnapped me to lure Caleb into the mine, kill us, then set off the explosives, entombing us together. *No bodies! No crime! I longed to be with Caleb, but not like this.*

Vermin had probably been watching Caleb and me back in Yuma, waiting for the right time to kidnap me. No one would question him and his brother's presence in town, nor relate them to the stranger Caleb had killed in the saloon. Strangers came and went all the time in Western towns, and he and his brother were just two drifters passing through.

Frantically, I searched for a place to go, not if, but when Vermin set off the dynamite. There was none. The timbers above us were ready to fall with the slightest vibration. It was a death trap, no matter how I looked at it. There was no sense of becoming irrational. I was due to die all over again.

Furious, Vermin's yelling escalated when he struck his brother on the side of his head with the butt of his rifle. Instinctively, I let out an echoing scream as Stubbs fell silent to the ground. My scream caused the overhead rotting beams to groan, sending small rocks and dirt raining down upon us. Afraid Vermin would strike me next, I didn't know if I should go to Stubbs or stay where I was. Going against my Hippocratic Oath, I remained seated. *"Hadn't intervening in the ER gotten me into this predicament in the first place?"*

"Damn fool. I hate to kill my own kin," Vermin said, standing over his brother with his pistol pointed at his head.

"No! Wait!" I shrieked. Pleading, "Please, don't kill him." Not moving from the crate, I raised my hands, "You don't need to do that." Shrugging for effect, "Besides, you might need him later." I was serious. I needed Stubbs alive more than Vermin wanted him dead. He might be my one and only key to helping me escape.

"Ah, hell, lady. Yer ain't no fun," Vermin replied. Sniggering, he shot off his gun into the dirt next to Stubbs' head.

Recoiling back, I closed my eyes, hoping I wouldn't be next. The sound of the shot ricocheted off the walls sending larger rocks tumbling down from above. Terror filled my heart since Vermin obviously had a very short fuse. I knew that any more shots within the mine shaft would have the walls collapsing and entombing all three of us. These men were not who I wanted for eternal roommates.

╰⌒ 41 ⌒╮

Rebecca

RUBBING THE SLEEP from my eyes, I walked into the clinic's kitchen, only to find my brother sitting at the table with his chin to his chest, sound asleep. Looking around, I asked, "Where's Emily?"

Slow to rouse, he mumbled, "What? Emily? Oh, she must have gone upstairs."

"No. Her bed hasn't been slept in, and she's not on the sofa in the parlor. I thought maybe she'd be in here with you having coffee." Concerned, I asked, "Where do you think she could be? With a darting gaze to the door, I asked, "You don't think there was a complication with Abigail and the baby, do you?"

More alert now, Caleb sat up straight in the chair, stretching his back and answering, "She probably decided to stay at the saloon." Looking around the kitchen, he asked, "Is Doc Sweeney here?"

307

"No. Not that I know of. But I'll go knock on his bedroom door." Taking the stairs to the second floor, I knocked on his door. Receiving no response, I opened the door a crack. Peeking in, Doc wasn't there, and his bed hadn't been slept in.

Concerned, I went back downstairs to find Caleb staring out the kitchen window as the golden hues of sunrise were edging their way over the eastern mountains. "He's not there. And, it doesn't look like he came home last night." Anxiously standing next to my brother, it became evident to us both that neither had returned from the saloon last night.

Without turning from the window, my brother said, "I saw her last around three this morning." Rubbing his hands over his face, he added, "Before I left the saloon, she asked me to put on a pot of coffee for when she came back." Raising a hand to his cheek, I watched him grin. "She kissed me and wished me a Merry Christmas." Turning his attention to the cold stove, "I must have fallen asleep before making the coffee. Maybe Abigail and Holly needed her."

Caleb

Could I tell my sister what I really thought happened? All the emotional pain and humiliation I'd gone through with Anna came flooding back as I gripped the edge of the counter. Hanging my head in defeat, I couldn't understand why Emily told me she loved me, all the while she'd been planning to leave. Had she just been saying it so I wouldn't follow her? No! She wouldn't do that. Yet, I couldn't ignore this sinking feeling in my gut that she wouldn't be coming back. *How can I go on without her?*

Going over the events of the evening before, I knew it would have been the perfect opportunity for Emily to leave after sending me back to the clinic. Slamming my fist on the counter, I yelled, "Why didn't I think of that?"

Rebecca flinched. "Think about what?" When I didn't respond, she continued, "Caleb, maybe something went wrong with Abbie or the baby, and Emily needed to stay at the saloon." Her tender touch was little comfort as she laid her hand on my forearm. "You should go over there and find out. Anders may need you."

"You're right." Pushing away from the counter, I took in a ragged breath and closed my eyes when a loud pounding at the back door brought me out of my surreal nightmare. Cursing, "Who in the name of heavens could that be at this hour?"

Irritated, I pulled the door open so hard it slipped out of my hand, hitting the wall with a resounding thud. There, standing in the entry, was Henry, who didn't seem so overbearing at the moment. In his hand, he held the satchel that I knew to be the instrument bag Emily had taken to the saloon for Abbie's birth.

"Caleb. Mam." Henry nodded. He was trying to catch his breath while holding onto the door jam. "I just stepped outside the saloon for some fresh air when I found this bag and Emily's shawl lying in the mud. They were near the hitching post."

A sharp spasm of pain hit me at seeing Emily's bag. Bending forward, I winced.

Henry grabbed my arms, and both he and Rebecca guided me to a chair.

Turning the chair around, I straddled the seat, leaning my head forward onto the top rim waiting for the pain to ease.

"Caleb," Henry and Rebecca said in unison.

I didn't look up.

"What's going on?" Rebecca asked, kneeling down beside me and placing her hands on my thigh. "What does this all mean?"

Shaking my head, I didn't know how to answer her. Rubbing the back of my neck, I asked myself, *How do I explain what Emily has done and why? I can't tell them she's not from our time.* Clenching my jaw tight, I knew *they won't believe me.*

"Caleb, you have to find her," Rebecca said as she began to pace behind me. "She didn't strike me as the type of person to just up and leave willingly like this." I watched her move back and forth in the small room while running the velvet ties of her dressing gown through her hands. My ordinarily demure sister raised her voice, "Something terrible has happened. I just know it."

Feeling a throbbing pressure pulse in my head, I calmly walked to the kitchen wall. Violence was not something I usually reverted too. Still, drawing back my arm, I slammed my fist into the fading wallpaper creating a jagged hole. Screaming, "She can't do this to me. I love her." Shaking my fist, I now had another form of pain to deal with.

"Henry. Please get the sheriff and bring him back here," my sister asked.

Henry looked between my sister and me before he left. Not questioning Rebecca's request, "I'll be right back. But first, I need to make sure that Abbie and the baby are OK before I pull the sheriff away. In the meantime, I'll get the word out through the men in the saloon to gather everyone they can to be ready to ride out and search for Doc Emily."

"Thank you, Henry," my sister answered before turning to me. "Caleb Young! You look at me right now!" she ordered.

With both hands leaning against the wall, I raised my hanging head.

"You need to tell me what's going on," with a no-nonsense look, she stood inches from my face. "And you'd better tell me the truth!"

Cradling my head in my hands, I answered, "Oh God, Rebecca, I've lost her. She's gone back. I didn't think she would do it. I thought she was happy here with me."

"Caleb, you're not making any sense," Rebecca said, placing her hand on my shoulder.

"She said she needed to try. She wanted to make sure that she really had died."

"Died! Gone back. Where? Caleb, what are you talking about?" Rebecca paced. Softening her voice, but demanding, "Please, Caleb, tell me what's going on. You're scaring me."

Rebecca sounded just like our mother when she'd been angry with the two of us. What did she expect me to do? We weren't kids anymore, and we couldn't run to our mother to make things right.

Looking up at Rebecca, I answered her. "You wouldn't understand. I didn't, at first, and maybe I still don't."

"Try me," my sister demanded, bringing me out of my self-deposed pity. Rebecca's face now red, her voice had risen to a point I could no longer ignore. Never had I seen her so angry. I knew she would be relentless until I told her the whole story. Before she realized how loud she was yelling, two small blond heads popped around the kitchen door, eyes wide with fear.

"Momma. Why are you yelling at Uncle Caleb?" Porter asked, moving to his mother's side. "Has he been bad Momma?" asked Daniel.

Rebecca knelt down, gathering her son's in her arms. "Oh no, my dears. Uncle Caleb and I were just having a discussion," she answered, looking up at me through steel blue eyes. "Now, don't you two worry. It's Christmas morning and still too early for you to be up," she said, steering them back to the stairs. "You go back to bed, and I'll be up soon."

Staring back and forth between their mother and myself, Daniel asked cautiously, "Momma, father didn't find us, did he?"

Porter took his brother's hand, tugging him up the stairs before his mother could answer. "No, silly, he won't come. He doesn't know where we are."

Rebecca ignored my questioning look.

Pushing away from the wall, for the moment, I ignored my nephew's comment. Through clenched teeth, "There's no time. I've got to go find her before she has a chance to go back."

Rebecca held out my coat and hat as I slipped into it. Holding onto my side, I could feel beads of sweat forming on my brow. I wasn't up to riding, but I'd do anything to find Emily.

"Caleb, sit down. You look like you're ready to fall over," my sister implored, pointing to the chair.

I hadn't eaten hardly a thing since the day before. Taking her hand, I allowed her to lead me to the chair. Placing the back of her hand on my brow, I knew I didn't have a fever. "I'm fine, Sis. Really, I am," kissing her hand and rising slowly. "I have to go after Emily." "Tell the sheriff where I've gone when he gets here."

"You don't even know where Emily went. So, you're not going anywhere until the sheriff gets here. Do you understand?" she said, indicating for me to stay in the chair.

"Rebecca . . .," my voice gently rising. "Remember, I'm your older brother. I can take care of myself."

Waving her hand. "Don't I know that? But right now, it doesn't look as if you're doing a very good job. Besides, I can still boss you around like I always did."

Smiling, I replied, "That's only because I let you."

"Whatever you say. Now sit! I'll make us some coffee, and you can tell me what this is all about while we wait for the sheriff."

Rebecca was filling the coffee pot at the pump when the back door slowly creaked open, and in walked a weary-looking Doc Sweeney. He'd been gone since yesterday morning and knew nothing of what had transpired in the past twelve hours.

"Mornin' to ya," he said, making his way in. "Is tat coffee ye be making?" he asked, gazing at my sister. They'd never met, but he smiled as Rebecca made herself right at home in his kitchen.

Doc sent me a questioning look. "And who might this lovely lass be?" he asked, putting on his spectacles.

Sitting at the kitchen table, with my hat in hand, I answered him, "I'm sorry. Doc, this is my sister, Rebecca." Turning to my sister, I said, "Rebecca, this is Doc Sweeney. This is his home we're staying in."

"I'm pleased te be making ye acquaintance, miss," Doc said, shaking her hand.

"Rebecca came all the way from Boston to be with me. Emily sent her a telegram to let her know I wasn't feeling well."

Doc laughed. "Not feeling well ye say! Is that what you'd be calling shot full of holes?" he said, placing his coat and hat on the hook near the back door.

I hadn't exactly told my sister the truth about being shot. Seeing the way she looked at me now, I knew that would be yet another heated discussion we'd soon be having.

Doc looked around the kitchen as if missing something. "Where's me beautiful granddaughter tis fine mornin'?" Meeting him with blank stares, neither Rebecca nor I replied. "What's goin' on?" he asked. Leaning his hands on the back of a chair for support, "Something's happened, hasn't' it? What is it?" he demanded.

～ 42 ～

Caleb

"**D**OC," I SAID, pointing to the chair. "You'd better sit down so we can talk."

Raising his voice an octave, he looked directly at me. "Don't Doc me. I don't want ta sit down. I want ta know where me granddaughter is't." His brogue thickened, the angrier he became. Raising his hand, "By all that is Holy. I can't leave tat girl alone fer five minutes with ye, and something happens." Glaring at me, "I knew ya was trouble the minute I laid eyes on ya."

Abruptly standing, my chair tipped over. "Now see here old man." My blood was boiling. Fists clenched tightly at my side, I moved to stand toe to toe with the Doc.

Rebecca rushed forward, separating the two of us, one hand on each of our chests to keep us apart. I had no intention of becoming physical, but the Doc had gone too far.

I didn't have the opportunity to finish before he yelled at me. Demanding and shaking a clenched fist in my face, the vein at his temple bulged and pulsed. "Well, say somet'ing boy before I kil' ye with my bare hands."

Doc's face paled as we each took hold of Rebecca's hand that lay across our chests, keeping us apart.

"I knew it," he spat out. "Somet'ing bad has't happened," slumping weakly into a chair. "God, no. Not again. Please tell me she hasn't been kilt."

"Doc, I'm so sorry," placing a hand on his shoulder, I quickly jerked it back as he began swearing in Gaelic. Whatever he was saying, he was probably cursing me to hell.

"Doc, listen, I think Emily is trying to go back, and I need to stop her." For the first time, I noticed his faded violet eyes were the same color as his granddaughter's. "You can hate me all you want. But I thought I made her happy, and she wanted to stay here with us." Pausing, I added while looking at his clenched fists, "I must have been wrong."

"No!" Doc cried out, slamming a fist on the table. "I tolt her she couldn't go back. That the gift is't irreversible. Why would she even try?" Running his frail hands through his silver hair, he added, "But no, she wouldn't listen to reason. That stubborn woman!"

The pained look in Doc's eyes was my undoing. Placing my hands on his shoulders, "I'm going to find her and bring her back. I'll go back up into the hills by the cabin where we first met. Maybe she's gone there."

Placing a hand over mine that rested on his shoulder, he confessed, "Son, it's me entire fault. I'm sorry fer yellin' at ye." Looking up at me, he added sadly, "I should have left her to lay with her parents."

Towering over him, I said, "Don't say that. Please, Doc. Emily has brought us both so much joy in the short time we've been together. We would have never been given this chance to find each other unless you had intervened."

"Well, this is all fine and dandy gentlemen," Rebecca chimed in. "But while you are reminiscing and feeling sorry for each other, Emily is out there, God knows where, and you're doing nothing to bring her back."

Stunned, Doc and I turned to look at Rebecca when she added, "Well, what are you going to do about it?" Hands on hips, she continued, "I don't understand what either of you are talking about, but I wouldn't be sitting here when the woman I profess to love is out in the cold waiting to be rescued."

Coming to stand between us, she added, "You two get out there right now and start looking." Facing me, "When you bring her back home Mr. Young you'd better settle your differences, or I'll take my children and head to California on the next train."

Looking like boys having been taken to the woodshed, we both replied at the same time, "Yes, ma'am!"

Grinning, Doc nudged me, "Aye, that sister of yers, ist a feisty one. Ye sure ye both aren't a wee bit Irish?"

Slapping him lightly on the back, I turned and gave my sister a hug. "I love you sis. I don't know why I was so stupid to keep you out of my life these past five years."

"Neither do I, but that's in the past. We'll talk later." Tearing up, she pushed us both towards the door, "Now get out there and find Emily."

Opening the door, all three of us stared down at over twenty townsmen on horseback with lanterns and shotguns in hand. I recognized the sheriff and some of the riders. But, to the sheriff's left, astride a beautiful black stallion, was a man I'd never seen before.

Sheriff Johansson looked up at the three of us standing in the open doorway, with looks of amazement etched across our faces. "Miss, Doc, Caleb," he nodded to each of us, pointing to the man on the stallion, "Tis is Nathaniel Burns. He owns te Burnside Mine up in te hills outside of town. I tink ya already know ta rest of ta men."

Eyeing the group, I was at a loss for words. "I don't know how I can ever thank you, gentleman. Descending the stairs, I reached up and shook the sheriff's then Mr. Burns' hand. He obliged, but the direction of his attention was focused on the porch where my sister stood. Following his gaze, I grinned. "Mr. Burns, may I introduce my sister, Mrs. Rebecca Ackerman."

I watched his smile fade as he tipped his Stetson, then said, "Pleased to make your acquaintance ma'am." I noticed Nathaniel continued to stare. I had to admit, Rebecca was stunningly radiant. But, out of his reach being a married woman.

Rebecca

Feeling my face flush, I looked down at Nathaniel Burns astride his beautiful horse. How did I not know he was bound for Yuma when we first met on the train? Maybe it was because I had been so flustered at the time, eager to be free from Elliot's snare. Mr. Burns had been the epitome of a proper gentleman. Something I'd missed being married to Elliot. With the boys and Pearl accompanying me at the time, we had kept our conversations light and on simple matters. He had attracted my attention then, but now, he held my eyes captive.

Thankfully, Mr. Burns didn't let on that this wasn't our first meeting. The heated stare of his emerald eyes made my heart flutter and breath quicken, now, as when we'd first met. I'd never felt this way before. Taking hold of the porch post with one hand, the other stroked the base of my throat as my eyes fixated on his muscular form. Feeling like a schoolgirl with her first crush, I pushed aside all thoughts of my husband, Elliot.

Nathaniel was the most handsome man I had ever laid eyes on. I shouldn't be having such thoughts since I was a married woman, after all. But, that was a secret I'd kept to myself since arriving in Yuma. No one needs to know about my past. My brother was the only one who knew my husband Elliot from five years ago, not the man he'd recently become. For now, it was better this way.

Caleb

I looked between my sister and Mr. Burns, seeing the immediate chemistry between them. I knew that feeling. *Has my sister so quickly captured Mr. Burns' heart like Emily did mine?*

Clearing his throat, the sheriff got everyone's attention. "OK everyone, mount up!" Looking up, the sheriff pointed to Doc Sweeney, informing him that he wasn't coming with the posse, using the excuse that Abigail and the baby may need him. The Doc looked relieved as he nodded to the sheriff, knowing he wasn't cut out for trudging up and down these hills on horseback.

"If ver done with all the introductions, times 'a vastin," he yelled. "Let's ride."

I caught Mr. Burns taking one last look over his shoulder at my sister as we rode away. I'd have questions for her when I returned. Glimpsing her radiant silhouette fading into the dim light, I only hoped she would provide me with honest answers. We had both kept secrets from each other for far too long.

43

Sheriff Johansson

BY EARLY AFTERNOON we came across a campsite that had recently been used. Kneeling, I placed my hand over the fire's cooling gray embers. Looking around, I concluded that three people had stopped here during the night. Searching the perimeter, I found a piece of fabric hanging on a low branch, recognizing it from the dress Emily had been wearing the night before when she delivered my daughter.

"What did you find?" Caleb asked as he walked River over to where I knelt.

Turning, I tried to hide my concern as I held the cloth up for Caleb's inspection. "It's a piece of fabric." While pointing towards the bushes, "It was caught on a branch back there."

Leaning forward over River's neck, he took the fabric from my hand and swore. "Damn. That's from Emily's dress she was wearing last night. Now we know she was here." Searching the faces of the men surrounding him, his horse side-stepped, causing Caleb to almost lose his balance. Grabbing his side, he let out a low groan as he listened to me address the posse.

Looking at Caleb, I announced, "Men, ve'll take time here te rest te horses."

"Sorry sheriff, I'm not stopping. I can't waste any more time. I'm going on ahead." Turning River around, Caleb started to ride off calling behind him, "You can catch up when you're ready."

Emily

"Can I check on him?" Pointing to Stubbs, I noticed the pistol still holstered at his side.

"What do ya want to do that fer?" Vermin asked, around a wad of chewing tobacco.

Hoping to keep Vermin's attention on me, and away from his brother, I just shrugged. Taking a chance, I knelt next to Stubbs, using my skirt to cover his pistol. In the darkness, it was hard to see if he was breathing. Moving my hands to his neck, I was relieved to feel the steady rhythm of his carotid pulse.

Gran. Are you here?

I'm here dear.

I'm terrified.

I know. Don't be dear—God is with you.

Can you just stay with me please, I asked, looking heavenward. *As if being killed once wasn't enough! I don't think my grandfather or Caleb can get me out of this one.* I had no more tears to shed. Besides, it would do me no good.

Oh, piffle. You're getting out of here if I have anything to say about it.

Stubbs stirred. Rubbing the side of his head with dirty hands, he opened his eyes to see me kneeling over him. Placing my fingers over my mouth, I urged him to remain quiet. Nodding his response, I felt he understood me.

Grasping my hands in his, Stubbs untied my binding ropes that had cut deep into my wrists, leaving behind crusty dried blood. Despite their filth, I took one of Stubb's hands and mouthed "Thank You." I wasn't sure if he understood, but it was the best I could do in the darkness. Surprised, Stubbs rewarded me by placing his pistol in my hands, then closed his eyes. I would soon find out what Stubbs kept safely tucked away in the side of his boot.

Keeping my hands out of view, I couldn't let Vermin know what his brother had done, or he'd kill him for sure. With Stubb's pistol hidden in the folds of my skirt, I moved back to the empty crate.

Vermin stopped rummaging through one of the containers. Turning, he sent me a sinister sneer and asked, "Is he finally dead?"

"No!" I hadn't given him the answer he wanted to hear. Pulling out some dried jerky and hardtack, he threw me a piece. I caught myself before bringing my untied hands forward. At the sight of food, my stomach growled. I couldn't remember when anything inedible looked so mouthwatering. Waiting for Vermin to turn back around, I leaned my head back against the damp stone wall and closed my eyes, savoring every morsel of the leathery meat.

Caleb

Two hours later, the posse caught up with me. With the sheriff now leading the way, Nathaniel and I rode side by side. He tried making light conversation, peppering me with questions about my sister. I wasn't in the mood. But that didn't stop him.

"How long has your sister been in town?" I didn't answer. "Will your sister be staying long?" I still didn't answer. "Is she a widow?" I turned and gave Nathaniel a warning glare, halting his inquisition. "We'll find your woman," he said.

The ride into the hills became grueling. With a death grip on the saddle horn, each pounding step River took found me leaning further forward. By this time, I was taking short, shallow breaths as beads of sweat dripped down the side of my face. In pain, I struggled to remain upright. I wouldn't give up. Still, after everything I've been through, this may be the one thing that killed me.

The sheriff called out from behind me, "Young, vait." I pulled my horse to a halt, thankful for stopping. "Don't be foolish. Give yerself and yer horse some needed rest. Ya look like ya're ready to fall flat on yer face. It von't do Emily any gut if ya can't make it because ya died trying."

Turning my horse around to face him, I pointed toward the hills, "What would you do if that was Abbie out there?"

I could see in the sheriff's features that he understood the unmitigated fear and frustration that I was going through. "Probably te same ting," he replied. "But I don't hav't two bullet holes in me, now do I?" he said sternly.

Taking a firm hold of River's reins, the sheriff looked at me, "Now. I'm not asking ya to vait. I'm telling ya, its fer yar own goot, and tat of te whole posse."

Stretching my back, I eased off on River's reins.

"Ve've been pushing tese men, and teir mounts hardt and te need their rest." Taking my silence as a means of my giving in, he added, "It von't be fer long." He looked around at the men who all nodded their agreement.

Son, don't be foolish. Listen to the sheriff, I heard my mom whisper in my ear. *He knows what he's talking about. He's thinking with his head while you're acting on your heart.*

Under my breath, I answered my mother. *You're right. It's just that I'm going crazy not knowing what's happened to Emily.*

I understand, son. Just be patient.

Grudgingly, I agreed with the sheriff, "OK. I'll give you thirty minutes. If you're not ready to move out by then, I'm leaving without you." As River stepped in a circle, all I could think about was that Emily hadn't left me. She was still here.

"Deal," the sheriff answered as I dismounted.

The men in the posse didn't take the time to light a fire since we weren't going to be here long enough, but they did eat the biscuits with bacon that my sister and Mrs. Mueller had prepared for them.

Before thirty minutes was up, I was pacing back and forth between the men. Time was wasting. My biggest fear was that Emily was no longer alive, or she had unwillingly gone back to her time. *How could that happen?* I couldn't remember if she told me how, or if she could go back. All I could focus on was the last time we spoke. *She said she loved me and wanted to stay? How am I ever going to live without her?*

Refreshed, the men mounted up, following the path we thought to be Emily's. "I know this place," Nathaniel spoke. "It belonged to an old recluse miner that would wander into one of my mining camps two or three times a year to stock up on supplies." Nathaniel looked around and added, "He's been gone for years now, and the mine's since been abandoned."

"Well, I don't think it's abandoned now," said one of the posse members, pointing to the ground. "The tracks we've been following end here at the mine's entrance."

I was the first to dismount. Taking a wide path not to disturb the pre-existing footprints, I stood to the side, encountering three sets, two large and one small. Somewhat relieved, I silently nodded to the sheriff and Nathaniel while pointing down the shaft. The question was, was Emily still alive?

Emily

I watched Vermin as he ate his jerky. I knew Stubbs wasn't uncon-scious but lay watching his brother's every move under heavy eye-lids. He made me curious as to what he was planning, wishing he could somehow tell me.

Abruptly standing from the crate he'd been sitting on, Vermin walked over to where I sat. I shuddered as our toes touched. Turning my head to the side at the stench of his foul breath, I scooted myself further back on the crate. I held my breath with my hands hidden within the folds of my dress. I couldn't let Vermin see that my bind-ings were gone and that I held Stubb's revolver in my hands. *Not yet anyway.*

"Well, little lady," Vermin said, sliding a chaw of tobacco from the right to the left side of his cheek. "We didn't finish what we started last night."

Leaning in closer, Vermin commenced unfastening his fly but-tons. Clenching the cold steel in my hands, I'd had enough. He was close enough that I could see his temporal vein on the right side of his head, ticking a silent rhythm. Licking his filthy lips, I let him take hold of my shoulders, pulling me up off the crate. I'd never killed a man before, but this was justified in my mind. The closer he was, the deadlier my shot would be.

"Maybe now we can have us some fun?" Vermin smirked, rais-ing his eyebrows.

He was right where I wanted him. Heart pounding, I felt my pulse race and adrenaline surge. Every nerve and muscle in my body went on high alert as I pushed the muzzle of Stubb's revolver stead-fastly into Vermin's gut.

"What the . . . How'd yer get yer hands untied?" he screamed, looking towards his brother's prone body.

"That's not what you have to worry about." Pushing the muzzle in deeper. "All you need to know is that I will pull this trigger! Now, back away."

He took a single step back. "Now, missy, don't ya go givin' ole' Vermin here no trouble. We'll both enjoy this."

"Not in this lifetime," I said as my fingers gripped firmer around the cold metal.

The next few seconds moved by in a blur. I started to squeeze the trigger when Vermin's right hand shot out, catching me off guard and causing Stubb's gun to fly out of my hand. Cursing, I should have shot him when I had the chance. Out of the corner of my eye, I saw Stubbs sit up, reaching for the knife he'd kept hidden in his pant leg, throwing it towards his brother. In one fluid motion, the Bowie arched in the air, plummeted downward, piercing deep into the right side of Vermin's chest. A look of shock etched across his face as he stumbled backward, but not before firing his own gun, hitting his brother.

Without thinking, I lunged for Stubbs revolver before Vermin could turn on me. Our eyes met, and I fired, hitting Vermin in the abdomen.

Without remorse, I watched his arms splay open, his body jerk, then fall back against the rock wall, as his weapon fell out of his reach. Breathless, I shook uncontrollably.

Caleb

Hearing gunshots, I ran towards the mine's entrance.

"I'm going in," Sheriff Johansson yelled, holding me back. "You two stay here and wait for my call."

"No, you're not," I said, grabbing his arm. "Emily's my concern, not yours."

"I'm te sheriff, and I say tat I'm going in first," shaking off my hand.

I knew I would regret my next move, but it was for the sheriff's own good. "Sorry, sheriff, that's where you're wrong," landing a swift punch to the sheriff's jaw, knocking him to the ground. Quickly turning, I made my way past the staring posse and into the mine's shaft. Keeping to the side, I hoped to stay out of the range of gunfire as I quickened my steps until I felt someone grab my arm from behind, pulling me back.

"What the hell are you doing?" I asked, jerking my arm out of Nathaniel's grasp.

"Saving your hide man," Nathaniel hissed out. "You're smarter than that, Young. Running in here without a plan is suicide, and you know it." Nathaniel turned me to face him as he continued. "Listen, I know what it's like to helplessly lose someone you love. But if you get yourself killed before you find out if Emily is still alive, you're not doing either of you any good."

I knew Nathaniel was right. For the first time in five years, I had people who cared about me, and vice versa. Wincing in pain, I let out a pent-up breath as Nathaniel released my injured arm. Leaning back against the wall, I knew I had never been at such a loss. This being in love was turning out to be more than I bargained for. But, I wouldn't' have it any other way.

Rubbing my side to ease the dull ache, I turned to Nathaniel.

"Listen, Caleb, you can't take much more before you collapse. It has to be me to go in first. I'm familiar with this mine." Toeing the dirt with his boot, he added, "Besides, if anything should happen to me, I have no one to leave behind." Shrugging his shoulders in despair, he added, "You have a woman that loves you."

"Thanks. But you should know that there are people who care about you too. I'm sure the whole town does. This is my fight, not yours. Now get the hell out of here, Nate, before I shoot you myself."

Leaving Nathaniel behind, I crossed into the darkness, allowing my eyes to adjust to the lack of light. I hadn't gone but ten feet when Nathaniel grabbed my right shoulder from behind. "I thought I told you to get out of here," I whispered.

"You did," Nathaniel replied. "But I'm just as stubborn as you are. And, I want to make sure you and Emily come out of here alive." Cautiously pushing me forward, he added, "I know these mines, and you're going to need my help."

"Damn fool," I whispered. Inhaling sharply, I conceded. "I appreciate the help. Let's go." We both continued down a narrowing path whose dampness was strongly evident in its musty odor. Cautiously, I eased my way forward knowing that at any given moment I could take a wrong step and find myself at the bottom of a watery pit.

Catching sight of dim light, I caught the whiff of spent gun smoke. Heart pounding, I could feel Emily was just within my reach.

44

Nathaniel

I COULD SENSE CALEB'S urgency to move forward. It was all he could do to remain calm.

"Hello in the mine," I called out as my voice echoed down the long shaft causing small rocks to tumble from above.

"Damn it, Burns," Caleb said, knowing I was taking a big chance.

Vermin

"Well, your man has finally arrived," I ground out through clenched teeth. Daggers of pain shot through my chest as I coughed. Warm blood oozed from the side of my mouth. I knew death was near, but

I had to finish what I started. The numbness in my legs crept upward. Soon, I wouldn't feel a thing. I knew the Devil hovered close by, ready to take me.

Turning my head to the side, I glimpsed the main fuse box I prepared earlier. Knowing I wasn't going to make it out of here alive, at least I could take them all to hell with me. That would be my sweet final revenge. *Maybe this will end the way I planned after all.* "I've been waiting weeks for this moment," I hissed, raising my head to look at Emily.

Caleb

"Caleb! Is that you?" Emily yelled.

Relief washed over me, hearing Emily's voice. Moving forward, I came to a wide opening as fading lamplight cast shadows on the wall. Emily was kneeling next to a body, one hand caressing a man's cheek, the other pressing into his abdomen.

Flashbacks of her kneeling in the dirt beside me doing the same rushed through my memory. I thanked God she was alive. I could see that her face was bruised and bloody, and the top of her dress had been torn and hanging off one shoulder. Anger surged through me when I caught sight of a man near the entrance lying against the rock wall. Blood was saturating the front of his shirt at a steady rate.

"Well, well. Who do we have here?" the man rushed out in gurgled breaths. "Finally, we meet face-to-face, Young." Coughing, he pushed his hand deeper into his chest. "You killed my brother in cold blood." Gasping for air, "I should have made sure I finished you off in the hills."

Raising his hand, he stared at it as if mesmerized by his own blood-covered fingers. "Your little lady, there is a pretty good shot with a gun. Didn't figure she'd use it though," he smirked. "It doesn't matter now. We'll all be in hell soon."

"Maybe so," I answered, seeing the pain etched across his face. My only concern was to get Emily out of the mine alive.

I watched the man's head fall back, letting out a sinister laugh as Nathaniel made his move into the light, urging me towards Emily. Dropping down next to her, I saw the bruising around her face and her blood-soaked dress. "Thank God, you're alive." Running my hands feverishly over her face and arms, I stared into the violet eyes I'd come to love. "Emily, what has he done to you?"

"I love you Caleb Young. Remember that!" Emily rushed out. "But we haven't got time. We need to get out of here." Turning her head from side to side, she added, "He has dynamite everywhere."

"Tell me that again when we're alone," I said, quickly kissing her back.

Emily took Stubbs' hands in hers, mouthing the words, "Thank you."

Quickly pulling her hands to his mouth, Stubbs kissed them, closing his eyes for the last time, freeing himself from his imprisoned silence.

"Revenge is mine now," Vermin yelled from behind us. "You see, I have a debt to pay. I'm here to finish what I started up in them hills." Sneering, "You should have died up there, Young. If it weren't for your little woman there, you would have."

Urging Emily closer to the entrance, I kept an eye on Vermin. His sickening tobacco-stained smile sent shivers down my spine.

With his dying breath, he spewed out, "Now, I get to take ya all to hell with me."

Emily and I followed the direction of Vermin's eyes, catching sight of the fuse box lying next to him. "Why, you Sonofa . . . I yelled, giving Emily a hard push towards the entrance.

Thinking I could prevent the inevitable, I started towards Vermin as a single shot rang out from Nathaniel's gun, hitting Vermin mid-chest.

Stunned, all three of us watched in slow motion as Vermin's last deed was to have his limp hand fall on the upraised handle of the fuse box.

The three of us took off running down the long dark mineshaft dodging falling rocks and rotten pilings, leaving the brothers entombed together. Flashes of orange, blue, and yellow lit up the darkness as more dynamite roared to life.

Halfway through the portal, Nathaniel screamed in pain. Silence followed while smoke and dust skewed our vision. Yelling to Emily over the pandemonium, "Go. I'll get Nate."

"No," Emily yelled back, grabbing the front of my shirt. "We'll do it together. I'm not leaving here without you."

"You! You are the most stubborn woman I have ever known," I answered, pulling her in for a quick kiss. Turning back, we didn't have far to go when we came across Nathaniel lying in gravel with his left leg caught under a beam.

"Get out of here, you two. Save yourselves," Nathaniel grunted out.

"No! We won't leave you," I told Nate. Thankfully alive, Emily was at his side, doing a quick assessment of his injuries. At the same time, I tried moving the beam off his leg. With my own injuries still causing me a great deal of pain, the beam was too heavy to move on my own. I needed help, and hoped some of the men waiting outside could hear me yelling.

"I don't think your leg is broken, Nathaniel. But you do have a large laceration on your thigh that's bleeding heavily and will need stitching when we get back to the clinic. In the meantime, I'll need to use your belt as a tourniquet."

In short order, two men from the posse came rushing down the mineshaft. Using their combined strength, they were able to remove the beam from Nathaniel's leg.

"Can you stand Nate?" I asked.

"I can try," he replied, groaning. With his arms over the men's shoulders, they carried him forward with Emily and I close behind.

Sheriff Johansson

The earth around us trembled, and a deep roaring belch came from within the bowels of the shaft. A gush of hot air and debris rushed out of the opening while we watched in horror.

My heart sank, thinking I'd lost five of my friends, including Emily, Caleb, and Nate, to such tragedy. I had no idea how I would go back to town and tell Caleb's sister and Emily's grandfather that their loved ones had perished in a mine explosion. Taking my hat off, I hung my head in defeat, sending a prayer heavenward.

Rubbing my eyes, someone in the posse yelled, "Sheriff, look!"

Rushing past him, I looked up at the incredible sight. My dirty bloodied friends came tumbling out from a white cloud of smoke as if they were running from the gates of hell. I couldn't believe what I was seeing. Rushing forward, ignoring Caleb, I took hold of Emily, hugging her to my chest. "Tank God yer alive. Yer all alive."

Caleb

Wiping the dust off my face, I stared at the sheriff with Emily tucked firmly in his arms. "Ah, sheriff," I said, trying to get his attention. He ignored me. Finally, tapping him on the shoulder, I coughed out, "That would be my woman you're hugging."

Letting go of the sheriff, Emily rushed into my arms, crying so hard her tears left brown rivulets running down her dirty freckled cheeks. She was beautiful and finally right where she belonged.

Looking up at me, flashes of pain crossed over her violet eyes. In a shaky whisper, she said, "Caleb, I killed a man. I didn't mean too."

Drawing her closer, I held her shaking body tightly to my chest, ignoring my own pain. Resting my chin on the top of her head, I tried reassuring her. "It's OK Angel. You did what you had to do."

"Hey! What about me?" Nathaniel spoke up as he lay against a bolder. "Don't I get a hug?"

Walking over to Nathaniel, the sheriff teasingly opened his arms. "Uh, no. That's OK, sheriff. I think I'll wait for someone's sister to oblige me."

We both chuckled as I continued to hold Emily in my arms. I would never let her go again. Going back to her time was no longer an option. My heart wouldn't survive it. As she looked into my eyes, was that love I saw? I certainly hope so. Heart pounding, I worried she was going to tell me she was leaving. Holding my breath, she began to speak.

"Caleb Young, I don't ever want to leave you again. I'm here to stay if you'll have me."

Looking down into the violet eyes of the woman I'd fallen in love with that fateful night in the desert hills, I smiled then answered, "Doc, my Angel, I will never let you go. I will love you, *Till My Last Breath.*"

45

JANUARY 1881 TWO WEEKS AFTER CHRISTMAS

Mother Young and Grandma Sweeney

THROUGHOUT THE CHURCH, hundreds of white candles flickered with a wavering light that danced off the walls. Dried desert wildflowers, tied with crisp red satin bows, had been attached to the ends of every other pew by the town ladies. Thrilled, once again, to see their beloved church come alive with such a joyous occasion.

Sheriff Anders Johansson, the groom and my son, Caleb Young, the best man, stood to the side of the altar, looking uncomfortable in their starched white shirts. Black string ties, black evening coats, and black boots shining like new silver dollars rounded out their attire. Both men presented a fetching picture any woman would fall in love with. But we knew, beyond a shadow of a doubt, which woman's heart belonged to which man.

Amused, we watched Anders pull out his pocket watch for the third time in five minutes, then fidget once again with his tie. Next to him, Caleb anxiously checked and rechecked his pocket for the rings Anders had entrusted into his care that morning.

In the vestibule, Abigail stood next to Henry in a borrowed wedding dress. Her girls had spent days redesigning and sewing it, so it barely looked like the original. Henry turned Abigail to face him. "You must know that I love you like my own daughter, Abbie. All I want is your happiness."

"I am happy, Henry. Knowing I now have the two men I love most in my life."

Placing a chaste kiss on her cheek and Holly's downy head, Henry pulled the gossamer veil over Abigail's face.

Mrs. Mueller began playing the pump organ. Hands shaking, Abigail moved from one foot to the other as she took in a long deep breath. Handing Holly to Rebecca, Henry began to escort Abigail towards the narthex of the church. First, to come down the aisle was my granddaughter Emily looking even more radiant than the bride. Her smile, only for Caleb, was as bright as the sun that shone on this crisp January day.

We chuckled at the light banter between Anders and Caleb as they both couldn't take their eyes off the women they loved. Anders followed the direction of Caleb's gaze. Teasingly, under his breath, "Ya better not be making eyes at my bride, Young, or I'll have ya behind bars until tis is over." Smiling, he added, "You have yar own woman."

"Don't worry, sheriff. As soon as we get you and Abbie married off, I'm asking Emily to be my wife."

"Well. It's about time ya put a ring on tat girl's finger. Otherwise, she's liable to find herself another man."

"Not going to happen," Caleb said, turning to Anders. "Your tie's crooked, sheriff," teasingly adjusting it. Anders batted Caleb's hand away.

The music changed, and all eyes turned towards the back of the church. Abigail, resplendent in a gossamer gown confidently made

her way towards a new life and the man she had secretly loved for
so long.

We both were so happy that Anders planned on leaving his office
as sheriff to take up ranching on a small spread outside of town.
We had heard that at his age, he thought he and Abbie better have
as many children as they could before he "became too old to chase
after them."

My sweet granddaughter planned to stay beside Caleb as they
both settled down in Yuma, hoping to start their own family.
Gradually, Emily would take over her grandfather's medical practice
in this dusty town she'd once despised. Now, Yuma would be lucky
to have such a learned and experienced physician. And, her soon to
be husband, Caleb, would begin a law practice as soon as they were
wed. Which couldn't happen fast enough as far as I was concerned.

In the front row sat Nathaniel, recovering nicely from his injury.
Leg propped up on the pew, his face held a pensive look. *What was
he thinking about?* Rebecca, sitting in the back row, looked so content holding baby Holly. I hadn't seen my little girl smile like that in
a long time.

I knew Nathaniel had become very fond of my daughter and her
boys. I only hoped she would remain in Yuma, allowing their relationship to blossom. There was just one wee bit of a problem. Elliot!
Trouble with her marriage and Caleb's injuries had brought her to
Yuma. Alone. Thankfully without that wretched husband of hers. I
never did like that dolt!

I felt sorry for Nathaniel since Rebecca had been far from truth-
ful to both Nathaniel and Caleb regarding her past. I worried about
her safety. Eventually, she would have to tell them both why she was
here without her husband.

The ceremony was short, yet left not a dry eye in the church as
the bride and groom walked back down the aisle. Picking up Holly
from Rebecca's care, they made their way out into the bright Arizona
winter's day.

Well, Mrs. Sweeney, I do believe our two children finally realize that they belong together no matter what year or century they come from. Don't you agree?

Yes, Mrs. Young. I agree wholeheartedly. Our two children make a lovely couple. Soon we'll be back here for another wedding, and won't that be a grand day?

Indeed it will, Mrs. Young. Indeed it will.

About the Author

DEBORAH SWENSON is an author who is at home writing from an island in the Pacific Northwest. I love everything country from our pristine mountains, raging icy rivers, and freshly plowed fields, right down to the sweet smell of a barnyard.

After an extensive and rewarding career in health care, I turned to my love of writing Western Romantic fiction. When I am not writing, I enjoy spending time with my family and friends, spinning fiber, quilting, photography, reading, and volunteering at a Therapeutic Horsemanship Program.

deborahswenson.com